STRUCK O..

Struck Off

John Killah

HOBNOB PRESS

First published in the United Kingdom
by The Hobnob Press,
8 Lock Warehouse, Severn Road, Gloucester GL1 2GA
www.hobnobpress.co.uk

British Library Cataloguing in Publication Data
A catalogue record for this book is available from the British Library

ISBN 978-1-914407-15-4

Typeset in Adobe Garamond Pro 11/13 pt
Typesetting and origination by John Chandler

Cover illustration by Alice Keegan

This novel is a work of fiction. Names and characters are the product of the author's imagination, and any resemblance to actual persons, living or dead, is entirely coincidental.

Acknowledgements

As a debut novelist I am hugely indebted to John Chandler at Hobnob Press for his wise counsel, inspiration and enthusiasm. Likewise, my thanks also go to novelist and writer Crysse Morrison for her support and her ability to point a beginner in the right direction. I am also eternally grateful to my friends (you know who you are!) who took the time and trouble to read the early drafts and come back with such positive ideas, guidance and contributions. I owe you all big-time. A massive thanks must in addition of course go to my wife Deb for her tireless patience and meticulous interventions ensuring that the final published script works.

 **John Killah** was born in Aberdeen, Scotland. *Struck Off* is his debut novel. Before qualifying as a solicitor, he read English at the University of East Anglia and lived and worked abroad as a teacher. Following an early legal career in London that included working for a specialist film, television and music practice, John then moved to the West Country where he established himself as a criminal defence lawyer. In addition to being a solicitor, he also ran his own marketing business as well as writing and campaigning on legal issues including the erosion of access to justice. He now concentrates on his creative writing and is currently working on his second novel. He is married and lives in Somerset.

THE HIT

KENDRICK MACLEAN was in a deep sleep, protected by the warm duvet enveloping his body. Then came the four heavy knocks on the front door. He opened his eyes and blinked, wondering where he was. Then four more loud bangs, immediate and unforgiving in the darkness.

The luminous face on the digital alarm clock by the side of the bed told him that it was 02:08 on Wednesday 17th April.

Kendrick Maclean was now wide awake, eyes staring at the ceiling wondering what to do next. Why didn't whoever it was do the normal thing and just press the front door buzzer in the porch. He felt safe living in the middle of Somerset. He loved it down here. However, he never believed all that keeping the doors unlocked bollocks. Thirty years of living in south west London, even if it was latterly in Barnes and then Kew, had taught him that there were thieving bastards everywhere. When he bought Bradstock Farm nearly two years ago, any commitment to investing in local business did not extend to the security system. Kendrick Maclean declined to use the recommended local Somerset firm and instead had hired his usual trusted security alarm people who had near anonymous premises quietly tucked away on a trading estate in Vauxhall. With Bradstock Farm there would be no risk of all his alarm codes and details being sold to the highest bidder in some shitty little village boozer that still had sawdust on the floor. Any local rural peasant who was even thinking of robbing Dougal Kendrick Maclean was in for a disappointment.

Then came the scrunches. A few months beforehand, Kendrick Maclean had arranged for 3 separate deliveries of gravel for the driveway and front entrance of the house before he finally settled on the 20mm Dorset Flint as providing the exact sort of driveway surface gravitas that was commensurate with the property that it was now part of. The scrunches were now moving away from the front door.

Next to him, Ronnie had slept through the commotion but in the near darkness Kendrick Maclean could still make out that she had her mouth half open, eyes shut and arm slung lazily across her face. Kendrick Maclean slipped out of bed and crept over to the window where he parted the curtains enough to be able to look out. The movement-activated security lights were already on and made the fully illuminated front entrance look like The Cottage as seen from the walk along Bishops Park from the tube at Putney Bridge to the ground on a midweek evening match. However, no more scrunches and no person or persons to be seen but someone was definitely out there taking the piss. After a few more seconds, the lights flicked themselves off leaving just the fast-diminishing warm glow of the halogen bulbs.

Kendrick Maclean contemplated going back to bed. Too late. He was now wide awake. Instead, he bent down under the bed and reached for his trusted old Gray-Nicolls, a relic from the days when he used to be a tail-ender. Sporting his striped pyjamas and clutching his bat, Kendrick Maclean tip-toed out of the bedroom and down the old creaking wooden stairs. It was at times like this he wished he had a dog in the house. A proper dog, not one of those poncy lap rats that Ronnie kept going on about getting. For the present however, he was on his own.

Kendrick Maclean now stood in front of the inside of his entrance door at what was Bradstock Manor. It was a proper fuck off front door that he was well proud of, surviving three and a half centuries of keeping its inhabitants safe and the scumbags out with its ten inch deep solid oak structure. It also had a solid iron lock with a key to go with it that any self-respecting jailer would be proud to have swinging from the ring on his belt.

To the left of the door, next to the suit of armour he had picked up for a pittance at the auction at Crewkerne, Kendrick Maclean punched in the security code and de-activated the state of the art security system before it went ape. It needed all of the strength of one hand to click the door key clockwise. The metallic thud signified the door was now unlocked. Kendrick Maclean suddenly started to feel uneasy. Who banged on anyone's door in the middle of the night? Police? Had something happened to the boys? If it was the plod come with some bad news then surely as well as using the proper door-bell they would have identified themselves by now. Instead there was just silence both inside and outside the house. There was not even the welcome interruption of the occasional screech of the barn owls that lived nearby or the barks and screams of the local fox population. Until he had actually moved to Somerset he had no idea what silence actually was. It was so quiet on some nights that the silence was deafening as he tossed and turned in bed for hours before being able to get to sleep.

Kendrick Maclean now had his hands on the large old iron handle of the door. He suddenly felt even more unease about not knowing what was on the other side of the door. For a moment, he contemplated replacing the faithful Gray-Nicolls by either extracting the sword from the knight's scabbard or alternatively tip-toeing down to the house cellars and retrieving his up and under from the gun cabinet. However, he was not sure where the keys to the cabinet were and in truth he had only just got his firearms paperwork through and was not yet that confident on how the shooter actually worked. He was still trying to remember which direction the safety catch should be pointed when he reminded himself that all that had happened was that someone had knocked on his front door at what was for Kendrick Maclean the middle of the night.

'Breathe in and get a grip,' he told himself.

The Gray-Nicolls was just fine. With one hand still clutching the frayed rubber handle covering on the bat, Kendrick Maclean lifted the latch and the ancient hinges swung the door in towards the hallway.

Kendrick Maclean peered out. Even without the security lights on it was obvious there was nothing there. He did not really expect to see anything.

It was only when he was about to slam the door shut again and retire back to the warmth of his bed that Kendrick Maclean felt something was not quite right. Instead of easing the door shut, he pulled the door wide open so that the lights in the hallway illuminated both the inside and outside of the door.

Kendrick Maclean had not been mistaken. He had heard noises when he was lying in bed. There was no one knocking on the door however. Instead, front paws smashed as a hammer had banged in the nails through the front feet and neck dangling backwards and loose was a crucified badger. Kendrick Maclean had only ever seen badgers before when they were road kill. There were always plenty of them littering the side of the Somerset roads as well. He was nevertheless still taken aback by its size, as it managed to cover all of the upper part of the ancient oak door.

Blood from the animal was already starting to drip on to the flagstones of the hallway, just missing Ronnie's Persian carpet in the hallway.

Kendrick Maclean could not miss the piece of folded A4 neatly folded in to the mouth of the dead creature. He eased the wet paper out between the teeth and unfolded it.

Some of the ink writing on the paper had smudged in the saliva but the message was quite clear.

'Wellcome to Somerset' was written in large capital letters with a black felt tip pen.

'Cunts can't even spell', thought Kendrick Maclean before slamming the door shut, the lower part of the badger's rear legs bouncing off the oak. As he turned the key anti-clockwise to once more secure the door he could have sworn that he heard the scrunch of the gravel in the darkness way down by the gates to the entrance of Bradstock Manor.

~ ~ ~

A few hours later at the large detached family home just outside the thriving Somerset market town of Sedgeton, Eaun Wright had also managed to quietly slip out of the matrimonial bed so as to not wake up his sleeping wife, Victoria. However, as soon as he had silently closed the bedroom door behind him and stepped out on to the landing, Eaun Wright knew that something was wrong. A hesitant lean over the bannisters confirmed his worst fears. They had taken a hit during the night.

There was no doubt. The reek was pungent and sharp. His shower would have to be put on hold.

Eaun furtively crept down the stairs and keyed in his burglar alarm de-activation code before walking through the open kitchen door where he guessed that the violation had taken place. However, even before he flicked on the lights, he had spotted the tell-tale small puddles at the bottom of the kitchen table legs. There was of course no sign of the perpetrator, but Eaun knew exactly who it was; the same skinny and mangy ginger that had taken it upon himself to periodically enter and soil the Wright family kitchen, aiming his foul smelling spray once more at the innocent and blameless kitchen table legs. Once, Eaun had caught the wretched animal in the act as he came down early one morning to see its short legs in a cartoon-like frantic circular action, slithering on the parquet flooring before the claws finally brought some traction as he shot through the cat flap smashing its head on the portcullis and taking half the flap with him, with Eaun in hot pursuit.

Over the years the Wright household had hosted the usual array of small pets, from hamsters, to guinea pigs and rabbits, each species being greeted with excitement and adoration by the two girls before inevitable boredom and indifference set in. With the exception of one of the rabbits' unfortunate encounter involving the neighbour's Weimaraner, all the previous pets had eventually come to a peaceful if somewhat neglected end in the designated but unmarked burial ground behind the shed at the bottom of the garden.

On the family pet roll of honour, the two brothers Vlad and Ivan were now the sole survivors. When first collected from a farm at North Brewham, they were advertised as 'fearless farm cats'. However, this morning, as with previous similar occasions, of Vlad and Ivan there was no sign.

There was nothing for it. Eaun donned his garden galoshes stacked by the back door and headed for the cupboard under the sink.

Twenty five minutes later, Eaun considered the task well done. He was grateful that the hits to date were at least limited to the hard surfaces of the floor and the kitchen table legs. There had as yet been no graduation to more vulnerable carpets and soft fabrics. The odorous and foul stench in the kitchen that had been wafting through the house had been truly appalling. Serious remedies had been required so Eaun had had to pour generous dollops of kitchen floor cleaner, disinfectant and washing up liquid into the bucket so that the final mixture resembled a frothing witch's concoction. Their work completed, Eaun stored away the yellow rubber gloves and red bucket together with what was left of the now near empty cleaning fluid containers. However, as Eaun was about to leave the kitchen and go upstairs to jump in the shower to de-fumigate and re-start the day, he still managed to detect the slight but unmistakeable smell of cat urine. He returned to the cupboard, extracted a top of the range furniture polish and liberally sprayed both floor and kitchen table legs two or three times over. Job done. Mrs Wright would later come down to a kitchen to enjoy her muesli and freshly-crushed orange juice as if nothing had happened.

As Eaun eventually managed to make his move out of the kitchen and back along the hallway he noticed a shape through the frosted glass front door window. He usually only shut the curtain across the front door in the winter, in an attempt to keep the place warm. An easily identifiable red blur of a baseball cap and the matching red face mask told Eaun that it was only the paperboy. As the daily newspaper was rammed through the letter box, Eaun shouted a quick 'thank you' to the boy, before grabbing the folded paper and striding upstairs to the shower. It was only as he waited for the interminable time it took for the water in the shower to move from tepid to warm and then finally hot, that he realised the only piece of clothing that he had to remove before entering into the shower were his pair of galoshes. He made a mental note to return the incriminating evidence to the shoe rack by the back door before leaving the house.

Eaun spent at least twice the usual time in his postponed morning shower, methodically selecting from the ranks of assembled shampoos, shower gels and soaps together with other assorted personal hygiene aids belonging to Mrs Wright the purpose of which he was not entirely sure. His hands, lower legs and genitalia received special attention to ensure that there was no trace of animal spray or domestic cleansing agents left on his body.

Satisfied that he was no longer unclean, Eaun stepped out of the shower and dried himself off with one of his wife's luxurious white bath towels. Eaun stepped into his work uniform of two piece suit, crisp blue oxford style button down shirt and a plain red silk tie. Mrs Wright often enjoyed an early morning lie-in, so the evening before Eaun usually stationed his work clothes for the next day in the bathroom.

Eaun felt parched. He had had no breakfast or even a cup of tea, his time being taken with having to deal with the repercussions of the night time attack on the family home. He would treat himself and get a proper drink on the way into work. Eaun slipped on the final piece of his attire, his hand made brown leather shoes, just before exiting the bathroom. His grandmother had lectured him as a child on how he could compromise on anything in life, but never shoes.

There just remained the final task of saying goodbye.

As he entered the darkened matrimonial bedroom, Eaun picked up the newspaper that he had earlier dropped by the door on the way in to the shower. As he unfurled the publication, he inwardly cursed. The numbskull paperboy had delivered the *Daily Express* instead of the usual Mrs Wright-favoured *Daily*

Mail. Decades after the event, the front page of this morning's *Express* promised yet another exclusive on the death of Princess Diana on pages 3, 4, 5 and 6. It seemed that even the *Express* had now got bored on reporting on The Plague. The old pre-Plague news order was perhaps now being restored after all. Eaun curled up the newspaper in his hand so that its title and identity was not immediately apparent. He would be well on the way to work before the delivery error would be noticed.

Eaun crept through the gloom up to the huge emperor sized bed where despite its vast acreage, his wife Victoria was curled up in a foetal ball perched on the precipice of the mattress. He gently nudged the hidden shape until there was a twitch.

'Have to go. Am dreadfully late,' said Eaun in a loud whisper. 'Here is the paper,' he added, making sure that it did not unfold as he released it from his hand and placed it near the bottom of the bed.

A head then shot up from under the duvet.

'I need to speak to you urgently,' said Victoria Wright, wide awake.

'Can't. Am really late with clients waiting. We can speak this evening.'

'Lunchtime. It can't wait. I will call you this morning.'

Eaun kissed the top of the head and with a 'Bye darling' headed for the bedroom door. He had nearly made it when he heard his wife direct at him:

'What is that dreadful disinfectant odour? Place smells like poor Aunt Molly's care home.'

Eaun mumbled something indecipherable before saying that they would speak later.

Within moments, Eaun had escaped through the front door, clicked the driver's door on the Volvo open and started to settle in for the short journey to the office in Sedgeton. The clock on the dashboard told him that the time was 7.25 am. He knew that he was late and the actual real time was 8.25 but following the recent change to British Summer Time the clock in the car had not been put forward the hour. In truth, the instruction manual had been lost years ago and Eaun did not have a clue how to change the time on the car's clock. He had just got used to adding an hour during the summer. Eaun shifted the car into first gear and he was soon heading down the drive and out of the gates. Despite the unpromising start to the day, Eaun felt that things could only get better.

~ ~ ~

Eaun's family home was just on the outskirts of town and on one of the executive housing estates that were all the rage in the late 1990s, when the property had been purchased. It was supposed to be a short-term purchase before Victoria eventually found somewhere more to her taste a few centuries older nearer the centre of town. Eaun himself was perfectly happy where he lived (except for the immediate neighbours). The family home slowly became a permanent fixture although Eaun did sometimes wonder whether it would still qualify for the 'executive' status.

Eaun's office was normally only a five minute ride in the car into Sedgeton. His daughters had for years accused him of killing their planet by driving into work. Didn't their father know that if he really didn't fancy the exertions of pedalling then on his income he could easily afford an electric bike? However, today he was very late and any electric bike would have to wait.

Just as he was approaching the middle of town outside St Christopher's First School, the traffic in front of him ground to a halt. He could see a couple of PCSOs standing in front of a crowd of loud demonstrators, some holding placards. Whilst waiting for the traffic to move on, Eaun scanned the crowd. He knew several of the faces. The recognition was hardly surprising as he had worked and lived in the area for well over 20 years. Several of the faces he knew either as clients or as mothers of clients that he had successfully managed to extract from the police cells. None of the town's usual community activist brigade that were usually to be seen these days whenever any protest was in the offing seemed to be around. A professionally printed and official-looking banner on the school wall behind the crowd pleaded 'Save St Christopher's'. The messages on the placards were of a similar vein, one stating 'What Local Democracy?' and another urging the council to 'Save Our School'. Eaun also noted a far more direct message hand-painted on the largest of the posters, inexplicably urging 'Hippies Go Home'. One of the women demonstrators, sporting a vintage Kate Bush Heathcliff-era hairstyle was speaking animatedly into a microphone held by someone with an official looking lanyard and tab around his neck. Eaun reflected that there hardly seemed anyone walking the streets these days without a message of belonging dangling around their necks.

Even Eaun had heard about St Christopher's being threatened with closure. Like everyone else in town, for years he had relied on the weekly *Sedgeton Courier* to keep him up to date with what was happening locally, from WI meetings, births and deaths to the details of every sports result and league table within a 15 mile radius. Over the years the *Courier* had started to get thinner and thinner, becoming almost devoid of adverts, with their depleting pages filled with quizzes and news from distant and alien places that the paper's readership knew little about and cared even less for. With the once loyal readership increasingly unwilling to even pick up the paper only to read what was happening in other towns, some of which were even across the county border, last year's eventual closure of the *Sedgeton Courier* seemed inevitable. In the final edition, the editor lambasted The Plague for the paper's demise, but everyone in town knew that the paper had started to lose the plot (and indeed its readership) well before the coronavirus reached our shores. However, after 125 years Eaun still felt a pang of sadness that like the livestock market, the court, police station, post office, council offices and the library, yet another part of the town's heritage and identity had disappeared for ever. From his own family to the girls in the office, everyone kept telling Eaun that he had to get on to social media and join local groups to now find out what was really happening in town. Eaun did not do either Facebook or Twitter and was not quite sure what Instagram was. It was therefore with a certain amount of pride that by just listening to people in ordinary conversation, he at least knew that the Council were trying to close St Christopher's First School. Eaun also made a mental note to later check out how and why this involved the hippies.

Eventually the traffic moved forward and Eaun headed towards his reserved parking space in the private car park at the back of the Black Dog, just a few doors down from his office.

He was now extremely late. Happily, Wednesday was his 'work' day when everyone knew to leave his diary empty so that Eaun could then get on with everything else he should have done days, weeks and even months ago. He was so late that the exact time of his arrival now made little difference. He was after all the Managing Partner and owned the business jointly with his fellow partner Julian Darby-Henderson.

On locking up his car, Eaun remembered that he had drunk or eaten nothing whatsoever that morning. By now his throat was rasping. He could not face the slops that passed itself off as the premium instant blend coffee that Julian and he supplied and paid for by popular demand in the office kitchen, so he made a brief detour down the hill towards the queue at the Blue Parrot Café on the Market Place, just before the metal archway that announced the entrance in to The Artisan Quarter. Eaun had been using the Blue Parrot Café for years. Unlike many of the other café establishments in Sedgeton, this was still a relatively normal café serving old favourites such as bacon butties and fried egg sandwiches where the yolk oozed deliciously from the white doorstep bread. The mandatory wearing of face coverings had ceased a long time ago, but the Blue Parrot was also a place where at the request of the owners, the vast majority of customers still felt happy to wear a face covering whilst waiting to be served in the queue. Despite the traditional feel of the Blue Parrot, the place had not ignored changes in public taste. Oat milk may not yet be on the menu but flat whites, vegetarian pasties and even decaffeinated lattes had now become mainstream.

After much industrial gurgling and slurping of the hot milk on the gleaming coffee-making equipment, Eaun was eventually served his usual flat white with one lump. Once he had encouraged the plastic lid to fit on to the top of the cup without taking the skin off his fingers, clutching coffee in one hand and briefcase in the other, Eaun strode up to his office to get stuck in to his day. The unfortunate earlier incidents involving the household disinfectant and Vlad and Ivan's dereliction of duty had long been forgotten.

~ ~ ~

It was only 9 a.m. but the telephone system already had three of its outside lines flashing simultaneously. On arrival at the office an hour earlier, Ludmila (she had long given up on the English ever calling her by her correct name of Ludomila) had picked up the request on the messaging system from Alex, the firm's criminal defence solicitor. She would explain later but she had to go to the cells and could Mr Wright please cover the Hudderston case in Bath for her that morning. There was then a second message from Alex saying that she would email through all the details of the case that Mr Wright needed to know.

Shortly before the office was due to open at nine, Ludmila had just finished her office-issue instant coffee and watered the indoor office plants when in through the front door came Mr Wright himself. This was really late for him. He liked to be in early, check the post and be one step ahead. Instead, he looked a little flustered. Before Mr Wright could take the stairs with coffee and briefcase in hand at his usual three steps at a time, Ludmila blurted out the urgent message from Alex about covering for her at Bath court that morning but that the good news was that an email had been sent to his screen from Alex before she left from her home for the cells.

Ludmila knew that Wednesdays were Mr Wright's 'office day' when to all enquiries he was definitely out and not available. Wednesday was the sacrosanct day when he caught up with all his paperwork and made sure that he was generally one step ahead. Ludmila expected an outburst of indignation from Mr Wright on hearing news that his protected Wednesday had now disappeared. Mercifully, all that was returned was a brief nod of acknowledgement before he disappeared up the stairs.

As Mr Wright fled to his office, the telephone reception module now had all five incoming lines flashing simultaneously. Ludmila took the first call in the queue. It was the firm's bank, Western Provincial. The actual caller she recognised as none other than the firm's account manager himself, Mr Curtis. He wanted to speak to Mr Darby-Henderson, the senior partner. He was normally in the office by this time, so Ludmila explained that he was not yet in. Mr Curtis then asked to speak to Mr Wright as a matter of urgency. Once again, profuse apologies were offered and a promise made that the request to call back would be passed on immediately Mr Wright became available. Ludmila loved how accommodating the English language was in being able to communicate a lie without in any way offending anyone.

Ludmila noticed that the return number to call Mr Curtis had a Bristol dialling code, but before she had time to email the details on to Mr Wright, he once more appeared in person at the bottom of the stairs, this time on the way out of the office with his leather brief case and a file of papers. Ludmila quickly passed on the message to urgently call back the bank and that she would email the number on to him.

Eaun Wright gave a quick smile of appreciation to Ludmila, said that he was late and that he would call the bank on the way to the court in Bath. He also asked where Julian Darby-Henderson was. Ludmila did not know. On hastening to the firm's reserved parking spaces in the rear yard of the Black Dog a few yards away in the Market Place, Eaun wondered what the bank were phoning him about on a Wednesday morning with something urgent. Also, where was his partner Julian Darby-Henderson? He was usually in the office before he was, yet when he went upstairs a few minutes before, there was no sign of him and the post lay stacked and unopened on the post room table where Ludmila had earlier deposited it. It was therefore no surprise that on walking down the side alley of the Black Dog, there was only his own slightly tired-looking Volvo estate parked there. Julian's reserved spot for his Tesla was empty. Still wondering why his business partner was not in the office, Eaun jumped in to his vehicle and headed towards the Market Place and then on to the main road for Bath. He was late and the client Mr Hudderston had already paid all of his fees up front.

Five minutes later Ludmila was still fielding the stream of incoming calls at her reception desk, including a rare call from Mrs Wright asking to speak to her husband and the man from the bank still wanting to urgently speak to one of the partners.

~ ~ ~

Eaun soon hit the A36, joining the long line of traffic heading from Salisbury and the South Coast towards Bath, Bristol and South Wales. He had faced ridicule from his own children and incredulity from his associates and clients as Eaun had still managed to hold off installing a hands-free mobile facility in his faithful Volvo. He had no idea whether his ageing vehicle was even able to host such a facility or not, but what it did mean was that he was therefore forced to abide by the law and turn his mobile off once in the car. Before he had even left the precincts of the Black Dog, the mobile lay silent and turned off on the front passenger seat.

As the A36 snaked its way slowly towards Bath, in the absence of the dead CD player and undiscovered Bluetooth, Eaun turned on the radio. The default station in the Volvo was 5 Live but this morning the participants in the phone-in were even angrier and more shrill with indignation than usual, so he pushed the Radio 3 button and settled back to listen to a string quartet.

It was not very often these days that Eaun got out and about to court and was on his own in the car. This was however a very precious me-time, when after a morning of mild

the procession of HGVs, Eaun felt generally grateful for what had happened to him professionally in the last ten years and more. He managed to laugh off the public perception and perennial accusation that he had nothing to worry about, being a 'millionaire solicitor'. It was true that both Julian and himself had made a decent living from the firm over the years, enough for Eaun to bring up and look after his family. However, it also involved sometimes brutal hours working during the evenings and weekends. It also involved the occasion when there was not enough funds in the office account to pay the VAT bill as well as the time when inadvertently the firm was non-compliant with no regulatory COLP or COFA having been appointed. Like everyone else in business who had ever had difficulties meeting a demand from HMRC, Eaun knew and understood what a real sleepless night was. It may well be that in London there were 'millionaire solicitors' working within the Magic Circle, but down here in the West Country, Eaun was certainly not aware of any local solicitor with such untold riches in his or her bank account.

As the road side signage told Eaun that he was now just a mile from the city centre, he pondered on how he felt a genuine gratitude for the people that he worked with. Everyone played hard and most of them worked hard as well, being financially rewarded with salaries above the regional norm for the sector. That investment in their employees had paid off handsomely for the partners as WHW Legal LLP prospered when The Plague started to hit at the beginning of 2020. Eaun felt a genuine pride in what 'his' team had managed to achieve in the worst economic blizzard to hit the country in living memory. The best man at Victoria and Eaun's wedding was Robbie Carmichael. Robbie was a property solicitor based in West London, but his firm had merged so many times he was not sure what it was called these days. Whenever Robbie came down to see Victoria and Eaun at Sedgeton, which was usually every couple of years, Robbie had seriously invited Eaun to make him an offer to entice him out of London.

As the A36 morphed into Pulteney Road Eaun knew that he had almost reached his destination. He also reflected that in all his time living and working in the county of Somerset, Eaun was not aware of any professional colleague who had been left a bequest from a client. Or at least they had never dared mention it to Eaun.

BADGER

KENDRICK MACLEAN had returned to bed to find that Ronnie was still asleep. However, he knew that after what had happened he had no chance of getting any shut eye. His mind was racing. Why would someone choose to nail a badger to his front door? Kendrick Maclean had only been in Somerset for just less than two years. He was trying desperately to think who he had managed to upset. Over that period he had used a lot of local tradesmen and suppliers and on occasion had to find a replacement. It is true, there had been some run-ins, but only very minor ones relating to shoddy workmanship, disputed bills, ignoring deadlines and such like. The usual builders and assorted tradesman behaviour that seemed universal. No one had ever actually threatened him before as far as he could recall. He was working on a huge project at Bradstock Manor, investing nearly £2 million of his own money on building a family home that was second to none plus a row of quality holiday lets in the old farm buildings. By the end of the summer, a swimming pool and tennis court will also have been built. The house itself was completed first so that Kendrick Maclean and his wife were no longer having to pay crippling rental fees in the local village. Kendrick Maclean would not forget the moment when he had had to explain to Mrs Kendrick Maclean that his idea of them both buying a mobile caravan and living on site whilst the house was being done up was in fact just a joke.

At the first hint of dawn, he got up and dressed in the bathroom so as not to wake up Ronnie. He suddenly remembered the first electrical contractors that he had hired. Some bloke from Shepton Mallet. Kendrick Maclean had at the outset decided that he would seriously invest in the local economy as much as possible. Except for the security system of course. Good investors in the community were supposed to hire local, or so he was told. So, except for the security system when the usual boys from Vauxhall came down to install their system and sort everything out, Kendrick Maclean always made a point of hiring local. Seems that unfortunately some people then thought that that this enlightened 'shop local' policy was a green light to deceive and thieve from the naïve bloke from London who didn't know what the fuck he was doing. At least that is how Kendrick Maclean saw the situation as he fired the Shepton sparky and replaced him with someone else who was not going to charge him for work that was never done. However, on reflection, although the Shepton sparky had turned out to be a robbing bastard, there was no way he seemed the sort of bloke to be prowling around in the dark looking for places to crucify a dead badger. In any event, he had settled that dispute out of court, along with most of the other trade disputes at Bradstock.

As he pondered what to do, it crossed Kendrick Maclean's mind that it may be an innocent case of mistaken identity or even address. Before actually moving in to the house, Ronnie had decided that the existing and historic name of the place they had bought, Bradstock Farm, did not properly reflect the ambience of what they were trying to create. So, after more than three centuries Bradstock Farm had now become Bradstock Manor and all the appropriate authorities including the Royal Mail were advised of what Ronnie liked to call her 'Bradstock Re-Brand'. The woman who had sold them the place had definite issues. He remembered her name. Mackenzie. She must have been in her late sixties and wore short skirts and long football socks turned outside her mud-caked Wellington boots. He had heard rumours that she had since died. Even the estate agents had warned them never to approach her to measure up anything unaccompanied. Having signed contracts, the lady had then announced via her solicitors that she was refusing to leave the property. She was definite trouble and was the sort that would attract dozens of nutters wanting to nail a dead badger to her door or even to her. Maybe therefore there had been some sort of muddle at the change of name. The postman had already delivered mail to the wrong place, particularly as there was a place called The Manor just down the road.

For a few minutes Kendrick Maclean thought that the mystery had been successfully solved. It was all really aimed at the nut case previous owner. Then he recalled the message on the piece of lined A4 and the message of welcome to the county. He also recalled that the agent had told him that the loony farmer's widow had lived there for 40 years. She would hardly now be expecting a message welcoming her to Somerset. Especially as rumoured she was now dead. The message, it seemed, really had been directed at Kendrick Maclean.

Before Ronnie woke up, Kendrick Maclean had figured out on what to do.

~ ~ ~

Eaun turned right under the railway bridge at Pulteney Street, but then had to wait in the traffic in North Parade Road. Nothing was moving. The city's Magistrates Court was easy to identify just ahead and on the right, with an assortment of dogs and Special Brew drinkers crowded around the locked public entrance. Eaun only needed to go forward a few more yards before he could park up on the near empty newly-developed Cricket Club car park on the left. One of the cars queued up behind him honked their horn briefly in a mixture of frustration and enquiry. It was still not yet quite 9.30 in the morning. Most of the shops in town would only just be opening their doors.

Another honk from behind. This time more prolonged, less enquiring and more indignant. The driver in front of Eaun got out of his vehicle to see what was happening. Eaun gingerly followed his example. Several of the cars in front of him were indicating to turn right in to the Court's car park. This facility was of course not there for the use of the public nor even professional users such as Eaun who actually used the public building. The car park was there solely for 'Official Court Use Only'. This was meant to be the actual people who worked there permanently as well as the local great and the good, the magistrates themselves. This exclusive and highly valued city centre park was guarded by two wooden barriers that answered only to the operation of the key or more usually the flash of the coveted car park pass at the entrance.

At the barrier to the car park stood a gentleman in a black gown. Dressed in grey flannels and a dark V-necked jumper the Gown looked like a history master from one of the several public schools that peppered the city and its surrounds, but instead of holding chalk in his hands was holding a set of keys.

A conversation was taking place between the Gown and the driver of the lead car who had by now got out and was remonstrating with the Gown. The driver was tall, with grey hair parted at the side and wearing a distinctive two-piece pinstripe suit. Eaun recognised Pinstripe from somewhere. He was fairly certain that he was one of the court's magistrates. Eaun could clearly hear the Gown patiently explain that the car park was full and that another car parking space in the city would have to be used. The explanation clearly had no effect on Pinstripe, who from his dominating height continued to smile down in exasperation, gesticulating that the Gown should now be ever such a good chap and open the barrier for him. However, the Gown chose to hold his ground and held his fore-arms aloft with palms outstretched, indicating that there was no way in to the car park, for anyone. Pinstripe jerked his head back, said something that Eaun could not hear before demanding that the Gown just do as he was told and please open the bloody gate. The smile on Pinstripe's face was becoming weaker and his face was slowly turning a deeper red. It was at this point that Pinstripe started to walk towards the Gown, raising his arms as he did so. Instinctively, the Gown moved a step back where his rear end collided with the bollard. On impact with the bollard, the Gown wobbled but just managed to keep his footing and now stood directly in front of Pinstripe. Eaun could clearly see that words were being exchanged between the two men but as the noise from the car horns increased, could not decipher any of the actual words being used. When the Gown then started to admonish Pinstripe by shaking his head and waving his forefinger in unison, Pinstripe obviously thought that this public display had gone far enough and it was time for him to beat a tactical retreat, turning round to smile at the waiting audience of queuing drivers behind him before climbing back in to his own large saloon. Through the open driver's side window and the still fixed grin on his face, Pinstripe made it known to the Gown that this was far from the end of it and that he should know that the matter was being reported. The Gown just stared back before starting to walk down the slope beyond the barrier towards the private rear magistrates' entrance to the courts. There was also a separate gate and portcullis providing a secure entrance for the meat wagons so that the prisoners could be transferred into the cell complex. Before he clambered back in to his Volvo, Eaun heard the gunning of a car engine and a short sharp squeal of rubber on tarmac.

Having witnessed what had just happened, the several cars ahead of Eaun who had originally indicated to turn right in to the court car park had now decided to flick their indicators to turn left into the Cricket Club car park. At least the queue in front of him had vanished and Eaun quickly followed the traffic and found a marked parking space on the ground floor of the new multi-storey structure just beyond the roped mid-wicket boundary where even he, with his limited parking skills, was able to place the Volvo between the lines of the narrow bay. Eaun only had the one client to see but would need to pay for a morning's stay. His wife Vicky always complained about what she termed the 'extortionate' cost of parking in Bath, but Eaun had a soft spot for cricket and did not mind paying to help a local sports club improve its facilities at the expense of those who could afford to pay. Having fed the machine he then returned to his car, placed the ticket in the windscreen before grabbing his briefcase, locking the vehicle and walking over to the wooden seven-bar gate to cross the road to the court entrance. His day at The Circus was about to begin.

~ ~ ~

Kendrick Maclean had first come across Griff before he had even bought Bradstock. Without ever understanding the legalities of any contractual relationship, Griff seemed to have been on some sort of feudal retainer to Mrs Mackenzie. Griff had always looked the same, with cloth cap pulled down over the eyes, ruddy complexion with an alternating red or blue nose, an immaculately knotted green tartan necktie and of course the mud splattered Barbour lookalike replica top. There was always knotted baler twine holding up his green check woollen trousers. Griff was one of these men who could have been aged anywhere between 35 and 70. He spoke rarely but when he did it was almost impossible to hear what he was saying, with a mixture of near impenetrable West Country accent coupled with some sort of mild speech impediment. He had also proved to be a great help to Kendrick Maclean even before he became the master of Bradstock, letting him know when Mrs Mackenzie was out or away, so that he could then nip in to the farm's outbuildings and take detailed measurements for the planned construction and development work ahead. When the completion of the purchase of Bradstock Farm eventually took place, Kendrick Maclean found no difficulty in offering a weekly wage to Griff for him to carry on with his general duties at the farm.

It had only been half an hour since Kendrick Maclean had made the phone call to Griff. He had explained about the difficulty regarding the badger currently adorning the front door and asked that Griff quickly come round to have a look for himself. Before he could finish his brew in the kitchen, Kendrick Maclean had picked up the approaching sound of Griff's hard Land Rover tyres ploughing through the immaculately laid driveway gravel.

Kendrick Maclean walked through the hallway to the knight in armour and opened the front door, clutching his mug of tea marked 'Boss' whilst studiously avoiding sight of what was nailed to the door.

Griff's land Rover was as filthy as he had ever seen it, the ancient black and white front metal number plate rendered indecipherable under the layers of country and agricultural mud and worse.

Kendrick Maclean watched Griff turn the ignition key to kill the engine, before letting the door swing open on the hinges and stepping down on to the gravel. Griff walked around towards the front door before stopping and audibly sucking in his breath through his teeth. Kendrick Maclean thought he heard Griff mutter 'Not good' whilst shaking his head at the same time.

Griff approached the door for a better inspection, peering at how the claws had been smashed by the force of a blunt instrument, probably a hammer, smashing into the four-inch nails now embedded in the oak door. Whilst Griff was looking at the night's work, Kendrick Maclean started relating again from the beginning what had happened and how he had no idea who would do such an appalling act. He never felt comfortable with silences and knew that it was more a nervous reaction to say anything rather than wait until there is something actually worth saying.

Griff took a step back.

'Not good at all,' he said, clearly and distinctly this time. 'It will need sorting.'

Griff moved to the back open section of his Land Rover before bending over and returning with a large metal box, which he then proceeded to open and extract a selection of knives, pliers and other partially rusted instruments.

'You go in and see that Mrs Veronica stays away,' added Griff. Kendrick Maclean had rarely heard him so loquacious.

Kendrick Maclean wanted to know what was planned.

'I will sort it,' said Griff.

'What are we going to do with it,' came the next question from Kendrick Maclean, although what he really meant and understood was what Griff was actually going to do with the corpse.

'I'll take care of it,' came the response. 'That A36 be a dreadful place for badgers being run over.'

With that, Kendrick Maclean knew that there was nothing else for him to do. No, Griff didn't want a cup of tea but could he please have a bowl of warm soapy water.

Ten minutes later, whilst still at the back of the house in the kitchen making another brew for himself, Kendrick Maclean heard the old engine of the Land Rover cough into life. Before he could make it to the front door, Griff's Land Rover was already half way down the drive eating up the gravel. Of the badger there was no sign. The blood had been washed down and swilled away, with the upside down bowl and wrung cloth placed by the front doorstep. Griff had done a thorough job. The nail marks in the old oak of the front door were hardly noticeable, especially when considered with all the other assaults on the ancient portal that had taken place in the last 300 years or more.

Since moving to Somerset, Kendrick Maclean had always wondered why he always saw so many dead badgers on the side of the road. Surely, not all of them had been crucified before being thrown on to the road so that any evidence of wrong-doing disappeared under the wheels of a 48 tonne HGV making its way down the main route from Bristol to the docks at Southampton.

Before moving back in to the house, Kendrick Maclean picked up and pocketed from the driveway the still neatly folded and damp lined A4 personal message of welcome to the county of Somerset.

~ ~ ~

The outside wooden door into Bath Magistrates Court grounds had finally been opened and the early Special Brew crew with their accompanying slavering canines had moved to settle down on the relative comfort of the metal seats near the main sliding entrance doors. Eaun could see a huddle of people already inside the court building. He decided to run the gauntlet towards the entrance, but not before one of the pit bull lookalikes made a lurch towards his left trouser leg. The string around the beast's neck jerked violently.

'Back Goebbels. Back!'

As the string gradually knotted around the dog's throat pulling it away from the flannel of Eaun's suit trouser leg, Goebbels choked spat and salivated in rage. Eaun tried to look cool and not to panic as he headed towards the sliding glass front entrance doors of the court. Eaun heard a sniggering behind him as he at last made it into the building.

Eaun was grateful to join the queue of people already inside the building. A handwritten sign was attached with fraying tape to a trestle table by the security team, warning everyone entering court today that machetes, bladed instruments, knives and other such items were not allowed in the building and should be placed on the table. The queue was hardly moving. Most of the people in front of Eaun were suits, with the occasional lost and perplexed looking citizen who was only there to answer a road traffic summons. It was too early for the hard-core court regulars to put in an appearance. Eaun then noticed yet another handwritten sign, this one announcing that the body scanner was not working. Whilst Eaun was waiting his turn to be searched for machetes and any other bladed weapon that he may have had on his person, he used the time to extract his phone from his inside pocket, turning it on before the message screen lit up. There were a couple of emails from Alex about the case he was dealing with that morning as well as messages from Mrs Wright with suggestions of which secluded country eating establishment they could meet for lunch. There were email messages from Ludmila, letting him know that the man from the bank had phoned twice more. Could he please also ring back a Mr Farquhar, whoever he may have been. Finally, could he please get in contact as soon as possible with Frank. He didn't know anyone called Frank, before quickly realising that this must be Rita's Frank. He was the only Frank that he could think of. Rita Thornham was the firm's Practice Manager.

Eaun suddenly clicked why the court was so busy. Alex had already mentioned this to him on several occasions. Today was actually the day that Bath Magistrates Court was closing. For good. For ever. It was not alone. At least 50 other court buildings that had been dispensing local justice for hundreds of years were also due to disappear before the end of the financial year, in order to 'improve both quality and access to justice' according to the Ministry of Justice mantra that Eaun had read with every court closure. The Ministry bean counters would no doubt be delighted at the very substantial funds about to be raised by the sale of the site of one Bath's prime and most sought after properties.

Sadly, the demise of the Bath court came as little surprise to anyone. Least of all Eaun. The building was actually on the list for closure back in 2016. It was common knowledge that it was only because of pressure from the powerful political class in the city that the less fashionable but more convenient Yate Magistrates Court in South Gloucestershire was axed instead.

The earlier incident at the court car park entrance now all made sense to Eaun. That was why he had seen the previously unheard of queue to get in to the court car park. All of the local magistrates had it seemed wanted to get in on the act and turned up to witness the grand farewell. It also explained why this morning all of the fixtures and fittings in the building had different colour labels attached to them. This is what had happened when the East Mendip Magistrates Court was closed back in 2011. A few days before the actual day of closure, the men from the Estates section at the Ministry turned up on a day when the courthouse was being unused and then labelled everything that was to be kept, retained for further use or disposed of. The blue, yellow and green labels were attached to everything, exactly as they were this morning at Bath Magistrates

Court. Years later, after the East Mendip closure, neither Eaun nor his colleagues were ever able to ascertain what fate befell the two magnificent coats of arms bearing the motto 'Dieu et Mon Droit' that once adorned the building's two courts.

Eaun was next in line for the full body metal detector. It had a green label attached to it. As it did not work, Eaun assumed that it would be soon heading for the skip.

Most of the security staff at the desk and detector still chose to wear face masks, although it had been some time now since the government decreed that it was once more no longer compulsory to wear face coverings in public buildings, including the courts.

'Well, well, if it isn't Mr Wright. Come along to witness another last rites?'

The muffled voice came from one of the security personnel. The mask covered the face but Eaun recognised the voice as one of the old security team that used to work at East Mendip. Under the black mask he could not see the missing upper incisor but the give-away was the undone button at the bottom of the tight cotton white shirt covering the man's belly together with the string vest underneath. He was either Gary or Larry. Eaun could not remember. He was getting really bad at remembering names.

Gary or Larry's colleague was doing the hard work inspecting every briefcase and carrying out a desultory frisking of each entrant with a squeaking apparatus that looked like it had been taken straight from a kid's garden swing ball game.

'Don't worry about our Mr Wright,' said Gary/Larry to his mate. 'He won't be bringing any of his knives and machetes into court with him today.'

With nods of thanks and acknowledgements all round, Eaun was now finally in the bowels of the court house at last and started to head upstairs to check out where Mr Hudderston was on the daily lists posted on the walls.

~ ~ ~

It should have been Alexandra Hilton that was walking into the main concourse at Bath Magistrates Court looking to see on which of the three criminal court lists the name of her client Mr Hudderston was typed. Alex was supposed to be handling all of the criminal defence work at WHW Legal. Until she had joined the firm four years ago, Alex's boss Eaun Wright carried out all of the litigation work in the firm, from PI to divorce and of course crime. On her arrival at the firm, Eaun had quickly started to hand over his criminal file workload to Alex, leaving himself to concentrate on his growing family law practice as well as being able to spend more time managing the firm.

Two years ago, Eaun had finally called an end to his stint as a Duty Solicitor, a role that he had undertaken since arriving in Somerset all those years ago. Alex was now the firm's sole Duty Solicitor and it was she who was on call when her Samsung chirped into life jut after 4am earlier that Wednesday morning.

'Duty Solicitor Call Centre here,' said the woman caller in the warehouse with her broad Yorkshire accent. 'I have a call for you at Keynsham Police Centre. A male adult. Can you take it?'

Alex flicked the bedside lamp switch on and fumbled for her plastic folder containing all the forms that she would ever need. She also grabbed her wooden pencil case. Colleagues may well have scoffed at Alex's retro work accessory but its bulk and weight made sure it was never lost or nicked and that she always had an available an array of writing tools that all worked.

Alex eased one elbow on to the pillow, leaving her right hand free.

She wrote down the details of the detainee. One Charles Battingsdale. An unusual name. Never heard of him. His date of birth, time of arrest and arrival at the police centre were given.

He had been arrested on an allegation of dangerous driving plus intent to supply, both familiar interim catch-all offences used when someone had the misfortune to be arrested in a vehicle with suspicious substances on board and the police had yet no idea where to go with it.

Did Alex require anything else?

Yes please. The unique DSCC reference number. Without this the firm would not be paid. In her first month at the firm, Alex had taken 3 or 4 calls in quick succession and had omitted to record one of the reference numbers on her paperwork. The resulting icy lecture the next morning from Rita, the firm's uncompromising Practice Manager, ensured that she never again submitted any police station attendance forms without that information.

The call ended but with the bedside lamp still on, Alex laid her head back on her pillow and shut her eyes for a few moments. The sleep that she had been woken from had been fitful in any event. The only thing that connected being on duty and flying off on holiday early the next day was the lack of any decent sleep. However unlikely that she would sleep through a telephone ring with the volume on maximum only inches away from her ear, the fear of missing the call or a flight was equally intense. Remaining half awake whilst on duty had just become an occupational hazard.

So, this morning it was to be Keynsham. Detainees ceased being taken to actual traditional police stations several years ago. Happy days, thought Alex, when a police station was actually in a town centre and housed a cell block, CID and even scenes of crime. There were even Enquiry offices to welcome members of the public. The local force, Wessex Constabulary, like other regional forces, now used almost identical new so-called police 'centres', many placed just off the motorways outside the major urban conurbations. These 'centres' at the edge of industrial estates did not encourage the public to come anywhere near them. The tall intimidating fences together with the security locks on all the gates were clearly designed to keep people out as well as keeping them in. Like the ancient notion of every self-respecting English town having its own town hall and courthouse, the idea of the traditional 'local nick' had long disappeared. With the concentration on the 'super centres', the traditional town police station had become a disappearing breed. For the few surviving outposts that remained nominally open, there was often little to encourage any contact from the general public. From her own experience, Alex also knew that it was not unheard of for some buildings housing the local nick to be actually empty of any police officers at all.

Whilst her eyes were still closed, Alex took a further moment to reflect on where she was with her life and her career. Most of her old friends from uni and law college thought that Alex had lost the plot. Most of them were now aged around 30 and were in good jobs earning good money in accountancy, marketing and finance. Alex had a couple of friends who were now teaching Years 2 and 4 respectively at Primary School and even they were earning more than her. Then there was Marcus. They had started to go out as a couple whilst still at law college and stayed together whilst they both started their first jobs as qualified lawyers. After his traineeship, Marcus was offered and accepted a post in the Mergers & Acquisition team at one of Bristol's most prestigious firms, with flash offices overlooking the harbour. Alex had spent all of her professional career working at WHW Legal. Even whilst starting off as solicitors, Marcus's salary was twice what Alex was earning.

The excitement of the new jobs also enticed Alex and Marcus to move in together. They became the envy of all their friends, even their old friends who were now living in London. There were regular articles in all the posh papers together with the glossy weekend supplements about how Somerset's Sedgeton really had become the place to move to, with the town boasting a theatre, galleries, a cinema, one of the country's largest Sunday open markets selling great street food, antiques and every kind of contemporary arts crafts and invention. In addition to a glittering new array of cafes and eateries, catering from vegan to french peasant cuisine, Sedgeton also had its very own Artisan Quarter. The town's new Free School was attracting hundreds of new pupils (and more importantly their cash-rich parents) from near and afar with its promise of new ideas and free-thinking education. Sedgeton was already seen as being the destination up. Should warn you Alex that the OIC is looking at a fairly early preliminary interview on this one.'

Alex thanked the officer for the information and could hear the echoes of the click clicks as the phone was carried down the cavernous long corridors of the custody suite. A metallic cell hatch could be heard slamming down.

'Your brief', resounded the custody sergeant's voice.

Charlie Battingsdale confirmed that it was he and gave his date of birth confirming that he was just 19 years of age and that as far as he could ascertain no one else was listening in to the conversation. He told Alex that he had never been arrested before, 'except when he was a kid'. Alex asked whether he had spoken to any other solicitor on this matter. Charlie said 'no'. Alex then said that she was here to give independent legal advice to him and went on to explain that she would go through all the details with him when they met up, probably in a few hours' time. Charlie sounded apprehensive and jumpy which given his age and the charge he was potentially facing was hardly a surprise. Charlie asked whether Alex could call his Mum and Dad to tell them where he was. Alex told Charlie to ask the police in the custody suite to arrange for them to be told where he was. They were obliged to do this. Charlie should also ask that his request be entered on the custody record, although Alex knew that if it was Matty Houseman was still on duty then this would indeed happen. Before hanging up, Alex told him to try and get some rest and under no circumstances was he to speak to anyone else regarding his case, particularly the police.

Alex knew that the last thing that Charlie or herself would be doing was getting any sleep. Alex now just had to wait till custody called her to let her know when she was needed for interview.

Alex's pen was returned to the pencil case on the bedside table. It looked like there was a long day ahead.

THE CIRCUS

THE LISTS for all three courts looked long, with the authorities no doubt trying to deal with as many cases as they could before the court doors were closed for the final time. Court One, which usually served as the remand court, had the longest list, but Eaun spotted the name of Piers St John Hudderston on the Court Three list of shame, advertised within a glass and light oak display case by the entrance into the court itself. It was only during the journey to Bath that Eaun realised that the WHW Legal court tablet was still with Alex. A few years ago it was decided by the authorities that the Crown would send out all communications electronically, including the advance disclosure papers on a case. Eaun skipped through the Piers Hudderston folder and noticed that a request for disclosure had already been made by Alex to the Crown Prosecution Service, but without the tablet and its secure password there was no way for Eaun to actually receive and read the papers on his client's case.

Eaun went through the double doors of the entrance to Court Three. There was no one there except the legal adviser sitting under the raised benches behind him, where the presiding magistrates sat.

'Well, well, well,' said a friendly voice. 'Come to see the untimely demise of the Circus then?'

The speaker was Dai Evans, who had been serving as a court clerk (long before they were re-named as legal advisers) for many years. Eaun explained his predicament that he had no tablet and no means of accessing the advance disclosure papers from the Crown. Eaun also knew however that the papers on each case not look in the mood for letting anyone in. He recognised him immediately. It was The Gown. He looked suitably restored following his earlier incident at the car park entrance.

'Mr Wright from WHW isn't it,' asked The Gown. Eaun was impressed, but also becoming increasingly concerned at how other people could remember him but that his own ability to remember a name and a face simultaneously was rapidly diminishing. 'Your client, Mr Hudderston, over there by the noticeboard.'

Eaun thanked The Gown for saving him the embarrassment of having to have his client called and identified for him over the court public address system. The man being pointed to by The Gown was identifiable wearing a cream linen jacket with a leather bag slung over the shoulder and a smart pair of deep royal blue chinos. Under the jacket the man had on a crew neck sky blue jumper. On his feet, Eaun's client was wearing a pair of Jesus sandals over black socks. Mr Hudderston appeared to be engrossed avidly reading the posters on the Public Information Board advising on the help that was available for sexually transmitted diseases. Experience had taught Eaun that anyone wearing a suit or who was otherwise well presented in court, but not acting in any official capacity, were inevitably there attending as a defendant for alleged wife beating, fraud, sexual deviancy or imploring the court not to disqualify them from driving.

'Mr Hudderston, I presume?' The man turned around and nodded to Eaun, who then introduced himself, apologising for the delay and piling all the blame on the Crown for not getting the papers to him in time.

On being face to face with his client, Eaun was immediately taken aback by the thick shock of snow white hair, eyebrows and moustache. The hair was neatly tied back in a tidy pony tail. Mr Hudderston was also wearing red framed spectacles. Before proceeding further, Eaun remembered to apologise for Miss Hilton not being in court for him today, but that she had a trial go over for a second day in Bristol and had to return there. Eaun made sure to tell Mr Hudderston that the excellent news was that he was effectively getting a service upgrade, now having his case dealt with by the Head of Litigation at WHW Legal himself. A visible look of relief and gratitude seemed to sweep Mr Hudderston's face.

'We do however need to have a chat,' said Eaun.

~ ~ ~

As Gustave Paterson swung the steering wheel of the vehicle to the left, the big Mercedes SUV swung through the imposing gates of The Sedgeton Grange Hotel & Spa. His wife Anabel was leaning forward in the passenger seat, applying the last of her final morning make-up before she started her day's work. She audibly cursed Gustave as he straightened the steering out heading towards the large mock Jacobean building in front of them, causing her to slightly smudge her lipstick. There were no cars parked in front of the building with its imposing entrance and large porch. Only guests were allowed to park at the front. Gus (all his friends called him that) followed the roadway around the side of the building to a large open yard where several cars and vans were already parked up by the beer barrels and laundry waiting to be collected.

Even now, when parking up with the staff cars, Gus still felt a shiver of excitement and anticipation on driving up to the imposing building. Anabel and he had met nearly 10 years ago when they were both ensnared in the death throes of their respective first marriages. They had been introduced to each other by mutual friends at a dinner party in Chalk Farm. Gus thought that it sounded ridiculously wet and unmanly to admit aloud, but it really was a case of love at first sight. Within 6 months of both of them receiving their decree absolutes in the post, they had once more tied the knot at Camden Town Hall. Happily, despite the crippling expense of having to pay off his first wife and being obliged to pay the school fees at Gordonstoun until both the boys had completed their 'A' levels, Gus was still able to rely on the not insubstantial regular funds allocated just outside the protected perimeter. Security cameras dangled from the underneath of the first floor of the building, where the long rectangular windows reminded Alex of the arrow loops used by archers in medieval fortifications.

Alex parked up, rang the bell by the front door and waited. Alex imagined that the only employees working at this time of the morning would be those in the custody suite. A few minutes later, Alex heard a bang and a female Detention Officer appeared from along the corridor and pressed an internal button which allowed the glass front door to slowly slide open. Alex was ushered inside and guided into another door marked 'Solicitors' just down the corridor.

'The sergeant said that we were all ready to go once I got here,' said Alex more in hope than expectancy.

'The officers in the case are not here yet,' said the DO. 'Rest assured that the custody sergeant will be with you as soon as he is able. He is currently dealing with another case.'

Alex sighed. The DO was young but carried with her that air of certainty and conviction that came from being in a position where it was rare for anyone to ever answer back. Alex knew that it was useless to argue the point with her. Alex therefore settled down on to a chair next to a table with a phone on it. She knew that as soon as the DO shut the door behind her, Alex would be locked in until someone opened it from the outside. Like the rest of the custody suite, there were no windows or access to natural light. The good news was that there was by the other wall a drinks machine offering delights from Diet Coke to Cappuccinos. The clientele were obviously changing, with Earl Grey and Mountain Stream Sparkling Water also now being offered to the punters. The bad news was that Alex had come away without any change on her. She was desperate for a drink but it would have to wait.

Instead, whilst waiting, Alex started to sort out her day ahead, a day that had already been turned upside down. She started with making a brief call to the office leaving a message for Eaun to help her out. She knew that Wednesdays were supposed to be his dedicated work day and he would not be happy. However, the reality was that there was no way that she would be finished in Keynsham before she had to be at Bath Court by 9.30. It might have worked if the client was already on remand and was waiting for her in the cells in Bath. He would not be going anywhere. But Alex knew full well that the client was Piers Hudderston and that he had paid money up front to be privately represented. Eaun would just have to cover for her. After all, she had done many favours for Eaun in the past, ensuring that the firm maintained a happy clientele. Alex knew that the telephone message would be picked up by Ludmila straight away and be passed on to Eaun without delay. Ludmila was reliable and thorough.

Alex then dragged the tablet out of her work bag and started drafting a full email of explanation to Eaun to supplement everything that was already on file. She warned Eaun in her email that Mr Hudderston was likely to be on edge and would probably need careful handling. She then pressed 'Send' on the tablet.

Alex then waited. Nothing happened. For very nearly two hours.

Alex eventually heard the door to the Solicitors' waiting room push open. The teenage DO had been replaced by the cheery smile of Sergeant Matthew Houseman.

'Sorry for the dreadful wait Alex. Good to see you. Looks as if we are all set to go now,' he said.

~ ~ ~

Eaun was certain that he could not be alone in his belief that over the past half century, buildings constructed for public use usually had the one constant: the designers and architects responsible were oblivious to what the visiting public actually needed. In the case of Bath Magistrates Court, the visiting public included the defendants, their lawyers and witnesses. Every self-respecting court in the country used to have a Robing or Advocates Room, where entry was usually by electronic code. These lawyers' enclaves provided a quiet haven to prepare cases, make confidential calls, as well as find out what the hot gossip was on the local legal circuit. They also often had their own toilet facility as well as exclusive access to the cells in the basement underneath. Sharing a public urinal with a prosecution witness standing next to you who had just been remorselessly shredded in your ruthless cross-examination of him was, in the extensive experience of Eaun, never either comfortable nor always entirely safe.

It was only after a short period following the opening of the court that the advocates' room disappeared. This was at the time when the interests of witnesses had become the latest 'paramount' priority for the government of the day. Having been advised that they were no longer paramount, the lawyers were told to remove themselves, which of course they duly did. The several dedicated legal interview rooms also started to disappear one by one, being taken over by other more worthy causes such as Witness Support, Probation, Youth Offending and the video link team. The court Duty Solicitor of the day at least had the benefit of the windowless stationery cupboard housing the photocopier, behind the arrival check in desk at the top of the stairs. Not being the court Duty Solicitor, like the rest of the solicitors and counsel that morning, Eaun was left to forage for the least crowded public spot available. He then saw someone whom he recognised as a barrister from a Bristol set of chambers tentatively wave towards a suit, no doubt her client, who had just entered on to the concourse and was reporting at the desk. The woman then made the error of moving forward to greet her client, taking her bag and papers with her. Eaun pounced and shepherded Mr Hudderston into his new and relatively secluded space behind the Out of Order hot drinks dispenser machine. The days of the WRVS café that once served lemon drizzle cake and proper coffee had long disappeared. A large green label was taped to the top of the drinks machine. Its fate was sealed.

Unlike many of the other advocates in the room, Eaun's new office at least enjoyed some privacy plus wall space to take vertical notes.

The charge against Mr Hudderston was straightforward enough, an allegation of exposure, contrary to s66 of the Sexual Offences Act 2003. The charge sheet provided most of the paperwork in the file. A PNC printout told Eaun that Mr Hudderston had no previous convictions or cautions, what was euphemistically referred to in the trade as 'being of good character'. There were no witness statements available, with all the details of the offence being contained in the half page Summary of Key Evidence sheet that had been prepared by the OIC and was placed at the top of the bundle. It was alleged that Mr Hudderston had been seen at a local layby off the A36 that was habitually used as a site where offences of a sexual nature had been carried out over a long period of time. The Summary went on to state that the Wessex Constabulary, alerted by the concerns of local people in the community, had been carrying out regular patrols on this part of the A36. On the night in question, the OIC and a uniformed colleague travelling with him in the passenger seat of the marked police vehicle drew up at the lay by in question and from the headlights of the vehicle were able to witness Mr Hudderston walking from behind some trees, fiddling with flies on his trousers but with his penis quite clearly exposed to the elements and obvious for anyone to view who happened to be using the layby. The Summary went on to say that Mr Hudderston was arrested at the scene, taken to Keynsham Police Centre and interviewed by the OIC himself. During interview, Mr Hudderston had made full admissions that he was alone on a public road, the lay by, and that his penis was placed outside his trousers for anyone to see.

Eaun now understood why the bundle of papers in his hand was so thin. Mr Hudderston's case had been placed in the GAP court, for those cases where there would be a Guilty Anticipated Plea. The police and the CPS were fully expecting Mr Hudderston to plead Guilty today.

'But I am guilty,' said Mr Hudderston. 'What the police officer says is true. I did as they allege that I did. When can we go into court and get this over with?'

Piers Hudderston was looking at Eaun intently through his bright red spectacle frames. It was only when he moved slightly away to gain a little more breathing space that Eaun was able to have a proper look at his client and realised how tall but painfully thin his client was. He really was built like a rake, with Eaun imagining that the belt holding up his client's chinos must have had several extra holes perforated in the leather to ensure that they actually stayed up. Eaun also realised that he already knew his client. The give-away had been the Jesus sandals and the black socks. The only other person that Eaun knew who habitually wore sandals and socks every day of the year and for every occasion was a social worker with bad teeth who worked for Children's Social Care at County. It was clear that Mr Hudderston did not recognise Eaun from earlier encounters, but to avoid any later embarrassment, Eaun decided to mention his recognition now.

'I think that I may already know you,' Eaun stated. Mr Hudderston looked mystified.

'Must have been 10 or 15 years ago, you came to look at our house just outside Sedgeton when we were thinking of getting an extension for the back. Nearly didn't recognise you. Think that you had long black hair in those days.'

What Eaun did not mention to his client was that Vicky and himself had ultimately chosen the design proposals of another local architect, who submitted a far more inventive and cheaper proposal. Eaun also omitted to mention the fact that after several visits to the house, he had remembered how his wife Vicky announced that Mr Hudderston was 'really creepy' and that there was no way he was coming to the house whilst she and the girls were there.

'Ah yes,' that was in an earlier life,' volunteered Mr Hudderston. 'Gave up being a proper architect several years ago. Got fed up of clients expecting to be given free advice all the time and then not paying their bills for their hideously boring little lean-tos and lookalike extensions. Plus, everyone with a Drafting Board and some nasty cheap software was setting themselves up as providing 'architectural services' when they did not then need to have to bother with boring stuff like professional regulation or indemnity insurance. So, I got out. Best thing that I ever did.'

Eaun felt quietly satisfied that for once he had managed to correctly identify someone, even though he could not remember the actual name. There was however, one fact that still niggled.

'Your hair, it is very distinctive,' said Eaun politely. 'I am not certain but did you not have a great deal of jet back hair back when we last met?'

'Absolutely right,' responded Piers Hudderston. 'The wife walked out the front door one day and said that she was never coming back. Within six months all of the hair on my body had turned white.'

Eaun was tempted to ask for more details but decided that this was neither the most appropriate time nor place. Eaun then got stuck in to the task at hand. After just a few minutes, Eaun had ascertained that not only did Mr Hudderston not know that that particular lay by on the A36 was an historic and popular dogging site, but from the nature of his responses Eaun was fairly sure that his client had no idea what the sport of dogging entailed either. On asking what he was doing at the layby outside his vehicle in the hours of darkness, Mr Hudderston was immediate in his response. He had been caught short. He had been having some UTI problems and was now having to go to the toilet 3 or 4 times a night. Yes, he had contacted the GP. Doctors never actually see their patients any more but after a telephone consultation with the nurse practitioner, he was given a prescription to collect from the pharmacy. He wasn't sure whether the medicine was working or not. He was fairly sure that he had called the practice before the incident. They would have a record. It was correct that his 'todger' (to use Mr Hudderston's terminology of choice) was outside his trousers when the police found him, but he had had a wee behind the tree and was in the process of tucking himself away and doing up the buttons on his trousers when the full beam of the patrol car headlight illuminated him.

Eaun then asked Mr Hudderston to confirm that he had indeed been interviewed by the police as the case summary stated. Yes he had, but he had been well treated by the policeman and definitely not been forced to say anything against his will. Yes, he had also been offered the free services of a solicitor to help him. However, he was told by the officer that the solicitor would take several hours to get there and that in the meantime Mr Hudderston would have to stay waiting in the cells. Anyway, at that stage he genuinely believed that he had done nothing wrong and was therefore happy to be interviewed without a solicitor. Did Mr Hudderston not explain to the police officer in interview that he had been caught short? No, he did not think that he was ever asked and did not think to mention. Eaun carefully explained what a police caution was and had Mr Hudderston ever been offered one? No, he hadn't.

Piers Hudderston turned to face Eaun directly.

Mr Hudderston told Eaun that it was only towards the end of the formal interview when the police officer had explained what the law was to him, that he realised that he had done wrong, even though it was unintentional.

'Look, I now know I made an error of judgement not having a solicitor represent me in the police station,' explained the client. 'I have never had any dealings with the law before, except for buying a house. I don't want to go to prison and I want the court to make a direction that my name is not going to be made public. I want you to do something about this. I have my good name to consider and this includes my position as Honorary Secretary in the Wessex Monuments & Historical Buildings Society to consider. Don't get me wrong, I am not religious or anything like that but because I have obviously always had an interest in ancient architecture, I am also a church warden at one of Somerset's oldest village churches. This must remain a secret and it is imperative that none of this ever gets out.'

Eaun hardly knew where to start.

'Firstly, the good news is that you won't be going to prison,' replied Eaun. 'From what I have heard to date, I am also fairly sure that you have not even committed any offence of Exposure.'

'But how long will I get? What is the worst scenario?'

Eaun hated these questions. But they were inevitable. Everyone asked and demanded to be told. Whatever happened, there was no way that Mr Hudderston was going anywhere near a prison. But from experience Eaun also knew that if he did not tell Mr Hudderston 'the worst', then he would within minutes of leaving the court precincts be clicking on the internet to find out anyway.

'Six months imprisonment in the Magistrates Court and two years maximum in the Crown Court and in some cases you may have to sign on to the Sex Offenders' Register. But just let me re-iterate once more that you are not, I repeat not, going to prison on this matter.'

The response from Eaun seemed to have little effect on Mr Hudderston, who remained silent.

'Now let me deal with your second point,' continued Eaun. 'The court cannot make an order prohibiting the publication of your name. This is a public court where the public are allowed to sit in and where proceedings can be published in the media. However, the good news for you is that last time I looked in Court Three, there were no members of the public queuing up to sit in the gallery and no journalists either who were there to fearlessly report on your case or indeed any other local case today. They already have their 'story' of today, being the last day that the court remains open. Unless you have committed a shocking murder, are an MP caught with the snout in the trough or their trousers down, play for a Premiership football team or regularly appear in the pages of Hello or OK magazines, the local press gave up a long time ago covering what went on in their local courts. In your particular personal and local circumstances Mr Hudderston, the *Courier* is not even in existence any more to even report of the allegations being made against you,'

'Just the one more question before we can make progress on this,' said Eaun. 'Did you ever intend that when you were putting away your willy, sorry todger, anyone should actually see it? When your todger was outside your trousers was it your intention that on seeing your todger that person would become upset and distressed at what they saw?'

'No, of course not. The whole thing was a ghastly accident.'

'That being the case, my definitive advice to you is to plead Not Guilty. The offence has not been committed. You should never have been charged. There is no evidence against you.'

'But I admitted that I did it,' responded a confused Mr Hudderston. 'My todger was exposed. But I am definitely not going to jail?'

'Actually, you have admitted nothing. You are innocent. And indeed, you will not be serving any custodial sentence.'

If the drinks dispenser had worked, Eaun would have called a temporary halt to the proceedings so that his client could gather his thoughts over a cup of coffee, even if the slurry was undrinkable.

There was one more line of questioning that Eaun still needed to explore with Piers Hudderston.

'You mentioned earlier that you 'gave up' from being an architect,' said Eaun. 'Can you tell me what you do now for a living?'

'Absolutely. I am a now a therapist and counsellor,' replied Mr Hudderston. 'Four weeks on an online training course where I picked up all the right lingo that I needed and I have never looked back. Like my old rivals the architectural consultants, I can call myself what I like and charge what I like and answer to no one. The great thing about Sedgeton and its surrounds is that everyone wants to have their own analyst and are more than happy to pay me a minimum £85 in advance for a 50 minute session, never complain and think that I am absolutely wonderful. All I have to do is to wait for them to start speaking, occasionally nod whilst they ramble on endlessly about themselves and then give them either a metaphorical hug in sympathy or alternatively a brief lecture on how to demonstrate a bit more of the old moral fibre in order to get on more successfully in life. Works a treat. Every time.'

Piers Hudderston was quietly smiling to himself as he described his current gainful employment to Eaun.

'Look Mr Wright, I really appreciate everything that you are saying but I just want everything to be over and to be able to get on with things once more. You have already said that there will be no press in there. That will mean I can go in there and plead guilty this morning and you have already said that I will not go to jail. Whether I get a fine, probation, community service or whatever they call it these days it will mercifully at least all be over and ended today.'

'Think that there may be a small issue here, Mr Hudderston,' explained Eaun. 'You currently are a man of no convictions. Leaving aside the matter of whether your name ends up on the Sexual Offences Register, what happens if one of your clients in Sedgeton makes the not unreasonable request from you that they want to see a DBS result before they start disclosing all the dark secrets of their life to you? You will know better than myself, but I imagine that news of your appearance at Bath Magistrates Court today may well spread quickly and signal the end of your career in that particular sector.'

Piers Hudderston was silent for some time as he absorbed what he had just been told.

'However, not only have you committed no offence in my view,' explained Eaun. 'But if you plead Guilty this morning or are found Guilty at a later date then the cost to you, financial and otherwise, will be a great deal more than any court fine.'

Mr Hudderston looked crestfallen and his crown of snow white hair seemed to go a little whiter.

'I suppose that you are right,' Mr Hudderston eventually conceded. 'I was starting to panic and had not really considered all of this. Thank you.'

For Eaun, there was one further difficult part of the conversation to come. The good news was that Mr Hudderston was by now actually starting to believe that not only had he committed no offence but that in addition he would not be going to jail. The next inevitable question was when the case would be dealt with. How long would it take to get a trial? In the magistrates court, many months. In the Crown Court, there were already extreme delays in holding trials before the coronavirus arrived, but especially post-Covid at least a year and possibly several years wait said Eaun, who could already feel Mr Hudderston's new-found belief in justice begin to fray at the edges once more.

There was also still one further difficult hurdle to cross.

It was Mr Hudderston who said that at least when he finally wins his case, either in the Magistrates or the Crown Court, he would then mercifully get all of his legal costs back.

'Er, no,' replied Eaun, who then had to explain how in order to prove his own innocence, Mr Hudderston on winning the case would only get a fraction of his costs back.

'I am not sure that I understand this,' said Mr Hudderston. 'I do as you suggest and plead Not Guilty today. I am found innocent after a later trial (assuming that there is still a trial) but I still have to pay most of my own legal costs to prove my own innocence?'

'Yes, I am afraid so.'

It was at times like these that Eaun felt deeply ashamed of the criminal justice system of which he was a fully participating and card-carrying member.

Half an hour later however, Eaun had agreed a strategy with Mr Hudderston, who had eventually agreed that he was indeed Not Guilty and that he could not and should not plead to something of which he was innocent. Eaun would now speak to the prosecutor and Dai Evans the legal adviser about being given time to make representations for the whole case to be kicked out. On the financial side, another £1000 plus VAT (in addition to the original £750 plus VAT already paid) was agreed to be paid to Eaun to make all the necessary representations to the CPS and to appear at the next procedural magistrates' court hearing, wherever and whenever that may be. The costs of trial (if it happened) would be discussed nearer the time. Mr Hudderston assured Eaun that when it came to protecting his good name, costs would not be a problem and that as soon as he got the account from WHW Legal he would arrange for his mother to have it settled immediately, as she had done the first account. If Eaun had earlier known anything about the mother's involvement, he thought that he may well have asked for a revised figure to be paid on account.

With a tap of reassurance on Mr Hudderston's stick-like upper arm, Eaun headed off to Court Three to arrange for his client's case to be formally called. Whilst speaking to Mr Hudderston, talk of his client's urinary afflictions had caused Eaun to move the weight on his legs and even to wince a little. However, he would put off the ultra violet lighting of the court's public toilet facilities until he had completed his work at court for that morning.

~~~

When she unlocked the office door that morning, Ludmila had been hoping for a quiet day. She had not even had time to ask Madge to relieve her at the office reception desk half way through the morning as usual, for her to get a restorative cup of coffee, even if it was instant.

Mr Curtis from Western Provincial had called twice more. He seemed to have accepted that Mr Darby-Henderson was regretfully not in the office, and all his efforts were now concentrated on being able to speak to Mr Wright. Yes, he appreciated that Mr Wright was in court. Yes, he also appreciated that it was not always easy to contact someone who is on his feet in court, but did not she (ie Ludmila) understand that that it was really essential that he, Mr Curtis, speak to one of the partners without any further delay or prevarication. Ludmila responded that the office was doing everything that they could to get the messages safely to Mr Wright, in the absence of Mr Darby-Henderson.

Talking of whom, the biggest mystery of the day was what had happened to Julian Digby-Henderson. In all the time that Ludmila had been working for WHW Legal, she had always known him to be punctilious and reliable, even more so than Mr Wright. He was always in the office well before Ludmila, to open the morning's post. She could not remember the last day that he had 'pulled a sickie' as Ludmila's English colleagues called it during the office gossip breaks in the kitchen. What was particularly odd was that there was no message sent through as to where he was and when he would be back in the office. When she eventually turned up at her usual time of 9.30, Mr Digby-Henderson's secretary, Felicity Lawton, claimed to know nothing of her boss's whereabouts. With Felicity however, there could be no certainty of anything. She was not known to all her work colleagues as The Poison Dwarf without reason.

Ludmila had earlier explained to Mr Curtis at the bank that she had even telephoned Mr Darby-Henderson at his home address. This was actually true. As she waited for the phone to be picked up at the other end, Ludmila imagined the ringing tone echoing around the large and extravagant imposing glass and concrete modern brutalist structure where Mr Darby-Henderson resided alone just outside the nearby village of Oakhill. And no, she was not able to give his home number over to Mr Curtis.

Almost rivalling the shock non-appearance of Julian Darby-Henderson, was the unknown whereabouts of Rita, the firm's Practice Manager. Rita Thornham must have started at the firm in the days when double entries on paper ledgers and adding machines were still all the vogue. As the firm had computerised and moved forward over the years, so also had Rita Thornham. The days when Rita was in charge of just petty cash and salaries had long gone. As Practice Manager, Rita now merited her name and job title embossed on the accounts department door. Not only did she now control and manage all the firm's finances, but she was also now running HR.

For a few seconds the reception switchboard fell silent. Ludmila thought that she might have enough time to nip upstairs and make a quick cup of well-deserved coffee. Before she could ask Madge to pop on down and give her a few minutes the phone rang again. It was Mr Farquhar again. No, he could not say where he was phoning from. And yes, it was still imperative that he spoke to Mr Wright without any further delay. As soon as the receiver had been replaced on the cradle, the telephone console started to flash again. A male voice, but on this occasion the caller was neither Mr Curtis nor Mr Farquhar. Ludmila recognised the deep lugubrious tones from somewhere, but couldn't quite place the voice.

'Frank here,' said the caller. Ah yes, recalled Ludmila. Rita's husband. He had asked to speak to Mr Wright earlier and she had passed the message on. Checking up on her already and it is not even half way through the morning.

'Good morning Frank,' said Ludmila. No, Ludmila had no idea where Rita was that morning. She had little idea where anyone seemed to be that morning. She confirmed that there had been no sign of Rita and no messages left. Had he tried her mobile? Yes, of course he had. He was not an idiot. Ludmila quickly picked up that this was not a casual social call. Frank sounded genuinely agitated. Ludmila offered an explanation that she had probably had an appointment with the doctor, dentist or perhaps even slipped in a visit at her favourite eye lash studio in town.

'That does not explain why she did not sleep in her own bed last night,' said Frank. Instead of expressing immediate concern and solidarity with Frank, the way that he had explained 'her bed' unaccountably started Ludmila painting an immediate picture in her head of Frank being banished to the single bed in the Thornham household's guest room while Rita enjoyed for herself the spacious delights of the matrimonial double bed. She could not envisage Rita ever choosing to sleep in any guest bedroom in her own home.

'I don't know what to say,' said Ludmila. She genuinely was lost for words. How and why did Rita not return home the night before? Ludmila knew that they had both been living in

Sedgeton for most of their lives. Frank clearly needed someone to speak to and today everyone wanted to be speaking to Ludmila. He confirmed that he had checked with both the local cottage hospital and the Royal United Hospital in Bath. There was no sign. When the police eventually answered the phone on their non-emergency number, they said that someone would call her back. Two hours later, he was still waiting for the call.

Ludmila did all she could really do, by promising that she would spread the word and be back in touch with him as soon she heard anything.

Ludmila replaced the receiver. Happily, the Easter holiday weekend was starting on Friday morning, when she could then escape from all this madness for at least a few days.

The red lights of the telephone system lit up once more with the metallic ring following a second or so later.

'Kurva!' Ludmila audibly pleaded under her breath whilst throwing her hands in the air. No one was around to hear.

THE FORCES OF LAW & ORDER

THERE WERE now just 652 to see out. DC Denise Halloran, collar number 1274, knew that all police officers anywhere near her vintage were aware of the exact number that applied to them: the number of days to go until they retire from the force. There were times when she felt sad that she even knew the figure. She was fairly sure that there were some that she had helped send to prison over the years who crossed a line off in their cell wall every morning as part of the countdown to their release date. As soon as anyone started a criminal sentence, the first thing that they were told at prison was their release date.

It wasn't even that she disliked her job. True, like every job there were parts that she hated, but that was true with every occupation. There were still parts that gave Denise a big buzz. It was only a month before that she had rushed out of Crown Court in Taunton and punched the air in elation as the chairman of the jury announced a finding of guilt for historic sexual offences on a case that she had been working on for over a year. Real justice actually being seen to be done.

It was just that the job was getting less fun and more stressful. Perhaps it was just an age thing that can happen to anyone. She definitely felt a great deal more tired these days and any energy was prone to disappear quickly.

Today she was on earlies. Although based in Yeovil, as part of the Criminal Investigation Department in the Wessex Constabulary, Denise and her colleagues covered all of Somerset as well as other parts of the West Country.

It had already taken her nearly an hour of her day to drive from her home just outside Wells to the Keynsham Police

Station. Once she had been allowed into the complex and found an empty desk and chair she had a cursory look at the papers in front of her. Suspected stolen Beamer, jumped the lights on the A361 just outside Clark's Village in Street and then an ensuing chase with two suspects eventually apprehended but only after an expanded tour of The Levels and an unexpected termination courtesy of the spiked Stinger across the A39 heading towards Bridgwater. DC Halloran was quietly impressed at the level of police co-ordination. A third suspect had fled the scene. A subsequent search of the vehicle found a large packet of what was suspected Class A. The alleged offences had taken place in her 'home' division of Yeovil in South Somerset, but for reasons that she could not fathom, the arresting wooden-tops had taken the suspects to Keynsham rather than the far more convenient and closer custody centre at Bridgwater. In an earlier age the suspects would have been taken to Yeovil Police Station, where today the expansive custody suite lay sealed off, redundant and unused.

When Denise had started off in CID, she remembered being told by her then DI that she could expect a constant work load of between six and eight cases for her to be working on at any one time. Anything more than that and you will not be able to do your job properly, she had been told confidently. If today's case was going anywhere that would bring her active files total to 31. Denise simply did not have the time to work properly on all of these files, ranging from fraud and kidnap to serious assault including use of weapons. She also had a year-old firearms case where she was still waiting to hear back from the armourer and she had had to bail the defendant for yet another three months. Denise dreaded answering the calls from both victims and witnesses, asking what was happening to their case. Often, nothing was happening because there was no one around to work on the case. It was not just CID that was under pressure. Denise knew that there were occasions when she was working nights that if there was a major incident occurring in somewhere like her home town of Wells, there were in fact no officers left to send out. A thin blue line indeed.

It looked like she had been assigned Phil Jefferies for this case. He had just messaged in saying that he was driving past the rowing club at Saltford and would be with her in five minutes. Denise looked at the suspects' names on the paperwork. She recognised neither. She had also been informed by the custody suite that one of the dynamic duo waiting to be interviewed had now demanded the immediate services of a well-known large Bristol criminal defence solicitors' firm. The other had asked for the duty and Alexandra Hilton had already arrived and was waiting. Things were looking up. Phil was easy to work with and great on the details that Denise seemed to increasingly miss these days. Alex was also a pleasure to work with, even if she did work for the forces of darkness. Young but determined. Even when things were fraught, Alex was at least always polite with everyone. To anyone who has ever worked in the criminal justice system, they would know that waiting around goes with the job. Denise had spent many hours over the past few years sipping a coffee with Alex and chewing the cud on how their respective personal and professional lives could be immeasurably improved.

Denise picked up her file of paperwork and headed for the custody suite. From tomorrow, only 651 days to go.

~ ~ ~

As soon as he re-entered Court Three, Eaun could sense the tension. The Gown was standing by the dock and with theatrical authority invited the court to rise. The three lay magistrates then trooped in to their seats on the bench facing everyone else. The chair for today in Court Three was no less than Pinstripe. Over the years that Eaun had been in court before him, Pinstripe had always sat as one of the two wingers. However, Pinstripe must have been attending on all the right MOJ courses for here he was sitting as a Chairman, with all the power that went with such a position.

The Gown was standing in front of the dock with his head proudly tilted high, eyes firmly fixed on the clock above the witness stand opposite. Pinstripe welcomed everyone to his court, managing to constantly smile through his deliberations. As he scanned the court before him, Pinstripe's sight travelled nowhere near the Gown.

Actually inside Court Three, Eaun was able to get a far better and closer view of Pinstripe. The woollen cloth of his suit was dark grey with a thin chalk stripe. The shirt was sky blue but sported a white collar, the style that was once all the rage more than 30 years ago. Eaun wondered whether the collar was detachable. He suspected not. A matching red necktie and silk handkerchief in the breast pocket of the jacket completed the attire. If he had remembered to wear the essential but missing waistcoat, Eaun would have sworn that Pinstripe was trying to pass himself off as a practising barrister circa 1984. In the magistrate's court, of course, there was no need for barristers to wear their wig or tabs.

Pinstripe had a look of grim unhappiness across his face. The prosecutor, who looked just about old enough to be doing her week's work experience at the CPS, stood up to say that she was not yet in a position to deal with the case that had just been formally called. Regretfully, by this stage, everyone connected with that case was already present in court, waiting, including the scowling shaven-headed defendant in the dock dressed in his HMP regulation grey track suit top and bottom. The prosecutor eventually confessed that she needed a brief adjournment to check a bail address with the police before conditional bail could be considered for the young man in the dock.

To Eaun, the request from the Prosecutor seemed neither unusual nor unreasonable. However, the look of grim unhappiness on Pinstripe's face quickly changed to complete bafflement and perplexity.

With barely hidden pomposity, whether intended or otherwise, Pinstripe responded that the request for an adjournment was simply not understood. Did the prosecutor not realise that justice delayed was justice denied? The whole situation was little short of scandalous.

'That's right, Your Honour,' chimed the by now grinning defendant in the glass enclosed dock. 'You tell 'em.'

'That is enough from the dock,' admonished Pinstripe. 'Any further outbursts and you will be taken back down to the cells.'

Eaun thought that Pinstripe could also have commented to the defendant that there was no need to call him Your Honour. A simple 'Sir' would have sufficed. However, Pinstripe simply looked to the ceiling before eventually returning his gaze of utter puzzlement to the unfortunate Prosecutor.

'I am not happy. The Court is not happy. This should have been prepared properly before you stood up. However, on this occasion you really leave the court no option. I will allow a five minute adjournment. No more.'

With that, Pinstripe stood, turned and waited for his two wingers.

'Court will rise,' boomed the Gown, slightly late thought Eaun. Pinstripe glanced behind him with irritation as he and his colleagues retreated towards the sanctuary of their retiring room. The wretched prosecutor, dressed in her standard court uniform of black skirt and jacket with white blouse and her dark hair tied back in a bun, made a half-hearted attempt to run out of the room to make the necessary call to the police to check out the bail address. The unexpected interruption at least gave Eaun the opportunity that he had been looking for. He nodded his head to the Gown with the notion of having a quick chat at the back of the court away from everyone else waiting for their case to be called.

Eaun immediately complimented the Gown on the way he handled such a delicate situation at the car park barriers earlier in the morning. A small glow of both acknowledgement and appreciation crossed the Gown's face. Yes, three of the cases listed to be heard before Mr Hudderston's case were unrepresented. These three would therefore have to wait, the Gown announced. Two of the other cases on the list had requested to see the court duty solicitor for the day, but he was currently tied up downstairs seeing the prisoners in the cells. To facilitate the continued smooth running of the court, Eaun confirmed that the case of Mr Hudderston was now all set to be called. Yes, in the circumstances of course Mr Wright could go next. It would be the final case before the luncheon adjournment.

Whilst waiting for the return of the Prosecutor, Eaun quietly enquired of the Gown whether he was expecting anything more of the promised repercussions following the events earlier that morning at the car park entrance. The Gown told Eaun that he had already spoken to his union and they were looking at harassment at the work place, a possible criminal charge of common assault plus a personal injury claim for damages. So, no, as far as he was concerned, he was certainly not expecting any action to be taken against himself. The Gown also delivered a very large and visible wink in Eaun's direction.

Two minutes later the prosecutor was hitching up the hem of her skirt above the knee and was by now managing to successfully half-trot back into Court Three as quickly as she was able. Eaun learned from Dai Evans that she was called Miss Ponsonby. Eaun also imagined how on her return to chambers later that day Miss Ponsonby would no doubt be checking with her clerk what the chances were of her changing career direction to specialising in taxation, land law, planning or even admiralty. In fact, anything except criminal law. On return to her chair, gulping for air and glowing from her exertions, Miss Ponsonby announced disconsolately that the police still needed more time to check the validity of the proposed bail address for the defendant in the dock.

All of the older more experienced prosecutors that Eaun used to deal with had gone, either made redundant, pensioned off or in a couple of cases had just disappeared without trace.

It was at this point that Dai Evans, the legal adviser, took charge of the situation. He was not going to allow his final day in court be ruined by anarchy and general collapse. Whilst Pinstripe and the other two magistrates were still in the traps in their retiring room waiting to be summonsed back in to Court Three, Dai announced to everyone connected with the current case that they should return at 2pm. Even from where he was seated several rows back, Eaun was sure that he could hear Miss Ponsonby whisper a desperate 'thank you' towards the clerk. The defendant in the dock just shrugged his shoulders and accompanied his jailers down the steps to the cells, mumbling resignedly that 'no one knew what they were fucking doing any more' before making the audible and specific demand that he did not want 'any green stuff' in his sandwiches for lunch.

With Court Three now near empty, Dai Evans then picked up the telephone on his desk and spoke quietly into the mouthpiece. A few seconds later, accompanied by a 'Court Rise' the magistrates returned to their seats. As Pinstripe made himself comfortable in the centre chair, Eaun could see Dai stand up, turn around and give an explanation to the bench of what had been happening. After a few seconds, Dai turned round and spoke in to the microphone on the desk to announce 'Piers Hudderston to Court Number Three please. Piers Hudderston Court Three please.' Eaun could hear the metallic tone of Dai's slight Welsh lisp reverberate around the cavernous public concourses outside the double doors of Court Three.

Eaun got up and moved from the back of the court to guide his client Mr Hudderston towards the single chair just in front of the enclosed glass dock. Before the legal adviser was able to formally introduce the parties and read the charge, Pinstripe was already leaning over his desk and lectern.

'No, no. This is a serious offence. I think that we will have the defendant in the dock for this one,' announced Pinstripe. The Gown unlocked the door and then ushered Mr Hudderston in to the empty glass dock. Mr Hudderston looked as if his world was about to crash around him.

'You will be fine,' whispered Eaun through the thin gap in the glass to his client who looked thinner and whiter than ever before.

Formal identifications and introductions eventually took place.

Mr Hudderston's case should have been listed for plea and

review before listing for trial. Eaun fully expected a stand up fight with the prosecutor, as he stood up and requested that the case be adjourned so that actual trial papers could be served on him so that a proper trial preparation sheet could be prepared, with details of witnesses and time estimates as well setting out in detail what the issues in dispute were.

Dai the legal adviser looked across at Eaun with an unspoken warning not to cause any trouble in his court.

However, what had been happening previously in her court that morning had obviously served as some sort of knock-out blow to Miss Ponsonby. As he looked across the advocates' table at his Learned Friend for the day, Eaun felt a wave of sympathy for the crumpled crown prosecutor, who, managing to pick herself off the canvass, nodded through everything in agreement with Eaun. Any hint of the usual ritual sparring contest had long disappeared. If it had not been for the earlier warning sign from Dai the court's legal advisor, perhaps he should even have pushed a little more and asked Miss Ponsonby to dismiss the case altogether against his client.

Pinstripe had been listening to the two advocates below him with what started off as a smile before becoming more of a grin then a grimace. He spluttered that it was yet a further outrage that a case clearly correctly marked by the police as 'Guilty' should see the offender change his mind at the last minute in court. Was not everyone aware that the new court plea procedures were supposed to put paid to all this nonsense. Eaun thought of standing up and responding that the defence argument was that no offence had actually been committed, which was why indeed his client Mr Hudderston was pleading 'Not Guilty'. He also contemplated mentioning that Mr Hudderston was not an 'offender' but at the current time was facing 'alleged' offences. However, raised eyebrows from both the Gown and Dai to Eaun told him to waste neither his time nor energy and to let the comment pass.

Before announcing that the court was going to be adjourned for lunch, Pinstripe once more leaned over his lectern in front of him aiming his words directly at Eaun's client. Mr Hudderston had been on unconditional bail since the moment that he had been charged by the police. However, in his lugubrious style and with his effortless air of entitlement, Pinstripe delighted in advising an increasingly terrified looking Mr Hudderston that although he had decided to grant him bail on this occasion, Mr Hudderston should be under no misapprehension that if he failed to attend Court at the next hearing, then he would immediately be arrested and could expect to spend the time up until trial in custody. Eaun saw his client visibly twitch at the mention of the word 'custody' and glance towards the door leading to the steps down to the cell block. No jailers appeared. Did Mr Hudderston understand and did Mr Hudderston have any questions? By now, his client had lost all colour that was in his cheeks, as if expecting to be sent in to custody there and then. Yes, Your Honour, Mr Hudderston quickly confirmed that he did understand everything. But when was the next court date when he would have to appear in court? Pinstripe was silent.

'Clerk, do we have a date?'

Sitting below Pinstripe, the legal adviser Dai twisted round and spoke up to Pinstripe that what with the court closures, no one really knew what court venue or date the next court would be, but nevertheless reassured Mr Hudderston that he would be advised by the authorities in due course. With that, Pinstripe finally rose announcing to all that lunch was now finally being taken.

As Court Three emptied, the Gown unlocked the door to the dock and Eaun guided his shaken client out on to the concourse. Mr Hudderston was quite clearly an intelligent and articulate individual, but he was also still in a state of recovery following his encounter with the criminal justice system in action. Eaun confirmed that he would set out everything for him in writing and that they would speak again shortly. Piers Hudderston offered profuse thanks to Eaun before turning on his heels and heading for the stairs and the exit, with his white pony tail swinging behind him.

At last Eaun was now able to head to the Gents where after a prolonged morning listening to someone else's inability to hold it in, he embraced the purple gloom of the stainless steel toilet facility. Happily, the place was not being used by anyone else, whether legitimately or otherwise. As he relieved himself at the urinal, subconsciously aiming towards the chewing gum stuck on the bottom of the tray, Eaun could not miss reading the one piece of graffiti etched in to the stainless steel above the urinal making it quite clear in the most robust of terms that one user of the court services had been left particularly dissatisfied at how justice had been dispensed by the Major. Eaun felt it fitting that after all of his former colleagues had departed the building for the final time later that day, the Major's legacy would remain engraved within the precincts of the court.

By the time Eaun had made himself respectable and left the Gent's, the concourse outside was empty. Downstairs, Eaun offered a quick cheerio and good luck to Gary/Larry and his mates. Since he had entered the building earlier that morning all of the seats in the lower foyer now had green labels attached to them. The automatic front doors of the court swung open to disgorge Eaun from the building for the Circus for the very last time. Outside, even the crusties and the Special Brew crew had departed from the metal bench, which by now also had a green label attached to it. Eaun supposed that even Goebbels had to have his lunch.

On the road outside the court, Eaun waited for a gap in the traffic so that he could get to his car at the Cricket Club car park. In the meantime he turned on his phone. There were numerous messages, texts and calls from Ludmila, all more desperate than the previous. There was also a final recorded message on his phone. This one was not from Ludmila but from his wife Victoria. When it was a casual call she was Vicky. Today she was very much Victoria.

'Victoria here. You complete shit. So much for our lunch. We need to speak and I don't give a damn how busy that jumped up cow on reception says that you are. Five o'clock this evening at the house. Be here.'

Eaun had that inner feeling of dread and foreboding travel from his throat all the way down to is legs.

Fuck, fuck and fuck. He had forgotten lunch with Victoria.

~ ~ ~

In the meantime back at the WHW Legal office in Sedgeton, things were becoming rapidly more frantic. It was approaching lunchtime. Mr Curtis had obviously had enough of the telephone and had decided to become more personal. He had just walked in to the office and presented himself before Ludmila, standing almost to attention and clutching a briefcase by his side as if it held the country's secret nuclear launch codes. He still looked like bank managers should look, thought Ludmila to herself.

Ludmila confirmed that she was indeed the person that Mr Curtis had been speaking to on the phone. To avoid possible unpleasantness over any suggestion that may have been forthcoming that the earlier calls from Mr Curtis had been simply ignored, Ludmila greeted the man from the bank with the excellent news that Mr Wright had just telephoned in to say that he was on his way back and would of course be more than happy to see Mr Curtis.

'Good, good,' responded Mr Curtis. Ludmila had checked Eaun's diary on her screen. There were no appointments in his diary for the afternoon, which came as no surprise as Wednesday was supposed to be a designated work catch up day. Mr Curtis would come back to the office to see Mr Wright at 2.15 sharp. Ludmila was also able to confirm to Mr Curtis that regretfully there was still no sign of Mr Darby-Henderson.

Mr Curtis left the office with a frown but at least in part placated.

The telephone console was flashing again. Ludmila picked up the receiver with a smile and after announcing the name of the firm asked how WHW Legal could be of help? The caller wanted to speak urgently to Julian Darby-Henderson. Ludmila felt like inviting the caller to join the queue but instead simply said that Mr Darby-Henderson was out and it was uncertain when he would get back. This was actually the truth. The caller was getting loud and irate. His son was being held unlawfully by the police and was there anyone else who could help? Ludmila apologised that Mr Wright was not yet back from court and that Ms Hilton was already in the police station. Could she get Ms Hilton to call him back? Yes she could, but it would not be immediate as she was already seeing a client in the cells. The caller told Ludmila that he would get someone in London who was actually bothered to help. With that, the line went dead.

In the meantime, minutes after the front door had clicked shut behind Mr Curtis, it opened again. Blocking off most of the light was the unmistakeable figure of Sammy Ferguson. Mrs Ferguson was a big lady in every way. Her large extended family, including in particular her own biological off-spring were also responsible for providing a steady flow of clientele to the firm both down at the police station and at the both the Magistrates and Crown Courts. Ludmila was indeed aware of rumours that the Ferguson family terrorised at least one of the estates in Sedgeton and despite the occasional arrest, Ludmila also knew that the local constabulary were in constant denial that they were actually in fear of the Fergusons and even for minor offences, would only pick any of them up on dawn raids when there was full heavy back up from the Support Group.

However, Ludmila never had any problems with the Fergusons, including of course their matriarch, Sammy.

On this occasion Sammy Ferguson was already in full flow, dressed in her slippers and ankle socks directing her general feelings of outrage at the current course of events to Ludmila. It seemed that Alex was supposed to have called her back earlier that morning to give an update on the police harassment case regarding her son Henry. Ludmila then had related to her in full detail by Mrs Ferguson the disgusting behaviour of the Wessex Constabulary, who had stopped our Henry without any reason, hauling him off his bike and accusing him of having nicked the coils of scrap metal wiring that were carefully balanced on the bike's handlebars. Our Henry had done nothing.

Whilst the verbal complaints continued, Ludmila noticed that another suit had entered through the office door, but this time holding one of those large black document cases on wheels, much favoured by air crews as they strode down the airport aisles in packs dressed up in their braided uniforms en route to board their allocated flight. She gave a quick nod of acknowledgement as the gentleman stood a safe distance behind Mrs Ferguson.

'That Eaun Wright, now he would of called me straight back,' exclaimed Mrs Ferguson. 'Anyway, where is Alex what's her face?'

'I reckon the behaviour of the police is just fucking cuntish if you ask me,' added Mrs Ferguson.

Ludmila dare not look at the man in the suit standing behind Sammy Ferguson. Ludmila had been speaking fluent English for most of her adult life, ever since she finished her languages course at Wroclaw University. Both her girls, Julia and Natalia, even complained that their mother now spoke a little like her own daughters these days, with an identifiable West Country accent. To her continued surprise, Ludmila still found that she came across new English words every day. The adjective 'cuntish' was a first for Ludmila, although she guessed that this particular word of description may well be unique to the Ferguson clan.

Ludmila knew that her sympathetic nodding towards Mrs Ferguson at her description of the police excesses would have to suffice on this occasion. With a promise that Alex Hilton would of course give Mrs Ferguson a call on her return from the cells, satisfaction seemed to have been achieved.

Muttering further curses regarding the general behaviour of the Wessex Constabulary, Sammy Ferguson turned and waddled out of the main office door, leaving the suit with the pilot's bag now standing in front of Ludmila. The man sported no braid on his cuffs.

'Apologies for keeping you waiting,' said Ludmila. She was not very sure whether the man standing in front of her had either heard or understood the newly discovered adjective just used by Sammy Ferguson.

'I have telephoned earlier. Several times in fact. Name is Farquhar. I am here to see Mr Darby-Henderson and Mr Wright. And no, I do not have an appointment,' announced the latest arrival.

The visitor declined to tell Ludmila where he was from or why he was there at all.

'I will come back to see the partners at 1.30,' announced Mr Farquhar. With his black briefcase trundling behind him, Mr Farquhar opened the door and was about to depart out on to the street when he stopped, turned and with a softer tone spoke to Ludmila.

'Look, I have been on the road for over two hours, where is the best place to get a spot of lunch?' Ludmila hardly knew anyone who had 'lunch' any more.

'If you fancy something vegan, vegetarian and which is also locally-sourced and definitely organic, then turn left at the bottom of the hill and head up towards the dozens of restaurants and cafes in the Artisan Quarter. They will sort you out a bowl of kale and rooilos chickpeas, washed down with a vegan non-dairy pecan smoothie in no time at all. However, if you fancy something semi-normal and full of gluten, then best head for The Blue Parrot just down the hill.'

Ludmila thought that she detected the hint of a smile on the man's face as the door clicked behind him. Now she would have to explain to Mr Wright on his return that his afternoon of being alone to catch up with his work was disappearing fast. There was also something strange going on with everyone demanding to see the partners. And there was still no word from either Mr Darby-Henderson or the practice manager Rita. Before Ludmila had time to ruminate further, the telephone console started to flash and ring once more.

It was the police. An Inspector Thompson. Ludmila started

to explain that Miss Hilton was already in the cells seeing a client.

'It is with Mr Wright that I need to speak,' interjected the Inspector. Ludmila should of course already guessed that it was Mr Wright that he wanted to speak to. Everyone wanted to speak to Mr Wright. Ludmila explained that Mr Wright was expected back in the office shortly and she would make sure that he returned the call. An extension number was left with Ludmila. And no, the Inspector was not able to relate to Ludmila what the call was about.

Knowing that he would not pick up, Ludmila sent a text to Mr Wright warning him that his afternoon ahead was rapidly filling up.

~ ~ ~

Gus had now been in his office for a couple of hours. It was situated near to the kitchens with a glazed door that looked out on to the entrance hall and reception area of the hotel. For Gus, the office was in the perfect spot. He was at the epicentre and could keep an eye on everything that was going on in the establishment, both staff and guests.

As soon as the renovations started on the old school building ten years ago, Gus and Anabel naturally fell in to their respective responsibilities. Gus was very much the figures man, with his cash flow projections and business plans. He ensured that the business made a good and healthy profit. Anabel was front of house who made sure that everything worked for the guests to perfection. Everyone commented on how well they worked as a team.

In the early years The Sedgeton Grange Hotel & Spa got rave reviews as the 'go-to' place in unexplored Somerset to go for the long weekend. It was rare that there were any vacancies for Fridays, Saturdays and Sundays. However, somehow, the 'dirty midweek break' as Anabel referred to it, simply did not attract the necessary numbers from Fulham, Islington and Dulwich, wanting to jump in to their Range Rover Vogues and Sports to sample the delights of The Sedgeton Grange Hotel. When the 3 nights for 2 Midweek Special Offer failed to stir much action, Anabel announced to Gus that it was time to think outside the box.

The seeds of The Sedgeton Grange Private Members Club being started were planted when Anabel flew off for a hen party 'do' to Amsterdam with one of her old school chums from Benenden who was about to enter into her second or even third marriage. Except for the next generation of younger family members, it had now been several years since Gus and Anabel had actually been invited to a first wedding ceremony of one of their contemporaries.

Gus fully understood the unwritten rules of these sorts of pre-nuptial events. Over the years he had been on enough rugby and cricket club tours to understand and appreciate the full benefits that what goes on tour stays on tour. However, as soon as Anabel had piled out of the taxi that had picked her up at Bristol Airport on her return from the trip, she could not be silenced. She was bursting to tell Gus how her idea would ensure that The Sedgeton Grange made them financially secure for life, as well as being what she promised would be 'great fun'.

The next six months meant extensive telephone calls to Gus's trust people in Edinburgh as well as Anabel making a couple of personal visits to her father's home in Holland Park. Eventually, his own spread sheets were able to tell Gus that Anabel's Members' Club idea could indeed actually work financially.

For a joining fee of £1000 and an annual subscription of £2000 (or just £3000 per couple), potential new members would be vetted by the formal Membership Committee, all personal friends of and chosen by Anabel. Membership to The Sedgeton Grange 'Private Members' Club was certainly not automatic. Written references (which were all checked) were required to be produced.

The local lawyer Darby-Henderson had managed to come up trumps again. There had to be substantial work done on the licensing of the premises to ensure everything was fully compliant. He had sorted all of this and in addition also presented Gustave and Anabel with a rules structure for their new club that made certain that although called a 'Private Members' Club', it was the two of them who called all the shots including being able to dismiss anyone from the club for breach of any code of behaviour.

Gus never did find out from Anabel what happened in Amsterdam on that hen party weekend, but the end result was that now, when not operating as a fashionable boutique hotel at the weekends, attracting the well-connected as well as the occasional 'name', the Grange now boasted Monday through to Thursdays, an extremely discreet, private and high quality adult social club. Before the renovations for this idea began, the hotel contained an old semi-basement that had originally been the boot room and Boys' Changing Rooms for outdoor sports. The initial conversion from a school facility to a multi-purpose 'function room', even if re-branded as 'The Hinton Charterhouse Room' never really took off. It looked and felt just like a function room and still smelled of dubbin and boiled cabbage. As part of her extensive midweek re-brand, Anabel had the signage on the heavy oak door leading to the steps down to 'The Hinton Charterhouse Room' removed, to be replaced with the new weekend sign of 'No Entry' (with the door firmly locked). However, for midweek the door now sported a stunning new sign of 'The Dungeon' printed out in large bold gothic font, which Anabel had asked one of the young graphic design creatives in the Artisans' Quarter in Sedgeton to put together . As part of the re-fit, whilst Anabel was happy for her new Dungeon venue to remain dark, it was certainly no longer either dingy or smelling of school greens and old rugby and football boot polish. The aura of the old function room had vanished. During the renovation work, Anabel had returned to Amsterdam with a budget that had been approved by Gus. Anabel had a fearsome reputation of being able to drive the hardest bargain. Over the next few weeks, one small shipping container and several large boxes with Amsterdam addresses on them arrived at the hotel. After the old Hinton Charterhouse Room had been extensively redecorated and carpeted, Anabel had then arranged for what she called her 'facilitator' to fly over and stay at The Sedgeton Grange hotel with a free bar tab for four whole days in order to direct and supervise everything, whilst all of the ordered equipment was unpacked and duly assembled in what was now to become The Dungeon. Gus occasionally peered through his office window wondering what the usage of some of the bars, chains, shackles and winches were actually for, before they disappeared down the steps. Anabel appeared to have bought a great deal of paraphernalia in Amsterdam. Gustave had not yet looked at the invoices in detail, but on her purchases she had kept to the agreed budget. The only overspend on The Dungeon was when Anabel insisted that to ensure authenticity and realism, the shackles should have the benefit of having the village mason and farrier apply them securely to the wall. Anabel stressed that as relative new-comers they should use local labour where at all possible.

The Dungeon proved to be the main burden on Gustave's spread sheets as the midweek conversion took place. The outdoor swimming pool and saunas and the existing Spa needed little more done to them. An outside jet hot tub was purchased and placed behind the evergreen foliage on one of the garden borders.

The only other piece of major expenditure was on the Attic Floor. When originally a school, this cramped space under the eaves was used as a dormitory for the boys who had just entered the prep school. There was still a board at the top of the stairs naming all the school monitors in the Remove class between 1946 and 1972. Gustave had always wondered what had happened to the monitors before and after these dates.

The Attic Floor was originally planned for conversion into at least four extra rooms for the hotel, but it was deemed that the likelihood of guests smashing their heads on the low sloping ceiling was simply unacceptable. What may have been suitable for prep school children was not acceptable to guests paying over £300 per night. Instead, the Attic Floor had now become 'Seventh Heaven'. Like the Dungeon, new designer signage courtesy of the Artisans' Quarter creatives told midweek Private Club members where the new upstairs playroom facility was situated, but curious weekend hotel guests were told that the area was very definitely 'Staff Only'. A secure lock also ensured that the door remained firmly bolted during midweek.

Anabel seemed particularly proud of Seventh Heaven. On one of her trips to see her father in Holland Park, Anabel had obviously made a detour via Conran, Heal's and Liberty. Large deliveries a few days later confirmed these visits, as once again through his office window Gus witnessed an array of assorted divans, carpets, bean bags, throws and cushions be carried through the hall and upstairs. Gustave wondered aloud how or why just one cushion could cost £140 but he trusted Anabel to know what she was doing. Further local labour had to be employed to install the cutting edge Conran lighting that would give just the correct subdued atmosphere required. With most bodies being horizontal, Gus surmised that there would now be little risk of banging the head against the ceiling in this re-vamped room.

And so it was that The Sedgeton Grange Private Members' Club came into being. It had quickly become an unqualified success. As every other hotel took a hammering during the coronavirus, and public confidence took time to return, it was the Club that saved Gustave and Anabel. The Club now boasted 500 members with a waiting list of several months. Not for the first time, Gustave thought, Anabel had been proved spot on with her commercial judgment and acumen. The great and good who lived nearby really did want somewhere to go, where they could be guaranteed utter discretion, great surroundings with fine foods and wines as well of course as adult conversation and good clean adult fun. And all of course completely lawful and in the best possible taste. Gus also recalled that Anabel never ceased to remind him that the very selective admissions procedure coupled with the prices charged to the private members, kept out what her father once described as the great unwashed.

It was Wednesday so tonight was Members' Club night with no 'normal' hotel guests. Gus glimpsed a plastic stone arch through his office window, as it was being brought round to the garden at the back. This must be part of the outdoor drinks bar. He remembered, tonight was the special Caligula Roman Orgy event. Following the stone arch, Gustave then saw a giant dancer's cage being deposited in the hallway as part of the same delivery together with a basket of tunics and togas also hired out especially for the night. Gustave wondered whether a dancer's cage was one of the usual accessories to be seen at a standard Roman party taking place in one of those villas that overlooked the Tiber. No doubt Anabel would reveal all to him later on, thought Gus as he checked on his most recent spreadsheet that there were enough tiger prawns ordered for the sell-out event.

BATTLESTAR GALACTICA

RELIEVED AT being rescued from the locked solicitors' room, Alex walked side by side with the Custody Sergeant down the long corridors, with the smart lighting on the ceiling flickering into life as it picked up the motions underneath. Alex had always made it a point to get on well with everyone that she worked with, and this included the police. With the one exception (there was always the one), she enjoyed a good working relationship with most of them. It was stupid in her eyes not to at least try to form a good working relationship with everyone.

Alex had now reached the main control hub of the custody suite. There was a barrier that was chest high that surrounded the control hub. There were also Perspex screens running most of the length of the wall-barrier, but Alex could not remember whether they were there originally or were a hangover from the pandemic. Every time she entered the building at Keynsham, or any of the other similar new custody suites at Bridgwater or Melksham, she was reminded of what it must have been like to be one of the crew on the Battleship Galactica. On the wall behind the barrier, was an impressive battery of screens that would have put most television studios to shame. Those officers working the control hub were on a raised level, so that they looked down on the unfortunates below them. Clearly, a great deal of time and trouble had gone into the design of the barrier. Any detainee, or indeed anyone else wanting to take issue with one of the custody staff on a personal level would have to negotiate the upper half of the barrier which was sloped at 45%. There was nothing to grasp on to. Alex had always admired the ingenuity of the designers who had made the barrier effectively insurmountable even with a running jump, yet still looking innocuous at the same time. A couple of DOs were tapping in to the screens in front of them, perched on their wheeled high-back leather desk chairs. On every side of the control nub were corridors, housing dozens of cells, an intoxilyzer suite, interview rooms, fingerprint, photograhic facilities, medical rooms and a small kitchen. In front of the barrier where Alex now stood were large red lines with accompanying signage inviting all detainees to stand at the far side of the red zone markings. Alex was not a detainee but nevertheless still found herself backing away from treading on the red demarcation line.

'Here you are,' said the custody sergeant Matt as he handed Alex a couple of sheets of paper that he had just printed off. 'I have just called the OIC and she and her colleague will be down here in a minute to fully brief you. They are just finishing off with speaking to your client's mate. In the meantime, can I get you anything?'

A couple of minutes later, with the freshly printed custody record documentation under her arm, Alex was following Matthew Houseman down one of the corridors and into one of the interview rooms, the lights flickering to life on signs of movement below. Alex was clutching a mug of tea made of real china as well as a slice of carrot cake on a plastic plate. It appeared that today was the youngster DO's birthday and Matt Houseman had had mercy on Alex and had sorted out a late breakfast for her. As Alex was left on her own in the interview room, she sat down on one of the four chairs surrounding the table. She then instinctively started to pull the chair in towards the table before remembering that the chairs were of course all screwed down into the floor.

The rooms were all sound-proofed. Alex could just about make out the very soft electronic tick of the interview room clock. Grateful for Matt Houseman picking up that she was both parched and starving, Alex started to get stuck in to her tea and cake. Matt had told her that the cake had been home-made and brought in by one of the custody staff that morning. The custody suite kitchen facilities did not extend to being able to offer Alex her usual preferred Jasmine Green tea, but the industrial strength builders' tea that helped wash down the excellent carrot cake made her feel rejuvenated. What made Alex feel even more appreciative was her knowledge of the quality of the ready-made hot drinks and microwaved meals that were available to the unfortunate detainees. Years of customer feedback from her own clients had informed Alex that if you had to drink and eat anything then the least sickening items on the menu were the hot chocolate and the meat curry, the latter because it seemed that the curry powder managed to disguise any possible taste or texture.

A trail of crumbs littering the table from the plate to her lap, Alex set out the two page custody record in front of her. It gave the usual details about when, where and why arrested. The name given was Charles Battingsdale. The address given was Bradstock Farm just outside of Sedgeton. A local lad then, thought Alex. Matt at custody had earlier divulged to her that the only thing on his record was a Referral Order for possession when he was still in short trousers. Charles was now just 19. So, effectively no previous and not a name that Alex had ever heard mentioned locally.

There was then a knock on the door. Before she could answer, the door swung open and clutching her trademark clipboard and standard issue blue hardback A4 notebook, in strode DC Denise Halloran.

'Hello stranger,' said the detective. 'It has been at least a week since I have seen you.'

Alex was clearly on a roll. Not only was the custody sergeant on the day a real human who dispensed cake, but the OIC dealing with her case was also a fellow human and when not knackered after an 18 hour shift, even possessed a sense of humour. This morning, Alex thought that DC Halloran looked only mildly done in. Alex also wondered whether the bags under her own eyes matched those of the police officer.

Even though she must have sat in interview rooms similar to this on an almost daily basis, Alex noted that the officer still instinctively tried to pull the screwed down chair forward to make herself more comfortable.

DC Halloran explained that she was there to fully brief Alex on what was happening. She said that she would tell Alex what she already knew which was not a great deal. Briefly, a BMW had jumped the lights at Clark's Village in Street and a chase through the bumpy dark roads of the Levels had ensued. The speed the vehicle was travelling at was 'excessive' and on one occasion, a vehicle travelling from Meare towards Glastonbury in the opposite direction had to take evasive action. DC Halloran went on to explain that it was only because of prompt and unexpectedly efficient police procedure that the deployment of a stinger device ensured that the vehicle came to a halt. One gentleman had exited the rear passenger door and fled the scene. Officers were currently searching the locality but it was feared that by now he was some distance away. The driver of the vehicle was seen by officers also trying to escape apprehension, but was quickly grabbed, taken to the ground and handcuffed. He had volunteered his name to the arresting officers as Nicholas Thornham. Something sounded vaguely familiar but Alex was fairly sure that she had never heard of that name either.

'No previous, at least officially,' added DC Halloran. 'He is also the registered keeper of the car, with tax, insurance and MOT all paid up. However, between you and me I suspect that Nicky has been a bit of a naughty boy. The intel that we have on our Howard Marks wannabee is that he has recently been mixing with all the wrong sorts in Bristol, so that the local populace in and around Bath and most of the northern part of Somerset can be reliably supplied with all their recreational requirements. That intel has been graded A1 as well. He has also picked up some Bristol habits along the way, like calling out his brief from a Bristol law firm with a quick flick of his fingers. And it is the actual solicitor brief who turns up as well, not some trainee at the bottom of the legal world's food chain. After confirming his name, it was of little surprise that after seeing his brief that he then went 'No Comment' on everything.'

'Right, I will arrange for custody to bring your client up from the cells for you to take instructions,' said DC Halloran. 'It turns out that there were three suspect packets hidden in the boot of El Chapo's BMW. Preliminary tests are looking like cocaine and quality resin. Oh, one last thing. Your boy gave an address of some farm just outside Sedgeton. Have to say that on first appearances he doesn't really look like a standard card-carrying member of Somerset Young Farmers. He should know that my colleague DC Jefferies was planning to be here but has been redirected and is currently on his way to carry out the section 18 search at Tractor Ted's as we speak.'

As is often the case with a prolonged car chase, Alex asked whether the shared police helicopter with Wiltshire and Dorset had seen action.

'No,' replied DC Halloran. 'The boys will be well pissed off that on this occasion they were not pursued by Whirly Birds, thus ruining their upward elevation in street cred. View was taken by those above that there was no threat to life or anyone lying on the ground injured but undetected so it never made it out of the hangar. That bit at least has cheered me up.'

'I will sort out and collect your client for you,' added DC Halloran as she headed out of the door.

~ ~ ~

Kendrick Maclean had spent the rest of morning working on one of the former out-houses that was being converted into self-catering accommodation. According to many of his old London mates, all of these sorts of lettings were now best done through Airbnb and this was definitely where the future lay. His eldest stepson Tarquin was already heavily involved in the local property market and he had told his stepfather that he thought that the idea would fly. And unlike other members of the family, Tarquin knew what he was on about. Most importantly, the project also had the full approval of Ronnie, so that was that.

Talking of Ronnie, earlier in the morning he had had to broach the subject of why Griff had been spotted on site earlier on. She had this woman's instinct of instantly knowing if Kendrick Maclean was lying or not. He had therefore had to learn how to adapt and in turn Kendrick Maclean was now highly adept at telling wholly credible part truths. Some sort of explanation as to why the flagstones at and in front of the oak front door had been scrupulously washed was provided. She will have known that it was highly unlikely that he even knew that they had any cleaning appliances, let alone where they were stored. Kendrick Maclean therefore told the truth that during the night there had been an incident involving a dead badger being thrown at their front door. It was all some dreadful misunderstanding, but the mess then had to be cleared up which was why Griff had been there. No, he did not know what Griff had done with the corpse. He also left out the bit about the animal being nailed to the door. He did not want Ronnie made unduly upset or even frightened. She seemed to have accepted the sanitised version of events.

Kendrick Maclean liked to think of himself as being the Project Manager at Bradstock Manor. After all, it needed someone of his weight and authority to ensure that the thieves and scoundrels that he used on the site actually did what they were asked to do for once. He prided himself on the good working relationship that he had now established with all the various contractors that he had hired.

Lunch with Ronnie was beckoning, but Kendrick Maclean decided to place one final call before heading off to the trough that he knew Ronnie was preparing. His call had just been picked up and he was about to ask why the scaffolding was not yet there for the tiling job due to commence on Friday, when he heard the scrunch on his gravel as a vehicle travelled up towards the courtyard. It was a police estate car. Kendrick Maclean would have to give the roofer his pre-emptive verballing later and said he would call him back before he killed the call.

Several thoughts then quickly flashed through Kendrick Maclean's head. Police. What the fuck did they want? Although he personally had more or less kept his name out of police records, life experience had taught him that the boys in blue were never good news. He quickly thought through why they would want to speak to him. He was after all a model citizen and as far as he was concerned no one anywhere had anything on him, least of all down in this part of the world.

By now, Ronnie had been enticed away from getting lunch sorted in the kitchen and had stepped outside to see who the visitors were.

Then Kendrick Maclean suddenly realised. Unbelievable. Just hours after the criminal damage attack on his antique front door, here were the local boys in blue come to follow up the incident. Those wankers in the Met could learn a couple of things about how to do proper policing by following the examples of their country cousins here in darkest Somerset.

As the police car came to a halt, two plain clothes officers got out and walked towards him.

'Gentlemen, I am impressed!' exclaimed Kendrick Maclean. 'Some scumbags crucify the West Country's favourite but most persecuted animal by nailing him up to an oak door and within 5 minutes the local Sweeney is at the scene in order to hunt down the evil perpetrators. Am I impressed or what!'

Not only was Kendrick Maclean marvelling at the efficiency of the local constabulary, but they didn't waste any time by sending down a couple of uniformed but instead sent down the serious mob from the CID. Respect.

It was at this point that the two plain clothes officers stopped in their tracks, both looking quizzically at Kendrick Maclean. Ronnie, having just come out of the building to tell her husband that his lunch was ready was also staring at him across the courtyard.

Fuck. It was now slowly dawning on Kendrick Maclean. He had dropped a bollock. Of course he had never called the police about the previous night's activities. He was sure as hell that Griff would have had his finger nails pulled out before he was ever tempted to say anything to an outsider, least of all the local filth. Time to move on. Quickly.

'Pleasure to see you. How can I be of assistance, officers?'

The driver of the vehicle introduced himself as DC Jefferies. The other one he did not catch the name of. Both officers thrust their warrant cards towards Kendrick Maclean who made as if to carefully scrutinise them. He had been able to read the large capital letters on the badger's death message without difficulty, but without his reading glasses he could not read the small written details of identification on the warrant card and the photographs looked a blur.

'Thank you. As I say, how can I help? My name is Dougal Kendrick Maclean and the lady standing by the entrance to the Manor House is my wife Veronica Kendrick Maclean.'

'It is about Charles Battingsdale. He has given his address as Bradstock Farm. I assume that this address is indeed that address.'

'You obviously mean Bradstock Manor. Same place,' said Kendrick Maclean, who then went on to explain to the officer that Charlie (no one had called him Charles since he was presented with the Duke of Edinburgh Award at school summer term assembly all those years ago) was his stepson. He was the son of his wife Veronica's first marriage but like his elder brother Tarquin was treated by Kendrick Maclean as if he was his own son. And yes, Bradstock Manor was owned by Veronica and himself.

'I have to tell you that Charlie has been arrested and is currently assisting us with our enquiries,' said the officer who had identified himself earlier as DC Jefferies.

Kendrick Maclean did what he then did at any moment of panic or stress. He bought time by biting the inside of his lip. What the fuck. What the actual fuck, he thought. Charlie had a little bit of trouble when he was a teenager back in London. He still remembered the day at Wimbledon Youth Court when he and Ronnie had to sit in front of the magistrates as Charlie, hunched in between them both, was given a 12 month Referral Order. Still, he had done the order, had been as good as gold and all that was now supposed to have been spent. After that court appearance, Charlie had been hauled out of the local comp where he was mixing with all his low life 'mates' and a small fortune then spent on sending Charlie to one of the country's finest public schools at Westminster. Despite the nightmare of having to cope with Covid, Charlie had actually stuck at it and secured a place at Warwick University, starting in September after this his supposed gap year. Now, here Charlie was, pissing it all away. What the actual fuck indeed. Why couldn't he be more like his brother Tarquin?

'Charles. Sorry, Charlie, has told us that he lives here with you his parents. We need to look at his room. Are you happy to consent to us having a look please?'

At this request, neither officer could fail to see the head of Veronica drop a little forward as if a line had been crossed.

'No you fucking can't,' replied Kendrick Maclean. 'Unless you have a fucking warrant you can both get the fuck into your poxy Noddy car and just fuck right off my land.'

There then followed a long silence. This time it was the turn of DC Jefferies to slightly lower his head with a sense of resignation.

'Actually sir, all I need is a section 18 search authorisation signed by an Inspector. Here is a copy of the authorisation for yourself sir,' as a yellow copy was handed over Kendrick Maclean who grasped it and looked to read it, except that he still did not have his glasses. DC Jefferies had momentarily deliberated on whether to tell Kendrick Maclean that the world had moved on from Dixon of Dock Green and The Bill but quickly thought better of it.

It was at this point that Ronnie lifted her head and took charge.

'Charlie hardly sleeps here,' she said directly to DC Jefferies. 'He is 19, no idea where he is most of the time. You got kids? He has only just recently come down from London. I take it that you do not want to search the rest of the premises, only Charlie's room? All that you will find there are old FIFA and Super Mario games and controls that he can't be bothered unpacking and taking with him to wherever he is living.'

The officer nodded in response.

'Then you had better follow me,' said Ronnie, 'His room looks as if it has already been trashed by the police. Either that or burgled. Or both. Don't suppose you can make it any worse.'

The two officers were gone only for 5 or 10 minutes, leaving Ronnie and Kendrick Maclean in silence to shuffle their feet in the gravel and wait for the search to be completed.

'We have seized only the one laptop,' said the officer with the forgotten name. An evidence bag with the orange labels was tucked under his arm, with a small grey laptop clearly visible inside.

More paperwork was handed to and accepted by Kendrick Maclean but only with reluctance.

'So, my son is arrested and no one even tells me. Where is his brief, does he even have a brief or is he at the mercy of you lot?' asked Kendrick Maclean.

As he tucked himself back in to the marked police vehicle with his colleague, DC Jefferies thought about replying that as far as he was aware, Charlie would have been asked whether he wanted anyone told of where he was. Like most kids, the last thing that he probably wanted to happen was for his parents to know that he had been arrested for suspicion of intent to supply. However, he did not wish to aggravate the situation any further and with a brief nod, the car engine coughed in to tired life and slowly scrunched its way down the long gravelled drive.

Kendrick Maclean retrieved his mobile from his gilet pocket that he habitually wore on site. He then started angrily punching in the numbers.

'Not so fast Dougal,' said Ronnie. It was only ever 'Dougal' when something bad was about to happen.

'You never mentioned anything about a badger being nailed to my door,' announced Ronnie. 'Whilst I am re-heating your quiche for lunch you can explain exactly what is going on. We can also dig up that leaflet about the Anger Management course as well'.

As he followed his wife in to the house, Kendrick Maclean knew what was coming next. It would not be pleasant. And everyone knew that real men do not eat quiche.

~ ~ ~

Ludmila was fairly certain that she had actually signed a contract of employment when she joined the firm. She was also fairly certain that somewhere in the document it spelled out her entitlement to an hour's break for lunch every day. However, today was like most of the other days and Ludmila could truly not remember when she had last enjoyed a relaxed whole hour's lunch in one of the several local cafes boasting a garden, where she could chew the cud with her friends whilst soaking up the sun. Luckily, on this Wednesday, Mr Wright's secretary/assistant Madge was popping out for herself and offered to get Ludmila her usual ham and salad roll with strictly no spread or butter.

Whilst waiting for Madge to return with her lunch, the front door to the office opened and the figure of Mr Curtis from the bank once more stood in front of Ludmila.

'I am so sorry,' said Ludmila. 'I did not think that you were coming back to see Mr Wright until after lunch. I am expecting him at any moment but he is not back yet.'

The bank manager looked tense and ill at ease.

'I will wait here,' replied Mr Curtis as he headed for the waiting room door and placed himself in the nearest chair to the glass screen that afforded him a full view of who was going in and out of the office. Ludmila noticed that that morning's edition of The Times still lay unopened on the waiting room table. Mr Curtis also left that month's edition of Somerset Life untouched.

Seconds later, the office front door was once more pushed open. Mr Wright had at long last returned to the office. He was clutching his briefcase in one hand and a small brown bag sporting the branding of The Blue Parrot in the other hand. Lunch.

'Am I glad to see you,' said Ludmila in a soft voice. 'Mr Curtis from the bank is in the waiting room waiting to see you. He has been waiting to see you all day.'

Mr Curtis was already on his feet and was starting to open up the briefcase in front of him.

'I am really sorry,' explained Ludmila. 'I tried to get him to wait for you but he wasn't having any of it,' whispered Ludmila, by now in a loud whisper. 'You should also know that there is another gentleman who wants to speak to you urgently. He is called Mr Facker or Mr Fucker or something. Surely it can't be Mr Fucker. Anyway, he is coming back but wouldn't say where he was from. I have also had Mrs Wright phoning again several times. You must call her urgently. There is also a policeman who wants to speak to you. His number is on your screen. And Frank.'

Ludmila knew from experience that her boss would have not looked at his screen. He had entered through the front door just a few minutes before with a calm smile on his face. Now, as he turned to look at Mr Curtis through the glass, Ludmila could both see and feel her boss's smile disappear in front of her.

'It is lunchtime, there will be no one else around, I will see Mr Curtis in here,' said Mr Wright as he headed for the glass-fronted waiting area.

Ludmila heard the 'Good afternoons' exchanged between the two men before the hydraulic door action began to click in and the voices were slowly silenced.

Unable to lip read, Ludmila tried to look through the glass without making it obvious that she was doing so. She had seen Mr Curtis gesture to Eaun Wright to sit down which he duly did directly opposite. Mr Curtis then started to read something from the papers that he had picked up from his briefcase. Ludmila could see that Mr Wright looked quizzical and it looked as if he was asking Mr Curtis to explain what he had just said again.

Mr Curtis duly did so. Mr Wright did not move or even say anything back to Mr Curtis, who then started to speak a few sentences. Whatever was being said by Mr Curtis seemed to be having no effect on Mr Wright, who was now just staring blankly at the remaining paperwork at the bottom of Mr Curtis' briefcase.

There was then just silence between the two men. The telephone console in front of Ludmila flashed and rang and told her that another call was coming in. It could wait.

Eventually she saw Mr Curtis ask what looked like a question to Mr Wright, who continued to stare into the bottom of the case. The question was repeated. Ludmila could not hear what Mr Wright replied, but there was a definite shrug of the shoulders. A couple of minutes later, Mr Curtis returned his papers and clicked his briefcase shut. A piece of paper was handed to Mr Wright who just nodded and remained seated whilst Mr Curtis stood up. It looked as if he was wondering whether to offer a handshake or not. It was clear that Mr Wright was still staring downwards so Mr Curtis eased the waiting room door open, slipped past Ludmila with a curt nod of acknowledgement and was then out of the front door back to the safety of his bank.

Ludmila could not help herself. Something was clearly wrong. Any colour on the face of Mr Wright had disappeared completely. Ludmila had occasionally heard the English, especially sports pundits, use the phrase 'ashen-faced'. For some reason football managers were always 'ashen-faced.' That was exactly how Mr Wright looked now. So, Ludmila opened the waiting room door and carefully closed it behind her. She could still see if any clients came in.

'You OK?' asked Ludmila. She had never seen Eaun Wright like this before. 'What has happened?'

Mr Wright started to sit up and looked as if he was going to give an answer to her. However, before he had the chance, both of them caught the front door of the office open once more and the man in a smart suit trailing an air pilot's bag enter.

'This is the man who came in earlier,' whispered Ludmila,

conspiratorially.

Eaun Wright stood up and brushed himself down.

'I know, replied Mr Wright. 'It is okay, Ludmila, this man is neither Mr Facker nor Mr Fucker. Mr Curtis from the bank has explained. The man in reception is in fact Mr Farquhar from the SRA with whom I must now speak.'

With that Mr Wright picked up his briefcase and the lunch bag.

'Mr Farquhar I assume,' said Mr Wright. 'I have just been speaking to Mr Curtis from our bank. You had best come up to my private office. Let me at least offer you a cup of tea,'

However, Mr Farquhar declined the offer and the two men disappeared up the stairs to Mr Wright's office. Ludmila had seen Mr Farquhar spot the Blue Parrot insignia on Mr Wright's lunch bag. Whatever was happening was clearly not good and she only hoped that her recommendation of The Blue Parrot was a success and would not adversely affect whatever the two men had to say to each other.

Ludmila had heard the name SRA used before in the office, but never in a complimentary setting. To Ludmila, she had heard the letters SRA mentioned in the same sort of hushed tone that her parents and grandparents in Wroclaw mentioned the old SB. She knew enough to know that it was never good.

Ludmila sat down in front of her screen again and typed in 'SRA' on her search engine.

~~~

It was not so long ago that traffic cops were the 'go to' fix for television production companies that did not have the wit, imagination or money to put together a real documentary that actually made a difference. In the past few years, traffic cops had ceded way to what happened in the custody suite. Denise Halloran had actually sat through one of these programmes with her husband, who did not make the end and fell asleep on the sofa. As with all these fly on the wall police documentaries, there was always a small element of truth coupled with a larger part that simply did not reflect what really went on. What astonished Denise was how the television cameras had failed to even hint that for substantial chunks of the shift, nothing really happened. Anyone who had ever worked in a custody suite would know that the best part of the day was usually spent just hanging around waiting, bored rigid, for criminals to get lifted and brought in.

Whether it was for the duty brief to show up, Social Services to actually pick up the phone and send an appropriate adult or to wait for an interview room to become free, a large chunk of Denise's day was actually spent in the custody suite just waiting with nothing to do.

This Wednesday morning had been no different. In fairness, the duty solicitor had got here quickly. However, there had been no one else around to carry out the section 18 search so as soon as he had got to Keynsham, her colleague DC Jefferies had been sent back to check out Bradstock Farm. Denise was now waiting for the duty solicitor to fully brief her client, take his instructions and then advise accordingly. It was already nearly lunchtime and for some reason, whether because of a hangover from coronavirus or not, there was only one interview room in operation and the chances were that she would lose her slot. Denise had also noticed that whilst slices of carrot cake were being consumed by virtually everyone in the custody suite, none had been offered in her direction. She was supposed to be on yet another starvation purge so probably just as well. With her job, grazing and waiting went together.

Her mobile chirped in to life. It was Matt at the control hub downstairs. Yes, the duty brief was ready to go for interview and the detainee had in the meantime been returned to his cell. DC Jefferies had also just phoned in with the result of the section 18 search. She was hoping that her colleague would be back in time for interview, but she was not going to be hanging around for another hour. Time to get on with it.

A quick walk downstairs. Denise was barely over five feet three inches tall and could only just see over the barrier to the custody staff at the other side of the Perspex.

'I will get Mr Battingsdale out of the cell for you. I already have Alex in the interview room ready. You should be all set.'

As she thanked the custody sergeant who had shown her down the corridor and towards the interview room, Denise saw the detainee Mr Battingsdale approach from the other end of the corridor, accompanied by a female DO. Unlike his mate who was driving the car, there was virtually no police Intel on Master Battingsdale, only the confirmation of a Referral Order for possession of some dope when he was still a kid at school. Since then, absolutely nothing. There was no agricultural look about him either. He just looked like a 19 year old kid, scared and nervous about being in a police station. At least he did not have a knowing snide smile across his face like his mate the driver, Master Thornham. The sleaze-ball lawyer was next to Nicholas Thornham throughout the interview, but Denise was fairly certain that Thornham knew exactly how to say 'No Comment' without any help from his brief strategically kicking him under the table.

Now, DC Denise Halloran was seated in front of Charles Battingsdale. Sitting alongside the interviewee was his brief, Alexandra Hilton. As she usually did, Alex came straight to the point as to what was happening. Her client would be letting Denise have a Prepared Statement. Given the paucity of evidence that there currently was, Alex explained that her client would not be answering further questions after handing over the Prepared Statement.

For Denise, this was a positive. She had had to deal with dozens of legal representatives in the cells during interview. She knew that Alex was a fully paid up solicitor who knew her PACE procedure rules inside out. But she also knew that many police station representatives were not qualified lawyers but had attended a short course and done the exam which meant that they were then entitled to advise an arrested person what they should say, or indeed not say, in interview. In fairness, Denise knew some police station reps who were extremely good and knew how to do their jobs. Denise often wondered if those in the police stations being interviewed ever suspected that a great many of the police station representatives advising them on their future liberty were in fact once police officers themselves and had taken up their new occupation upon early retirement to supplement their pension and to make sure that they were out of the house and away from the missus on the days that they were not playing golf with their mates.

For today, Denise happily had Alexandra Hilton on the other side of the table.

The interview had started, the caution had been given and it had been explained to young Mr Battingsdale why he was there in custody. After establishing that he was definitely 'Charlie' and not 'Charles', his solicitor Alex read out the Prepared Statement on his behalf.

It was short and to the point and gave nothing away whatsoever, confirming what was already obvious. Of course, the Statement said that at no time was Mr Battingsdale responsible for the manner in which the car was driven. He was only the passenger and had no control over the vehicle. He knew nothing about the identity of the man sitting in one of the rear passenger seats who had fled the scene. Mr Battingsdale in his statement had not implicated himself and had skilfully given the police no information about what they did not already know. The statement even gave the impression that Mr Battingsdale was going out of his way to be of help to the police. It was very tidy.

Both Alex and Denise knew what was going to happen after the Prepared Statement had been handed over. There then commenced the ritual theatre of all the questions that needed to be asked being put directly to Charlie Battingsdale and with him then responding No Comment to every question put.

Denise Halloran used to become irate at the No Comment responses. Why did some detainees still go No Comment even when it was clearly in their interests not to do so?

These days Denise just got on with her job. What had happened earlier that morning with the smirking Mr Thornham and his arrogant knob of a lawyer in his Ted Baker suit was often how things worked. Denise knew that the smirks and the arrogance came about in the belief that they were making things so much more difficult for Denise. In fact, these days the DC was more than happy to be presented with a No Comment interview. It meant that she did not have to stay extra hours later in front of her screen making copious notes of what had been said during interview.

Once the formal interview was over and whilst collecting all her paperwork, DC Halloran warned Charlie Battingsdale that the police would be looking at his computer that had been seized from his parent's house as well as his phone which had been taken from him when he arrived at the police centre in Keynsham. He would need to be bailed to a later date.

Denise then opened the interview room door and walked out down the corridor, leaving Alex and Mr Battingsdale together. Denise knew what Alex would be telling her client, that if indeed what he had told her was the truth, and that he had never seen any packages in the boot of the car or indeed touched any such packages, then he had little to worry about. If there was to be any driving charge, then that also would not involve her client. Alex would also probably be warning him that he was now on the police Intel system and that he should be keeping a low profile. She was correct.

Denise walked down to the barrier where there was enough room for her to see over the top. After signalling for his attention, she spoke up to Sgt Matt Houseman and filled him in on what had happened. After a bail date had been agreed, the sergeant told Denise that someone was waiting to see her in a side room.

'All very strange. Best that you follow me,' said Matt Houseman.

In one of the rooms behind the custody desk stood Thornham's greasy brief. He was juggling a plastic cup between his fingers trying to ensure that his hand was not burned by the scalding hot liquid of a drink inside that the custody staff had just served him.

'You will remember me from earlier this morning. Axelby is the name. Representing Mr Thornham.'

'Of course I remember,' replied Denise, lying that she had indeed remembered his name.

'There have been developments,' said Mr Axelby. 'I am also here to represent Charlie Battingsdale. His step-father Dougal Kendrick Maclean has explained that he cannot get hold of his usual solicitor Mr Julian Derbyshire Henderson today. He therefore contacted the Chambers that he uses in London and they recommended myself. I would like to see my client now,'

'As I tried to explain when you returned to the police station earlier and completely leaving aside any issue of conflict, Mr Battingsdale is already legally represented and indeed has just been interviewed,' explained Sergeant Matt Houseman. 'You are I fear a little late.'

'No, you do not understand,' said Axelby. 'I have just been expressly requested by my client's father to look after the legal interests of his son. I am not here as some duty dogsbody. I am here representing him in a private capacity. I trust that my client's right to legal advice will not be denied.'

DC Halloran was going to say something. However, this was the domain of the custody sergeant and the look on his face said told Denise that he would deal with this.

'Follow me,' said Sgt Houseman. Denise decided to follow on just to witness the confrontation, if nothing else. The small procession marched down the corridor to the interview room and the door was opened by the custody sergeant. Inside, Denise could see Alex placing her wooden pencil box in to her briefcase and clearly was about to leave.

'Mr Battingsdale, Mr Axelby is here as he has been asked to represent you by your father,' the custody sergeant carefully and patiently spelled out. 'However, as far as I am concerned you already have the benefit of legal advice, with Ms Hilton here to represent you.'

Mr Axelby tried to intervene but the sergeant was having none of it.

'Charlie, are you happy to have Ms Hilton as your legal representative?'

Tossed in to the middle of a most unedifying and embarrassing legal tug of war, Charlie Battingsdale looked nonplussed.

'Er, yes,' said Charlie.

'Do you want to instruct Mr Axelby here as your solicitor? It appears that that he is here at the request of your step-father.'

All eyes were on Charlie who looked to Alex for what to say.

'Alex is my brief,' muttered a mystified Charlie.

On those words the custody sergeant ushered Mr Axelby out of the room. Instead of heading back to the control station behind the barrier, Matthew Houseman asked Mr Axelby to follow him to the exit.

By now Mr Axelby was a very deep purple. Threats were made by Mr Axelby to the sergeant that he would ensure that he was disciplined and that there would be formal complaints made about his preposterous behaviour to no less than the Chief Constable.

DC Halloran saw Mr Axelby being escorted down the corridor and off the premises. She had not seen such good entertainment as this for a very long time.

~ ~ ~

Kendrick Maclean's lunch had been both tense and mostly silent. He had managed to hold out till he had swallowed the last piece of Ronnie's quiche lorraine. By now Ronnie was leaning with her back against the rail on the AGA, waiting for her husband's explanation.

'OK, but you are not going to like this,' started Kendrick Maclean.

'Dougal, there are many things that I do not like. Just get on with it,' came the riposte from Ronnie.

Kendrick Maclean took the linen napkin in his hand and touched both sides of his mouth before standing up and making his way to the side of the kitchen away from the AGA. He knew that in a flash Ronnie could be round in front of him, her face and hands inches from his, but he felt far safer standing opposite the AGA and resting his weight against the huge pine Welsh dresser that took up most of the wall on that side of the kitchen.

Kendrick Maclean knew that having got this far, he would have to explain what had happened during the night. Which he did, leaving out no details. When he had finished relating the tale, he then apologised for not being straight at the outset and that he was only trying to protect his wife.

'I don't need protecting,' said Ronnie.

This may be true, thought Kendrick Maclean.

Ronnie then launched a series of relentless questions at her husband. Ronnie had never liked or trusted Griff and regretfully his involvement in the clean-up operation had done little to improve the atmosphere.

'Snivelling incoherent rat sent by you to do your dirty work,' was her estimation.

The two questions that Kendrick Maclean could not explain were who had carried out the atrocity and why.

Like his wife, Kendrick Maclean had gone through the growing lists of those that he may have upset, usually in the local building sector. However, everyone had eventually been satisfactorily paid off and he pleaded with his wife to believe him that there was no unfinished personal business with anyone that would attract such extreme action. Even in Somerset.

He was genuinely upset and told Ronnie this. This was his new life and he had made new friends and was being accepted in to his local community. Their membership application to the exclusive Sedgeton Grange Members Club had just been accepted and Kendrick Maclean had recently been invited to join the East Somerset Hunt (which reminded him to re-start the riding lessons). He had also now got a proper Firearms Certificate so that he could go on the local shoots when the season started later in the year. This was not like living in Straw Dogs country in Cornwall where he had heard that unless your family had lived there for generations, everything stopped when you entered the local boozer and within minutes the customers in there were whispering about burning down the houses of interlopers. This was modern-day Somerset for fuck's sake. No, he could not tell Ronnie who did this to the badger, because he genuinely did not know.

'It might have something to do with Charlie,' suggested Ronnie.

Charlie.

'Why haven't you done anything about getting him out of the police station?' enquired Ronnie.

Ronnie knew why. It was not like when Charlie was out of control annoying the good people in nice and leafy Barnes when being lifted by the police meant an instant call to the worried and embarrassed parents. Charlie was now 19. Kendrick Maclean knew that everyone was allowed the one phone call in the police station. For whatever reason, Charlie had chosen not to make that call to Ronnie and himself. He was about to decide that as he was now a consenting adult aged 19, Charlie could look after himself. Then Ronnie broke his chain of thought.

'Why don't you do something for your own son instead of standing there feeling sorry for yourself and a bloody badger,' spat Ronnie.

Kendrick Maclean retrieved his mobile from his gilet pocket and punched a number in.

The number was quickly picked up as Kendrick Maclean waited for the introduction to come to an end. He demanded to speak to Darby-Henderson as a matter of extreme urgency. He was out. Who else could help? They were out too, he was told.

'Useless fucks,' thought Kendrick Maclean aloud, as he jabbed the button that brought the call to an immediate premature end.

'What was the name of that proper barrister from the posh set of Chambers that we went to see just off Chancery Lane?' he asked his wife. 'You know. When we had the spot of bother with the Official Receiver.'

Ronnie knew instantly. Of course she did. Five minutes later Kendrick Maclean was speaking to the Chief Clerk of the set. Unfortunately, they were not able to assist with police station representations, but they knew an excellent firm of solicitors in Bristol who would no doubt be delighted to assist. The contact number would be sent through by text straight away. Thirty seconds later a ping on his phone told Kendrick Maclean that the number was on his phone and five minutes later he was speaking to the criminal defence department of what their website described as one of the West Country's 'top criminal defence firms'. Kendrick Maclean said that he believed that his son was in Keynsham nick. He stressed that he was also happy to pay privately and did not want some second rate useless legal aid lawyer looking after the legal interests of his son. Kendrick Maclean was reassured that they would be delighted to advise and indeed, they already had one of their top lawyers at the Keynsham Police Centre. They would be able to act immediately.

The call was made to a Mr Axelby in the presence of Ronnie. Mr Axelby was extremely helpful and said that he would be pleased to help and would sort immediately. In order to prevent any future misunderstanding or recriminations, Kendrick Maclean nevertheless still presented to his wife a full update of events.

Unfinished business. It was also time for Kendrick Maclean to make one further call before he returned to the outbuilding to recommence work on Ronnie's dream Airbnb holiday stay conversion. There was still no sign of the roofer's wagon with its load of scaffolding pipes, planks, crossbars and ties. Kendrick Maclean extracted his mobile once more and punched the buttons with right index finger.

'I am really just not in the mood for this. Let's just hope that he is not going to fuck me about,' thought Kendrick Maclean to himself, before his roofer picked up the call at the other end.

THE FERALS

Ludmila noticed that Mr Wright had been up in his room now with the man from the SRA for more than hour. Madge had also told Ludmila that as well as meeting in Mr Wright's office they had also shut the door behind them in the accounts and Rita's room. In the meantime, the telephone console had continued to flash with incoming calls, usually asking to speak to people who were not there. The telephone calls included Frank. Rita had still not returned home but the police had finally called him back. They were useless and told him to do everything that he had done already and that statistically there was little doubt that she would return home soon. Inspector Thompson also called back, becoming more restive that he was still not able to speak to Mr Wright. He would be extremely appreciative if Mr Wright could call him back within the hour. Victoria Wright had also called in again and accused Ludmila of deliberately preventing her from speaking to her own husband. If she was not allowed to speak directly to him could Ms Nowak or whatever her name was at least have the courtesy to pass on the message that she was expecting him back home for 5 pm. Without fail. Ludmila said that she would pass on the message and had actually sent an email to her boss before she heard Mrs Wright slam the phone down.

The WHW Legal office had also received a steady stream of visitors as well. An elderly couple had popped in to say that they wanted to change their Will. It had been Douglas Wainwright that had drawn up the original. Ludmila explained that Mr Wainwright now worked only as a consultant two half days a week. However, they both said that Mr Wainwright understood them best, so Ludmila fixed a meeting for them the week following the Easter break. She had also filed off an email requesting that the couple's original Will be retrieved from the archives, ready for the meeting next week.

The next visitors to the office were a couple who identified themselves as Cosmo and Miranda. They never did volunteer their second name or names. They were followed in by two children of indeterminate sex, both with long unkempt hair and who must have been no more than 6 or 7 years old. Both children headed immediately for the rubber plant that Ludmila had carefully been nurturing every day, over several years, where they now started to tear the leaves off. Ludmila asked that the parents tell the children to desist.

'Marley. River. Careful with the lady's plant,' asked the presumed father Cosmo.

It was at this point that Ludmila noticed that despite it only being April, both feral children wore just shorts, flip-flops and T-shirts. The words of admonishment from Cosmo appeared to have had some effect. Marley and River had now restricted their activity to just flicking the leaves with their fingers.

'Look, we are just down from Isleworth where we have already sold our house, the cash is in the bank and we have seen the exact house that we want to buy here for £750,000 and our offer has been accepted,' explained Miranda. 'We have already spoken to the Free School and they said that they could accommodate the boys after half term. Cosmo even has a space lined up for him and his business at the Creatives' Co-operative studios. The town's Well Being Clinic has also said that they are really interested in introducing my interpretation of Ashtanga yoga. We have seen your website and that says you would charge £1,400 for your conveyancing costs. But listen, we are cash buyers and as you can see are now all set to go. We just need to know what sort of discount you could do us as cash buyers. You came recommended from the estate agents down the road and they said that we should speak to you direct.'

Ludmila had never seen this couple before. The man wore a

Fez hat and the woman had an old woollen jumper and a midi skirt prominently displaying old Doc Martens' with the top laces loose and untied. Ludmila prided herself on her reasonable knowledge of English geography but she had no idea where Isleworth was.

She was far more concerned that Marley and River were now diverting their attention towards the small printer and photocopier in the corner where they had just extracted a pile of the firm's notepaper from one of the printer trays and were heading to Ludmila's desk to help themselves to the pens, pencils and crayons stacked up in their attractive glass cylindrical container.

'I myself can't authorise any discount,' said Ludmila, her eyes never leaving the marauding Marley and River. 'You will need to speak to one of our fee earners.'

At this point Ludmila thought of asking Felicity, the Poison Dwarf, to come down and sort it all out but she also thought that any meeting between Felicity and these prospective new clients could become unpleasant very quickly.

The couple, now stood in front of Ludmila, persisted.

'You don't seem to understand,' explained Cosmo. 'We are cash buyers. We are giving you work and in London they would be snapping our hands off to get our instructions.'

Ludmila had been to London on several occasions and she suspected that solicitors' firms there were probably not hugely different to WHW Legal.

However, more seriously by now the firm's headed notepaper was being torn into small pieces by Marley. His brother River was now concentrating on making shapes with a pair of scissors that he had picked up. Both parents were oblivious to the increasing carnage around them.

Ludmila rarely did this, but she then decided to make an executive decision.

'Actually, we don't do discounts,' she announced, quickly and authoritatively. She thought of the legal rivals that she disliked the most in town.

'However, I am fairly sure that the solicitors Maddison and Robinson just 50 yards down on the right can help you out,' added Ludmila.

Disappointed looks crossed the faces of both Cosmo and Miranda.

They both turned and started to herd their two offspring towards the door. River still had the scissors in his hand.

They opened the office door and Cosmo said to Ludmila.

'Sorry to hear that. Thought that businesses down here were supposed to be welcoming of entrepreneurs and wealth creators. No worries. Your loss. We are off to speak to your rivals. Have a nice day.'

With a click of the front door, Cosmo and Miranda had disappeared, together with their delinquent offspring.

Ludmila walked from behind the reception desk to the front of the office where she started to pick up the torn and cut paper as well as the shredded rubber plant leaves. She was not certain whether it would ever recover from the assault. She would explain the lost business to Mr Wright and also to Mr Darby-Henderson once he had returned from wherever he was. She would pay for a new set of scissors out of her own pocket.

Ludmila was bending down, with her back facing the stairs, picking up the final pieces of devastation, when she heard the voices and footsteps of both Mr Wright and Mr Farquhar approach her from behind. Ludmila had stood up and moved out of the way by the time both men had reached the bottom of the stairs.

As both Mr Farquhar and Mr Wright moved across the reception area towards the front door, she heard Mr Wright tell Mr Farquhar that he would telephone him by 11am the following morning, as agreed. Both men then shook hands by the door.

Before the door clicked shut, Mr Farquhar turned towards Mr Wright.

'And thank your colleague for the excellent recommendation for lunch. Splendid.'

Mr Farquhar then looked over Mr Wright's shoulder and gave a nod and a smile towards Ludmila, who smiled and nodded back in return.

Before Ludmila had time to explain why she was tidying up the wreckage in reception, Mr Wright had turned and was striding up the stairs with purpose.

'I need complete privacy in my room for the next hour,' he shouted back to Ludmila. 'I have several important and confidential phone calls to make and I want to be left alone. I also need you to ensure that there is a staff meeting in my room at 4.30. No exceptions. You can lock the front door.'

Before Ludmila could respond to the requests, she heard the door of Mr Wright's office upstairs close behind him.

Locking clients out in order to hold a staff meeting? Nothing like this had ever happened before. She felt no sense of anticipation, only worry as to what was coming next. In the meantime, she would see whether the rubber plant could be saved from death after its savaging by Marley and River.

'Kurva,' exhaled Ludmila quietly, for the second time that day.

~ ~ ~

Eaun did not have a lock on his door but if he did have one then the door would have been firmly locked, barred and bolted. He sank into his leather swivel chair and gave himself a gentle spin.

He had just spent the last hour, mainly listening, to the men from the bank and the SRA respectively, Mr Curtis and Mr Farquhar. He had several choices that he had to make. He then made the first. Colleagues laughed and even members of his own family scoffed, but Eaun still used his Filofax. He kept all the important stuff in here. He delved in to his briefcase. Sure enough, here it was, hidden under the Hudderston disclosure papers. He then got to work. With its Meetings and Action pages, the Filofax was the perfect tool as Eaun then set out in writing exactly what he was going to do. With the Action list taken care of, Eaun then picked up his mobile and started to work his way through the people that he had to telephone on his list. Eaun was habitually lazy about entering phone numbers on his mobile and in truth was not really entirely sure how to make certain that the number stayed as a mobile number and not a land line or email. The Filofax had always seen more reliable and certain.

The next hour saw Eaun's phone pressed to his left ear, leaving his right hand to take copious notes on the blank Filofax pages. At one stage his assistant Madge had furtively opened the door and enquired with the aid of a touching forefinger and thumb and her little finger tipping up and down whether he wanted a cup of tea. Eaun waved her away, but later realising that she had probably just popped her head through the door to check that he was actually okay.

Eaun had just finished the final call on his list when there was a nervous knock on his door and Madge once more nudged her head through the door.

'It is 4.30 Eaun,' she explained. 'You asked us all to be here for a staff meeting. We have brought chairs. Alex has just got back from the cells. The rest of us are here except Julian and Rita, who have not been here all day. Ludmila is just seeing to someone downstairs and as soon as she has locked up she will be here.'

Ludmila was the last member of staff to squeeze in to Eaun's office, dragging a large carver chair behind her.

'Sorry about that,' she said. 'The office is now locked with a message on the door apologising and confirming that we will be open tomorrow morning at nine. I have also just had to get rid of Frank again who seems to think that you have kidnapped Rita. Inspector Thompson from the police also rang. Again. He insists that you call him before close of business this afternoon. Oh, and your wife rang again to remind you that you are seeing her at five.'

Eaun waited till everyone had found a seat or had brought an extra one in.

Seated behind his desk with the semi-circle of seated personnel in front of him, Eaun felt a little like one of those pre-internet solicitors who used to perform the formal ritual of reading the Will of the deceased before the assembled family.

Alexandra Hilton was to Eaun's immediate left. Being a millennial, the only thing that she had in front of her was a small screen. Alex was next to Madge Appleby, talking through the day's events in the cells. Always vigilant and always prepared, Madge had rested on her lap her notepad and pencil to take notes. Alongside Madge, in her strident pink trouser suit was Felicity Lawton, Julian's secretary. Madge had once disclosed to Eaun that Felicity always got her clothes from M&S, but this information could no longer be correct as Eaun could not help but notice that Felicity's quite stylish suit jacket had flapped open at the bottom to reveal a different label called Autograph. Felicity may well have moved on in her fashion tastes but this afternoon her glum face still looked as down as it always did. Felicity had a reputation for occasional ferocity and Eaun knew that the other girls in the office referred to her as the Poison Dwarf. Eaun felt that Felicity only tolerated him out of sufferance. However, she was extremely good at her job and all the clients loved her. At the end of the semi-circle, Ludmila was positioning the carver in to its optimum position.

'What with Julian and Rita having 'gone walkies' for the day as you English say, you now have everyone here,' Ludmila told Eaun.

'Not quite,' replied Eaun to everyone. 'There is one more attendee to come. Would someone mind getting an extra chair in?'

At that point there was a noise downstairs of a key in the front door, the door closing again before being locked. The footsteps of the final invitee could be heard starting to mount the bottom of the stairs.

~ ~ ~

Back on the building site that was soon to become a highly desirable top of the range holiday let on Airbnb, Kendrick Maclean was unable to fully concentrate on what he was supposed to be doing. It was never the sort of thing that he would ever admit to anyone, but Kendrick Maclean had been spooked by the badger nailing. How would anyone even manage to get hold of a badger that had yet to be squashed by the side of the road? Someone had gone to a great deal of trouble to upset him. Since arriving in Somerset, Kendrick Maclean had heard the rumours of farmers taking matters into their own hands to protect their cattle, shooting the animals in the head themselves before getting rid of the evidence under the wheels of a 48 tonner artic. However, in this case, with the exception of the smashed paws and the wide open mouth, the animal looked remarkably untouched by any .22 or similar. It all looked very personal. If Kendrick Maclean knew who he had upset he would have been far more at home dealing with it. There had always been tossers who had hated him, just because he had made a few more quid than them and done better. In all his years working at Canary Wharf and later at Leadenhall Street he had never had anything like this happen before. The worst that he could remember was once when he was in a lift alone and about to get the Drain from Bank heading for Waterloo and the train back to Barnes, when two blokes got in from the floor below, one of them then advising Kendrick Maclean darkly that he should never pull a stunt like that again – 'or else'. He never did have any idea what the particular stunt was that he was supposed to have pulled. However, he did remember that just as the lift doors opened on to the crowded Ground Floor, he laughed. In any event, the 'or else' never materialised and until now Kendrick Maclean had thought no more about it.

This, however, looked and felt very different. This felt very personal. What was really bugging him was that he had no idea who it was passing on the request that he leave Somerset and find somewhere else to live.

He was also worried about Charlie. Yes, he was now over 18

and he could still behave like a plonker, but he was also family. He meant everything to Ronnie.

Kendrick Maclean stared at where the scaffolding was supposed to go when it was eventually delivered and then decided to write the afternoon off. There was too much going on. He needed to do some digging around. He placed several calls, made from the privacy of the future luxury Airbnb site. When he had made his final call, Griff, in response to the first call made, was already pulling in to the parking space in the middle of the Bradstock development. Kendrick Maclean could have sworn that the old olive green Land Rover with its split windscreen and spare tyre attached to the bonnet was dirtier than when he had seen it earlier that morning. The fumes from the exhaust seemed even more noxious and suffocating.

Griff was asked in to the shell of what was supposed to be the future living area of the holiday home and invited to make himself comfortable on the pile of breeze blocks still awaiting attention.

Kendrick Maclean enquired whether everything went okay with the disposal of the badger.

Griff nodded. No other information was offered and Kendrick Maclean decided not to pursue that particular point any further. However, he did open up and explain to Griff that he remained most unhappy about what was in effect a threat against him and his family.

'Bad,' concurred Griff eventually.

Kendrick Maclean then went on to explain that he really needed to know who this message came from. He was investing his money, his home and his future here in Somerset and he did not want some fucking wanker out there ruining it all for him. Griff lived locally, knew what was happening locally and had he heard of anyone planning this sort of threat being delivered to his employer?

Griff shook his head.

'What about down in the local boozers?' enquired Kendrick Maclean. 'Everything that happens eventually becomes common knowledge in those dark infested pits.'

'Not many dark infested pits left these days,' replied Griff. 'My mates and I, our old pub became one of those posh food places. They didn't want the likes of I or the village cricket team doing their drinking there. They even got rid of the trophies.'

Griff had rarely ever been heard to talk so much, so Kendrick Maclean decided to move in and strike while the iron was still hot. Did Griff have any idea how and from where a fresh and pristine badger could be sourced from? After all, it was hardly the sort of animal that you could pick up at the local Pets R Us?

Griff nodded his agreement.

'Let's think this through,' mulled Kendrick Maclean. 'Whoever did this must have spent time and cash getting their hands on the animal in such pristine shape. This should help. Who would provide a possible live badger on demand? Not a farmer. How about the local gypsy fraternity? I had only been at Bradstock the one week and they had my angle grinder. Got to be them. Let's go up there now and get some names. I have cash.'

Griff was silent in response.

'Well?' enquired Kendrick Maclean.

'Maybe,' ventured Griff finally and with some hesitancy. 'However, it might be for the best if you let I handle this sort of thing, sir?'

Kendrick Maclean knew that Griff was both loyal as well as diplomatic. He now remembered that having had the angle grinder stolen from under the nose just after he had bought Bradstock, on receipt of certain information he had decided to go up to the gypsy site on the outskirts of Sedgeton. He went alone. There was a single file approach road to the site, with the odd abandoned washing machine and old lawn mower by the side of the road. It was when the closed gates to the site came in to view, Kendrick Maclean's almost brand new Range Rover was then ambushed, coming under a sustained barrage of stones. He particularly remembered the hasty retreat that he had to beat back down the lane.

By Griff saying that he would 'handle' things, Kendrick Maclean now knew that Griff would be making the required introductory phone call before the trip, giving the make and registration of his vehicle so that there were no misunderstandings at the other end. In any event Griff said, they had known him for a long time, some even from primary school days.

Griff nodded in agreement with his employer when Kendrick Maclean proclaimed that in his view it was unlikely that members of the local travelling community had anything to do with the crucifixion itself, but given their local knowledge and range of contacts, it was quite possible that they might be able to provide a name.

Kendrick Maclean peeled off £150 in used £10 notes from a roll in his back pocket and handed the amount over to Griff.

'Try to make it £100 max. It is not Christmas,' he said.

With that, Griff had swung the metal driver's door to his vehicle open and with a cloud of dense thick dark grey smoke, Griff's Land Rover scrunched its way down the Bradstock driveway.

Kendrick Maclean spent some more time on the site, checking that measurements for the forthcoming scaffolding delivery were correct. His phone then went again and was retrieved from the gilet pocket.

He confirmed his name.

It was the boy's brief, Axelby.

'Just reporting what happened,' Axelby opened the conversation.

'I assume that Charlie is OK and on his way home,' asked Kendrick Maclean.

'I am not sure. I imagine so,' came the response.

'What do you mean 'I imagine so'? You are the one I am paying £250 an hour to look after my boy and you don't fucking know what is happening?'

'Things turned out to be a little more complicated than both you and I originally thought,' Axelby started to explain. 'I did eventually get to see your son but he was already represented and had even been interviewed by the time I was allowed to see him. I fear that he had been told probably by the police as well as the duty solicitor that as he already had a lawyer then he could not instruct myself.'

Axelby then launched into the decisive actions that he was proposing, including complaints to the Chief Constable when he was quickly stopped in his tracks.

'I really don't give a flying fuck who you intend to complain to,' said Kendrick Maclean. 'You came to me recommended by a top London set of Chambers as being the dog's bollocks in the West Country. You are asked to do something simple. And you fuck up. Unbelievable.'

With that, the call was terminated. Kendrick Maclean knew that he would have to wait till he spoke to the boy before he got anywhere near the truth on this one. What really pissed him off about lawyers as a breed was not only their extortionate hourly rates and the fact that they always had to be chased to do anything, but the ease with which when something did fuck up the blame was always apportioned to someone else. The fuckers always knew who to complain to but never knew how to take responsibility.

Before Kendrick Maclean had time to tuck his mobile back in to the warm quilt of the gilet jacket, it sounded off. Incoming. It was his elder son Tarquin. There had been developments, he told Tarquin. No, he could not explain now but there would be a family supper that his mother would get ready for 6.30 sharp this evening. And he was expected to be there.

Before any excuses could be offered, Tarquin was told that time and date were non-negotiable and he would see him later and not to be late.

His phone then told him that he had missed a call when speaking to Tarquin. Griff had been trying to get hold of him. Fitzroy immediately hit the Return Call button. A couple of rings later, and he was speaking to his employee.

'Bloody hell Griff, you aren't fucking around are you. What have you found out?

'Best we don't speak on the phone, sir. I think there may be a bit of a problem.'

'Problem, what do you mean, problem?' shot back Kendrick Maclean. 'Was the Land Rover stoned? I will pay for any damage.'

'No ambush and our friends here been extremely helpful. However, we need to speak face to face. I think that there may be a bit of a problem. Possibly a very big problem.'

BETRAYAL

ALL EYES were fixed on Eaun's office door as it was eased open and the ruddy but friendly face of the firm's Senior Consultant, Douglas Wainwright MBE appeared. Douglas Wainwright had been a partner back in the old Wainwright & Wainwright days. For the last 10 years he had been the renamed firm's Senior Consultant. In fact there never was any 'Senior' bit, he was in fact the firm's only Consultant. Any client over 40 years of age knew who Douglas Wainwright was, as did all the local dignitaries. It was just over ten years ago that he had been awarded the MBE for services to the community and the legal profession.

'Good afternoon everyone,' said Mr Wainwright as he nodded individually to each person sitting in the semi-circle around Eaun. Finally, he looked at Eaun who in turn nodded in return.

Ludmila looked around the table. It was clear that no one knew why they were there and Mr Wainwright was only in the office on the odd day. What was he doing here?

'We have everyone here now,' said Eaun. For the first time Ludmila detected a shakiness in Eaun's voice. She also noted that he was using notes in an old Filofax that he had spread on his desk, next to the brown Blue Parrot sandwich bag that had remained unopened.

'This is the most difficult day that I have ever had,' he commenced. 'It is all extremely painful for me. However, before starting I would ask that all of you, and I mean all of you, keep what you will shortly be told to yourselves and do not discuss even with your families.'

All eyes were firmly fixed on Eaun.

'There is no easy way to explain what has been going on, so here goes.'

At this point Ludmila was sure that she was not the only one who thought that Eaun was starting to well up. She felt herself begin to tense up and even start to become tearful. However, Eaun then coughed, sat up ramrod straight in his chair, the Filofax spread open before him.

'I don't often use notes but I am using notes this afternoon so that I do not miss anything,' he commenced.

'You may have noticed that we have had lots of comings and goings in to the office during the course of the day. The first visitor was Mr Curtis from our bank. He came to tell me personally that £5 million pounds has disappeared from our client account.' Eaun was squinting on to the pages of the Filofax trying to decipher his own writing. 'The actual amount that has gone is £4,975,000. As most of you will have discovered on busy completion days, our accounts system has a sophisticated security operating with our bank. For years it worked seamlessly. For any payments over £250,000 on either office or client account, the digital signature, which involves a constantly changing security code linked to the bank must be authorised by at least two people. The authorised signatories for WHW Legal are Mr Darby-Henderson, myself, Douglas and Rita, Mrs Thornham.'

The room was silent.

'The system has in-built safety systems, including the 2-signature authority. It also signals an automatic alarm system to the bank in the event of more than £1 million a day or an accumulative amount of £5 million over a period of time being withdrawn and sent to any unusual or unauthorised accounts. It seems that over a period of five days, the amount of £995,000 was withdrawn from our client account every day, making the total of £4,975,000. I know that many of us may curse the bank at times for their regulatory and compliance demands, but on this occasion they must be given credit themselves for spotting that something was very much amiss and telling me as soon as they were aware.'

'So, someone has stolen nearly £5 million of your money,' said Madge, almost whispering.

'I wish it was my money,' replied Eaun. 'Regretfully, all of the funds taken do not belong to me but to someone else. Our own clients. This brings me on to the second visitor at lunchtime, Mr Farquhar.'

'But who took the money?' blurted Madge, with all eyes centred on Eaun for the answer.

'The investigations at the bank are still ongoing,' explained Eaun. 'They are being as helpful as they can but their immediate task is to ensure that they remain 'clean' and cannot be blamed for what has happened. I do not blame them for that. It appears that the two digital signatories that authorised the payments were sent from this office last Friday evening, after the office was shut, during the weekend at about lunchtime on both the Saturday and the Sunday and late in the evening on Monday as well as last night. The digital signatures of authority were those of Mr Darby-Henderson and Mrs Thornham.'

No one in the room said a word.

'The investigations of the bank inevitably alerted the Solicitors Regulation Authority, for whom Mr Farquhar works,' continued Eaun. 'Most of you will at least have heard of the SRA. They regulate what we as solicitors do and ensure that we comply with their rules and regulations, particularly on matters such as finance and money laundering. Their powers are extensive. These powers include being able to what is called Intervene in any firm where there has been dishonesty. What this means in layman's terms is that they effectively have the power to shut us down immediately and ask another firm to look after the affairs of our clients. The SRA does of course also have the power to refer a solicitor to a disciplinary tribunal where he or she can be struck off.'

Ludmila noticed that along the row of seats, Mr Wainwright had his head bowed. She was trying to imagine what it would be like with those dreadful people at Maddison and Robinson telling her to get out of her chair so that they could take over.

We, I, have had to make some very quick and immediate decisions,' continued Eaun.

'Firstly, it appears on the face of it that there has been a mammoth fraud and/or theft. The monies appear to have been transferred to a company account in Spain. Mr Curtis will shortly be letting me have the details. Regretfully, this may well be why there has been no appearance today by either my partner Mr Darby-Henderson or indeed Mrs Thornham. This does however mean that I have no option but to formally advise the police on what is happening. Madge and Alexandra, can I have a quick word with you later re the mechanics on this?'

Both women quickly nodded but remained too stunned to say anything.

'Mr Farquhar spent time looking at our accounts today and he is sending in a full inspection team tomorrow morning. However, the one piece of good news is that he accepts that there is no further risk to client monies, the theft having already been discovered. The second piece of good news is that he is not taking any immediate steps to Intervene. It looks as if I am likely to be given a period of a few days, to try and retrieve and return the monies ourselves. This very short window has been allowed and for this I will remain eternally grateful to Douglas. We have been speaking at length on the telephone earlier this afternoon. Between us both, we will ensure that the bank have enough cash and collateral from us both to cover any immediate risk to clients.'

'I will not be taking this lying down. I have our reputation, good name and the well-being of all of you to look after. I have no idea how, but I am determined to rectify this. I do not even know where our colleagues Mr Darby-Henderson and Mrs Thornham have disappeared to.'

'Finally, I appreciate that you are all in a position where your jobs, immediate financial security for your families as well as possible careers have all been put at risk. I will fully understand if you wish to stand up and leave now. I will personally ensure that you will receive full recompense and you can depart with my blessing. I am just so very, very sorry.'

Ludmila could now see that Eaun was indeed beginning to well up. She always felt ill at ease at the idea of men crying so felt she had to say something.

'So, what is that word you English use? Elope, that is it. Julian and Rita have gone off and eloped to Spain with our money?'

Ludmila felt certain that she was not alone in feeling both horrified and completely mystified as to how the suave and smooth Julian could go off on a liaison with straight-laced Rita who lived the quietest of lives with husband Frank and who would not even join in the £1 a week firm's lottery pool as she thought the venture too much of a risk.

'Of course I am staying here,' added Ludmila. 'Kurva!'

Douglas was the next to speak.

'As you will know, I have already put my faith in Eaun on this. I am not going to let a lifetime's work and achievement be destroyed.'

'How can I help? asked Madge. 'Anything that I can do then you need only ask. You know that.'

Alex was the next. Recently qualified, facing the risk of being tainted with a firm that had been taken over by the SRA, Ludmila knew that of all of them Alex probably had the most to lose.

'At my interview Eaun, you said that working with you would never be boring. You were correct. Of course I am in for the duration. This certainly beats Mergers and Acquisitions,' she said, possibly a little too bravely.

That just left Felicity Lawton, the Poison Dwarf. To date, she had said nothing. She very rarely said anything, other than to bad-mouth clients and anyone else who had the misfortune to cross her path. She had been secretary to Julian Darby-Henderson for many years. She had also been loyal and unstinting in her service to him. Ludmila also knew enough to know that Felicity was extremely good at her job, so that when Mr Darby-Henderson went on one of his extensive holiday trips, he knew that everything back in the office would continue to run like clockwork under the watchful direction and eye of his trusted secretary, Felicity Lawton.

Ludmila suspected however that the support for Mr Wright may well find issue with the Poison Dwarf.

'I have never seen anything like this,' the Dwarf started, with her legs crossed and stretched out in front of her as she remained seated and still looking as grumpy as ever. Ludmila was certain that both she and the others were now waiting for her to uncross her legs and head for the door. After all, she had been as thick as thieves with Mr Darby-Henderson for as long as she had worked there.

The Poison Dwarf now continued.

'I am utterly disgusted. I have given the best part of my working life doing all the donkey work for this man who then walks off with £5m in order to get his filthy way with that trollop and hussy Thornham. Too bloody right you have my support.'

Ludmila was shocked. She had never heard the Poison Dwarf swear before, even mildly. She had also never seen her so downright angry.

When Felicity Lawton had finished her deliberation there was a very short silence and then someone started to clap, slowly at first, but then gaining momentum until everyone around the desk was clapping loudly and looking at Eaun, who by now had had a tear running down his face.

'Thank you Felicity,' choked Eaun.

It was however Douglas who was to have the final words, his jaw now no longer resting on his chest and his head held high.

'Now is the time that we start to fight back,' he announced to all.

~ ~ ~

The afternoon at The Sedgeton Grange had been manic. Gustave had been answering the phone most of the afternoon telling disappointed members that regretfully the Roman Orgy evening was sold out. However, one of the calls coming in did manage to put a smile on Gus's face.

When the suggestion of the Roman orgy evening was first mooted, Anabel came up with the idea of adding a bit of spice and authenticity to the proceedings by asking her godmother and long-standing family friend 'Aunt Cressida' along to give a talk. It turned out that Aunt Cressida was a Professor Emerita in Greek and Roman civilisations and was an acknowledged expert in Roman architecture. Aunt Cressida was it turned out also a good sport and expressed enormous enthusiasm at being invited to such a prestigious event and following detailed talks with Anabel, it was agreed that she would present a talk early on in the evening entitled 'Debauchery in Caligula's Rome: A Modern Perspective.' Slides were to be included. The inclusion of the talk as part of the evening entertainment subsequently went out on all of the invites to members, including the weekly newsletter.

However, as Gustave had learned to his cost on many occasions, nothing to do with his wife's family was ever straightforward or easy. True to form, the evening before the Caligula event, things had gone wrong. Aunt Cressida had left a message on the hotel answering service saying that she had been in North Africa working on the archaeological site at Carthage when there was an outbreak of the coronavirus. Before she could return to the UK she had been told that regretfully she would have to isolate in Tunisia for ten days, regardless of whether she was fully vaccinated or not. The Tunisian authorities were not letting anyone out. She would therefore not be able to make this evening's event. She sent all her love to Anabel and she was sure that the event would be an enormous success.

The immediate reaction of Gus to this piece of news was to check that there had been an outbreak of Covid (yes, there had been a surge of the disease in Tunisia and travel restrictions had been imposed). The reaction of Anabel was to immediately sort the problem by finding a suitable replacement.

The call that Gus had just taken and that had caused him such relief and delight was from one of the club members. Yes, in response to the plea from Anabel, as President of the Wessex Monuments & Historical Buildings Society, he was delighted to say that he had just come off the phone with the society's Honorary Secretary, who not only was an acknowledged local expert in Roman architecture in Britain, but after some uncertainty as to whether or not he would be available to give the talk, he had now confirmed that yes indeed he would actually now be free on the evening in question and would be there at 7pm to get everything ready. It seemed that the replacement speaker was also a trained architect and expert in local Roman buildings. Once more, the mightily persuasive charms of Anabel seemed to have come up trumps.

Gus enquired what the name of the replacement speaker would be. Certainly. It would be a Mr Piers Hudderston. Gus was assured that he was ever such a good chap who everyone got on with. Mr Hudderston had already been requested to come along in Roman clothes if at all possible. Gus was also able to confirm that once the talk had been given, then Mr Hudderston was more than welcome to stay and enjoy the evening's activities of which there were likely to be many. Gus was assured that the message would be passed on. Would refreshments be available? Of course. Mr Hudderston would be able to consume as much food and drink as ne wished. Gus also gave an assurance that a cheque in appreciation would be sent to the Society from The Sedgeton Grange. Account details were duly provided to Gus.

Anabel would be absolutely delighted to learn of this development.

Gus had to bring in some extra staff for the event. The staff who normally worked the Hotel during the weekends also had the option of working during the midweek evenings. To date, none of his staff had turned down the opportunities on offer. Why would they? Gustave made it worth their time, the wages and bonuses on offer being well above the local going rate. To ensure confidentiality for the members and their guests, Gustave had had Darby-Henderson draw up NDAs for all the staff as part of the employment package. All of the staff were of course prohibited from indulging in the hidden delights of either the downstairs Dungeon or Seventh Heaven at the top of the stairs. Gus conceded that they may however well be witness to a little bit of unexpected flesh on display elsewhere on the premises, especially outside at the pool and Jacuzzi and in the gardens. The first week or so following the opening of the club brought a few initial nervous giggles and sniggers but thereafter, as Gus had predicted, no one thought any more of it.

Tonight's party was sold out. This was not unusual for a special event evening. Within the last few months, the club's Marquis de Sade evening and the Monks and Nuns bash had both been spectacular successes. Gus had thought that Anabel's initiative of holding a special BDSM 4 LGBTQ+ event was probably a step too far and would back-fire in rural Somerset. However, this proved not to be the case as the evening managed to attract large numbers of the younger hipster membership down from London to start their new life in the country. Gustave recalled totting up the profits on his spread sheet the following day, just as he still remained pleasantly surprised at the amount of money they had made from the Strictly Face Coverings Only event held to mark the 'official' end of the coronavirus. As well as being good clean fun, the Special Events evenings were also definitely great for business at Sedgeton Grange.

However, Gus still wondered whether for this evening he ought to arrange for some extra security. There had in the very early days of the club been the occasional pervert from the village who, having clambered over the old school wall, had had to have been chased away from behind the hydrangea bushes. Just as Gus and Anabel had remembered on their very first visit to the school when it was waiting to be auctioned, there was very little that could be seen from the road and the pools were in any event hidden on the other side of the house. As well as the occasional local adult deviant, the early weeks of the club opening also saw attempts by the local acned youth from Sedgeton and the surrounding villages to scale the wall and observe what carnal delights were available for viewing. The town of Sedgeton was only a few miles away. The increasing popularity and attraction of the town had persuaded both Gus and Anabel to include its name in the full title of The Sedgeton Grange Hotel & Spa. It all made sound marketing sense.

Older members had related to Gustave how in the 1960s there were then countryside or seaside establishments called nudist colonies that habitually used to attract local pre and pubescent kids peeking from behind the vegetation. However, at Sedgeton Grange, after promises of 'a little slap' from the security team from Bristol that Gustave had initially employed when the midweek club opened, the problem seemed to then largely disappear. Gustave also surmised that in reality, viewing largely unclothed middle aged people trying to get in and out of the swimming pool and jacuzzi through the swaying pampas grass may not have been as alluring and exciting for the youth of Sedgeton as perhaps they originally imagined. Playing games on the computer at home seemed to be providing the far greater excitement.

At busy events, it sometimes just paid Gustave to have a couple of young, fit but low profile security people in their black tie outfits stand at the entrance to Sedgeton Grange. However, tonight was an all-member event and Gus and Anabel knew most if not all of the members personally. The members tended to self-police and if there was ever any inappropriate behaviour from a guest or member, then a quiet word with the veiled threat of instant expulsion usually worked. In truth however, Gustave could only remember a couple of occasions when this had ever happened. For this evening, Gustave decided that there was no need to hire outside security from Bristol. This would save the hotel several hundred pounds. To compensate, Gus had however arranged for two of the hotel's gardeners to dress up as Caligula's Praetorian Guard and stand at the entrance to greet the guests as they arrived.

Gustave went down in to the kitchens to ensure that Chef and his team were on top of things. Huge silver and gold plated platters were lined up, ready for the Roman feast to be loaded up and taken upstairs for the enjoyment of the paying membership. Gustave had noted with satisfaction that Anabel had managed to source several dozen big goblets, no doubt similar to what was used by the Romans themselves. Gustave, the hotel's self-appointed sommelier had proudly ordered a dozen cases of Italian wine for the event, including one case from the Lazio region, so that a real authentic Roman taste was brought to the evening. Back upstairs, Gustave had made certain that the projector had a table to sit on for the replacement speaker in what was once the school library. The magnificent panelled oak built in shelves still lined one of the walls and Gus remembered how before the hotel had opened, he had had to go down to the Bookbarn at High Littleton and spend a small fortune bringing back three deliveries of hardbacks in the hotel transit just to fill the shelves on the one wall of the old school library, there for the delight of all the hotel guests. Gustave suspected that most of his purchases from the Bookbarn had never actually even been removed from the shelves. Still, the lines of books impressed Gustave and he felt they contributed a genuine weight and grandeur to the place, especially as for many years the building had been a school.

The door to the Dungeon was open and Gustave glanced in to see that all was ready. It was still in preparation mode. Bright neon ceiling lights illuminated the whole of the old function room. Two of the hotel's uniformed maid service team, Gustave thought that their names were Brittany and Erin, were hard at work. One of the women was working the Henry vacuum over the room's extensive deep pile black carpet, dragging the reluctant and whining suction machine behind her. The other member of the domestic team was using the feathered duster on the chains and manacles dangling from the wall. It really was worth going that extra mile on the local artisans to ensure that the black metalwork on the stone looked so fantastically imposing and above all else authentic. There was a hint of wax polish in the air. Gustave could see one of the committee members down in Purgatory Parlour in the corner of the Dungeon, setting out various implements ready for use on the bench with the sets of furry and padded hand cuffs hanging from their large brass hooks. Members were of course encouraged to bring their own dress and accessories to events, but the club, just like any good tennis or bowls club on members' nights, always ensured that there was a full and constantly rotating set of paraphernalia and assorted aids available for use by the general membership, particularly the newer recruits. The committee member in his yellow Marigold gloves was wearing ear phones and was nodding to the beat but saw Gustave and gave a smile and wave of acknowledgement before Gustave let him get on with his job of meticulously lining up a large variety of whips, canes and other spanking paraphernalia in a straight line, ready for individual selection, on a polished late seventeenth century oak table. Another committee member, also sporting yellow Marigolds was applying the final polishes to the gleaming set of stocks. Gustave left them to their work and returned to his office.

Gustave was now just waiting for the sounds people to turn up. They were however a resident set and always made sure that they were ready to start on time. The Sedgeton Grange was now almost ready for their first ever Caligula's Roman Orgy Evening.

~ ~ ~

At the end of the staff meeting in Eaun's office, together with Madge, Alex had remained seated at the earlier request of Eaun.

'You both may well wonder why I have asked you to both remain behind. There will from now be a close involvement with various police and law enforcement agencies. Madge, you worked for several years with Wiltshire Police. Alex, you already have many contacts with inside knowledge,' said Eaun.'

Eaun then stopped speaking. Madge and Alex both looked at each other. Eaun's face was drained. He looked punch drunk, like a boxer on the ropes who no longer knew what was happening. It was clear to both women that as the silence continued, Eaun had burned up with all his energy expended in trying to explain to his staff how he had brought disaster to them under his watch. Alex sensed that unless something was said immediately, Eaun could start on a downwards spiral. She depended on Eaun for her job and future career. She also genuinely liked Eaun. From the horror stories that she had heard about experiences from her former colleagues at Law College, Alex knew that she had very much landed on her feet at Eaun's firm.

Both Alex and Madge looked at each other at the same time, smiled simultaneously with Alex pointing a finger at herself.

'Right, we are all hear to help,' addressed Alex to Eaun. 'You have just been through what no one should ever go through in a professional lifetime. Let me be blunt, you are reeling. However, you are not flat out on the canvas. But you cannot do this alone.'

Eaun had been listening intently to what Alex had been saying. He nodded gently. He was clearly in no position to fight back.

'To help you, we need your help,' continued Alex. 'Where are all the papers that the bank and the SRA left with you?'

Eaun pointed to a pile of papers, business cards and envelopes on his desk.

'It is all here,' explained Eaun. 'Everything that they have and know about what has happened to the money. That includes personal phone numbers where I can get hold of them if necessary. I think that the only thing that you do not yet know is that the only reason that we are even having this conversation is because of Douglas Wainwright. Before we all met up earlier, I had been speaking at length with Douglas on the phone. He is making arrangements as I speak for substantial funds of his own to be transferred to our office account and then together with the bank an agreed amount will then be transferred to client account to ensure that all our liabilities are covered. I feel personally embarrassed by the enormity of what he is doing. I had no idea that Douglas was financially in any position to make such significant immediate payments to the bank, although he did mention something about Peggy. In addition, we have both undertaken to somehow repay every penny stolen whilst at the same time obviously going after the £5 million taken from the firm. It is only because of the actions of Douglas that the SRA have agreed not to immediately intervene. However, unless we get all of the money back within days then the likelihood is that the patience of both bank and the regulatory authority will run out and the firm is likely to be closed down as an entity and all of our files taken over and run by another firm. I will also likely face personal bankruptcy including the loss of my home. I also face the very real prospect of being struck off. In short, we have been given a very short window to see what we can produce.'

Madge then chipped in.

'How about the firm's professional indemnity insurers?' she asked. In a pecking order of fear and trepidation within the legal profession, Alex knew that after the SRA the firm's insurers were probably on the next rung below, if only because she knew that every year it took Eaun at least a week in his locked office to complete the indemnity application forms.

Madge continued.

'I know that the PII people may not be your favourites, but during the time that I have been working for you I know that on several occasions you were really impressed by what they did, offering and suggesting really helpful solutions that pleasantly surprised you. You will know better than me, but it may well be that under the terms of the insurance, you may well be covered at least in part for what has happened.'

Alex could have hugged Madge. For the first time, there was a glimmer of a smile on Eaun's face.

'You had better not hang about however,' added Madge glancing down at the screen on her phone. 'It looks like their office shuts at 5.30 and it is already gone 5. If it is a potential claim that we are talking about then as you were always telling me, there should be no delay in calling it in. I have just sent a text message on to you with the contact number.'

'Madge, you are a star!' said Alex. 'Eaun, you need to alert the firm's insurers now and also call the SRA and the bank just to let them know what you are doing. Your wife is expecting you back at 5 so don't forget to call her and let her know that you will be late.'

Alex and Madge both started to gather up the paperwork on Eaun's desk.

'We are taking over the Conference Room,' directed Alex. 'Madge needs to call home to make sure that her kids get fed and she is not reported to social services. The two of us then need to sit down and think through a plan and strategy on what to do. Once we have done this we will call you at home Eaun and let you know what our options are.'

Eaun rose and walked round to the front of the desk. He still looked slightly tearful but at least he had some colour back in his face. Alex then saw Eaun hesitate in front of Madge, whose arms were now filled with papers. For an instant she thought that he wanted to give Madge a hug, but quickly retreated back to his chair behind his desk.

'Get on with those phone calls that you need to make now then get yourself off home to see poor Victoria,' ordered Madge. 'No need for you to come back in here just yet. We will call you.'

In the conference room the two women started to sort out the paperwork and also set up the flip chart with marker pens at the ready. Jobs to do and calls to make were listed on the chart.

Ten minutes later Eaun announced that he had made his calls and was finally leaving the office, by gently knocking on the conference room door and saying a quick cheerio. A minute later, the latch could be heard on the front entrance door to the office.

'Right, let's get started,' said Alex.

On Alex's first call, a female voice eventually answered.

'I am really sorry to have to bother you. I suspect that by now you are on your second G&T and about to settle down to watch the latest exciting episode of 'Flog It!' started Alex.

'However, I need your help. Big time.'

~ ~ ~

'There have been developments,' said Griff. 'No trouble up there. Long as they know who I is and what I am driving then they are as good as gold. The gate was even left open for me and the look-outs were waving me in towards Barnaby's caravan.'

Yes, yes, just get on with it,' Kendrick Maclean exclaimed with impatience. He was wondering who the hell Barnaby was.

'A few days ago Barnaby, who basically runs the show up there, got word of a very strange request. Someone wanted a badger. Not a live one for they be as wild and dangerous as fuck when you piss them off proper.'

'And?'

'They also demanded that the badger concerned was not scraped off the road covered in muck and dirt. Anyone could go along scraping corpses off the road. They wanted one that looked in good nick.'

'Well?'

'It seemed that finding out where the local setts were is extremely easy,' explained Griff. 'A free range chicken with a slit throat and filled with rat poison was thought enough to do the trick. Seems however that it made the unfortunate badger very sick and ill. I was told that things then got a little messy as they tried to bash it on its head but once dead they were certain that when delivered you could never have told that it had also got a small clubbing on the head just to put it out of its misery. Have to say that I never noticed any lumps earlier today.'

'I don't need to know all this.'

'I am just filling you in on what happened as I think that they thought that I was there to complain that the animal had not been delivered in pristine outward condition.'

'Well, the request for the badger was made by someone driving a silver Mercedes estate,' started Griff, trying to make sure that he left nothing out. 'When they came along a few days later to take delivery of the badger, with a polythene sheet all laid out in the boot, it was the same two blokes that came along. The driver, he have a local accent Barnaby says but the other bloke he say nothing throughout, just got out and stood by the side of the car.'

'That is very good,' said Fitroy Maclean, eager to encourage his employee as much as he could. 'What happened then?'

'One of Percy's people said that the passenger he had the same sun glasses as Clint Eastwood in the 'Do You Feel Lucky Punk' films. Never took them off. What Barnaby and his cousins all said was that they had never seen neither men nor their car before. One might have been a baldy. They also looked like they had money.'

First Barnaby. Now Percy. Who the hell were these people, wondered Kendrick Maclean.

'Talking about money, what happened to my £150?'

'It only cost me £100. Barnaby was as good as gold,' Griff explained as he extracted some notes from his back trouser pockets and handed the £50 over to his boss.

Griff had actually done well. For a moment, Kendrick Maclean was tempted to give back all or some of the £50, but the thought was only momentary. After all, that was what he got a weekly wage for.

Kendrick Maclean was however uneasy at this latest development. At the back of his mind he was still concerned that whoever had arranged for the crucifixion of the badger had gone to a lot of trouble. Griff did not mention any fees incurred and payable for the delivery of the animal, but it could not have been cheap. Sadly, he concluded, this was not the work of a nutter and this was deeply troubling. Maybe Charlie could throw some light on matters when he eventually showed his face again. He had sent a text to him telling him to make sure that he did not let his mother down and to ensure that he was in time for tea at the allotted time.

As he turned round to return to the old Land Rover, Griff promised that he would keep an ear out locally to see what he could pick up.

'Oh, I nearly forgot,' said Griff. He walked back towards his boss and started to hand over a torn bit of paper that he then gave to him. Kendrick Maclean still had the £50 in notes gripped in his hand.

'What is this?' enquired Kendrick Maclean.

'One of the look out at the gates was Barnaby's boy, can't remember his name. A bright one he be. Took the number plate of the Mercedes while they were loading up our badger,' responded Griff. 'Seemed like it was a new car as well so he took down the name of the dealership on the back window as well. Here it all is.'

Even Kendrick Maclean was impressed as he exchanged with Griff the torn piece of paper for the £50 in notes in his hand. He also made a mental note to ensure that Griff kept his employer's generosity strictly to himself.

~ ~ ~

Eaun had just sat down in the family Volvo. Predictably, the parking space in the Black Dog car park allotted for Julian Darby-Henderson's Tesla was still empty.

He had felt a lot better having touched base with both the SRA and Curtis at the bank, just to let them know what was happening. He was not so sure what good the call to the firm's PII people had achieved but he felt better for making it. He had told them all that he was in the process of formally reporting the loss to the Wessex Constabulary. The call that he had yet to make was to his wife Victoria. He really could not have faced another tirade from her as to why he was late again. He wondered what sort of response he could expect from her when he told her that there was a very real possibility that she would lose the roof over her head. Instead, Eaun took a coward's way out of the problem and sent a text that there was something serious and urgent in the office and he would be back home very shortly.

Eaun remembered that he had still to call back Inspector Thompson. His calls had been insistent. There was no way that Colin Thompson could have been calling about the loss of the £5 million. That event would have passed him by and been over his head, as by all accounts his time working for the Constabulary was filled up in an office with organising shift rotas and the monthly crime analysis figures for the division. The only reason that Eaun knew of the Inspector was that he lived a few hundred yards from his own home just outside Sedgeton. They had met each other at a neighbours' drinks do jointly organised by Victoria during one of her spells when she thought that they should be meeting more new faces. Eaun had never come across the name of Inspector Colin Thompson on any operational police matter. He therefore dialled the number that Ludmila had earlier emailed on to him to see what he wanted. There was laughter and the clinking of glasses in the background.

'Ah, Wrighty old man. Good of you to call back,' came the voice of the Inspector.

'How can I help,' said Eaun.

'Yes indeed. Bit difficult to speak at the moment. Actually at the 19th hole at the club. Midweek Medal competition.'

Eaun recalled that following the original drinks do it was Victoria who pushed him to ensure that Colin Thompson could get through his application to the golf club. Eaun remembers trying to explain that the days when golf clubs had a 20 year waiting list and an application process more intimidating than the intelligence services had long since gone. Most golf club these days accepted any Tom, Dick or Harry and welcomed with open arms anyone who was offering them the signing on fee and a year's membership. Nevertheless, Eaun had duly supplied the names and the phone numbers and clearly Inspector Thompson now appeared to be a dedicated member of the local club.

'One of my officers knew that we were friends and suggested that I might have a quiet word with you rather than go through official channels,' said the Inspector as the background chatter increased in intensity. 'As I say, difficult to speak, old boy. Your number has come up on my phone. I will call this number later and let's speak once we both get home, maybe even have a chat.'

'Er, what is it that you actually want to speak to me about?' enquired Eaun.

'Really difficult to speak here and I can't hear a thing,' came back the reply. 'It is presentation time and I won longest drive on the par four seventh hole. Must go.'

The phone at the other end clicked dead and Eaun threw it on the passenger seat next him, before starting the engine and easing the vehicle on to the Market Place and towards home.

Before reaching out of town, Eaun was once again held up at St Christophers School. There was a small but still noisy crowd of people outside the school entrance. A megaphone helped choreograph the chants. The main poster about saving the school was still there. However, the earlier banner asking the hippies to go home had disappeared, only for Eaun to notice that it had now been replaced by a far larger being held aloft urging 'Fuck Off Hippies'. The broadcast journalists with their lanyards had obviously got their story and retreated. There were no police present either. The traffic had just all slowed down so that everyone could have a good stare and time to soak in the scene.

Eaun remembered that he had still not asked Ludmila what exactly the hippies had done or were threatening to do to St Christopher's. He would do so tomorrow.

~ ~ ~

Denise Halloran was not watching Paul Martin and 'Flog It!' when Alexandra Hilton called her at home. However, she did have her G&T with lots of lemon and not a great deal of tonic in her left hand. She picked up the mobile with her right hand.

'Hello Alex,' she responded. 'You know that I never watch trash daytime television. However, I will confess that I do have something in my hand to help me into the evening.'

Denise liked Alex. She was thorough at her job although she did work for the opposition. She was one of the few on the dark side that it was always good to speak to. Alex would surely not be calling for a social engagement. Denise could not remember the last time that Rod and herself even went out. During the pandemic, even more as a police officer, Denise did not socialise with anyone. She reflected however that even before the arrival of the coronavirus, Rod and she had effectively stopped going out as a couple. On the very few occasions that Rod and she ever did make it out of the front door to go somewhere social, it was always to meet other police officers. She was just feeling done in the whole time. Overtime used to pay for the family holidays. Now, she reflected that the overtime she spent just to try and keep her in touch with her increasing workload was having a real negative impact on her. Looking down at her body and taking another sip of the G&T, Denise felt that she was perhaps starting to let herself slip a little, physically and mentally.

'Anyway, how can I help?' asked Denise. 'Hold on, I think that I will need a pen and paper.'

Denise then spent the next quarter of an hour listening to Alex and occasionally asking the odd question or asking for clarification. Towards the end of the conversation Denise said to Alex.

'Bloody hell, you don't ask a lot do you?!' she laughed. 'And you need this information like now? I have books to read, friends to see and a lamb tagliata with watercress and tomatoes to prepare for my gorgeous husband. I do have a life you know.'

On the other end of the line, Denise could hear Alex snigger and then giggle.

'Give me an hour,' said Denise. 'I will need to do some phoning around and probably drag some of our finest out of public houses, at least those establishments that still remain open for business. I will get back to you as soon as I can. I am sure that the tagliata needs to marinate.'

Profuse thanks and gratitude were offered to Denise, who suddenly felt rejuvenated by the call. Here she was, about to start digging around, asking questions, exactly what she did in her real job, but on this occasion she already felt the spring in her feet as she got up from the sofa and went to get her black phone contacts book from the family paperwork drawer in the kitchen. She also liked Alex because she did not push boundaries or even think of putting Denise in a compromising position. None of the information that she wanted was a state secret, just near impossible to get your hands on quickly or even at all unless you knew the right people.

As she rummaged between the old bills, balls of string and historic Christmas card lists in the drawer, Denise spotted and retrieved her prize contacts book. It was too valuable to keep at the station where her colleagues might pinch her top contacts and inside information.

Whilst in the kitchen the M&S Meal for Two that Denise had earlier purchased on the way home from work was rammed in to the fridge, including the bottle of the supermarket's house Sauvignon that went with the deal. As she headed back to her phone and the sofa in the sitting room, Denise thought that it really was time for her to get a life and to get out more. One day she could even find out what a lamb tagliata was.

A replenished glass at her side and hunched over the coffee table in front of the sofa, Denise was all set to go. She started keying in the numbers on her phone.

LIVING THE LIE

It was only a five minute journey from seeing the placards outside St Christopher's School and driving through the gates of the Wright household. The journey was short but it was also the first time that it had truly sunk in for Eaun the extent of betrayal by his partner Julian. Two questions started to chip away at Eaun. Firstly, why had he not guessed that his business partner was even capable of stealing £5 million of his clients' money and at the same time chose as his co-conspirator in crime their very own office Practice Manager. Rita Thornham. Rita bloody Thornham. Eaun had seen her most working days for twenty years. He left her to get on with her job, making sure that the firm was compliant. Otherwise, Rita simply had never registered with Eaun, in her Hillary Clinton trouser suits, string of pearls and a hairstyle that would have looked dated even on Peyton Place. Eaun conceded that he knew very little about Rita. At the office Christmas parties (when firms still had these) and also the work's summer 'family' barbecue, Rita had been known to be 'shouty' after too much of the Bristol Cream sherry. On at least one occasion her husband Frank had to take her home before there was a scene. There were also regular occasions several years ago when her then Goth son, whatever his name was, used to come in to the office on the way back from school asking to speak to his mum so that no doubt he could cadge some money off her to buy fags, spliffs or cheap vodka to consume with his mates in the town's park. That was about it for Rita. Eaun knew hardly anything else about his key employee. Now, she had helped to utterly shaft him and had disappeared on a supposed shag fest with his business partner spending millions and ensuring that Eaun faced ruin. Eaun cursed his own blindness in failing to see what had been happening behind his back.

And what had he missed all along with Julian? Julian and he had joined the firm at about the same time. They were different in nearly every way but they both found out that their different skills and personalities were in fact complementary. Crucially, they both knew how a modern law practice worked and even more crucially understood how to make money in a sometimes difficult market. Eaun was married and had gone on and had two delightful daughters, Alison and Cassie. Julian had no family. He lived alone in his glass and concrete pile at Oakhill, overlooking a valley. This meant that Julian did not have two sets of university fees to pay or a wife to keep in a style to which she had become very accustomed. Julian could therefore afford to live in a designer house and drive a Tesla. When Julian was away on one of his many extensive holidays abroad, there was usually a huddle of the girls in the office in the kitchen, conspiratorially guessing whether Julian was gay or as Madge put it 'swung both ways'. Eaun had never thought of Julian's sexuality, or cared. He had had girlfriends, some had even stayed for extended periods at Oakhill and had been even been paraded for viewing at local social events. However, none of them ever stuck around for very long. If it was the 1950s, Eaun supposed that Julian would be known as 'a confirmed bachelor', for in those days it seems there really were such things. Eaun just assumed that he did not want a life of being tied down and wanted to continue to play the field. Over the years Eaun had admitted to an occasional pang of private envy at his freedoms.

The second question that perplexed Eaun, was why him? What was the level of contempt that could make Julian take decisions that he knew would lead to Eaun's ruin? He really had no idea. He also realised that he was still feeling stunned and pained by what had happened. Otherwise, why had he not immediately driven round to Julian's concrete castle and smash every glass window and door, of which there were many?

He conceded that even after all those years of working together, Eaun in fact knew nothing at all about Julian. Like he knew nothing about Rita.

The gates of his late twentieth century detached house finally came in to view and Eaun swung the Volvo on to the drive. He parked next to Victoria's mint green Fiat 500 hybrid. As he switched off the ignition, Eaun spotted Vlad the Impaler on the shed roof, on his back and stretching to the full in order to eke out the last of the evening sun, no doubt recovering from another hectic day of guard duty. There was no sign of his brother Ivan. Eaun picked up his mobile and got out of the car.

Eaun unlocked the front door and placed his briefcase on the small table by the entrance in the hallway, the sort of table where the family landline telephone used to be kept on a pile of directories. These days, it habitually housed Eaun's leather briefcase, so at least he always knew where it was.

There was no sign of his wife.

'Hello darling, I am home,' shouted Eaun up the stairs.

'There is no need to shout,' came a voice hidden somewhere downstairs. 'I am in here. The lounge.'

Eaun followed the direction of the voice and saw his wife Victoria sitting on one of the armchairs, next to the television. For one terrible moment, Eaun thought he was about to be reprimanded once more about his viewing habits. Several months ago, as usual Eaun had gone to bed last and had switched the television set off on the channel he had been watching. Regretfully, the next morning, when Victoria came to switch on the television, instead of the cheery tomes of Good Morning Britain, his wife was greeted to Channel Red Hot Babes and the number to call to speak direct to Red Hot Hilda. Eaun's protestations that he was just casually flicking through the channels before retiring for the night (this was actually true) unfortunately cut no ice.

Victoria would hopefully want to talk about something else. Eaun also felt deeply discombobulated, wondering why, given the earlier events of the day, he was even in the least bit worried about Red Hilda and her ludicrous promises.

'Where on earth have you been, you have deliberately been avoiding me all day,' scolded Vicky. 'Early this morning, then the promised lunch and then finally you turn up when you want to this evening. You having an affair? I have told you that we need to speak. Urgently.'

Eaun was about to say that the day had not been the best and that Vicky should know about what was happening because it would also affect her. And no, he was not having an affair. However, he never got the chance.

'Before we get on to the substance of what I need to say and in case I forget, you should be aware that I had to get out of my bath this morning and open the door to some mad witch holding her wretched brat by the scruff of the neck telling me that we have a sex pest living here in the house,' continued Mrs Wright.

Eaun had no idea what to say. Sex pest? What sex pest?

'I told them that it was nothing to do with us and that they should go away. They did, but I expect that you might be hearing further from someone,' said Victoria.

'Now let's get down to the reason that we are having this talk,' said Victoria.

'I expect that you already know what is coming but I will spell it out for you. You had better sit down.'

In fact, Eaun had no idea at all what was coming.

'Three things you should know,' started Vicky. 'Firstly, what has happened was inevitable. We effectively have been living separate lives. Since the girls have gone off to university I never see you these days, you never seem to be in the office and you hardly seem to be here at home longer for 5 minutes either. When was the last time we did anything together even before the months stuck together during lockdown? Even then, you claimed that you were a 'key worker' and always going off somewhere. So, this is now the end of the road for us. I am getting a divorce.'

The news of his pending divorce came as news to Eaun, but Victoria was now starting to get into her stride and she continued apace.

'The second thing that you should know is that I have become a lesbian. These things happen and it has happened to me. We had a great marriage and have two wonderful daughters but I can no longer live a lie. I am now at ease with my true feelings. I have now come out. Officially. I am a lesbian. So there. Now you know.'

Vicky paused for a moment. Eaun was pondering what coming out 'officially' meant. The *Courier* was no longer around for an old-style official announcement page so perhaps this involved his wife sending out announcements on Instagram to the whole world.

Vicky took a deep breath and continued.

'The final thing that you should also know about is that I am moving out of the house, starting my new life with Chris,' Vicky stated.

Chris? Who the fuck was Chris? Eaun felt himself sinking in to a sponge of confusion. The only Chris that Eaun could immediately think of was Chris, the scorer and telegraph of the Second XI at one of the nearby village cricket clubs. It was several years ago, but Eaun still remembered helping him out over an unfortunate misunderstanding with a member of the town's women's cricket team in the pavilion toilets. It surely cannot be that Chris that his wife was planning to spend the rest of her life with. In any event, she had just announced that she was lesbian.

'Chris. Chrissie,' said Vicky. 'For nearly 20 years she has been in your own house most days. If you had spent more time with your family rather than at your precious work, you would have remembered all this. You know, Alison's best friend. Chris, Chrissie or Christine. All the same.'

Eaun now remembered. Christine. Alison's inseparable friend, from nursery through to the sixth form. Eaun did indeed remember Christine. He couldn't be that bad a parent if he was at home long enough to at least remember her. Yes indeed. Always happy, always bouncy and always round at the Wright household. Her parents used to run the chemist's shop on the edge of town. Eaun remembered her as being pretty with blond hair, but nearly all of both Alison and Cassie's friends were pretty with blond hair. Eaun could distinctly remember her being at the Wright household on the occasions when the family had to face its darkest moments, including Chrissie being there sobbing hand in hand with Alison and Eaun had to excavate the impressively deep hole at the bottom of the garden for the burial of the unfortunate rabbit that had been singled out for attention by the neighbour's Weimaraner.

Not for the first time that day, Eaun was lost for words.

'You mean Chrissie, Alison's best friend?' he eventually asked.

'They were never that close after Alison decided to go to uni at Bristol,' replied Vicky. 'Look, I never planned for any of this but it has happened. We love each other. I appreciate that none of this is easy but eventually, you will be happy for us.'

Eaun then fell silent because there was nothing that he could think of to say. There was however a small inner wave of relief that it was not Chris from the village cricket club that she was planning to spend the rest of her life with. He had this image in his head of his daughter Alison and her best friend Chrissie, both in pigtails and holding hands and sobbing as Eaun lowered the bloodied blanket containing what remained of the rabbit into its final resting place, trusting that neither of the severed ears would escape from the blanket during the full rites of the burial ceremony.

'You should know that Chris and I have decided to live with each other, as from now,' said Vicky. 'I have already moved some of my clothes and personal things out already. The rest of my stuff I can come and collect over the Easter holiday.'

Eaun picked up on the phrase 'rest of my stuff'. After her clothes, books and records, Eaun figured that the rest of the 'stuff' in the house were things that they had bought and shared together over the last 30 years or so.

'For years you have been giving me your solicitor spiel that couples who split up should make sure that they keep the channels of communication open between them and only go to the lawyers once they know how things are going to be split between them,' said Vicky. 'We can decide about the sale of the house and how we split the proceeds over the weekend. Any questions?'

There were of course hundreds of questions starting to swirl round Eaun's head, but only two that he could currently articulate in any way. His mouth was dry and it was difficult to form any words at all.

'Yes,' muttered a baffled Eaun. 'The girls. Have you spoken to them? They are both in Bristol. Do you plan to drive up and speak to them, particularly Alison, to let her know the good news that her best friend is now sleeping with her own mother?'

'You are just going to have to get over and live with it, Eaun. I was planning to tell both girls about these developments after you had been kind enough to give me five minutes of your precious time. I will probably get in contact with them both either this evening or tomorrow. I don't expect you to be down there with the kids Eaun, but young people these days, including our own children, have a far wider and socially accepting attitude towards sex and everything else.'

'I am not quite so sure, Vicky,' responded Eaun. 'Think that you had better go and see both Alison and Cassie in Bristol this evening. This news had better come from you and not anyone else.'

'Can't go to their grotty little flat now, responded Vicky. 'I will call them tomorrow. Christine has got a piping hot delicious cottage pie waiting for me at her flat. Anything else or are we done for the evening here?'

What happened next Eaun had no control over. He did not even feel it slowly coming. As Vicky hauled on to her shoulder her giant handbag that looked more like something more likely to be taken to Base Camp rather than Waitrose, Eaun suddenly bent forward and at first guffawed and then started to laugh, not polite laughs, but full painful uncontrollable laughs that came from the pit of his stomach. Doubled over, Eaun could now feel himself gasp for air with his sharp intakes of breath in between the waves of laughter. Later, Eaun thought of how he once saw Billy Connolly in his early days at the Victoria Palace, when a man across the aisle could take no more. Exactly like Eaun was now doing, he was doubled up on the aisle floor, fighting for breath with tears running down his cheeks. Eaun could not stop his own belly laughs. The pain became worse. Could anyone ever actually die laughing?

'It's not funny,' uttered Vicky as she stormed out of the lounge. Eaun then heard the front door slam and the glass in its window shake with the force.

It took Eaun nearly ten minutes to completely stop his laughing outbursts and for the sporadic bursts of hysteria to cease.

At the end of his laughing bout, Eaun's chest was still sore. He decided to lie down on the sofa for a few minutes. Funny? He was in the process of losing his business, reputation, house and everything he owned. He had also just had his wife of nearly 30 years announce that she could take no more of him, decided that she was a lesbian and was now off to consume the waiting cottage pie followed no doubt by full-blooded lesbian sex with the best friend of their own daughter.

Staring at the ceiling from the sofa, Eaun let his eyes slowly close. Everything seemed to be turning gently but irrevocably upside down. He was supposed to be feeling the very worst of despair, anguish, humiliation, hurt, betrayal and extreme anxiety. Instead, following the catalyst of the belly laugh spasms, Eaun felt a gradual sense of liberation come over both mind and body.

Suddenly, a large and heavy shape landed on Eaun's chest. He sat bolt upright ready for his attacker.

It was Vlad. Vicky had clearly decided that feeding the boys was already no longer part of her job description. Fed up of waiting, Vlad had taken it upon himself to come back indoors and then to jump from the piano behind the sofa and on to Eaun's chest to gain attention.

Eaun cursed, but nevertheless followed Vlad into the kitchen where Ivan the Terrible was already patiently waiting for his dinner. Whilst searching where Vicky kept the bag of what must be the world's most expensive specialist cat food for adult British shorthairs, Eaun noticed the distinctive masthead of that morning's *Daily Express*, incorporating the Crusader with the shield, helmet and sword, sticking out of the waste bin. Eaun extracted the clearly unread newspaper from the food bin and placed it in the paper recycling basket by the back door. He then washed his hands and made a mental note to cancel the existing cat food order. For Vlad, Ivan and any of their visiting feline friends, bulk buy cat food from one of those cash and carry places that the girls in the office kept talking about was from now going to be the order of the day.

Eaun noted with satisfaction that there appeared to be no whiff of either disinfectant in the kitchen or indeed anywhere else in the house.

Eaun then disappeared upstairs to take a long hot shower, with a final two minutes under the shower head with the water on cold. Back in the bedroom, Eaun had checked under the pillows. There was no sign of Victoria's nightie.

Whilst Eaun was putting on a clean pair of jeans and a T shirt, his phone went. It was Alex.

'We have been busy,' she said. 'We have everything in the conference room. Be easier if you came here. See you in 20 minutes? Seven o'clock?

Eaun suddenly felt better. He found the trainers he wanted and was doing up the laces when the Westminster chimes of the front door bell went. Perhaps it was Victoria returned to apologise and say that it had all been a dreadful mistake.

Eaun walked quickly down the stairs and saw through the frosted glass that it was not Vicky but a tall male figure.

Bugger. Inspector Thompson said that he would be popping around. Eaun reached the door and opened it.

'Good time? said the Inspector.

'Absolutely,' lied Eaun.

~~~

Kendrick Maclean had just got out of the shower and only had a towel around his waist. His dusty and dirty work clothes he had thrown in the voluminous Ali Baba of a laundry basket. Those fuckers from the roofing company had still not called him back, so he had no idea what was happening on the scaffolding front. He felt upset. Ronnie would say that he was always upset but tonight he knew why his stomach was churning.

It was not the roofers. They could go fuck themselves.

It was Charlie.

Charlie had arrived back home about an hour ago. He did not see the vehicle that dropped him off and he carried on working in the holiday home conversion site until his son eventually showed his face and came to see Kendrick Maclean, who had been coaching himself to remain calm and collected when he did see Charlie.

'Sorry, Dad,' started Charlie.

'You know we have had the Old Bill here, barging their way in and helping themselves to stuff in your room? Your mother is beside herself with worry. What the fuck were you thinking about?' responded Kendrick Maclean, using all the powers of restraint that he had. 'What is going on? Tell me. All of it.'

Charlie related to his step-father that he had been messing around with his mate Nicky. He had mentioned him somewhere before, hadn't he? Nicky had a beamer, all legit, and he asked him whether he wanted to go for a spin as he had to pick up a mate in Glastonbury. He had nothing to do and he was bored so went along with it. They went to Glastonbury, went to some house behind the Abbey and then this bloke came out of the house with a sports bag. Nicky was next to him, outside the car. Nicky opened the boot and said to his mate that should put his kit in the boot. Nicky mentioned something about him staying a few days in Sedgeton with him and his friends. Thought no more of it. Bloke then got into the rear passenger seat.

Kendrick Maclean asked Charlie who this bloke was.

Charlie explained that he hardly spoke. At least until they got to Clark's Village in Street. That was when it all kicked off.

What do you mean 'kicked off'? asked Kendrick Maclean.

Charlie continued with his explanation, that the rear passenger shouted something about the police being behind them and then there was screeching tyres as Nicky went through the lights and towards Meare on the Levels. He was driving like a maniac. I told him to slow down or he would get us killed. At one stage we thought that Nicky had got rid of the police car but after we hit the main road to Bridgwater that is when the police stopped us with one of those spiked chain things across the road.

Charlie related how before the car had even come to a stop, Nicky's mate in the back had opened the door and fled the scene. There was no point in running, said Charlie. He had done nothing wrong. He and Nicky were then arrested.

Kendrick Maclean nodded, but he now wanted to know more. What happened next?

'Why didn't you call your mother or me?' asked Kendrick Maclean. 'Everyone knows that you are allowed the one telephone call. We heard fuck all.'

'Sorry,' said Charlie. 'I should have done. To be honest, I was scared and ashamed. I was in a police station, arrested and had done nothing wrong. The police mentioned something about possession with intent to supply, saying basically I am a dealer. I am not. You know that. After all that Mum and you have done for me, I was too scared to call.'

This was the juncture where Kendrick Maclean would normally let rip. He didn't, but went on to ask Charlie a further question.

'Why didn't you get yourself a proper brief? Police will get you to admit anything in those places. I actually spent time getting you the best dog's bollocks lawyer in these parts and he told me that you told him to fuck off.'

'I didn't tell anyone to fuck off', explained Charlie. 'You had always told me, ever since what happened in London, that if

I ever ended up in any police station anywhere, then I get a brief. That is exactly what I did. I had a woman called Alex come out to see me as Duty Solicitor. She was friendly, but she was also a bit of a hard cow. She told me what to do. There was no need to change any solicitor.'

Charlie went on to explain that he was bailed to a date sometime next month, but this Alex said that the police had nothing on me and unless anything new came up she was certain that the case against me would be NFA'd. I was given a bail date but Alex thinks that it will be cancelled. Think that she meant that that would be the end of it.

Charlie confirmed that the police had told him at the station that they had already taken his laptop from his room at the house. He said that he had already apologised to his Mum for what had happened. He then said that there was nothing of interest to anyone on his laptop, not even porn and of course he had given the password to the police. He had nothing to hide.

'By the way,' said Kendrick Maclean. 'Did you ever get to meet Mr Dog Bollocks lawyer when you were at the police station?'

'Yes. His name was Axel something. The police said I could have whatever lawyer that I liked. To be honest Dad, I didn't really like him and this lady Alex Hilton had been really great.'

'Think that you are right son. I spoke to Mr Axelby again this afternoon. Turns out he is a bit of a wanker.'

With that, Kendrick Maclean opened his arms and clasped his arms around Charlie in a man hug, slapping him on the back.

'Come on son, it is supper at 6.30 and I need a shower.'

As Kendrick Maclean stepped out of the shower, he started to feel his stomach turn as it always did when he was really worried. He was minded to believe what Charlie had told him but something was not right. Something was not right at all.

~~~

Eaun invited his neighbour Inspector Colin Thompson into the living room, where both men then sat opposite each other on the armchairs.

'How can I help?' enquired Eaun, still trying to fitfully absorb everything that his wife had said to him only a few minutes before. 'I think that it was you who wanted to speak to me?'

'All a bit delicate really, which was why when the matter came to my attention I decided to call you myself to see whether this is something that we can nip in the old bud,' explained the Inspector.

'It is about the incident this morning, Eaun.'

Incident? What incident? Had he somehow found out what Darby-Henderson had been up to, although Eaun could not have seen how?

'Not really sure what you mean,' ventured Eaun.

'I suspected that you may not know what I am talking about,' said the Inspector. 'Apologies, but there is not really an easy way of putting this across. We took a call this morning from an irate mother. It seems that in the course of delivering the daily paper to an address just outside Sedgeton, the 14 year old papergirl was confronted through the window by a naked male who upon the *Daily Mail* being inserted through the letter box then shouted at the child 'Fuck you'. It seems that when the paper girl mentioned all this to her mother, she was then escorted by her to your front door where she alleges the incident took place. The mother did knock on the door but received an unfriendly response from the middle-aged lady who opened the door. That was when the mother of the child then contacted ourselves. The newsagent also confirmed that your property is on the paper girl's round of deliveries and that you are the account holder.'

'This has been a dreadful misunderstanding, Inspector. You are talking about me. I was not in fact naked but wearing a pair of galoshes, after clearing up an utterly disgusting mess in the kitchen. I thought that it was a boy not a girl delivering the paper. It was also not true that the *Daily Mail* was delivered. The paper girl had in fact delivered the wrong newspaper and this can sometimes cause ructions in the household. Most importantly, I did not shout 'Fuck you' but 'Thank you' to the paper boy, sorry paper girl, as I went back up the stairs to take a shower.'

'I am utterly staggered at these foul and slanderous accusations being made against me,' continued Eaun, his voice starting to raise. 'Look at the front door that you came through, you can see the glass and that it is more or less opaque. What does the paper girl say that she saw? Me twirling around my member at her? I think not. It is utterly and completely preposterous and not true. I have had a challenging day and I apologise, Inspector, sorry Colin, but I am really not putting up with this.'

'If you want a formal interview with me then please arrange this through my criminal defence colleague, Miss Hilton,' added Eaun. 'I may be many things to some people but a sex pest I most definitely am not.'

Eaun did not mean to, but the strength and vehemence of his response to the accusation had both surprised and slightly frightened the Inspector, who was now pinned back and felt embedded on the sofa.

The Inspector waited a few moments before gathering his thoughts and daring to lean slightly forward on the sofa.

'Eaun, I thought that it must have all been some dreadful misunderstanding,' said the Inspector. This is why I have come to see you as a friend to have all this nipped in the bud. I spoke to the girl's father this afternoon, less volatile than the mother and he said that they just want someone 'spoken to'. No one wants to make a fuss on this but what with protocols and everything you will appreciate that I have to do something.'

Eaun felt his whole body start to become less tense. He wondered how Colin Thompson ranked himself as a friend, but he also thought that after a day like this Wednesday, he probably needed all the help he could get from anyone, whether a friend or not.

'Thank you, Colin,' said Eaun with as much grace as he could muster. 'I really do appreciate your help on all this'.

'No trouble old chap,' came the response. 'Give me a day or so. I will try and speak to the father rather than the mother, make all the necessary noises and that should then be the last you hear anything about all this. We really want to avoid any unnecessary paperwork.'

As both men started to rise from their respective chairs, Eaun ushered the Inspector towards the front door. The Inspector knocked on the glass and peered through with squinted eyes.

'Quite right, Eaun,' he said. 'Can't see a thing through this. Sorry I missed the delightful Victoria. I should have asked earlier, please pass on to her my best wishes.'

The Inspector turned and was about to make his way into the early evening and the brief walk to his own home when Eaun called out.

'Oh, congratulation on your longest drive medal. Impressive!'

The Inspector then carried on his way with a smile. Eaun conceded that he was now feeling a generosity of spirit towards him. Eaun also wondered whether the 'no unnecessary paperwork' was strictly police protocol on these issues, especially when allegations of a sexual nature are made involving a minor, but for once was nevertheless grateful for this pragmatic approach offered.

Clearly the Inspector had no inkling of the day's events at WHW Legal. He would no doubt shortly find out via the jungle drums in due course.

Eaun picked up his briefcase and car keys from the hallway table before shutting and locking the front door and heading off on his journey to the office to find out what was next in store for him.

~ ~ ~

Kendrick Maclean usually relished these family gatherings in the family home at Bradstock Manor, formerly Bradstock Farm. Ronnie had the knack of making the whole family structure thing work. There was always a delicious aroma emanating from the supper that was slow-cooking in the British racing green AGA. This Wednesday evening was no different, with the four places all set at the large and expansive old pine kitchen table. The family silverware, linen napkins and wine goblets were all laid with military precision. Ronnie did things properly for these family suppers.

However, Kendrick Maclean was still not feeling at ease. The incident with the badger had ruffled him, although he would not admit that to family. Griff had confirmed his fears. Someone had utilised the services of the local travellers' community and spent time, money and effort trying to scare him. Anyone who really knew him could attest of course that Kendrick Maclean did not do scared easily. To himself, however, he would admit to being unsettled. He had worked his bollocks off scaling his way up the greasy pole of reinsurance. To the uninitiated reinsurance may not have been the sexy beast of private banking or corporate investment. However, he had learned his trade, first working in insurance at a firm in Fenchurch Street, before doing his penance in Canary Wharf where for a spell Kendrick Maclean had worked as a Catastrophe Risk Analyst. For the final few years in the business, he had returned back to the City working out of Leadenhall Street, concentrating on reinsurance. He became an expert at successfully passing on risk. It was more than once that he had thought that everything was going to come crashing down, but his skills, knowledge of the market and a sixth sense had brought him a highly successful and remunerative career. There were very few people that Kendrick Maclean knew who were able to retire as early as he did so that he could create the exact life that he wanted here in Somerset for Ronnie and himself.

It was that sixth sense that had bought him such success in his career that now niggled away at him.

Ronnie had called all the family around to the table. Tarquin was based only a few miles away in Sedgeton where he was doing really well for himself and where he ran his successful property portfolio from. Even when the pandemic hit, property prices continued to boom in the West Country. Every time that Bruton or Sedgeton was nominated in a Sunday glossy as the place to move to, the local estate agents jumped with joy. Tarquin had been playing his brother Charlie on the snooker table that occupied the play room area (or recreation hub as Ronnie now called it). Ronnie urged them all to find their places at the table as she opened the AGA door and extracted the lasagne with the bubbling cheese on the top. A warm crispy baguette followed. A large bowl of salad was already on the table and Charlie had started to mix in the dressing. Ronnie's lasagne was what she called her family comfort food.

Charlie and Tarquin immediately got stuck into the steaming lasagne as soon as Ronnie had delivered their plates to them, with both boys helping themselves to the salad and bread that were also on offer.

Kendrick Maclean did not want to sound like some nineteenth-century autocrat who had formally summonsed the family together for an important announcement, but he had to start somewhere.

As the bottles of Perrier and Sauvignon made their way around the table, Kendrick Maclean went through the necessary preamble about how great it was the family all being together that evening, especially as it looked as if the boys might not be there for Easter itself. Both boys had by now been appraised as to what had happened with the badger being nailed to the door earlier in the day, but nevertheless Kendrick Maclean invited everyone to contribute their thoughts.

'I like it down here and I don't like it when some ignorant fuck pulls a trick like this. More to the point, I don't understand how and why it has happened, except that me or someone close to me has managed to seriously piss someone off,' started Kendrick Maclean.

'There is no need to swear at the table Dougal,' chided Ronnie. The two boys smirked.

Kendrick Maclean felt irritated, like it was quite legitimate to swear when he was away from the family table. Anyway, he hardly ever swore.

'You blaming me for what happened then,' enquired Ronnie as she cut up and divided the lasagne on her plate. 'Tell you what, I think that I may well have upset a couple of the girls at the last Book Club meet. I told them that I thought that they had completely misunderstood what Hilary Mantel was trying to say about Cromwell in The Mirror and the Light.'

Both boys sniggered as Kendrick Maclean remained silent. Ronnie and he knew each other well, almost too well at times, he thought. He also knew that being flippant was her instant reaction to what had happened. She did not want her natural order of things threatened, exactly as he did not. It was just that despite being married all of these years, there were some things that they just did not speak about but nevertheless instinctively knew what the other was thinking.

Kendrick Maclean then took the lead and gave his reasoning to what had happened. He sipped the mineral water, leaving the white wine untouched.

'Just before we all sat around the table I spent some time going through all of my invoices since the day we bought the place,' started Kendrick Maclean. 'Nothing. Absolutely nothing to cause aggro like this. True, there were some wankers at the start who thought that they could pull a fast one on the new city boy who didn't know what he was doing. Yes, with one or two there may have been a degree or two of unpleasantness but in all these cases there was settlement, either before or at the steps of the court. It may also be correct that one or two of the local trades cartel may not have me on their current Christmas card list. However, this was all business and not personal, even for down here. Further, and this is important, the last acrimonious business discussion that I had was at least six months ago. If there was to be any payback or throwing the toys out of the pram it would have been a long while ago.

I spend my life working like a dog on this place and don't have time to upset anyone else in the local pub, village or even the book club.'

Charlie had by now scoffed down what was on his plate and with a nod from his mother was helping himself to a second helping from the lasagne dish. The baguette had already disappeared. Before he got stuck in to his seconds, Charlie addressed the expectant members of his family across the table.

'I know that you are all looking at me,' said Charlie. 'Dad has something nailed to the door at the same time that I am arrested. However, I did not do anything and I have not been charged with anything. I have nothing to hide. I was in Nicky's car. I hang around with him. He enjoys the same things that I do. He does not hang around all day in his darkened bedroom playing computer games. We go out, meet our mates at KFC and generally have a laugh. There is nothing else to do around here. Yes, he did drive his car like a maniac when he spotted the police car last night, but that was his decision to do that. I kept telling him to stop. As I have already told Dad, exactly as I told the police, I have no idea who the bloke was that Nicky picked up in Glastonbury. I had no idea what he had placed in the boot of Nicky's car. It could have been his training kit he was taking to his Mum to get washed for all I knew. Nicky may well do a bit of blow with other mates, but never when I am around. He knows that it is not my scene. Look, I am really sorry about plod coming to knock on the front door. It was one of the most embarrassing and humiliating moments of my life but there was nothing I could have done to prevent it.'

Kendrick Maclean was going to add that if he did not hang around with such a brainless fuck-wit as his big mate Nicky in the first place, then he would never have ended up in the cells and caused so much mayhem to his mother and father. However, he had already had it out in full with Charlie so he let any further comments go. Instead, Kendrick Maclean turned around to his elder step son Tarquin. He had never been as emotionally close to Tarquin as he had to Charlie.

Tarquin and he had never had any serious run-ins beyond the standard arguments about parental overkill regarding sleep overs, curfews, smoking and how every other one of his peers have better and more understanding parents.

Tarquin was scraping his plate clean with his last piece of bread.

'Just forget it, both of you,' advised Tarquin. 'You chose to live in the countryside. It makes me laugh. All these lifestyle gurus come down from London to buy up Somerset's finest thatched cottages that are now way out of the price range of the locals and then they can't understand why the natives sometimes get a little restless. Since Covid, there has been wave after wave of urban interlopers arriving to escape the big city. These new shock troop immigrants do not have a clue about culture down here being totally different and none of them make any effort to assimilate. If you went in to Sedgeton to anywhere other than the builders' merchants you would see what is really happening. Locals are fed up as their local first school is being closed to accommodate the free school lot who all send their children to the education paradise where they can choose not to do maths if they don't want to and to spend the rest of the day whittling their twigs with sharp knives.'

However, Tarquin was not finished.

'It is not just in the towns that we are talking about. Here we are this evening, in the middle of the country and miles from anywhere. In my Sunday league team are a couple of teachers who work in nearby country schools, the ones that have not closed yet. They say that the real dark side of life for the peasantry in modern day Somerset is set behind the doors of these idyllic thatched cottages, where practices go on there that have existed for generations. Look, some of your local neighbours may not be very bright. However, trust me, there is no nail the badger campaign. Nutters happen. Let it go. Show that you don't care what they do, if indeed they are doing anything, and the problem will disappear.'

There was quiet around the table.

'Who knows that you live here, Tarquin?' asked Kendrick Maclean after a long silence. He had rarely heard his eldest son speak for such length and eloquence on a subject matter that did not directly affect him.

'The last time that I looked I had a penthouse 3 bedroomed apartment with two en-suites in an executive development at the old print works in Sedgeton. Think that you and Mum may even have been there. I am an open book. I don't hide away. My real name is on the top buzzer at my apartment block.'

Kendrick Maclean was not smiling. Neither had he yet touched his wine.

What was Tarquin hiding behind the outwardly confident and almost aggressive stance that he was presenting at the supper table? In truth, thought Kendrick Maclean, whilst he may be able to see straight through the idiocy of Charlie, he actually did not know a great deal about Tarquin. Tarquin had all the appearances and accoutrements of early success, but Kendrick Maclean also knew that very often meant very little.

'What were you up to last night?' asked Kendrick Maclean.

'I don't understand you,' said Tarquin. 'Perhaps there ought to be a place setting for a fifth person here so that they can answer for themselves what they were up to last night. What about that weirdo that you employ. Griffin or whatever stupid name he has. The one with the filthy Land Rover and has string to hold up his trousers. When he speaks you can't understand a word of what he is saying. Where was he last night?'

Kendrick Maclean could feel his hackles rise, but before Kendrick Maclean was able to respond, Ronnie managed to get in first.

'It is great to have you all here. Everyone's favourite for pudding!' she announced as she headed to the huge double door American style fridge to retrieve the tray of home-made crème brulee.

Tarquin had already announced to everyone that he had to leave soon as he had a party to go to that evening, but Kendrick Maclean had decided that he would have to run things past Ronnie when they were next alone. Nothing ever escaped her eyes, ears or sixth sense.

REVENGE & RETRIBUTION:
THE BEGINNING

L UDMILA HAD been in the office only ten minutes before Eaun himself had returned. She had popped home, spoken to her husband Grzegorz and made sure that their daughters Julia and Natalia were not going to be fed oven chips in her absence. Not only did the two girls speak far better English than Polish, but they had also now adopted a very definite and worrying Somerset lilt to their speech. Unfortunately, it looked like both girls were also finding affinity with the English diet.

Having made sure that the family all had a bowl of Rigatoni with a freshly cooked home-made sauce to share between them, Ludmila then quickly disappeared upstairs to make several telephone calls to members of her family. She also filled out the best part of an A4 page to hand to Grzegorz when she left the house to return to the office.

She told everyone to behave, do the washing up and that she would not be late.

Back in the office, Alex, Madge and Douglas were all waiting for her around the conference table. Ludmila then noticed Felicity Lawton, the former Poison Dwarf sat in the corner turning over the pages of her ubiquitous shorthand notebook. With her Edna Everidge style spectacles perched towards the end of her nose, Felicity beamed a smile at Ludmila who could do nothing else except smile back, adding a brief nod of the head in acknowledgement of their mutual new understanding.

A few minutes after Ludmila's return, Eaun entered through the door of the conference room. Ludmila knew from the messages that she had passed on that her boss was having a key meeting with his wife that evening. Whatever happened had obviously gone well, for Eaun now had colour back in his face, looked far more energetic and looked like his old self. He was no longer sporting that haunted look.

It was Alex who took the lead. Ludmila noticed that before her arrival someone had clearly made a trip to Maccy D's, as Alex had to push back empty cardboard boxes and brown bags, before she had room to spread her notes on the conference room table.

Alex should have felt exhausted after being woken up well before dawn, spending most of the day in the cells before returning to the office and then wondering whether she would even have a job the next day.

However, Ludmila thought that she had never seen Alex look more focussed. Alex looked as if she was about to address the bench in the most important address of her short career and for a brief second Ludmila thought that Alex was about to rise to her feet, before she nervously managed to disguise her movements into a quick adjustment of her seating position on the conference room chair.

'Right, it is probably easiest if I start and we can then all go from there,' commenced the seated Alex.

All eyes were fixed on her.

'Earlier this evening I spoke at length on the telephone with DC Denise Halloran,' said Alex. 'For those that do not know, Denise is a senior member of the Criminal Investigation Department of the Wessex Constabulary, based in Yeovil but serving the whole of the county. She is also dead straight. I told her everything that had happened. I was quite blunt and told her that we needed her help. Think that it is a huge testament to you Eaun, that over the time that you used to work as a criminal defence advocate here, you gained an enormous respect from the boys and girls in blue. I suppose it figures if you were the lawyer of choice for members of the local constabulary whose own kids managed to get themselves picked up by one of their own colleagues for possession of a bit of weed or indeed who themselves got themselves into a bit of disciplinary bother. Eaun, the message from Denise was that she would be delighted to help in any way that she could.'

Eaun nodded, and aimed his stare down towards his feet. Ludmila thought that she detected Eaun's eyes moistening. He still looked a bit fragile.

'Denise has just called me back after doing some digging around,' continued Alex. 'She has spoken to one of her colleagues at the main Fraud Office at police HQ, DI Steve Dibley. He is our man and she promises that he will be very interested indeed and already wants to know more. Don't think that it was a joke, but when you have your substantive conversation with the officer Eaun, Denise recommended that somewhere along the line you mention the word 'terrorism' in connection with what has happened. Don't spread this, but Denise said that if you do this then suddenly there will be untold resources made available to your case as well as a multitude of closed doors suddenly opening.'

Like everyone else, the eyes of Ludmila remained fixed on Alexandra.

'The excellent news is that our friend Steve Dibley has great links with Interpol in both France and Spain, particularly in Catalonia and the Balearics. This may be relevant when we hear what Felicity has to say later. Thanks to Brexit, the European Arrest Warrant has now gone, but it seems that the UK has not yet been permanently cast into the wilderness. Police forces in all the major European countries are for obvious reasons still extremely anxious to work with each other. Probably easier at this stage if I pass the lead over to Felicity. Felicity, all yours.'

Alex remained seated and gathered her papers in front of her. Felicity Lawton had managed to find time to go home and get changed. Ludmila reflected that she had actually no idea where Felicity lived. She had heard references to Felicity being married but had to her knowledge never seen her husband. Most spouses over the years, even Grzegorz, managed to pop their head through the office door to offer a quick 'hello' to the members of staff or even to put in a brief appearance at the obligatory office summer barbecue. In her changed attire of black leggings partly concealed round the waist by a long blue shirt with the top couple of buttons undone made Felicity look surprisingly contemporary and almost even a bit sexy, surmised Ludmila. Certainly, any image of the frumpy, grumpy Poison Dwarf had disappeared in its entirety.

'Little shit. Complete little shit. Shits. Both of them,' started Felicity. 'Apologies for that. I never ever swear and I am really sorry but I had to get it out first. Years of total loyalty and he steals from everyone before eloping with that tart. Apologies once more for the language. Let me start again. Properly this time.'

Ludmila noticed that there were a few nods and smiles around the conference table.

'You will all know that Mr Darby Henderson was always fairly secretive about his private life,' began Felicity. 'Nothing wrong with that. Every couple of years he asked us all out to the office summer party at his pile outside Shepton Mallet at Oakhill. There was little that he ever gave away about his private life. I should know. I was his secretary and supposed personal assistant for years. I bet none of you know where he even really went on holiday. Spain, France, Portugal and Greece are all huge places. I bet that none of you around this table have a clue where his actual usual holiday residences are?'

Before anyone had the chance to agree or disagree, Felicity ploughed on.

'I may not say a lot. Which word do you think 'secretary' is derived from? For me, loyalty and secrets are sacrosanct. I am old guard. Until now that is. Mr Darby-Henderson I suppose thought that I was stupid and had no clue what he did with his spare time. However, I managed to learn a great deal after years of taking messages from so-called friends and companions. He has a place in Mallorca. It is a private villa. Pretty grandiose as well. I even have the name of the town that it is near, a very odd name. Anthrax. The bacteria. Like they use in chemical weapons. With a name like that you wouldn't have thought that it would attract the holiday crowd but there you go. This is where the contemptible little man takes his companions, accomplices, associates and I have no doubt his trollops as well. Sorry. Apologies again. I have let myself down.'

'No need to apologise. Felicity,' said Alex. Felicity was looking down at the pile of hamburger boxes and the brown bags with the grease stains from the fries. Her explanation of events had clearly taken its toll on her, but Ludmila thought that Felicity also looked fiercely determined.

'This brings us on to the next discovery,' explained Alex to everyone in the room. 'I used the card left by Mr Curtis from our very own Western Central Bank. You never think of bank managers having homes but that is where I tracked him down to. He knew who I was. He even saw my ex Marcus and me when, incredibly, we were once considering getting a mortgage together and then living happily ever after. He remembered me, said that Eaun had given his consent for him to speak to me. To say that what had happened to the bank was also hugely embarrassing was an understatement. However keen Mr Curtis was on righting the wrong and for the bank to get the money back, I was not sure how much he was willing to tell me. So, we spoke largely in terms of 'what if' and other imagined scenarios.'

'Ignoring the 'what if' rider, what Mr Curtis said was fascinating. We at WHW Legal have an account with the bank that is supposed to be watertight. It is impossible for anyone to hack in. Even for withdrawals of less than a million pounds, such as this case where there were 5 separate withdrawals of £995,000 over a 5 day period, the actions of two persons is required. Here at WHW Legal, Julian and Eaun as partners had the authority under the system to transfer funds into and out of both client and office account, where the amount is less than a million. This authority is also given to Douglas as the firm's former senior partner and current consultant, as well as Rita Thornham as practice manager. Each authorised signatory is handed a small hand held device that allows numbered codes to be entered. The codes change randomly and automatically after every use. It does however require the authorised code to be entered by two people. This is in case of anyone ever deciding to 'go rogue'. However, what this security system failed to pick up on is what happens when two people decide to 'go rogue', as with Julian and Rita. Like every security system in the world, there is always one weakness. Human beings and the element of trust. If trust is to be broken, then any system is going to be vulnerable. As we now know.'

Alex let everyone have a few seconds break before she got back to the next page on her notes.

'According to Mr Curtis, all 5 payments of nearly a million pounds each were sent to a previously set up account with an international money broker via the CHAPS system. I am not a conveyancing lawyer but everyone else in the room will know that when the CHAPS system is used, then any transfer is almost immediate. What the international money broker did was quite legitimate. Our own bankers have already been in touch with them and they have happily passed on the details of the transaction to Mr Curtis' colleagues. CHAPS can only be used between UK banks but in this case what our friends Julian and Rita did was ensure that the CHAPS payment to the money broker based in the UK left our client account almost instantly. The international money brokers then sent the monies as soon as it was received via their Express Service. This service normally allows for the monies to be paid in within 24 hours. The brokers very kindly provided details of the overseas bank where the monies were sent. The Banca Calvia. It is not certain, but it is likely that by now, the near £5 million pounds sent from client account is now sitting in some account at the Banca Calvia. This ties in with everything that Felicity has been saying. Mr Curtis says that the Banca Calvia is based in Spain and has its HQ in Palma, the capital of Mallorca.'

Ludmila gave out a soft whistle followed by an almost inaudible 'Kurva'. Looks were exchanged around the table.

'I do not want anyone to get overexcited,' went on Alex. 'But this is where things start to become very interesting. The plan was to get the near 5 million out of the client account and safely abroad within the shortest time possible. We now know that by this evening, all or nearly all of the money is sitting in an account in a Spanish bank based in Palma. However, it does not require Sherlock to track down where the money actually is. The next stage of the process is for Julian and Rita to get the money out of the quite legitimate bank in Palma and then into funds or other assets which will be difficult or near impossible to trace. However, for a very short time this is where our duo are vulnerable. According to Mr Curtis and his colleagues at the bank's HQ, because of the amount involved, the money in Spain will take a little time before it can be moved. They are assuming that Julian is not a mastermind from organised crime able to utilise the resources of the dark web and is basically just a greedy criminal ready to exploit a system that as he sees it is there to be exploited. I think that they are right.'

'The reason that Julian and Rita are vulnerable for a short window of time is that the monies cannot be quickly disposed of from the Banca Calvia account. Like most banks, they have a £10,000 limit on their Fast Forward service. The CHAPS service cannot be used in Spain which leaves the remaining equivalent of the BACS system. This is a great internationally renowned system that everyone knows and understands. However, any monies that need to be transferred from the Banca Calvia will take three days to clear.'

Alex barely took a breath and carried on.

'I never knew that bankers had hunches,' she continued. 'However, Mr Curtis said that he did. And his hunch is that Messrs Darby-Henderson and Thornham are waiting for all of the monies to actually arrive in the account, either later this evening or first thing tomorrow morning before distributing and making the whole lot vanish within three working days.'

It was Douglas who intervened.

'Look, call me old fashioned and a dinosaur but if the

authorities know where the ill-gotten gains are, in a bank account in Mallorca, why don't they simply ask the bank there to hold the money there till things can get sorted and the monies returned?'

Ludmila thought that this was an excellent question which she would also have asked.

'Good point,' responded Alex. 'Firstly however, things in the international banking fraternity are never that easy or simple. Secondly, no actual crime was formally reported by Eaun until late this afternoon. A bank can only respond when they have been notified that a suspected crime has actually been reported. The final point is this. Easter is a big deal in Spain and most of Mediterranean Europe. In Spain, Easter starts tomorrow, Maunday Thursday, which just happens to be a national and bank holiday in the country. As from earlier this afternoon, all banks in Spain are shut. Shut shut. No one answers telephones even to their own kind. Everything now has to wait till next week.'

'Which brings us back to this,' continued Alex. 'There are no certainties, but the likelihood is that most if not all of our client account monies are in a bank account in Mallorca and we have a very short window of time to rescue that money.'

'But if the banks are now closed for the next few days, what can the police, the banks or anyone else do to get the money back,' queried Douglas.

'This brings us back to Felicity,' replied Alex.

Felicity had regained her composure and nodded that she was happy to proceed.

'Alex has explained it far better than I can, but what it comes down to is that with the banks now closed for a short period and the police yet to spring into action, if indeed they spring at all, we need to locate Darby-Henderson and Thornham fast. Really fast,' said Felicity. 'There are mates whom he trusts enough to take on holiday with him to Anthrax. The Sedgeton Grange crowd. The owners of the place, the Paterson couple, Gustave and Anabel, they are always on the phone to Julian talking about their next holiday in Mallorca. Think that he does not even charge them for the place when he is not there. God only knows what they get up to when they are out there in Mallorca. The Sedgeton Grange may well be a respectable family hotel during the weekends but midweek they are all at it. Like this evening. That Anabel woman dropped off two complimentary tickets for Julian earlier in the week. Couldn't resist opening the envelope to see what it was all about. Caligula's sex orgy or some sort of sordid event. I ask you. Here, in Somerset. Think that the main event starts at 8pm, in about 20 minutes time if anyone wants a freebie. The complimentary tickets are on my desk. Seriously, this is where you will find the Gus and Anabels' who will know all about where that little shit is hiding with his trollop. Happy to help in any way I can but you won't catch me in that place. Private members indeed.'

He had been quiet and contemplative throughout the whole meeting, but Eaun now spoke out.

'Needs must. Of course I will go,' Eaun interjected. 'They know me. They should also be quite open with me as well. I can explain that Julian had not been able to make it and gave the tickets to me.'

'We were all hoping that you would say that,' said Alex. 'Whilst you were at home earlier this evening, we were all talking through how best this can work out. We need to know exactly where to find their location. Thanks Eaun. We have also found a partner for you to go along to the party with. We would hate to see you stand around in your toga in Billy No Mates mode. So, Denise is going along with you.'

Ludmila felt her raise her own eyebrows at the same time as her boss, Mr Wright. She had to think twice who Denise actually was.

'Don't worry, she is well up for it,' reassured Alex. 'Her old man Rod thinks that it is all absolutely hilarious his missus going off to a Roman orgy with a local solicitor. Doing this all for work of course, playing the big important detective bit. I have never heard Denise sounding so excited, the thought of being able to get such unfettered and exclusive access to the glitterati of

Sedgeton and Somerset. She said that her colleagues would be sick with envy. Felicity and I have been through the invites, by the way. If you are unable to supply your own toga and or loin cloth then these will be supplied gratis at the event. Denise will be meeting you in the car park at 8.45. Lucky Eaun. I hope that Mrs Wright does not come over all jealous!'

For the first time there were smiles and laughter around the conference table. Even Eaun joined in briefly. He wondered whether this was the right time to tell everyone that he had been dumped by his wife of 25 years so that she could become a practising lesbian and run off with their daughter's best friend. On reflection, he thought that all this could be mentioned at a later time. His focus had to be on trying to salvage his professional life and the jobs of those who relied on him.

Madge had been silent to date but now chipped in.

'I know you, Eaun,' she volunteered. 'We all agree, you need someone with you and you can't do this on your own. We need someone there who will help you get the information that we need. Normally, I would of course have been delighted to be able to accompany you, but Norman is on lates and I will need to be home soon to look after the kids and also to do other stuff. However, if not myself then Denise is perfect. I know her from the golden age and she will also ensure that you will not do any big social gaffes.'

'Denise and yourself will need to get the information we need about the whereabouts of Julian and Rita as soon as possible, and certainly by the end of your advertised Roman orgy,' continued Alex. 'Ludmila will explain why.'

Ludmila had been biding her time nervously, waiting for her turn to explain her role on what was now being planned. Her English was impeccable and many clients and even her own neighbours actually assumed that she was English. For the first time in many years she had been rehearsing what she was going to say in her native Polish first, before translating in her head into English. She was anxious that she missed nothing out and got everything absolutely right.

'Here goes,' she started, with hands outstretched in front of her and looking around the table at the individual faces as she spoke. 'Some of you may know that I have a brother Jan who lives in Spain. That is where we try and disappear to every summer with the two girls, Julia and Natalia. The flights are cheap and Jan and his partner Reme have a spare room in their apartment but all our time is spent at the beach. Jan's apartment is just outside of Palma, the capital of Mallorca, so when Felicity mentioned Mallorca and the place Anthrax earlier today, we got talking.'

Ludmila could see Eaun glance at both Felicity and herself in mild surprise. He could not recall ever seeing or hearing the two women have a non-work related conversation before. Ludmila continued.

'So, I have been doing some phoning around. After work and before coming back here I have been speaking to my brother. Jan has now been living in Mallorca for nearly 15 years and he is now running his own building company. He services not only the expats over in the island, but most of his clients are now locals. He has qualified electricians and plumbers working with him. No fly by night stuff with Jan. He has to live in the community that he works for.'

'He also filled me in on Anthrax. It has nothing to do with bacteriological weapons but is almost certainly a place called Andratx. It is on the western tip of the island and Jan says it is only 25 minutes down the motorway. If we are able to give Jan just part of an address then with his contacts he said he should be able to track anyone down.'

Eaun wondered about the tracking down bit. What was going to happen when and if they did manage to track down Julian and Rita? Julian was hardly likely to say 'sorry' and then hand the money back. He knew and trusted Ludmila but he had never met Jan. Eaun almost found himself saying aloud that threats and violence were not the way. However, all of these thoughts were way premature, he realised. After all, they did not yet even know that Julian was actually in Mallorca. The island of Mallorca was actually a place that Eaun had never been to before, which added to his sense of general unease. Motorways on Mallorca? He thought that it was just beaches for families and teenage kids getting trashed in Magaluf. He also wondered whether he was starting to get a bit out of his depth.

Ludmila cleared her throat and continued.

'Eaun, you and I are flying to Palma tomorrow morning. The flight is at 7.40 from Bristol. Madge already had your passport details for when you asked her to sort the surprise weekend birthday trip when you took Victoria to Venice back in February. You will need me to get you introduced to Jan. As with your imminent trip to the private members Club at Sedgeton Grange, you will also need someone in Mallorca to make sure that you generally keep out of trouble. By the way, I need to be back home for the family Easter Egg Hunt on the Saturday afternoon.'

For Eaun, things were starting to happen very quickly. Venice? The trip was only two months ago but already Eaun could not recall anything.

'Last but not least, there is the question of funding all of this,' concluded Ludmila. 'This is where Douglas comes in. At the moment you have the office account which the bank have agreed not to freeze, but we do not know what is going to happen in the next few days. This is where Douglas has come to the rescue. He has already reimbursed Madge for the flights and he has given me a wedge of Euros for 'expenses'. We really do not know what to expect so Douglas has loaned us 5,000 Euros with more available if we need it.'

Eaun could see Madge touch Douglas' arm in appreciation and Ludmila give him a brief nod and a smile as she tapped the handbag that was slung around her shoulders.

Douglas then raised his head as all eyes turned on him.

'We have to right this terrible wrong. Whatever it takes,' decreed Douglas.

Before Eaun had time to express his gratitude to everyone for what was happening, Alex quickly took charge.

'No time to delay,' she said. 'Eaun, this is the number from Denise for you to phone Steve Dibley at the fraud office at the police HQ. He will then immediately get the ball rolling at his end. You must do this now before you leave for Sedgeton Grange.'

It was now Madge who chipped in.

'And you don't have to worry about leaving the office for the day,' said Madge. 'Alex and I will be here to deal with all the court hearings and police station work. Douglas has said that together with Felicity they will deal with all the conveyancing completions tomorrow. We will also clear the accounts room so that the team from the SRA will be able to access what they need. Sorted!'

Alex passed a yellow telephone message slip of paper across the table to Eaun, managing to avoid the discarded McDonald's wrappings.

'Mr Curtis from the bank is already in contact with his HQ,' continued Alex. 'You will also need to get in contact with Mr Farquhar at the SRA. You can do that tomorrow morning but make sure that you take his number with you.'

Eaun promised that he would do as he was told.

'You had better get your skates on,' said Alex. 'You need to call Steve at the fraud squad now. Don't forget to tell him that you are suspicious of terrorist activity! Then you are meeting your escort Denise Halloran at a quarter to eight. You have a Roman sex orgy to attend. Get to it!'

~ ~ ~

At the end of the family meal, Tarquin made his excuses and said that he had to get home to his flat in town and pick up his toga and sandals ready for the fancy dress bash later that evening. Charlie said that after his night in the cells at Keynsham, he was done in. He said that he was going to watch some football in his bedroom before closing the door behind him and heading for an early night. Kendrick Maclean remained at the table and helped his wife clear the dishes and stack the dishwasher. Ronnie asked him a couple of times whether he was alright. Kendrick Maclean said that he was fine but he had a couple of things to sort out and did Ronnie have time to chat through some issues that had arisen in the course of the last 24 hours? Of course she did, Ronnie replied.

As Kendrick Maclean helped give a final wipe to the large pine family table, Ronnie started to pour from the royal blue coffee percolator that had just completed its final cough, gurgle and splutter whilst warming on the AGA plate.

Husband and wife then sat down opposite each other, absent-mindedly stirring their full coffee cups.

It was Ronnie who spoke first.

'Look Dougal, I know that Charlie has been a bit of a handful recently, especially today. I also know that he manages to push all the wrong buttons with you but he is not a bad lad.'

'I agree,' responded her husband. 'But it is Tarquin that we need to speak about this evening, not Charlie.'

An hour later, Kendrick Maclean knew exactly what he had to do.

THE ROMAN ORGY

GUSTAVE ALWAYS felt nervous before an event at Sedgeton Grange. He admitted that he was a perfectionist, but it was precisely because both Anabel and himself worked so hard at getting it all just right, that the establishment had become such a success, especially the midweek private members' club. They now had the professional and commercial confidence that came with having a waiting list and a membership that spread from those not only living in and around Sedgeton, but from places like Bath, Taunton, Bristol, Wells and beyond. Even when the authorities had to temporarily re-impose some Covid restrictions, membership enquiries had remained both constant and numerous.

As always, Gustave and Anabel had both made the effort to dress for the occasion. Gus was sporting a short-sleeved knee length tunic and a pair of sandals that were usually only seen on Gustave when holidaying abroad. Anabel was wearing a sleeveless tunic with shoulder fabric that easily slipped down her arm. Gustave had earlier commented that her costume had looked 'revealing'. Anabel had shot back to him that of course it was supposed to be revealing. They were hosting a Caligula Roman orgy evening. What else was she supposed to wear? A shell suit?

The idea of hiring the wardrobe of Roman theatrical clothing had been well received. Most members had actually made the effort to dress up, but the two hotel gardeners who were spending the evening transformed as the Praetorian Guard at the entrance had made an excellent job of ensuring that those who had not made the effort were pointed in the direction of what was once a common room in the old school, where all of the costumes were kept in big old laundry baskets.

The replacement speaker for Aunt Cressida, Piers Hudderston, turned up early, hauling his own slide projector along with him. He struck Gustave as a somewhat strange looking fellow, with a mass of white hair tied back in a pony-tail, on top of a painfully thin frame. A good sign was that at least he was immediately entering into the spirit of the evening, arriving dressed for the part in a toga. The appointment of the replacement speaker had all happened extremely quickly and it appeared that in the rush no one had actually passed on the title of the proposed talk, 'Debauchery in Caligula's Rome: A Modern Perspective' to Mr Hudderston. Mr Hudderston himself had told Gus on his arrival that he had been asked by the local branch of the Monuments & Historical Buildings Society, of which he was the Honorary Secretary, to give a talk on local Roman settlements between Bath and Sedgeton, of which there were several. It emerged upon questioning by Gus that Mr Hudderston knew absolutely nothing about Caligula and even less about general debauchery whether in Rome or indeed anywhere else within the Roman Empire. When Gus suggested to Mr Hudderston that he might 'sex up' his proposed talk a bit, he received an initial blank stare in return, before Mr Hudderston started to warm to the idea and even volunteered that there was some evidence of houses of ill repute being kept for the Roman legions whose job it was to see that the ancient Fosse Way between Exeter and Lincoln remained open, secure and safe. Did Mr Paterson know that a sizeable chunk of the Fosse Way travelled through the modern county of Somerset? Was this the sort of local history that Mr Paterson was thinking about? Gus suspected that all of this may well have been bunkum but he responded that this was an excellent idea and could Mr Hudderston please base his lecture around this?

Asked whether he needed anything else, Mr Hudderston replied that he had just had an extremely trying and stressful day and a drink would be wonderful. It would also help settle his nerves, explained Mr Hudderston. Gus said that he would arrange for the kitchens to send up immediately a sandwich together with some genuine Roman beverage. Mr Hudderston was also told by Gus that as previously mentioned to his colleague at the Society, he was of course more than welcome to stay for the later celebrations. Mr Hudderston said that he would be delighted to stay and indeed had been keenly looking forward to the event all afternoon.

Gus duly went down to the kitchens where he asked the harassed Chef to sort a snack now for their guest speaker up in the Library. Before he managed to leave the kitchens, Gus could hear his order for the Library being delegated to one of the temporary staff brought in for the event.

Just before the talk by Piers Hudderston was about to start, Gus was pleased to see a steady flow of members move into the Library, anxious to obtain a premium seat from where to learn of what sort of exact filth the Romans really got up to in the time of Caligula. Twenty minutes into the talk, Gus popped his head around the door to see how things were going. He had to wait a few moments for members to actually leave the room first. Inside the Library, disappointingly there were now just a handful of guests remaining, bravely sitting through the monochrome slides of a fallen stone wall that could have been anywhere. Gus was alarmed. From what he had heard to date, there had not even been mention of any kind of Roman debauchery, even in the supposed whore houses along the old Fosse Way. What was however of more concern to Gus was that there was an empty full-sized carafe next to the lectern. A ham sandwich lay untouched alongside the empty carafe.

Gus wondered how trying and stressful the day could have been in order for the evening's star speaker to drink a whole carafe of wine within no time at all, so that he very quickly started to become slurred, repetitive and then drunk. Within a few more minutes, the slide show became jammed in the projector and before Piers Hudderston was able to commence talking about what the Romans were allegedly up to at their villa encampment just outside of Nunney, Gus walked out to the front of the Library, thanked him profusely for his talk and in particular for standing in at the last moment. The remaining audience of only four or five clapped politely, wrapped their togas around themselves and departed the Library for other more exciting entertainments.

Gus stayed in the Library for a few minutes and helped clear up the speaker's slides and notes. Anabel would now be having a great deal to answer for after all, thought Gus. Piers Hudderston, whose red framed glasses were starting to slip off, declined a lift home and pronounced himself 'absolutely fine' for the rest of the evening, as Gus left him resting from his exertions with his thin body reclining on the length of the Library's chaise longue and his bright white pony tail curled over the headrest.

Happily for Gus, a quick general tour of The Sedgeton Grange re-assured him that everything else was going as planned. It was still early in the evening, but a glance outside towards the South Gardens showed that several members were already taking advantage of the lit swimming pool and Jacuzzis, with flashes of naked flesh cavorting in the splashes. Neat piles of white togas and tunics surrounded the edge of the pool.

Inside the hotel, the catering staff, all dressed in their uniform tunics and leather apron with scarlet sash, were doing wonders with the food and drink, providing an endless stream of filled platters doing the rounds, piled high with spicy samosas, empanada, turnovers, bruschetta and devilled eggs. Chef had earlier assured Gus that these were the exact sort of canapes that were lustily devoured by all the ancient Romans. Gustave retained strong doubts that this was in fact the case but Chef had put an enormous effort into his 'genuine' Roman delicacies so Gus decided to just let this one go. Large jugs were also in a continuous stream offering the genuine red and white wine from Rome. For those preferring beer, the large goblets were kept filled with the Circus Maximus brew that had been specially concocted and adapted for the event by one of the many local artisan breweries located in and around Shepton Mallet and

Sedgeton itself. Anabel's idea of the bottomless leather aprons for all the catering staff had been truly inspirational.

The evening was still young and Gustave imagined it unlikely that anyone had yet made it up the stairs to the delights of Just Heaven. He would check it out later. However, the door to The Dungeon was wide open with loud drum and bass with the vibrations escaping into the main hotel hallway. The earlier neon lighting had been replaced by a few strategically placed flame-shaped uplighters. The main DJ set for the evening had yet to commence. Gustave stepped into The Dungeon and at the bottom of the steps he could see several male and female members dressed in rubber and pvc head balaclavas with not a great deal else on their bodies. The members that he saw with their distinctive headgear were the same ones that he saw congregate every week. However, he was still unable to quite get his head around why anyone would want to hang around chatting with something on your head that made it difficult to breathe and made you sweat like a pig. However, all of their subscriptions were up to date.

Gustave then retreated back in to his office just off the main hallway, his favourite spot where he was ignored behind the glass door but he could see what was happening and who was arriving. He was about to turn on the security cameras for the evening when there was a knock at the door. It was someone tall, made even taller by the brass breast plate and the plume of feathers on his helmet. It was one of the two Praetorian guards on duty.

'Sorry to interrupt sir, but there is a gentleman and his partner at the entrance who have a couple of tickets to get in. However, as you requested, we have checked the guest list and they are not on there. Man says he is a member here'.

Under the stooped helmet, Gustave could see that it was Jack the head gardener.

'That's OK Jack. I will come out and sort,' responded Gustave.

~ ~ ~

A few minutes earlier Eaun had pulled the old family Volvo estate on to the drive leading up to Sedgeton Grange. Before he had reached the building, temporary signposting pointed the way to the members' overflow car park for the evening. The field next to the house was the designated parking spot for the evening, with its boundaries lit every few yards by flaming bamboo torches.

He took a moment to think in his car before getting out. He let himself slide down into the driver's seat and sat still for a few moments. He had had no time to think. All he knew was that he no longer had any control of what was happening in his life. Who knows, maybe he really never had the extent of control that he once imagined that he had. Driving along on the way to the Sedgeton Grange, Eaun had tried to absorb all the efforts that many people were making on his behalf. He felt genuinely humbled, but at the same time also depressed that everything that they were all planning now may come to nothing. No one knew for certain where Julian even was. Then there was home. No one even knew yet that his wife had dumped him to become a lesbian living with someone who Eaun still remembered taking to the Soft Play Centre hand in hand with his daughter Alison. How could he explain all this, especially to the two girls? Almost certainly Vicky would be going to instruct the reptiles at Maddison and Robinson, if indeed she had not already done so.

Eaun was woken from his private thoughts by a loud hammering like a woodpecker on the passenger side window. A rotating hand was gesturing for him to wind the window down.

It had been a day of continual surprises but Eaun instinctively still felt safe enough that he was not going to be robbed or assaulted. He therefore pushed the unwind button by the side of the door so that the passenger side window hesitantly juddered down to be near level with the bottom half of the door. The glass then stopped moving and Eaun leaned to his left to see who it was.

'Long time no see, lover boy. Seems like you are my hot date for the sex party tonight.'

Eaun then remembered. Yes, Holloran. DC Denise Holloran. They used to clash swords regularly in the past. He rarely saw her now that Alexandra Hilton was in charge of all the criminal defence work at the firm.

'Sorry, Denise. Was in a different world,' explained Eaun.

'You will be in a different world in a moment sunshine,' she retorted.

Eaun got out of the car and went to greet the officer and his escort for the night. A couple of yards apart, he stopped in his tracks and they both raised a hand in formal greeting to each other. The Plague had not all been bad, thought Eaun, as at least he did not have to go through those awful rituals of deciding whether you should shake hands, touch elbows, give a man hug, kiss on the cheek or just say a quick 'hello'. These days most people seemed satisfied with a quick mutual wave of the hand.

'Nice to see that you made the effort,' she said, glancing at Eaun's casual dress of trainers, jeans and t-shirt. Denise herself was dressed in a full length toga adapted from one of the single white sheets that she had pinched from her bed linen cupboard. Eaun had never seen the officer in a toga before, but he also thought that she looked good, with her hair up at the back. Eaun reflected that he had only seen her before in work mode, exhibiting an air of tired resignation like everyone else and wearing clothes that looked as if they had never seen an iron, although he was sure that this was not the case.

'It's fine. I won't let you down, I didn't have time to go home and the invites say that costumes can be collected at the door.'

Eaun waved the two complimentary tickets.

'It may be a question of how long you are allowed to wear your Roman kit, Mr Wright!' said Denise with a wicked smile and a wink with her left eye. 'Look, seriously, Alex has filled me in on the picture at what has been happening today at WHW

Legal. Really sorry to hear this mate. I really am. I am sure that Steve at fraud will do all he can to help sort you out.'

Eaun was still trying to assimilate all the help that had been offered to date, including from DC Halloran.

'I am really grateful Denise. Thank you. That is part of the reason that I am late and did not have the time to go home and change. I called Steve on his mobile. Even took him away from watching the Champions' League quarter finals. He was incredibly helpful. Thank you. I dread to think what would have happened if we had used the local channels first. Yes, I also mentioned to Steve that I was not sure but there was some thought that there might be some terrorist connection involved. Hope I did the right thing, Gave no names.'

'You would probably have had to explain everything to me, what with all my experience of fraud including electric meter jobs and other such scams. You are fortunate.'

'I also know from Alex that we are here on a serious mission tonight,' continued Denise. 'You think that you can obtain an address in Spain for your cheating partner? Am I right? Probably from the owners? I have always had a soft spot for you Eaun, even when you once accused me years ago of suggesting to one of your less savoury clients that unless he confessed he would be a likely victim of 'severe repercussions' from my colleagues and myself. That Alex also has a soft spot for you, but like me thinks that on a mission like this evening you need to go with someone who is a bit of a mad bad cow with a sometimes handy vicious tendency. I am indeed your mad bad cow for this evening. And while I am about it, if I am going to be able to legitimately claim overtime, then I also need to do a bit of my own snooping around as well. This is after all an opportunity that I may never get again. Just in case, I have even brought my warrant card as well. Come on, let's get on with it.'

With that, DC Halloran thrust her hand around Eaun's elbow and arm in arm escorted him from the flaming torches of the overflow car park towards the Roman soldiers guarding the front of the building.

Eaun thought that it had been a very long time since he had to negotiate his way past what effectively were a couple of bouncers. On checking his name on the clipboard and finding that he was not on the list, even though he had a couple of invites to the party, Eaun even contemplated calling it a day and going home. However, assisted with a gentle kick on his shins from his companion for the evening, he then asked the guards whether he could have a word with the proprietor, whom he knew.

Happily, Eaun did know both Gustave and his wife Anabel. They were of course the friends and indeed major clients of Julian, but when the place first opened he had been given complimentary membership and a few partners' strategy meetings away from the office had been held at Sedgeton Grange.

The wait outside was bordering on becoming embarrassing when eventually the taller of the guards returned with Gustave.

'Hello old boy, delighted to see you at Sedgeton Grange!' said Gustave in the manner of an excited puppy. Eaun was fairly certain that Gustave was in fact several years older than himself.

Eaun explained that unfortunately Julian could not make the event but he had passed his tickets on to him. He himself was a member but as he was in fact just replacing an existing invitee, he hoped that there would be no problem. He and his partner (Denise Halloran performed a small curtsey and offered an enchanting smile) were really looking forward to the event.

'Absolutely no problem,' responded Gustave, as he moved between his two latest guests and with arms around both started to usher them both through the entrance doorway and into the imposing hallway.

'Just help yourself to everything on offer. Eaun, you will just need to slip in to the old common room over there and get some proper Roman kit on, there should be plenty your size. We also need to see Julian and yourself have a lot more of your highest level business meetings up here at The Sedgeton Grange as well.' With that, Gustave disappeared into the busy throng of togas and tunics, a throng that was getting busier by the minute.

Denise having agreed to wait in the main hallway for him, Eaun duly disappeared through the door of the old common room where he found two large curtains dividing the room with large printed signs delineating the private changing area for Viri and Feminae. On arrival, Eaun had noticed that several of the men were wearing rather smart looking togas that went down to their ankles. However, obviously all of the best stuff had gone and Eaun was left with a choice of fairly ordinary tunics to choose from. Hoping that he did not resemble looking too much like the plebeian Grumio, Eaun picked the least offensive looking tunic he could find to replace his jeans, t shirt and trainers. He had already decided that under no circumstances was he going to relinquish his boxer shorts.

Eaun went back in to the hallway, had a goblet of 'genuine Roman ale' thrust in his hand by one of the waiters in periodic top with a leather apron. It was only when the man walked away from him towards the next guest, that Eaun realised that the apron did not have a rear and that this particular waiter was exhibiting a well- rounded naked bottom.

There was no sign of Denise. She was supposed to be here as his minder. He thought of panicking for a moment. Instead, Eaun looked around. A few of the faces he vaguely knew, but most of the attendees seemed to be either from out of town or from circles that he made every effort to avoid. There was a tap on the shoulder. Eaun turned around and was face to face with Joseph 'Mac' MacBain who was chair of one of what was now the town's biggest and most influential networking concerns, Business Means Business. He had an attractive woman clinging to his arm, sporting a short red haircut and a toga that did not leave a great deal to the imagination when she moved around. Eaun assumed that the woman at his side was Mac's wife, but after the day that he had experienced he was not all that sure of anything.

Eaun knew Mac from work and with Eaun training his eyes to stay away from the mobile toga fabric adorning Mac's wife, the inevitable small talk began. Yes, business had never been better. Yes, against the odds the town is thriving and yes, hadn't our children done well. Eaun also knew that Julian was a leading member of Business Means Business so he asked straight up whether Mac knew where Julian was. No he didn't and why did he want to know this when after all he was Eaun's partner and surely he should know.

Eaun had always found Mac somewhat smug. For some reason, during all the time that he had been working and living at Sedgeton, no one had ever invited Eaun to join one of the several professional networking organisations in town.

With Mac asking Eaun to pass on his best to Mrs Wright, Eaun was only grateful that he was not asked why she was not there accompanying him. It was time for Eaun to quickly move on.

There was still no sign of his escort for the evening, DC Denise Halloran.

Eaun then walked through the hall and out of the open double doors to the gardens outside. One of the corners of the garden was dominated by a swimming pool and at least a couple of hot tubs. The guests occupying the jacuzzis all appeared in earnest discussion about something, holding their plastic flutes and goblets filled with real Lazio wine or the local Circus Maximus ale with one hand and with the other hand either gesticulating in the cool April air or attached around the shoulder or waist of the neighbour seated next to them. From his vantage point, it seemed that most of the guests seemed to be in a state of complete undress, as evidenced by the neatly folded tunics, togas and sandals adorning the small grotto next to the tubs.

Most of the real activity seemed to be centred in the actual swimming pool itself. There were a couple of guests exhibiting their athletic prowess as they swam up and down the length of the pool. They also appeared to be unclothed.

A shriek behind Eaun diverted his attention. A lady clinging to a towel to cover her frontage ran at speed past Eaun, quickly followed by a gentleman. Eaun could only see the rear of the man as he sped past, displaying a long white pony tail and a tiny behind in earnest pursuit. The woman, with long blond hair could be heard shrieking again as she headed in to the darkness trying not to slip on the damp grass. Her pursuer was obviously enjoying himself as he tried not to spill the liquid contents of the goblet that he was clutching with one hand, urging others to join in the fun chase with him. Eaun did not fully understand what the purpose of the game was, but the two were clearly enjoying themselves. Eaun walked over to the opposite corner of the garden where the guests were mainly in huddles under the gas heaters, a Roman tunic affording little protection against the Somerset spring chill. Loud R & B shook the ground around the bar area, where Eaun could see the DJ behind his extensive deck, dressed all in black, including large thick polo neck. He was also wearing a matching black face covering as if he was preparing to do a bank job. Except for a couple of waiters, this was the only face mask that Eaun had come across to date at the event.

Eaun also spotted a large metal cage next to the DJ set, but it was empty of man, woman or beast.

With still no sign of Denise, Eaun decided to retreat indoors, conscious that he was here with a purpose. Inside the old school building, it was crowded, as many guests seemed to have taken the view, no doubt as the original Romans in nearby Bath must have done, that only mad men (and women) would cavort around naked on a cold April evening in England.

Many of the guests now seemed to be headed through the door marked 'The Dungeon'. Eaun was about to follow the herd in search of Denise when he saw the light in the office off the hallway and inside was Gustave who was half looking at the bank of screens against one of the walls whilst unable to avert his eyes from what appeared to be a large spread sheet in front of him on the desk. He was alone and the timing could not have been better. Eaun gave a quick rat-tat-tat on the glass door. From inside, Gustave gestured for Eaun to enter.

'And what has happened to the delightful Mrs Wright,' asked Gustave with a broad grin. 'Trust that she is actually here enjoying the debauchery of our Roman evening. Would thoroughly recommend that you two sample the delights of Just Heaven before you retire back to the safety of Sedgeton. Have to say that the whole evening has been a real triumph so far.'

It dawned on Eaun that of course Gus had never had the pleasure of meeting Vicky. He was therefore assuming that Denise was his wife.

Gustave tapped his gold fountain pen on the spread sheet before him.

'From the figures to date, this evening probably tops the lot,' crowed Gustave. 'The midweek members' evenings are always good value, but it is the special events that manage to fill up the overflow car park. In the last few months, we have had special events to cater for every taste, persuasion and perversion. It is of course Anabel who is the inspiration of all these things. One week when takings were down, she managed to put together a FFLT party. No one had a clue what FFLT meant. It turned out that Anabel did not have a clue either, but the curious membership flooded through the doors to see what FFLT was actually all about. It turned out that it was just another evening of the usual naughty shenanigans but everyone loved it. A great hoot!'

Eaun was waiting to get a word in, but Gustave still managed to get in first.

'And where is my old mucker Julian?' asked Gus. 'He rarely misses these events and is usually the heart and soul of the party. I need to speak with him.'

'That's just it Gustave,' responded Eaun. 'He has disappeared off the face of the earth and no one knows where. I need to speak to him. Extremely urgently. Thing is, everyone seems to think that he might be at his place in Mallorca. He is not answering his phone but I need to speak to him without delay. The thought is that Julian may well in the past have invited Anabel and yourself to his place there. Somewhere called Anthrax?'

Eaun did not want to explain to Gustave that the reason that he needed to speak to his partner was that he had betrayed every trust there was and stolen £5 million that belonged to clients of the firm.

'Not sure I would have ever have written the address down old boy,' said Gus. The tone of the conversation had started to quietly shift.

'Surprised that Mrs Wright and yourself have never been invited out there yourselves. Fantastic place. I will ask Anabel of course but you will appreciate that in our line of business, even with fellow professionals, we need to be discreet. Our members and guests demand privacy and discretion at all times.'

Eaun took this answer as a 'no' to his request. However, before he could take the matter further, there was a rapid knock on the office door and one of the hotel waiters entered. It was the genuine Roman ale drinks dispenser with the tunic and leather apron, but fortunately he was front-facing to both Gus and Eaun.

'Terribly sorry to interrupt, Mr Paterson. There is a bit of an incident developing and I think that you should come and have a look for yourself,' said the flustered waiter.

With a mumbled 'sorry' and a flick of dismissal from the hand from Gustave, Eaun understood that that was the end of the conversation between the two 'fellow professionals'. He would clearly not be given any address of where Gus and Anabel Paterson had been staying with Julian in the Balearics.

Eaun decided to go once more in search of Denise. He left Gus' office and walked across the hall. There was by now a steady stream of guests heading upstairs on the wide staircase. He would leave upstairs till later. Instead, Eaun walked across the hallway and popped his head through the door marked The Dungeon. Inside, it seemed dark and badly lit. His vision was not helped by the periodic blasts of dry ice that came from the fog machine. As Eaun stepped in to the room and down the stairs in search of Denise his eyes could better focus on what was happening.

Eaun would have felt a great deal more comfortable if he had Denise, or indeed anyone, by his side. Stepping down through the dry ice and towards the spectacle of chains, ropes and contraptions with leather straps hanging from them that he did not fully understand, Eaun was desperate not to feel like an interloper and a voyeur, especially as he was one of the few people in the room wearing any kind of clothing.

There was no sign of Denise. Mercifully. He thought that he would most definitely not have wanted to find her here. A queue seemed to be forming in the pit of the room, with a stark naked large lady at the front ensuring that she was the centre of attention. She was insisting that she was next in the queue and that the gentleman dressed in the thong would have to wait his turn. It was the lady who was definitely in charge, issuing directions to the three or four colleagues around her, who were at the same time pulling items from one of those traditional old school trunks. One of the fellow near naked participants had donned a mortar board and was clutching a cane. Another was trying on military caps and hats whilst one of the women in the group was hitching up what seemed to be a short leather skirt. One of the gentlemen in front of the large woman, sporting an El Zorro hat and eye mask, was offering an assorted selection of whips on a tray from which to choose.

After the woman had made her selection of choice for the evening, she turned and bent down before her colleagues. There was a short wait as her colleagues started to apply and tie the leather straps from the device. Even over the deafening music, Eaun clearly heard the woman shout at the others that she wanted them to 'do it properly' and 'not fuck about like the last time'.

It was definitely time for Eaun to flee the scene as he headed towards the light at the entrance to the door of The Dungeon. Just as he stepped back into the hallway, even through the music, behind him Eaun could distinctly hear a woman's scream of what he supposed was pure pleasure, followed by a barked demand for more of the same please, except much harder.

Relieved to have escaped the excitement of the Dungeon, a quick spin around the ground floor still did not produce Denise.

Where was she? If he was not feeling so unsure and uncertain, Eaun would have followed the steady stream of guests climbing up the stairs to discover the pleasures of what was on the upper floors. He had however experienced more than enough sights for the one evening.

Before deciding where to search next, Eaun helped himself to some of the excellent canapes that were circulating on a regular basis. Eaun noticed that what marked the catering staff apart from the guests was that all of them, male and female, sported the bottomless leather aprons with the sash across. He wondered whether Gustave and Anabel were forced to pay above the living wage for this extra service provided by their employees.

Whilst looking around, Eaun could not help but notice another waiter supporting a large gold plated platter with the tips of the fingers on his left hand. On the platter was just a black notebook and a box of HB pencils. However, what distinguished this young waiter apart was that he was not wearing the otherwise ubiquitous leather apron of his work colleagues, as he took individual orders from around the room. Quite definitely a patrician in both looks and manners.

What the young tall man was taking orders for, Eaun could not tell. He seemed to be on both good and familiar terms with many of the guests, who clearly knew him and were familiar with him, even to the extent of calling him by his Christian name, which Eaun could not help but pick up. Tarquin.

At one stage Eaun thought that he was going to stop in front of him and ask what his order was, but instead he just looked up towards Eaun, gave a polite Hi! and then proceeded on to the next group of people who were clearly able to provide far better pickings and were already waiting to greet him.

Eaun once more headed for the outside, despite the plunging temperature. The hanger-arounds who had earlier been on the lawns had been driven off the grass, heading for either the warm glow of the heating lamps by the DJ set or alternatively to the heated pools and hot tubs where clothes were rapidly dispensed as naked bodies were submerged like hippos keeping warm under the surface. Eaun was sure that he could see some of the noses of the swimmers turning blue in the outside air.

As Eaun was scanning the scene in search of Denise, he heard a shout behind him as yet another lady ran right past him. She was turning around and screaming at someone behind her who had emerged from the darkness. That person doing the chasing soon ran past Eaun leaving a view of his behind. The mass of trailing white hair and the negligible posterior told Eaun that it was the same gentleman that had ran past him earlier in the evening, except that the previous woman he had been chasing had long blond hair, this one had short strawberry blond hair. The woman running on this occasion was of a similar shape as the one involved in the earlier game, with ample but very rounded curves. Except for a substantial selection of large modern silver jewellery adorning her neck and wrists, she was stark naked. By now the woman was panting for breath as the man with the flow of white hair caught up with her. Whatever had been keeping the hair neat in the pony tail had been lost in the fray and the long white strands of hair were now damp with sweat. With a final scream the woman jumped straight in to the far hot tub, creating a tidal wave tipping the water over the edges of the tub and on to the path and grass. Those bathers still in the hot tub spat out the water they had digested as the tsunami hit them.

However, the chase appeared to be continuing as rushing past Eaun now was both Gustave and a few seconds later Anabel and one of the Praetorian guards.

'Caught up with you at last, Mr Honorary Bloody Secretary!' shouted an incandescent Gustave. 'Just stop and come with us!'

It was then that it slowly dawned on Eaun what was happening. In fairness, he had never seen the emasculated naked backside of Piers Hudderston before and for a good proportion of the male population aged over 40 (at least the ones who still had hair) growing a pony tail now seemed seemed almost obligatory. Somewhere during the evening's excitement, Mr Hudderston had managed to shed his large red framed glasses as well as most of his clothes. It was however the pair of sandals with the ankle length black socks that was the giveaway. There was no doubt. The gentleman now perched, standing on the edge of the hot tub with the now terrified looking woman he had been chasing submerged on the other side of the tub was none other than Eaun's client, Piers St.John Hudderston. The same gentleman who, on the advice of Eaun, had earlier in the day pleaded Not Guilty to an allegation of Exposure under the Sexual Offences Act 2003. There was however no current signs of any nervous disposition.

There were in the small pool other naked bathers who had not yet had the time, or the ability, to haul themselves out of the tub without using the steps that were now stood over by Mr Hudderston. By now, a small crowd was starting to form behind Gustave.

Gustave was by now screaming at Mr Hudderston demanding that he immediately comes away from the tub, gets dressed and leaves the party forthwith.

Clearly however, Mr Hudderston had other ideas, no doubt greatly encouraged by the inebriating effects of the Lazio wine and the Circus Maximus ale which had clearly been consumed in large quantities. Eaun was directly behind his client now and mercifully shielded from a frontal view. By now, Mr Hudderston had both arms outstretched as if he was a Senator about to make an address at the Forum.

'You stuck up bunch of wankers,' slurred a swaying Mr Hudderston. 'You are all too scared to actually enjoy a real Roman orgy. What is the matter with you, my darling Florence or whatever your name is? I love you and am here at your command. I know that you really want my body!'

By now the watching crowd had grown in size and even the DJ had stopped his set to see what was happening. Those remaining in the hot tub looked petrified with fear. Before Piers Hudderston could do or say anything further, he was grabbed from behind by several figures who had rushed from the watching crowd. Eaun spotted Jack the head gardener and part time Praetorian guard, together with Gustave himself, grab an arm each of Mr Hudderston who was shouting in loud protest that his civil rights were being violated and that they would be hearing from his solicitors.

Mt Hudderston was then manhandled away from the hot tub with Anabel shouting in his face and wagging her finger, screaming that he was a disgrace and that he had ruined her whole evening and that she would see that he would never step foot in The Sedgeton Grange ever again.

Gustave and his gardener were clearly trying to manoeuvre Mr Hudderston around the back of the house and the side door for the old school changing rooms. Before they could get there and in the still full glare of the garden floodlights, another figure came running out of the hallway. The belly and breasts bounced and wobbled, travelling up and down over the stretched white Y-fronts as the man attempted to move as fast as he could towards where everything was happening.

'You filthy little pervert. You dare try to do that with my wife…'

This must have been the husband of the unfortunate and by now deeply traumatised lady identified by Mr Hudderston as possibly being called Florence. As the man waddled past him, Eaun's mind was racing in imagination as to what sort of act Mr Hudderston had tried to perpetrate on the unfortunate Florence. It could not have been good. The face that ran past Eaun was glowing with sweat. Eaun made a mental note that whatever any future temptation lay before him, he should stay away from the upper floors of Heavenly Bliss, the Sex Heaven or whatever it was called at the top of the hotel.

With beads of sweat now starting to run down his face, the Y-fronts man had managed to catch up with the still protesting Piers Hudderston, being frog-marched off the premises by Gustave and the Roman guard, with his white hair flowing like an old lion's mane behind him. Mr Hudderston turned around just long enough to see the chasing husband pull his right arm back as if to throw a punch. However, before anything else could happen, a long hairy naked leg shot out from the crowd in front of the man who then stumbled and rolled on the wet grass, staining his Y-fronts green down the left side in the process. The owner of the hairy leg emerged and stood over the man.

'I think we have all seen enough for one night,' said the man with authority. Eaun knew who the man was. They seemed to swap every year but the man had definitely once been the Mayor of Sedgeton. It seemed that half of the town were here for the event. The Mayor was wearing a short tunic and a wide leather belt but with large solid bracelets on both wrists, resembling a gladiator all kitted out and ready for his next contest at the Coliseum. The absence of his chain of office was made up for on the recognition stakes by the unmissable dreadlocks reaching down to just above his shoulders. Since the demise of the *Courier*, Eaun had more or less lost touch with local politics. He did not know the name of the Mayor, but knew enough about him to know that he was one of the leaders of the town's Sedgeton First bloc whose candidates had swept the board at the last local election.

The Mayor went over to the stricken fallen husband, offered him a hand and pulled him up effortlessly.

As soon as he was back on his feet the man in the Y-fronts was then clutched by the woman with the chunky silver jewellery and the short strawberry blond hair who had earlier been of keen interest to Piers Hudderston. Except now the woman had pulled a towel around herself, which covered most of her curves. Eaun assumed that this must have been the unfortunate Florence. The occasion had by now got too much for Florence's husband as actual flowing tears were now mixing with the sweat still pouring down his face.

'Let's just get you home, buddy,' said the Mayor in a deep west coast Scottish accent. By this time Florence had found another towel and was wrapping it over and around her husband's stained Y-fronts.

The Mayor ushered them both in the direction of the car park when someone from the crowd shouted 'Nice one Mayor!'

A weak cheer from the remaining crowd could be heard in response. As Eaun started to disperse with the rest of the crowd, he could not help but feel that even with the strawberry blond hair plastered to the scalp and the make-up running down the face, there was a quite remarkable likeness between 'Florence' and Mrs Compelling.

~ ~ ~

'Well hello gorgeous. Did anyone ever tell you that you just looked utterly irresistible in your Roman tunic?'

Eaun had just made it back in to the warmth of the hallway in the hotel, when he turned around to see who it was addressing him.

'And hello to you. DC Denise Halloran,' replied a relieved Eaun Wright. 'I seriously thought that I had lost you in this den of iniquity. Was figuring out how I was going to explain to both your husband and your DI how it came about that you got lost at a Roman orgy whilst in the line of duty.'

Denise ushered Eaun round to a small alcove near the hotel dining room where there were few guests and members.

'I am having the best time ever,' announced Denise. 'Yes, I did manage to catch the end bit of the lookalike Albert Einstein performance. Saw you near the front getting the best view of what was happening. There has been loads more happening as well. You tried Seventh Heaven yet? You could hardly see anything in the near dark but there were things going on there that after 25 years as a police officer, even I did not know which bits were from where. Compared with upstairs, the events in The Dungeon are like something out of Blue Peter. My hubby will be absolutely gutted when I tell him what he has missed. And I suppose that you have by now got the address that you needed of your thieving partner in Spain? Would be nice to get home. Rod will be wondering where I have gone, and with justification as well after what I have seen this evening.'

Eaun shuffled his Roman sandals uncomfortably.

'Er, not as yet, no,' replied Eaun. 'They were stalling on me. Gustave said that he did not know then went on to say that because of privacy and confidentiality and as Julian is their big mate, he thought it best that he say nothing further. So he didn't.'

Denise knew that this would happen and was therefore prepared.

'No worries, Eaun. You have had a bad day and just as well that everyone decided that you needed to be accompanied here by the mad bad cow. Your girls in the office, Madge and Alex, they know you inside out. Let's go cowboy.'

Eaun had no time to respond before he found himself following Denise in to the hallway and outside the door to Gustave's office. The toga hanging from Anabel's shoulders was hiding most of the front of her husband, but Denise and Eaun could both hear the raised voices of the two office occupants.

'Bloody hell, Anabel, this has been a total shambles,' said the male voice. 'Firstly, we make the promise to our members of a red hot lecture on Roman filth and depravity, with matching slides as well from a real academic, and your Aunt Cressida does what your family usually does, which is to let us down. What has happened to our credibility? If that was not enough you then hire a ninth-rate replacement from the local Historical Society or whatever they are called who does not even mention the word debauchery in his presentation before revealing himself as a lecherous sex maniac, alcoholic and public menace.'

'And what about you and all your procedures,' responded the unmistakeable voice of Anabel. 'Did you run a check on the perpetrator to see whether he had a record as a perv? No, of course you bloody well didn't. After what I have seen, I bet he has a record pages long. You are always going on about our success being down to due diligence.' Anabel paused for a breath of air. 'Not a lot of due diligence around this evening, was there?'

At this, Denise knocked on the door loudly and pushed Eaun in before her.

Both Gustave and Anabel stopped arguing and stared at Eaun.

'Anabel' explained Gustave, 'I am sure that you will remember Eaun Wright. Julian's partner at WHW the solicitors. He says that Julian has disappeared and wants his address in Spain off us. Eaun, I do apologise, but I fear that you will find that Anabel has exactly the same view as myself. No can do.'

'Too right, Mr Wright,' followed on Anabel, closing ranks. 'This is not a branch of Friends United. We have loads of issues going on to sort here so if you would leave us alone to get on with our business that would be appreciated. Never known Julian to be out of the limelight for long. Sure that he will turn up soon.'

The eyes of Anabel were staring at the still open office door through which she expected Eaun and his unknown female companion to imminently depart.

Instead, Denise, who was standing behind Eaun moved to the front and placed herself directly in front of the two proprietors of Sedgeton Grange.

'Let me introduce myself,' started Denise. 'I am with Eaun and he has asked that I accompany him this evening. Just let us have the address of Julian's place in Spain and we will then get on our way without causing any trouble to either of you.'

'I have no idea who on earth you are or who even let you in to this private event but please make a little effort to understand the English language. Just get out, both of you. The door is there. Out!' Anabel was now raising her formidable voice considerably.

Denise did not head for the door and could sense Eaun trying to cower behind her and being more than happy that she was in the front. Denise wondered what the eventual ramifications would be for Gustave when Anabel eventually found out that it was her husband who had welcomed Denise in to the event together with Eaun. Denise had never met Anabel before but she did not strike Denise as the sort of woman who would quickly forget such an error.

Denise just gave a gentle sigh, more of sorrow than indignation.

'As you actually requested this information, let me tell

you who exactly I am, Mrs Paterson,' said Denise quietly but precisely. Eaun was only inches behind her in the cramped office designed for one but now hosting four people. However, Denise could feel Eaun freeze as she then lifted her toga up in the front so that it bundled around her waist level. When Denise with her other hand then pulled the elastic out wide in front and plunged her other hand in to the depths of her big white undergarment to remove what looked like a small wallet, she was sure that she could both hear and feel the thumping of Eaun's heart.

Seated directly in front of Denise, Gustave's eyes had not moved an inch. 'The Romans have a great deal to answer for,' explained Denise. 'A handbag would be a great deal easier. What I am showing you both now is a Wessex Constabulary warrant card. To be precise, my own Warrant Card. My name is Detective Constable Denise Halloran, collar number 2072 and now you are going to stop wasting my own and everyone else's time. And thank goodness for my big traditional school gym knickers. I can tell you the level of their comfort was such that I hardly even knew where my warrant card was being stored all evening.'

Neither Gus nor Anabel said anything in response. Denise figured the silence may be more shock than resistance but she really did not want to be here all evening.

'Right, so be it,' said Denise. 'Not sure how much trouble you two realise you are now in. Have either of you two ever bothered to read the Licensing Act 2003? Especially the provisions surrounding the 'fit and proper person' provisions? No? Thought not. Which is why the local Council licensing team will no doubt be fascinated to hear what I have to report to them on. It makes no matter whether you are running a private members club or not. As the joint licence holders (I checked that it was both of you on the sign above the entrance door) I don't think that anyone is going to be impressed by inviting a known sex pest who is actually on the Register to an event where alcohol is being consumed and where there are acts of sexual assault and intimidation taking place. What explanation are you two going to give to the Licensing Committee for having an invited guest physically and sexually assault the wife of at least one member and then chase her, terrified, into a pool where he then shouts abuse and threateningly displays himself to all and sundry.'

Gus and Anabel remained silent. Whilst she paused for breath, Eaun behind her whispered something in to her ear.

'Ah, it gets better,' continued Denise. 'It seems that one of the ladies who is groped, manhandled, chased and threatened, the delightful Florence, or whatever her real name may be, is one of your important members and pillar of the community and that she will now be making a complaint.'

'There is also a multi-million pound theft that has taken place and yet it seems that you are both happy to obstruct that police investigation. Do either of you have any idea of what sort of sentence you could be looking at for conspiracy? If you still are not convinced about whether to assist with enquiries or not, then you might want to consider the issue of under-age sex. No one is going to lose too much sleep about the middle aged fatties with their bit of slap and tickle in the Heavenly Bliss room. Likewise, not sure that any sleep is going to be lost about your membership dressing up and being recipients of a good sound flogging in The Dungeon. What is worrying and worries me a lot, is the age of some of your catering staff going around with their cute little bums hanging out. Whilst they were hanging around waiting to pick up the next round of canapes for distribution, it was difficult not to overhear them talking about their A level exams next month. Did you actually check their ages? Employing children in a private sex club. Oh dear.'

'Finally, just from my brief visit this evening it is fairly obvious that you are running a drugs operation from this address, although in fairness I have to say that this is definitely the most salubrious crack house that I have ever had the pleasure of visiting. I suppose that you know all about that though.'

'But that just isn't true,' uttered Gus. 'You make us sound like criminals.'

'Tell you what,' replied Denise. 'My colleague and myself will wait outside your door and come back inside after two minutes when you will then have a piece of paper to give us with all the known telephone numbers and full contact addresses of Julian Darby-Henderson in Spain.'

With that, Eaun stepped outside following Denise, who clicked the door shut behind her.

The hallway was once again busy with some guests heading upstairs and others finding their way out to the garden. A few were venturing towards the open door to The Dungeon. The unfortunate earlier kerfuffle involving Mr Hudderston, Hon Sec of the Sedgeton branch of the Wessex Monuments & Historical Buildings Society, seemed to have been forgotten as the evening continued as originally planned.

'How did you know about the under-age employees?' asked Eaun.

'I didn't,' responded Denise. 'I just guessed. From their reaction of both going a deathly white, I imagine that they had probably just assumed that they are all aged 18 or over but of course neither of them had ever bothered to check.'

Eaun dare not mention to Denise that he had represented the 'sex pest' in court only a few hours beforehand and that he was rapidly approaching or had already reached the quagmire of professional conflict of interest. Already facing being struck off for the financial irregularities perpetrated by his business partner, Eaun now found himself facing another possible SRA probe. Eaun did of course already know the answer to his next question, but out of curiosity he could not resist asking.

'And how did you know about this man Mr Hudderston being on the Sex Offenders' Register?'

'Again, I didn't,' replied Denise. 'From what I witnessed this evening he certainly should be. I imagine that our generous hosts for the evening are also now of that view as well.'

Eaun remained silent.

'Since you are asking all these questions, I have no idea whether Florence is making a complaint or not. Who cares, it all helps. Have to say however that it is some time since I have enjoyed such a high level of job satisfaction,' added Denise. 'Come on, the two minutes must be up. Time for more sport.'

With that Denise barged back in to the office without knocking, assuming that Eaun was trailing behind her.

'Well?' asked Denise.

'This whole performance has been an utter disgrace,' proclaimed Anabel, who during the two minutes' interval had clearly decided to take charge of proceedings on her side of the desk. 'We both have a good mind to report what has happened to a senior officer. Several are members here, you know.'

'I have no doubt of that,' responded Denise. 'But let's cut to the chase. Are you going to co-operate with the police in their enquiries or is this the time that I formally caution you both?'

Anabel's hand glided across the table, pushing across the desk top a folded piece of hotel guest notepaper. Denise picked up the note and showed it to Eaun, who then nodded.

'There, that wasn't so bad was it?'

With that, Denise pushed the note down the front of her toga and departed the room with Eaun in tow.

'Right, an excellent evening's work but definitely time to leave the fun palace,' said Denise. She waited for Eaun to get changed from his plebeian tunic and sandals back in to his civvies in the former Common Room. When he eventually emerged, Denise handed to Eaun from the inside of her toga, the piece of paper with details of the contact address for Julian. By now there were no signs of the two Praetorian guards. They had probably had enough and sensibly retreated from the mayhem of Roman social life to the safety of their own potting sheds, thought Denise.

The floodlights at the entrance of the hotel lit up the drive most of the way to the overflow car park. When they reached where most of the vehicles had been parked, there were by now several empty spaces where guests had obviously decided that they had had enough of the evening's orgy and had decided to go home.

Denise and Eaun stopped to face each other before heading for their respective cars and then travelling home.

Eaun thanked Denise profusely. If it had not been for his remaining nervousness of The Plague, he felt that he would even have given her a quick hug of appreciation.

'All part of my job,' said Denise. 'One of the best evenings that I have ever had, honestly. Would not have swapped this for anything. Off you go, you have the address and you have an early flight in the morning. When I get home I will immediately call Steve Dibley so that he can start to get the wheels moving both here and in Spain.'

Eaun was about to head towards his Volvo and was wondering on which wheel he had left the car keys, when there was a loud squeal of tyres and a commotion as a black Range Rover hurtled around the curve and screeched to a halt in the first spot in the car park that was now vacated.

Both Eaun and Denise looked across at the vehicle as a squat broad figure smartly dressed in casuals with a shaved head alighted from the vehicle. Even in the half-light the man looked consumed with rage, slamming the car door behind him. It was lucky that he was not in charge of a less robust model, thought Denise.

The man saw Eaun and Denise, by this time both staring across at him.

'What you two looking at,' snarled the driver, by now beginning to head for the hotel buildings.

'Tarquin. Tarquin Battingsdale. Where do I find him?' came the order.

Denise was tempted to say nothing but instead shouted across the car park.

'He is taking orders for the canapes. You can't go in there looking like that,' responded Denise. 'You will need to get kitted out like a proper Roman.'

'Fuck the Romans,' came the response shouted across the roofs of the cars, as the man in the chinos and checked shirt headed towards the hotel.

With that, both Eaun and Denise smiled and mouthed a 'goodnight' to each other before heading towards their respective vehicles.

However, it was only once she had pulled all of her sheet/toga safely into the insides of her car before starting on the journey home that Denise picked up on the name that she had just heard Mr Angry shout out in the car park. Battingsdale. It was a different first name but there could not have been too many Battingsdales in the vicinity. What had started out as a casual fishing trip to child mind Eaun was turning out to be a golden evening with enough excellent quality A1 Intel to feast on for a long time. Her colleagues really would be sick with envy.

Eaun had no doubt driven off home by now, to get ready for his big day tomorrow. Denise contemplated returning to the hotel to see what the angry bald eagle was doing there shouting out the same name of one of her suspects that she had been interviewing only a few hours before. Denise also considered that so far she had only managed to get a quick peek into Seventh Heaven at the top of the house. What was going on there looked genuinely interesting and deserved a more thorough inspection. However, Denise also felt that that was probably a step too far and would be pushing her luck. In any event, she already had enough material to entertain Rod for half a life time.

Double checking that none of her toga had got stuck in the car door, Denise turned the ignition and started to head off back in the direction of Wells, the evening cocoa and her quiet life at home.

MONKS ON TOUR

IT WAS not yet 5am but already the dark night was being slowly transformed in to a dirty grey light in the sky. Eaun was starting to panic. Ludmila had given him precise instructions on where she lived with Gregor and her two daughters. He knew that they had just moved to a new rented property in the huge new housing development past the edge of town's retail park. The estate was so new that the street lights were not working and he could not make out the names on the road signs that had actually been erected. He was about to telephone Ludmila and wake her whole household up when he spotted a figure with a long pony tail and a rucksack waving frantically at him at the end of a road that still had dumper trucks and other construction paraphernalia ready for work later that day. As he drove up, Eaun should not have worried about waking the Nowak family. Husband Gregor was standing behind Ludmila with his arm around her shoulder and her two girls were on the doorstep in their dressing gowns excitedly jumping up and down. Predictably and embarrassingly, thought Eaun, he had forgotten their two names.

Eaun pulled up.

Ludmila opened one of the back passenger doors and flung her rucksack on the seat. There was then a dawn ritual of kisses and hugs with her family as Ludmila opened the front passenger seat and piled in.

Eaun gave a general wave to the departure party as the taller of the two girls shouted to her mother not to forget to send their love to Uncle Jan and Auntie Reme. Eaun noted that they spoke to their mother in English.

Before Eaun had even made it back past the retail park, Ludmila asked him to pull over by the side of the road. Eaun immediately did so.

'Right, let's have a spot check before we go any further,' said Ludmila.

Eaun was then forced to produce his passport which Ludmila then checked to see whether it was valid and that there was no post Brexit expiry date problems. She then demanded to see his phone which he then handed over and passed to Ludmila. He also told her his password. It took Ludmila just a few seconds to find what she wanted.

'In case we need to show something at the other end, your NHS App is fine. You also have the paper proof of vaccination as well?'

Eaun checked his wallet and nodded.

'Right, I have the tickets with a provisional return date of just after midnight tonight. If things take a little longer then no problems we can sort that easily. Mr Wainwright has also made sure that he gave me enough money. By the way, you should never give your password to no one, not even me. You don't know what I would do with it,' said Ludmila with an easy smile.

As the sky became brighter whilst the sun crept behind the clouds, Eaun made his way across the Mendips to Bristol Airport. Neither Ludmila nor Eaun spoke, both wrapped in their own thoughts. Eaun thought that today should have been a normal day whilst he was seeing clients in the office whilst downstairs in reception Ludmila was guarding the fort for everyone upstairs by keeping the clients at bay.

An old-style black and white rural road sign hand-pointed the way towards Lulsgate. It was only on the major routes that there were directions to what was now called Bristol International Airport. Eaun remembered how years ago one of his old clients, a tarmacer, had got into a spot of bother. At the time, the client and his gang were extending the runway and apron at somewhere that both he and the locals still called Lulsgate Aerodrome, a name that Eaun still fondly remembered.

It was only as they approached the airport itself that the early morning traffic started to build up. However, there were no hold-ups as after collecting the ticket at the barrier they parked up the vehicle in one of the numerous car parks available at the airport. The place had long since ceased to be an aerodrome. As they should be back within 24 or at most 48 hours, Eaun chose the short term car park, but not before noticing that the parking rates advertised there made those prices at the cricket club by the court at Bath look a complete bargain.

Eaun did not like air travel at the best of times. He hated flying and he especially hated having to get to any airport hours before take-off in order to wait interminably for security and everything else. The Plague had made the waiting far worse, of course. Last time he used the facility, Eaun counted four different queues that he had to stand and wait at before he was eventually allowed on to the plane to take his seat. He also remembered that that last time he was here was when Victoria and he made the trip to Venice. Eaun wondered whether she was already planning her escape from Eaun then, but he then decided to put Victoria to the back of his mind and to concentrate on his other more immediate partner of betrayal, Julian Darby-Henderson.

Once Ludmila and he had cleared baggage security, Ludmila said that she wanted to pick up a couple of items at what she called 'the smellies department' that all passengers were forced to deviate through on the way to the main departure lounge. Eaun said that in the meantime he would sort out a coffee for both of them whilst they waited for their flight to Palma to be called.

It took several minutes for Ludmila to catch up with and find Eaun. When she eventually returned, she was clutching an airport duty free plastic carrier bag. In the meantime, Eaun noticed that the bar upstairs was starting to get boisterous as a couple of dozen monks got stuck in to their Full English breakfasts washed down with copious pints of Guinness. Families were already beginning to navigate their way around and away from the monk party.

Even with supposedly fewer flights following The Plague, Eaun noticed that the airport were still not announcing flights over their public address system. Accordingly, Ludmila and Eaun took it in turns to stay awake and regularly scour the digital Departure board so see what was happening.

When it was Ludmila's turn for board duty, Eaun shut his eyes and leaned back on the chair, a chair made to ensure that no passenger ever felt truly comfortable and certainly had no chance of ever actually falling asleep in.

The night before, once he had got back from Sedgeton Grange, Eaun had eventually gone to bed but slept only fitfully. It took him a while to find his passport, noticing that Victoria's had already been removed from their safe customary hiding place. It was just as well that others had taken control of the situation regarding Julian. However, except presumably for those toads at Maddison and Robinson, no one yet knew of Victoria's departure from Eaun's life and the reasons for her departure. As far as he knew, his daughters Alison and Cassie were still oblivious of their parents' split. By the time he had got home last night it was far too late to phone them. He wondered whether his wife had yet contacted them both. He suspected not.

Eaun had however been proactive in at least one respect. Whenever Vicky and he planned to be away for more than a day, they had booked the two cats into somewhere called the Mendip Luxury Cat Hotel. Their daily rates far exceeded what a human was charged for a night at the local Premier Inn. Both Ivan and Vlad always seemed to be churlish and resentful upon collection. There were never any fond signs of recognition or gratitude that seemed to be lashed out on other owners. Having been fed on a gourmet diet of rice and chicken and fresh line-caught fish at the Luxury Cat Hotel, Eaun felt no sympathy for them as they were returned back to the land of what passed as boring normality.

On this occasion, Eaun knew that he might be away for a couple of days. When the girls still lived at the house there was no problem. On the days that they remembered, Ivan and Vlad were fed. However, just now there was no time to book the two animals in to their usual holiday residence and in any event with the Easter weekend approaching, no doubt the establishment will have been fully booked, even in these still sometimes uncertain times. Eaun wondered about leaving the key with one of the neighbours, but he disliked all of his immediate neighbours, especially the stuck-up retirees living either side. He then had a moment of inspiration. Looking back, Eaun still wondered why he had become first choice, but before leaving the house for the dawn run to the airport, Eaun wrote a scribbled note to DI Colin Thompson saying that Vicky and himself had been called away for a couple of days without notice on urgent family matters, here is the house key and the burglar code and could he please feed the cats. The message went on to say where the cat food was stored. He was also more than welcome to help himself to the *Daily Mail* each day.

Eaun had been told to prepare to be away from home for 48 hours, although the period may be less. Consequently, Eaun had packed just an overnight bag with his toiletries, a couple of clean t-shirts and three pairs of socks and underpants. Vicky had always quizzed him as to why he always took one more item of both socks and underwear than he actually needed. His excuse was that they might be needed for 'emergencies', although Vicky never actually challenged him on what those 'emergencies' might actually involve. Eaun had also thrown in to his bag a tube of Factor 30. Just in case.

Double-checking that he had his phone and passport, Eaun approached the front door before entering the exit code on the alarm system and heading for his Volvo. Colin Thompson's house was a half a minute's drive away. There was no sign of anything stirring when Eaun pushed the envelope containing note and key through the Thompson household letterbox.

As Eaun started to drift off on the airport chair, fighting off the periodic nods and jerks of his head involuntarily falling forward, there was a sudden dig in his ribs. It was Ludmila.

'Flight is called. Let's go.'

He followed Ludmila at the end of a queue by one of the gates. Eaun had checked when Ludmila gave him his Boarding Card. Yes, this one was not a dog eat dog scenario, they had designated seats. What was the point of queuing and standing up if they had a reserved seat waiting for them anyway?

Three queues later, Eaun and Ludmila finally made it up the front steps of the aircraft to be greeted by the ridiculously happy, smiling and cheery cabin staff. A perfunctory glance at the Boarding Card and they were all directed in the same direction down the aisle of the plane, the only direction of travel possible. Eaun felt quiet relief when they walked well past the monks who had all been placed near the front of the plane, as if someone knew that teacher or the Abbott was there to ensure that they all behaved.

Another final wait as the pilot announced that they had missed their original slot and they were now awaiting fresh instruction to proceed to take off.

Next to him, Ludmila announced that she hated flying. Eaun said that he did not like it either. No, responded Ludmila, she really did not like flying at all.

At the end of the approach, the plane turned to face the long and dipping runway ahead of it. Eaun wondered whether the tarmac that the plane was now standing on was the same as the tarmac laid by his client all those years ago. Then, with a roar and release of brakes, the aircraft lurched forward quickly gaining momentum. Above the engine noise, Eaun could hear the monks cheering as the speed of the aircraft on the runway gained momentum.

Eaun then suddenly felt a vice like grip on his upper right arm. As well as being clutched fiercely by both Ludmila's hands, her head was also now hard pressed against his neck, as she muttered what Eaun initially thought was a prayer but then realised was the word 'kurva' being constantly repeated. He could not help but smell whatever perfume that she was wearing, direct evidence of the trip through the smellies. The pain on his arm started to become excruciating when the plane finally took off to the accompanying roar of triumph from the monks. The grip on his right arm eventually slackened.

Eaun looked next to him. He had never seen Ludmila be otherwise than calm and collected at all times. She was now breathing quickly and still looked tense.

'Kurva. I am really sorry Mr Wright,' Ludmila eventually explained. 'I am just so, so sorry. I fly many times but I hate take offs. Usually of course it is Grzegorz who gets to suffer. Today, I am sorry but it is you who are my Grzegorz.'

Eaun immediately said that there was nothing to worry about and he did not feel a thing, which was a lie. He had no idea whether it was in a gym or was caused by total panic, but Ludmila had an iron grip that was fiercely strong and tight. He made a note to inspect the bruises later.

The flight to Palma was just over two hours. The shape of the seat and the constant announcements from both captain and cabin crew made the idea of sleep pointless. Instead, Ludmila reminded him that on arrival at Palma, he had several phone calls that he had to make. Eaun noticed that Ludmila had brought a small note-book with her, no doubt to tick box that Eaun was doing everything that he was supposed to be doing. Ludmila also briefed him on what was happening at Palma. Full details had already been passed on to her brother Jan who would be meeting them. He would be taking them back to some place called Calanova and this is where they would also be meeting some colleagues of Jan's. Ludmila said that Jan spoke quite good English, although not as well as her of course. There should be no problems.

Eaun commented that both he and others in the office had to often remind themselves that English was not Ludmila's first language.

'That comes from having great teachers at school,' responded Ludmila, 'After Senior High School I then spent three years studying at Wroclaw University. We could only afford to live at home but even on the daily journey in to Glowny Station I made sure that I read all the British newspapers and magazines that I borrowed from the university library.

'Your children sound as if they are from Somerset.'

'That is because they are, Mr Wright! Both Julia and Natalia were born in Bath and most of their class mates and friends are of course English. I sometimes have to scold them when they occasionally lapse into the local way of saying things.'

Eaun realised that during all the several years that he had employed Ludmila, he did not really know a great deal about her, except that she and her husband were Polish and were from Lower Silesia, although Eaun was not very sure where Lower Silesia actually was. Before Brexit he had tentatively asked Ludmila whether she and her family were all set for Britain leaving the EU. The response from Ludmila was that of course she had already obtained settled status. Next day she indignantly brought the paperwork in to actually show Eaun.

There was still half an hour before they landed in Mallorca.

'What language do you speak at home?' asked a curious Eaun.

'Everyone asks that question,' came the response. 'The girls and I speak English most of the time and sometimes a bit of Polish. Grzegorz also speaks good English, he has set up his own business so he has to. However, when Julia and Natalia don't want their father to know anything then they just speak in English. The only negative is when we fly back and see the grandparents in Wroclaw. They get all emotional sometimes when their own granddaughters don't always understand everything that they are saying in the Polish language.'

An announcement came from the pilot that they were about to land in Palma and that all passengers should return to their seats and fasten their seat belts. All passengers were already seated anyway, noted Eaun. Looking up and down the plane, Eaun also noticed that most passengers were still wearing a face mask, even though it was no longer compulsory to do so.

The whine of the engines decreased as the aircraft got nearer to landing.

'Do you want to borrow my arm again?' asked Eaun, as the fasten seat belt sign flashed on.

'You are safe. Just need your arm on take off.'

A few moments later Eaun could hear the slight screech of the landing gear on the runway and the roar as the jet engines went into reverse to slow the speed. This was accompanied by a round of applause from the monks seated towards the front.

As the plane taxied to an eventual halt, Eaun thought that whilst approaching the airport, the island from the sky seemed so much bigger than he thought. The place even had mountain ranges. With a warning that face masks were to be worn at all times within the terminal building, both Ludmila and Eaun retrieved their respective bags from the overhead lockers and headed back to the front of the plane where the cabin crew were still bright and cheery and wished them both a great day. Eaun nodded. Everything hung on today. Was the plan going to work? Were they already too late? Eaun thanked the crew for their good wishes. It really had to be a good one. There was no sign of the monks.

~ ~ ~

Alexandra Hilton had decided to get to the office before everyone else that morning, to ensure that she was up to speed and on top of everything that Eaun and she were supposed to be doing. After all, they still had a busy practice to run. It had never happened to her, but she had heard apocryphal tales of terror from professional colleagues about the missed diary entry, when they were at their desk quietly drafting the grounds for unreasonable behaviour for a divorce petition, or even on their way to the beach for a precious day off with the family, when there was the call from the court saying that the District Judge was wondering where they were as both the client and he was waiting in court for them.

Alex parked up her Mini in the town's nearly empty central car park and posted her annual season ticket on the Mini's cockpit, visible to all. Invariably, on most days, Alex found herself having to go somewhere and it was more convenient and quicker to have the car parked and ready just 2 minutes away in the main car park. None of the cafes in the Artisan Quarter were yet open and even the man at the Blue Parrot told her to come back in 10 minutes when they were ready to open.

On arrival at the office, Alex was surprised to see that the alarm system was already on 'Open'. In the reception area, the rubber plant did not look well after the unprovoked attack from the day before. With Ludmila away, Alex made a mental note to do what she could later to try and save what remained of the mauled plant.

Alex was even more surprised to find upstairs a hive of activity. There was a bright air of activity and purpose. The fast food wrappings from the previous evening's meeting in the Conference Room had all been cleared away and the window opened. Julian's office was now occupied by Douglas Wainwright.

He beamed a broad smile at Alex and boomed a hearty 'Good Morning' to her.

'Right, everything well under control here,' said Douglas behind the desk. On the few occasions that he came in to the office these days as a consultant, he usually did so in smart casual attire of blazer and slacks, like Alex's grandad used to wear. He always wore a tie, usually striped silk, but today he was kitted out in what Douglas called his 'Number One's' in his immaculate pinstripe suit, white shirt and shining gold cuff links, as well as the striped tie.

Felicity Lawton, once universally known as the Poison Dwarf, then came into Julian's office holding seven or eight files. She gave a quick smile and a 'Good Morning' to Alex, who reciprocated.

'These are the completions for this morning,' explained Douglas to Alex. 'Everyone always wants to get in before Easter so that they can then devote the long weekend down at B&Q

spending the rest of their money on DIY and decorating. Much impressed that this Curtis fellow at the bank answers the phone at half seven in the morning. He has just rang me back to confirm that there are no problems with any movements on the client account this morning. We are all set to go. Right, Felicity, let's get on with the first completion, Sale of 24 Hatfield Avenue. Paul and Jenny Harris. First time buyers by the look of it…'

Alex left them to it.

There was another voice coming from down the hallway. It was Madge, who had just put down the phone and emerged from her room to greet Alex.

'Right, have just come off the phone with chambers in Bristol,' said Madge. 'They are always there at the crack of dawn. Love it. Real commitment. Of course I didn't explain what or why, but did say that Mr Wright had urgent issues that he needs to attend to this morning. Could they send someone along to the Family Court in Bristol this morning for the 11am list? Johnson v Johnson. Eaun has a FDA. All the paperwork including the Form E has already been completed and I am just about to email everything over to them now. Not sure which counsel it will be that will be doing the First Hearing, but I warned them that it should be someone who does not look 15 and has just a little bit of gravitas about them. Our Mr Johnson is extremely jumpy about everything so they are calling me back shortly with a name and I will then tell Mr Johnson which legal eagle he can expect to meet at court. Eaun had loads of other stuff for me to get on with but I can cope with all of that here from my desk.'

'Alex, I know that there is also loads for you to catch up on as well. Just for today, can you also look after reception? I can tell you how the phone systems work. We still have an hour before we open the door,' continued Madge.

'Of course I will,' responded Alex, impressed and in slight awe of everything that was happening. She was also feeling glad that she could get stuck in and help in any way.

'When you are in reception if you can try and rescue Ludmila's plant that would be great. Her watering can is under her desk.'

'Of course I will. Already part of the day's Action Plan.'

'By the way,' added Madge. 'Rita's office has already been cleared so that the SRA people have somewhere in private. Just let them get on with it. Felicity and I will ensure that they get everything that they need.'

Alex went to her own room and collected all of the many files that she would need and then proceeded downstairs to set up her office for the day at the reception desk.

Before she settled down in the chair she retrieved her mobile from her bag. She typed out a brief text to Ludmila:

'About to carry out surgery on your plant. Full recovery expected. Tell Eaun that all well here and that Madge Douglas and Felicity have already organised the whole day! Nothing to worry about!! Alex xxx'

Alex then pressed the Send button, put her phone back in her bag and settled down for the day ahead.

~ ~ ~

Eaun was surprised at the size of the airport at Palma. It had taken Ludmila and Eaun several minutes just to get to Passport Control. He fell in behind Ludmila in the queue and started searching for his passport. It was then that Ludmila gently nudged him and pointed to a far larger crowd of people at the other side of the cavernous passport reception area.

Eaun looked up. Together with Ludmila he had naturally stepped in to line on the EU nationals queue. There were only a handful of people in front of them in this queue, waiting to be directed to the automatic passport machines that resembled ATMs.

'Think that you will need to queue with the monks,' said Ludmila. 'See you in a few hours at the other side of passport control.'

When Eaun was several yards away he heard Ludmila shout after him.

'Losers!'

Eaun trudged towards the end of the Non EU passport queue, which by now snaked around a multitude of posts and ropes.

Twenty minutes later, the queue had hardly moved. Most of those queuing seemed to be Brits, mainly families with screaming babies and toddlers looking for a few days away in the sand, sea and sun during the Easter break. Eaun surmised that much of their break was likely to be spent at Palma airport. There was also a sprinkling of the older tourist, one such couple being next to Eaun. Both the man and the woman were of the generation that still 'dressed' to go on holiday, the woman in her smart floral dress and the gentleman in a white linen suit and that morning's edition of The *Daily Telegraph* tucked under his arm as if he was straight out of a Graham Greene novel.

As the wait became longer, so the impatience and the ire of the couple increased. The man started to mumble about how the Spaniards had always had it in for the Brits ever since 1588. By now all of the queues for the EU nationals had disappeared. Eaun only hoped that Ludmila had remembered that she had to wait for him on the other side.

There was suddenly a kerfuffle towards the front of the queue. There were loud shouts and oaths that echoed around the huge passport reception chamber. Eaun stepped aside to see what all of the fuss was about.

It seemed that two airport security guards, with holstered firearms and sticks dangling from their belts, had got hold of someone dressed all in brown and were dragging him away, with sandaled feet trailing behind him towards a plain and unfriendly door marked Entrada Prohibida. The man being hauled away was shouting loudly, in English, that he was innocent and had done nothing wrong. He was also exclaiming that all he was trying to do was find his lost crucifix. Before the man had time to say anything else, the door slammed behind him. The shouts and screams were cut off. Of course, realised Eaun, the detainee must have been one of the monks on tour. Eaun felt momentarily sick to the stomach knowing that if this trip went wrong, then it could indeed be Eaun himself who was carted off by men with guns and sticks. Unlike the protesting monk, it was also highly unlikely that Eaun would be returning home on the next available flight back to Bristol.

As the wait continued, the elderly couple in the queue seemed to have focused all their attention on Eaun, blaming 'Johnnie Foreigner' for singling out the Brits for this sort of disrespectful behaviour. When Eaun responded that these days it might be little wonder that Brits were not universally loved throughout Europe, there then followed a loud harrumph and then an even louder silence from the couple.

To avoid any further unpleasantness and as there were only a couple of dozen passengers behind him in the Non EU passport queue, Eaun used the opportunity to carry out his allotted tasks for the morning and found a quiet spot behind a large Covid awareness sign and where he could also keep an eye out on what was happening to the queue.

Eaun called Mr Curtis at the bank first. He gave him an update on what was happening and said that he would keep him posted. Mr Curtis confirmed that he had earlier spoken to the 'utter gentleman' Mr Wainwright and that for today at least the bank would allow the client account to remain open and active. Additionally, he had set up the arrangements as previously discussed. Eaun thanked him and told him that he would keep him posted, even during the holiday period. He then placed a call to Denise's colleague Steve Dibley at the force's Fraud Office. Yes, Steve had taken all the steps promised and he said that as soon as there were developments, Eaun should call Steve again. Like Mr Curtis, he promised to keep his phone with him all day. Finally, he made the call to Mr Farquhar and gave him a full update. Pending the next update and the report from his inspection team, Mr Farquhar said that the SRA would hold off taking any further immediate action either against the firm or Mr Wright personally. Eaun confirmed that of course his colleagues in the office would this morning be affording whatever help and facility to the visiting SRA inspection team that was needed. Any issues and Mr Wainwright would be there to assist. To Eaun, Mr Farquhar did not seem as friendly and accommodating as yesterday. However, at least he had not been struck off yet.

His essential calls completed, Eaun turned his phone off and returned to the queue. Following the removal of the innocent monk, the queue seemed to have moved forward immeasurably quicker. It seemed that for those with UK passports, there were no user-friendly ATMs to help on the journey. Instead, along with all the other Non EU passengers, Eaun had to queue and have his passport physically stamped. Was he planning to stay in Spain more than 90 days he was asked? No, he most certainly was not came the response. A surly nod of the head under the peaked and braided cap and Eaun was through.

'Kurva!' she explained when Eaun eventually found Ludmila. 'You were so long, thought that they had found out about you and were refusing you entry. That queue will teach you Brits on voting for Brexit.'

'I didn't,' said Eaun sheepishly in response.

Ludmila was now in her stride, urging Eaun to follow her down the endless corridors and travellators. Armed with just their hand luggage, Ludmila and Eaun passed the carousels where the passengers from Bristol were still waiting. Eaun could not help but notice that included in the large waiting crowd was the party of the remaining monks. It was impossible not to overhear the furious argument going on between the brethren. It appeared to Eaun that the argument was over whether they should wait for their detained colleague or not. The consensus seemed to be siding with the lead brother with the gold crucifix around his neck and a large knotted rope holding in an expansive stomach who proclaimed 'Fuck Billy. He was behaving like an arsehole anyway. We are already losing valuable drinking time.'

'Brits. Why always the Brits,' said Ludmila as they left the arguing monks behind them.

Eaun thought that notwithstanding the fact that, as we all know, God moves in mysterious ways, the detained monk's pilgrimage had probably come to a premature end.

The monks left to their devices, Ludmila led Eaun through the green 'Nothing to Declare' gate and towards the waiting friends and relatives at the other side of the barrier. For a moment, Eaun had lost Ludmila, who then quickly reappeared on the other side of the barrier hugging a dark haired, tall man. As Eaun walked round to join up with them, they were both still talking excitedly and at a speed where nothing was comprehensible to Eaun.

Seeing Eaun, the embracing couple drew apart.

'Jan, this is my boss Mr Wright,' said Ludmila, proudly and loudly. 'Mr Wright, this is my brother Jan.'

'Just call me Eaun. Delighted to meet you.'

Eaun was still not sure what the protocol was on touching as a greeting post-Covid, especially in a place he had never been to before. He therefore just smiled back and waved. Jan reciprocated.

A couple of minutes later, the party of three had walked across to the large multi storey airport car park where they picked up what turned out to be Jan's family car, a Skoda saloon. Eaun let Ludmila sit in the front with her brother, whilst in the rear, Eaun removed one of the two child seats and settled in. Jan enjoyed driving fast as the car found the motorway signposted to Palma. Eaun soaked in his surroundings. He thought that it would be hot on the island but when they exited the doors from the airport, the temperature was disappointingly hardly warmer than it had been in Bristol. So much for the Factor 30. On leaving the airport there was a mixture of old broken windmills and industrial estates with the odd shopping complex boasting a Carrefour. Before hitting Palma, Jan came off one of the slip roads and followed the signs for Via de Cintura. Eaun noted that most of the drivers did not seem that bothered about any speed limits on the motorway, including Jan, who was still talking non-stop to Ludmila in the front of the car, usually at the same time. As the Skoda sped on, Eaun continued to take in the local scenery. An IKEA, sports facilities including a large football stadium with the mountains as the backdrop behind the tall and imposing stand. Eaun also noted that Jan passed what Eaun was fairly sure was a newly-built prison. He wondered whether and hoped that Julian would soon be an inmate of the establishment.

It was just before the car entered a long tunnel that Eaun spotted the sign. Andratx. Where Julian had his holiday home and where he was hopefully holed up with Rita. Eaun could not help but feel a twitch of both nerves and excitement. Everything that had been planned was based on supposition. Julian may not even be on the island.

'I didn't know that we were going straight to where Julian is,' interrupted Eaun.

It was Jan who responded.

'I am sorry. I should have explained. We are going to my house first. Luda wants to see Reme and the kids. We have also a few things to do first.'

'As you can see, Jan speaks excellent English,' said Ludmila.

'I have to,' explained Jan. 'Many of my customers here are what you call, ex pats? Most do not bother to learn Spanish so everyone knows a little bit of English, including me.'

'Really sorry,' added Ludmila. 'Got carried away speaking Polish to Jan. We come out here every summer as a family, but because of coronavirus we see each other far less frequently. There is lots to catch up on!'

'You carry on,' replied Eaun, happy to be looking around and wondering what would be greeting them in Andratx. How were they possibly going to get nearly £5 million back from Julian if the money is in the bank? The further Jan continued, the more nervous Eaun was starting to feel. Were they planning to rob the bank? He did not want to end up the one in the prison with the view of the Via Cintura.

A short while after exiting the tunnel, Jan took an exit from the motorway and quickly entered a town called Cala Major.

Eaun could see flashes of the sea as Jan drove past a long line of supermarkets, bars and cafes. Down a slope with a small harbour on the left sheltering a flotilla of sailing boats and Jan announced that they were nearly there. Calanova.

Up a steep hill and across some narrow streets and Jan pulled up outside an apartment block.

Three minutes later and a further session of hugs and kisses took place in the apartment between Ludmila, Jan, his wife Reme and two young children, the nephew and niece of Ludmila whose names Eaun had already forgotten.

Eaun had no idea where and how she had time to do so, but Ludmila, or Luda as everyone called her here, even had time to hand over a couple of small gifts, to the utter delight of her young relatives.

After coffees and something really tasty called ensaimada had been passed round the room, Ludmila took Eaun aside and guided him out to the terrace. There was a view of the sea and most of the expansive Bay of Palma, where a large blue and white ferry with Balearia painted on its funnel and sides was headed out to the sea.

'Apologies for all of that speaking in Polish. It was rude,' said Ludmila. 'Let me give you a catch up on what has been happening. Jan and his mates have been busy boys.'

Mates? What mates, wondered Eaun.

'As soon as you passed on to me Julian's address in Mallorca, I forwarded that on to Jan. Whilst we were arriving at Bristol airport earlier this morning, Jan and his friends were already carrying out a reconnaissance – is that the right word – mission to Julian's house. It is just off the road between Andratx and Peguera. Up in the hills. Quite palatial apparently but also quite cut off. Jan and the boys are getting quite excited. Jan loves this sort of thing. He also reports that the owner is in residence. Yes!'

Eaun was taken aback at everything that had already been done to set up what was going to happen next. Eaun was also starting to get increasingly uneasy at how he was rapidly getting way out of his depth. What had been lined up for Julian?

'You can leave your overnight bag here at the apartment,' added Ludmila. 'You will not need anything till later and we can pick the bag up when we get back. Let's get ready. We are walking down to Jan's lock up and where we will be meeting the boys. It is also where all the tools are.'

Eaun felt even more unease. What tools were needed to get money from a bank account in someone else's name? Could a hammer unlock a laptop or phone? Eaun thought not but he also knew that at least for now, he had no option but just to go with the flow.

After the goodbyes to Reme and the children, Eaun and Ludmila followed Jan down the stairs and out in to the street below.

'By the way, I have already had several texts and emails from the girls in the office asking whether you are OK. Mr Wainwright specifically says that there is nothing to worry about. Got the feeling that he is really enjoying himself. I was also asked to remind you to make all the calls that you had to make this morning.'

Eaun answered in the affirmative. The calls had all been made.

'Good boy! Everyone in the office is also trying to help my massacred plant. They think that it might live.'

Eaun had no idea what she was talking about but thought that there were probably more important issues ahead.

~ ~ ~

As her brother Jan's lock up started to come in to view, Ludmila started to feel a little guilty. For her employer the last 24 hours had proved an absolute disaster. She had learned that the firm faced something called an Intervention which from what she could find on Google sounded terminal for the firm. Mr Wright also faced the prospect of being disciplined and ultimately being struck off. She did understand what this meant. She knew that this also happened to doctors and other professionals. Eaun also faced complete public humiliation as well as losing everything personally. Her job was in the balance as was the financial security of Grzegorz, Julian and Natalia. Whilst she also stood to lose everything, she was here and enjoying herself on a trip to Spain for a surprise visit to see Jan and his family. More to the point, she also felt excited about what was happening and was enjoying a real buzz. This is not the sort of thing that normally happened working as a receptionist in a solicitors' office in Somerset. However, Ludmila could honestly not recall a better day than she had ever had at work.

As Jan, Ludmila and the following Eaun approached Jan's lock up, the metal rollers were already open and a couple of men in their thirties or forties were leaning against a large black pick-up truck, with two rows of seats in the passenger section and open at the back.

The two men shouted indecipherable greetings to Jan who responded back with a grunt and a wave.

On the way to the lock up, Jan had explained that the two men that they were meeting had been working for him for several years and that he would trust them with his life. Despite the previous holiday visits to Spain, Ludmila had never been allowed to see the work side of what Jan did. This lock up was new and spacious, holding a couple of vehicles and tools, equipment and materials galore. There was even room for a proper table football game by the kitchen at the rear of the unit.

Ludmila was impressed by what her brother had achieved in the 15 years that he had been living in and around Calanova. He had actually bought the apartment, had created a thriving business doing construction, plumbing and electrics and was properly qualified to carry out all of these activities. Jan also had the family talent at being able to speak other languages well, speaking almost fluent Spanish and English as well as Catalan, although Ludmila was not yet very sure how this differed from Spanish. Ludmila also knew that Jan spoke Russian which he had picked up at school when learning Russian was still compulsory.

Jan's two side-kicks were eventually introduced to Eaun and

Ludmila. They both waved a hand and said 'Hola'.

The thinner of Jan's operatives was it turned out called Georgi. He had a shaved head. He was Bulgarian but apparently spoke reasonable English and perfect Russian. He was a plasterer by trade. The larger and the bulkier of the two men was Maxim. He also had a shaved head. Maxim said in slightly hesitant English that he was from near St Petersburg and had been working for Jan for over 5 years doing everything. Maxim pointed to the Zenit badge on his replica shirt and gave a thumbs up.

Ludmila then heard Jan speak to his two boys, in Spanish, going through a check list of items and equipment. The power tools were loaded into the lockable box behind the cabin and the rest, including tin baths, cement and several large plastic containers were hauled on to the back of the truck.

Jan then asked Ludmila whether she had remembered what he had asked her to bring from England. Ludmila smiled and waved her Bristol Airport Duty Free bag in the air.

Finally, Jan threw a sports bag into the back and asked everyone to pile in. Ludmila noticed that Eaun was following whatever everyone else was doing.

Jan slipped in to the driver's seat next to Ludmila. The three men sat in the back row of seats. When everyone was seated Jan turned around and asked Maxim something that Ludmila could not fully understand. Maxim smiled and lifted a small cardboard box to satisfy Jan, who also smiled back. As they started to pull away, Ludmila noticed the metal shutters in the lock up start to automatically roll down and lock.

'A day out in Andratx. Better than a morning with criminals in the Magistrates' Court, eh Mr Wright?' enquired Ludmila, turning round to look at her boss. Eaun returned a weak smile.

A few minutes later and the vehicle was back on the motorway following the signs to Andratx and Port d'Andratx. As the pick-up started to approach a town called Peguera, Jan broke the silence and asked everyone to listen.

'Right, Maxim and Georgi have already been through everything with me so they already know what is happening.

Firstly, Mr Eaun, it is an honour doing this. My sister Luda and her Grzegorz have helped me out of a couple of real bad spots in the past, best that you don't know about. I have been asked to do something for her, so am honoured to help out. This is family.'

Ludmila turned round and gave a broad and knowing smile to Eaun.

'It also sounds pretty crazy as well,' continued Jan. 'However, we don't want this to go how you English say, 'breasts up'. No, 'tits up'. That is why it is really important that all of you do exactly as agreed. That way, no one is going to get hurt.'

Ludmila stared straight ahead. She knew that Eaun behind her would be starting to panic, asking what was this all about, people getting hurt? No one had mentioned anything about anyone getting hurt. However, Ludmila decided to stay quiet. For the remaining ten minutes of the journey before they turned off, Jan spelled out what the task of everyone was. He asked Maxim and Georgi in both Spanish and Russian if they fully understood what they had to do. Both answered with a short and emphatic 'da nachal'nik'. All was good.

Jan then asked Eaun whether he had everything that they would need. Happily, Mr Curtis had already forwarded him all the information that would be needed, which Eaun had also transposed on to a piece of scrap paper that Reme had given to him at Jan and Reme's apartment. The information was of course also on his phone but Eaun felt far safer with the piece of paper.

'Yes,' said Eaun. He wanted to ask about anyone getting hurt, but took the view that this was probably not the best time to do so.

'Sister. Ready to rock and roll?'

'Let the day's sport begin!' responded a visibly excited Ludmila.

'Two minutes and we are there,' announced Jan.

~ ~ ~

Back at The Sedgeton Grange Hotel it was very much the morning after. All of the staff, even those who had been serving at the previous evening's Roman Orgy event, were already at work in the hotel, trailing vacuums after themselves, polishing away the stains of the goblets on the hotel furniture and emptying the outside tubs and Jacuzzis. The several pieces of discarded clothing found both in the gardens and in the house were deposited in a large plastic container marked 'Lost Property'. Any evidence of signage pointing to the Dungeon and Seventh Heaven had already been replaced. The two venues had been made to disappear behind now locked doors.

A steady stream of vans and trucks arrived during the morning in order to collect the laundry baskets, hired glassware, the sound system and of course the Roman costume hire. Today, Thursday, was change over day at The Sedgeton Grange and the whole hotel had to be ready once more looking spotless for the first guests for the Easter weekend as they arrived shortly after 3pm.

Whilst the owners Gustave and Anabel Paterson allowed their staff to get on with readying the hotel for the weekend transformation, they themselves were behind closed and locked doors of the smaller Priddy Conference Suite, which in an earlier life served as the Third Form Junior Common Room.

Gustave had transferred his printed out spread sheets from his office to the main conference room table. They were now dominating most of the table.

It was Gustave who opened the meeting.

'The great news is that as you can see from the figures, it looks like we made a profit from last night, even quite a healthy profit. The late night pay bar collected an extra £1500 on its own. It seems that your idea of a bit of Roman naughtiness really did work, bringing in the denarii.'

Now the not so great news,' continued Gustave. 'It also looks like we now have reputational and other issues, which is why this meeting is taking place behind closed doors. Basically, the whole future of The Sedgeton Grange is now at risk. I am afraid that it really is that serious.'

It was now the turn of Anabel to speak. On the journey into work with Gus that morning, she had not uttered a word in the Mercedes SUV.

'The night was a brilliant success. The members loved it. When they were leaving, they were all saying that we should do another orgy evening as soon as possible. As usual, you are just trying to put me down and take the credit for everything.'

Gustave let a few seconds elapse before responding.

'Let us be quite clear what happened here last night. Who was it that let us down at the last minute? Your Aunt Cressida. These professorial academic types have always been completely unreliable and an utter waste of time. And who was it responsible for getting the drunken sex pest architect invited along as a replacement? I am afraid that is down to you again, dear Anabel. We have always prided ourselves on the members' midweek evenings being good clean fun, which up until the appearance of your friend Mr Hudderston last night, they generally have been. No one has ever had any issue with a bit of good honest slap and tickle. Assaulting, chasing, molesting and terrifying our female membership and then exhibiting his manhood in such an inappropriate manner at the pool in front of our polite, pleasant god-fearing membership is however crossing a red line. Any red line. There is something else that you should know about your favourite local Roman architecture expert.'

Anabel stared at the ground as Gus searched through a separate pile of data print out papers.

'Here it is,' Gus was pressing down his finger on the thin paper as he squinted to read the small print. 'Yes, it seems that according to our membership database, Mr Hudderston has twice applied for membership here and twice has been refused. A real rarity. The Membership Committee's comments are 'something pervy' about him and 'he just gives me the creeps'. So much for due diligence.'

Anabel was about to protest but Gus was in his stride.

'Further, we have to assume that the event was witnessed by the police officer, DC Hooligan or whatever the name was on the warrant card, which by the way looked very real indeed to me. Have you any conception of all the hard work and effort it took to get the Licensing conditions that we have? Not only is our licence at stake but we may even be subject to a criminal investigation thanks to your wayward invitations. It gets even worse. Following the comments from the Hooligan woman, as well as the membership database I actually checked the staff records this morning. We do of course have the dates of birth of all our members of staff. Right from the off we have also made it a rule that all staff working at the midweek sessions must be over 18. It seems that because we had a full house last night, at least a couple of 17 year olds were drafted in not only to serve alcohol but also to prance around with their pert little bums on show to everyone. This it seems included one of our 17 year old cleaners, Brittany, apparently only too keen to get kitted out as a waitress with her backside on display but who is still re-taking her GCSEs. I can hardly believe it.'

'I have spoken to the staff,' responded Anabel. 'They all had a lovely evening and appreciated the generous bonus payments as well. I have had no complaints from any of them, particularly the youngsters and that includes Brittany. You always try to ruin everything.'

'Anabel, I love you to bits but sometimes I really don't know what to do. If this police officer was to take this issue further I will tell you what will happen. We will be shut down. Finished. What you refer to as 'youngsters' are in fact as far as the law is concerned, children. That is the legal word. Children. I have looked it up on Google. How is it going to look on the front page of the tabloids, 'Children offer nudity and alcohol at booze-fuelled Roman Orgy".

Gustave had more to say, but decided to pause. Anabel's eyes were becoming moist and she started to slowly sob.

'You know that we have never done any harm to anyone so why are you saying these wicked things?' asked Anabel. 'We have also dropped dear Julian into trouble, although I don't know what trouble.'

Gus had almost forgotten about Julian Darby-Henderson. What was all that about a multi-million pound theft and the police and his partner wanting to know the address in Spain? It had nothing to do with Gus. Before coming in to work, out of old loyalty to Jools, he tried to call him on his mobile to at least let him know that the police had been sniffing around making wild allegations against him. His phone just went straight to voicemail where Gus left a message for Julian to call him back. To date, he hadn't.

Gus moved his chair up next to Anabel. She was still producing the odd deep sob so that her whole body shook. He put his arm around his wife.

'Look, we have been on stickier wickets before. I think that I know a way forward on this one,' Gus said. 'Just give me a little time to sort things.'

Anabel offered a silent sob and a nod in agreement in response.

Gus, trailing his multiple spread sheets behind him, then stood up, unlocked the door of the Priddy Suite and walked over to his own office. There was a whirr of domestic machinery reverberating around the inside of the hotel as all the staff were working towards the 3pm deadline. On the chair by his desk in the office was a telephone message that had been left for him.

The message was from DC Denise Halloran from the CID in Yeovil. She wanted to speak 'properly' to both Mr and Mrs Paterson at a later time but in the meantime could Mr Paterson have all his personnel files ready for DC Halloran to pick up and take away with her later in the day.

It was looking like Gustave Patterson had a lot less time to 'sort things' than he could ever have imagined.

Through the window of his office, Gustave also noted that those hopeless equipment hire people had failed to collect their cage. One more thing to sort.

THE SPANISH INQUISITION:
MALLORCAN STYLE

O N LEAVING the main Paguera to Andratx road, Jan had driven his truck along several country lanes, each becoming narrower, rougher and dustier. Eventually, he found a small parking space off the track. He stopped.

'This is where we checked things out earlier this morning. Señor Henderson has his villa just round the corner facing the next valley, but if we walk up the hill we can see everything, including whether anybody is at home.'

Maxim got out of the vehicle as Jan signalled for him to follow.

'The rest of you stay here,' ordered Jan as he and Maxim disappeared through the sparse bushes and up the hill.

Jan had only been gone a few minutes when the heat of the sun beating on the unshaded roof of the truck forced all of the passengers to seek the breeze and tree shade of the outside. Eaun thought that it was now getting surprisingly warm and he could already feel the skin on his sensitive scalp start to burn. He then remembered that the Factor 30 was back in his overnight bag at Reme and Jan's apartment.

Ten minutes later Jan and Maxim had returned.

'All okay,' said Jan. 'Señor Henderson and the senora are both at home and by the pool. Looks like they have just had lunch and are about to sleep it off by the pool in the spring sunshine. The site is perfect. Between here and the villa there are no other residences. No one will hear anything. There is also excellent WiFi connection here. I checked this morning. We can drive the truck to the entrance of the villa. Come on, let's go.'

Everyone climbed in to the same seats that they had occupied previously. Jan edged along slowly. He was right. There were no other houses near here at all, only some grazing goats and sheep that Eaun managed to spot.

Jan drove down a couple of hundred yards. As the truck came to a halt, Eaun noticed the sign by the entrance. 'L'Amagatall'.

'What does that mean in English?' asked Eaun.

'It is Catalan. Not 100% sure but think that it means the hidden place or the hideaway, something like that,' responded Jan.

'Not hidden away bloody well enough,' Eaun shot back.

Jan asked everyone to remain where they were whilst he performed a 5 point turn for his vehicle, so that it now faced the direction that they had just come from.

'Sure that a quick getaway will not be required but if it is, then we are all set,' announced Jan. 'Right, let's get moving.'

It took Jan, Georgi and Maxim some time to unload everything that they wanted from the back of the truck into large bags, ready for transportation around the corner and towards the villa. Eaun wondered what on earth the dented old tin bath, the sort of rubbish that you would see for sale for an extortionate £200 at the Artisans' Market in Sedgeton, was doing here on a Mallorcan hillside.

Jan and his boys declined the offers from Ludmila and Eaun to help carry anything. Everyone was now walking along the dirt drive into Julian's villa. As Eaun looked around, all he could hear were the crickets under the warming sun. There were indeed no other houses or sign of anyone else. A proper hideaway. The approach road to the villa then came to a fork, with outhouses on the left and the main dirt driveway sloping down to the villa itself. Eaun could see flashes of shining sun on water reflected from a swimming pool. Jan was leading the way but turned and faced everyone urging them to keep low and be quiet.

Jan then started to quietly issue orders to Maxim and Georgi. Eaun was fairly sure that he was speaking Russian but languages were never Eaun's strong point.

When he was finished, he turned his attention to his sister and Eaun.

'Right, Maxim and I are going in first. When we are ready we will come back and get you all to come down to the villa. However, at no time do you speak one word whilst in the villa. Leave that to me, Maxim and Georgi. And at no time do you take your uniform off.'

Uniform? Eaun thought to himself.

It was at this point that Jan took the sports bag off his shoulder.

'Courtesy of the Fancy Dress shop in S'Arenal,' said Jan, who then pulled out 5 pairs of rubber gloves plus the same number of identical Tina Turner hair wigs, followed by five large individual face masks of Batman, Mickey Mouse. The Joker, Pluto and Donald Trump. 'Right, everyone get changed.'

By the time that Eaun had reached the haul, the only face mask left was that of Donald Trump. He tried it on for size. It fitted fine but as always when Eaun had to wear any mask, he hated it, being unable to see properly through the tiny slits that were supposed to be eye sights. No wonder jousting knights hardly ever managed to hit their opponents. As soon as he put the Tina Turner wig on, it started to itch his already partly reddened scalp. The rubber gloves felt damp and sweaty immediately he had slipped them on.

When everyone had dressed, Eaun found it genuinely difficult to tell who was who. It was only when he spoke that Jan identified himself as being Batman.

Jan approached Eaun and Ludmila.

'Right, you two just wait here till one of us comes to get you. Look after the kit. No one should be coming to visit the villa but any problems then text me. Ludmila has my number of course.'

Then Maxim, Georgi and Jan were gone, taking with them just some coils of rope.

Eaun was starting to feel sick to his stomach. Sick at the thought that others were doing all this to help him (and he supposed a little bit for Ludmila as well), but also sick at what was actually happening. Did they even have the right house? What was all this kit they had brought with them? A drill is not going to be able to unscrew millions of stolen pounds from a bank account. Eaun also felt scared for himself. Eaun may well have voted Green and Lib Dem in the past. Twice he had voted for Tony Blair and at the local elections he had even voted for the cricket club vice-captain who was standing as a Tory candidate. But at heart he knew he was a conservative with a small 'c' who was risk-averse. He was a partner in a law firm in a small market town in the West Country. He remembered his title as described on his Practising Certificate. Solicitor and Officer of the Supreme Court of the Judicature. Eaun was fairly sure that the Supreme Court of the Judicature would be asking him serious questions as to why he was wearing a Tina Turner wig and disguised as Donald Trump with a load of tools and a tin bath hidden behind an outhouse in Mallorca. Eaun admitted to himself that he was actually scared. If this goes wrong then it could be Eaun who was in that jail that he had seen on the way from the airport. Being struck off might be the very least of his problems.

He looked across at Pluto.

'Exciting!' said Ludmila as she clapped her hands gently with the rubber gloves and yet managed to restrain herself from looking around the corner of the outhouse to see what was happening below.

The wait for the others seemed interminable. There was just the accompanying loud crickets and Eaun and Ludmila's own breathing through the face masks that could be heard. Eaun supposed that it was good news that there had so far been no screams, shouting or sound of gunshots. However, anxiety soon returned. What happens if the stolen money has already been transferred?

Eventually, a head popped round the corner gesturing to them. It was Mickey Mouse but Eaun had already forgotten whether it was Georgi or Maxim.

'Vamos,' ordered Mickey Mouse. Eaun grabbed the tin bath which luckily was not too heavy. The others grabbed the assorted bags and boxes.

Eaun followed the other two.

So, this was it. In front of the party of three was a splendid villa built in an L shape, surrounding a pool overlooking the valley below and the sea and Port d'Andratx way beyond in the distance. It was only April but already the gardens and the many flower pots were a burst of colour under the by now azure sky. By the pool there were loungers, drinks and various sun tan lotions on the matching poolside tables. By one of the loungers a paperback lay face down on the tiled surrounds. But of Julian and Rita, there was no sign.

Mickey Mouse/Maxim signalled to Ludmila and Eaun to stay outside and wait for his signal before coming through the set of open doors leading from the swimming pool terrace into the villa itself.

Whilst waiting for Mickey Mouse to give the signal, Eaun then saw the car. Not the Hertz hire car from the airport that was parked in the bay just above the pool, but the magnificent gleaming red convertible parked alongside it. Eaun's lack of knowledge of anything to do with engines was legendary, but even he recognised that it was a Jaguar E Type. Eaun felt a surge of relief. He knew that at least they were at the correct house. The vehicle with its GB plates could only have belonged to Julian.

It was at this point that Mickey Mouse signalled for Eaun and Ludmila to come into the villa. They both made their way to the back of a large spacious room, filled with quality furniture, paintings and framed photos. Mickey Mouse gestured for them both to remain at the back of the room and not to move. They were standing on a thick rug. In front of Eaun at the other side of the room sat Julian and Rita. They were seated next to each other, with their hands and ankles tied with rope. Julian looked ridiculous. He was always in reasonably good physical shape but the budgie smugglers that he was wearing made him look comical as his stomach spilled over the top of his Speedos. Next to him was Rita. Eaun hardly recognised her in the two piece swimsuit and with a new short hairstyle which Eaun thought made her look several years younger. Any Peyton Place look had disappeared. Eaun had never considered Rita as anything other than his Practice Manager, but here she was looking even quite attractive in a funny sort of way. Eaun also noticed that she must also have been escorted straight from her sun-bathing session to the cream sofa that she was now seated on, as the copious amounts of dark oil that she must have applied to her skin was now spread all over the sofa fabric.

No one spoke as Mickey Mouse and The Joker lined up a series of drills and other tools on the table in front of the sofa where both Julian and Rita were tied up and seated. Eaun had to convince himself that as far as both of them were concerned, they were looking at Donald Trump, not Eaun.

Eaun looked at the photographs around the room. Most of the pictures involved Julian, either at his villa and garden here in Mallorca or on a sailing boat with three or four friends. There were also pictures of Julian that had clearly been taken in England, receiving various awards or decorations at either what seemed to be golf clubs or black tie events. One black and white framed print showed Julian shaking hands with the forever grinning 'Mac' MacBain, in front of a Business Means Business banner. He recognised a few other faces on the photos, including those of Gustave and Anabel who had of course just betrayed his whereabouts only the day before.

Eaun was wondering where Jan was, when he walked in from one of the back doors carrying a laptop. He expected Jan to take the lead from here but it was Mickey Mouse who did so.

Mickey already had a deep voice which when speaking in slow broken English with a heavy Russian accent, sounded positively threatening.

'We find your laptop Mr Henson,' said Mickey. I get straight to point. You stole 5 million British pounds. Everybody on island knows this.'

Mickey paused. Both Rita and Julian were staring at the floor. Sweat was starting to drip down Julian's face. In the meantime, the tin bath and the big plastic containers had been moved by Batman and The Joker to behind the sofa where the two captives were seated. Eaun could hear the sound of liquid being poured into the bath but from where they were seated neither Julian nor Rita could see anything. The liquid must have been what was in the plastic containers that they had brought with them. Eaun then saw the cardboard box that Maxim had kept carefully on his lap on the journey out to Andratx. He then heard a plop as whatever was in the box hit the liquid in the tin bath, still concealed behind the sofa. Finally, Eaun saw a flash of Ludmila's Duty Free bag from Bristol airport and three further splashes followed by loud fizzing, popping and cracking.

Eaun looked across where Ludmila was standing with her Pluto mask on. He could see Pluto nod vociferously and Ludmila clutch both her hands showing the thumbs up sign to Eaun. What on earth had got in to the girl?

As Batman and The Joker had been attending to the bath behind the sofa, Mickey Mouse had been putting on a large black rubber apron and top, before pulling on an additional pair of rubber gloves that extended well past his elbow. He then leaned against the wall and stepped into a pair of industrial rubber wellington boots. Mickey was now covered in black rubber. Even Eaun started to feel intimidated and a little terrified.

By now, Eaun had noticed that the sweat running down his partner Julian's face was mixed with tears. For heaven's sake, he had started to blub. Rita remained with her eyes firmly fixed to the ground. The mascara or whatever the stuff women put round their eyes had started to create small rivulets running down her cheeks, but otherwise she remained with her fixed stare.

Mickey Mouse was now standing in front of the two tied and trapped captives.

However, it was Batman, alias Jan, who spoke next. He started speaking in a Slavic language, he assumed that it was Russian or Polish, before then switching to a most heavily accented and hardly decipherable English. He addressed the two captive figures in front of him.

'Good afternoon. Let me be quick. You two have stolen a big amount of money. We know about it. We want it. If you give us the money now we will not kill you both. We are Russian. We are reasonable people.'

Eaun started to tense. No one mentioned anything about threatening to kill anyone. All of this was going way too far. For a moment, he almost blurted out to Jan to stop it there. However, Eaun was also transfixed. In front of him was also the man who had plotted Eaun's professional and financial downfall. He felt torn between wanting to set Julian free and starting off himself on his kneecaps with one of the waiting drills.

'I will ask you just the once. If you don't tell me how to access the money then I will have to ask my friend Mickey here to start asking the questions. With myself,' Jan explained, 'I just work with drills and chisels. What do you English call this sort of method of extracting information? Old school. That is it. Old school.'

The accent was extremely convincing. Eaun was impressed.

However, there was still no information forthcoming from either Rita or Julian.

'I tell you what. Still don't want to tell me anything? Then we should begin.'

There was then a silence as Batman pulled the table with the tools on it away from the front of the cream sofa and in its place spread out some thick plastic sheeting.

'We don't want what looks like a nice Persian carpet ruined with acid, blood or other bodily fluids, do we? A shame, looks like I will have to wait my turn with the drills. Mr Mouse, over to you.'

With that, Mickey Mouse and The Joker appeared carrying the large old tin bath. It was now half filled with a greyish fermenting liquid, with what looked like sizzling foam literally bubbling on the surface. Even from where Eaun was standing at the back of the room, the contents of the tub smelled putrid.

Mickey started to speak, with a deep bass growl.

'You want to know why Mickey now dress like? It very dangerous. Anything gets on my clothes it will burn right through the skin and then start to eat the flesh. Rubber only thing that works. Excuse language. Big respect to drills but no old school fuck about here with Mickey. Acid works quick and good. You most welcome to new school methods.'

The atmosphere in the room changed immediately. Even Rita had moved her stare away from the carpet to the contents of the tin bath. She was also starting to cram her body in to the corner of the sofa where she was trapped, spreading even more of the sun tan oil over the cream fabric and leaving a brown trail behind her.

It was then that The Joker and Batman swung a length of rope over the old oak beam running across the centre of the room. Julian was yanked from the sofa by both The Joker and Batman, who then tied the rope around the already bound wrists of Julian. A couple of hefty yanks on the rope and Julian was suspended in mid-air, with the tin bath resting just a couple of metres away.

'Thank you for first volunteer,' said Mickey Mouse. 'Mr English, I will show you acid bath. How it works. Everybody should have one. This morning in my cellar a rat felled on my bath. I brought it here to show you.'

Mickey had walked across the room and picked up a poker and pair of tongs from in front of the open fire. He then slowly returned to where the tin bath was, closely inspecting the tongs and the poker in his hands. Mickey then swirled the poker around the foul liquid, as if looking for something. He then plunged in the tongs and extracted from the grey liquid a small object that he then dropped on the plastic sheeting right in front of Julian and Rita.

At first, Eaun had no idea what it was from the distance. It was just a small white and pink mass, before he realised that what he was looking at was what was left of a rat that had most of its fur and insides burned and corroded by acid. He felt sick looking at the skeletal remains that somehow still had the odd bit of fur attached to the cadaver. The rodent's jaw and teeth were sparkling white.

The effect on Julian was instantaneous. His blubbing had now accelerated to uncontrolled screams and gasping for breath. Eaun had never seen any man truly terrified before. Eaun himself was gripped with fear as to what would happen next. If he was terrified then how on earth was Julian feeling?

Mickey Mouse spoke again.

'All you have to do is to tell us where the money is being safely kept, transfer it to us and we will then go away. We are reasonable people. Very reasonable.'

Eaun thought that Julian was trying to say something but he was physically unable to get out any words, between the shakes, sobs and trembles.

There then came a voice, but from a place where Eaun least expected it.

'Don't tell him a bloody thing Julian,' demanded Rita. 'They are bluffing. They will do nothing to you. We have not worked for all of this for some jumped up Russian cowboys pretending to be hard men to then take it all away from us. Say nothing!'

Eaun recalled part of the conversation in the pick-up truck between Ludmila and her brother. They were speaking in English, maybe for Eaun's benefit. Jan had asked Ludmila which of Julian and Rita was the hardest. Eaun remembered Ludmila not even hesitating in her reply. She said that Julian was the soft touch and they would get nothing from Rita. It seemed that Ludmila had been correct in her judgement. Nevertheless, Eaun was still taken aback at how his Practice Manager had reacted.

Mickey Mouse by now had had enough.

'Then it looks like Show Time!' he announced with glee as he told Batman and The Joker to stay out of harm's way whilst he alone dragged the tin bath along the slippery plastic sheet covering to right under the body of Julian, who in order to prevent his feet coming in to any contact with the still bubbling and fizzing liquid immediately below, now had to keep his bent calves touching his thighs behind him. As his body now took the full strain of his body, there was now nowhere for Julian to place his feet.

Julian's face and whole upper torso was now soaked in sweat. His head was red and looked like it was going to explode. The sobbing and trembling had now changed in to a whimper and pleas for Mickey Mouse to just stop.

Regretfully for Julian, Mickey was by now well in to his stride with his new school methodology.

'We can start with the feet, as you can see. The record up to now is 17 minutes for someone to keep his legs in the air without dropping them,' advised Mickey. 'When you hit the acid, within seconds your skin will be removed. We can then move on to your hands and then finally your face. Lady friend here then no fancy you as much.'

A few moments later, Eaun noticed with acute embarrassment that Julian had wet himself. The accident was not immediately apparent as his whole body was bathed in sweat and fear, but the budgie smugglers were not able to lie.

Eaun himself had reached the limit. The whole idea of coming out here was insane. He should be letting the police deal with everything. He was about to move forward and have a word with Jan to call the whole thing off, when he received a sharp kick in the legs from Pluto who was also admonishing him with a finger.

Happily for Eaun, it was at this point that Julian had enough breath in him to mutter that he would do as they asked. He just wanted to be let down.

Through the eye slits of his Donald Trump mask, Eaun was just about to make out that Rita was staring up at her lover with contempt.

Mickey Mouse carefully pulled the tin bath away and both he and The Joker undid one of the knots on the rope and eased Julian on to the plastic sheeting on the carpet where he curled up in a ball. What remained of the rat remained where it had been earlier dropped, a few feet away from Julian's eyes.

As Julian lay by himself for a few minutes, Mickey went over to the other side of the room. Eaun heard a chink of glass and saw him return with what looked like a large brandy in a thick based tumbler. The drink was offered to Julian who sat up and quickly downed the alcohol.

'There. Mickey tell you. We Russians not unreasonable people. Now you must tell us. If no. Next time upside down.'

Jan then invited Julian to sit down again on the cream sofa. Julian still had his wrists and ankles bound so Jan helped him up. Julian was gesticulating to be put at the furthest corner away from Rita. Eaun then saw Jan, alias Batman, position himself on the sofa between Rita and Julian, managing to avoid the sun tan lotion trail left by Rita.

On Jan's lap, Eaun recognised the laptop that he had seen Jan take from a room at the rear of the villa.

'Look what I also managed to find in your desk drawer,' said Jan as he showed Julian the digital secure key with the Banca Calvia logo stamped on it. The match-box sized slim device had a display of numbers, coded buttons and a small screen.

There was a wait of several minutes as the machine warmed up. In this age of instant everything, Eaun was still at a loss as to why we still had to wait for a laptop to boot-up or whatever the phrase was. Eaun could also feel the sweat run down his own face under the Donald Trump face mask and the itch of Tina Turner's hair on his scalp was starting to become intolerable. The moment of whether all of this madness had been worthwhile was about to arrive.

Eventually, Jan gave a nod of approval.

'Right mi amigo, I have now keyed in to <u>www.bancacalvia. es</u> and I am now on their internet banking section. It tells me that we must type in your account name and also your password.'

Even from the other side of the room, Eaun could see that although they were still tied, Julian's hands were shaking uncontrollably. Jan would have to enter the information himself.

'Well, Julian let us start with the account name.'

'Rita Thornham and Julian Darby hyphen Henderson. In

that order.'

Eaun could hear Jan hitting the keys before turning to Julian.

'Regretfully, it tells me that the account name is incorrect,' said Jan. 'What a shame. Señor Mouse, get the acid bath ready once more.'

'No, no, no!' begged Julian. There must be a mistake. Do you understand hyphen? No?'

Eaun was once more reprimanded by a raised finger from the disguised Ludmila just as he was about to step forward and offer to help Julian.

'Here, this is how you spell my name,' as Julian moved his head towards a small table by the front door with some unopened post on it. The Joker brought a couple of envelopes over for Jan to look at.

'Thank you, Mr Julian. We no have hyphens in Russia,' thanked a grateful Jan. 'Password now please.'

'Don't be such a stupid prick Julian,' hissed Rita from her corner. 'Don't you dare bloody tell them.'

When Rita had finished, Jan absent-mindedly picked up one of his drills from the nearby table and turned on the hammer function as he hit the 'On' button. The machine gave a deafening screaming sound before Jan turned it off.

'I am ready to proceed, Mr Julian.'

By now however, even from where Eaun was standing at the other end of the room, Julian looked a defeated man.

'LAMAGATALL1968 with the letters all in upper case. Capitals.'

'There, that wasn't too painful, was it,' encouraged Jan. 'However, next time you try something like this, if there is a next time, you will have to do a bit better than the name of your love nest and your or Rita's year of birth.'

Eaun assumed after what he had witnessed that afternoon, that Rita took precedence on most things involving Julian.

Within a few minutes, Jan had easily found the relevant account at the bank and after keying in the date 1968 and the resultant other security numbers on Julian's fob, the amount in the account flashed up once he had pushed the Transacciones Recientes button. Jan then deliberately shoved the screen within inches of Rita's face so she could see the figures clearly, before getting up from the sofa and bringing the laptop over to Eaun and Ludmila.

'All yours from here. You will need the security key as well.'

This was the moment of truth. Eaun looked at the screen, where the account said that there were Euros 5,267,874 currently resting there. For a second, Eaun could not understand how there was more than five million there, before realising that the original amount had been transferred from Sterling in to Euros. Eaun's hands were also starting to shake, nearly as badly as Julian's were. As Mr Curtis had suggested might happen, all of the money was still in the account and had not yet been moved. Eaun wanted to scream with joy. Ludmila must have anticipated this so applied a further hack to Julian's leg to ensure that he said nothing.

Julian and Rita were by now starting to exchange words between each other as Ludmila used the opportunity of putting her Pluto mask next to Eaun's ear and offering to do the next stage herself if Eaun handed her the information given to him by Mr Curtis. Eaun was still shaking and was delighted for someone else to take responsibility.

With his shaking hands he was finding it difficult to turn his phone on, even before he was able to start looking for the relevant message from Mr Curtis. Instead, relieved and not a little surprised at his own forethought, Eaun retrieved from his pocket the information on the piece of paper from Reme's flat and handed it to Ludmila.

Ludmila moved quickly. Still on Rita and Julian's Banca Calvia account, she then clicked on Nuevos Pagos. As a new payee on Julian and Rita' account at the Banca Calvia, Ludmila would first of all have to key in the account details. With Eaun looking on, Ludmila keyed in the new payee recipient as being 'Holding Account:/:European Banking Services'. She then typed in the 6 number bank code and the 8 numbered account as instructed by Mr Curtis. Everything was then confirmed by the yellow button on the digital key.

'You happy with all this?' asked Ludmila, just above a whisper. Eaun nodded. He did not have a clue, but what Ludmila had done had looked pretty good.

Eaun could then see Ludmila return to the payments page where she asked for the total amount of Euros 5,267,874 to be paid immediately to the new payee whose details she had just entered and confirmed. She also keyed in the reference of Somerset Cider, as requested by Mr Curtis.

'You agree?' said Ludmila in hushed tones, although at the other end of the room, Rita was still directing venomous comments at her lover.

Everything looked fine to Eaun who was by now too nervous to really take any of it in. He asked Ludmila to double check once more herself.

'I don't need to, it is correct,' she firmly but quietly responded. 'Send?'

'Send,' whispered Eaun in reply, without looking at the screen.

The Send button pushed, a quick look back to Rita and Julian's Transacciones Recientes page confirmed that the amount in their account was nil. The whole of what had been in there a few minutes earlier was now on the way to Mr Curtis and the bank in England, if indeed it had not already flashed up on Mr Curtis' screen.

Ludmila nodded to Jan and took the laptop back to the still tied Rita and Julian. Jan held the screen in front of both so that they could see the nil balance for themselves.

'Spasibo. Spasibo,' Jan told them both. 'Maybe on next occasion you try when banks are not shut in Spain on national bank holiday day. Maybe time to find new career?'

Mission accomplished, Jan gestured to his colleagues to start collecting everything and get ready to move on out.

'Mickey, just chuck the acid in the swimming pool, which is where the laptop and the security key are about to go.'

Eaun was one of the last of the party to leave the room when he heard Julian's pleas to be released from being tied up.

'Leave them,' said Jan as he walked out on to the terrace and hurled the laptop and key in to the deep end of the pool.

Eaun was still feeling nauseous and was still visibly shaking, but he was also wondering how Julian and Rita did not even start to guess that two of their work colleagues had witnessed what had happened. Jan had done an excellent job.

Eaun eventually reached the parked up pick-up truck facing the right way back towards the Peguera and Andratx road. Just as everything had been loaded in to the truck, Ludmila gave a sudden shout of Kurva! and ran off back towards the villa. Eaun had no idea what she was up to. He imagined that she might have become merciful and decided to release them, or worse, commit some ghastly bodily harm to either or both of them. Everyone had by now packed their face masks, wigs and gloves back in Jan's sports bag, but no one else seemed perturbed at Ludmila running off like that.

However, Eaun definitely was concerned, particularly as they had achieved everything that they had set out to do. So, he ran after her. It was just as he reached the curve of the dusty drive leading in to the villa complex that Eaun saw Ludmila. She was up on the raised parking lot by the side of the convertible Jaguar. The handbrake had clearly been released, the driver's door was open and Ludmila was pushing the vehicle with all her might towards the garden slope that led down to the pool, with one hand steering the leather driving wheel. With a final effort from Ludmila, the Jaguar gathered momentum on the slope before Ludmila let go as the car demolished the bed of geraniums before hurtling past the spring-diving board and splashing into the deep end of the pool, the Jaguar's iconic bonnet creating a large wave that caused the water to cascade over the sides of the pool and envelop all of the surrounds, taking the soaked paperback in its wake. With the driver's door open and the roof already down, the Jaguar took in water rapidly, before starting to sink in a film of filthy oil and leaking petrol. Eaun then saw Ludmila turn and shout 'Yes, Yes. Yes!' and run back towards where Eaun was, pumping her fists. By the time Eaun had decided to follow Ludmila back to Jan's vehicle, he took one final look back. Only the Jaguar's elongated bonnet was above the surface, as it too slowly began to sink.

'Yes!' shouted Eaun as he also ran back to where the others were by now waiting for him. He had stopped shaking.

~ ~ ~

Alex had actually started to enjoy her day as honorary receptionist at WHW Legal. She managed to catch up with most of her police station paper work and had even started to prepare for the cases coming up after the Easter break. As well as taking the many phone calls that came in, Alex had to admit that she also enjoyed the interaction of speaking to both clients and potential clients as they came through the door.

As lunchtime approached, a familiar figure entered the office. Sammy Ferguson, today wearing a fetching green top with intermittent brown gravy-like stains down the front. On her sockless feet, Sammy Ferguson was wearing a pair of Green Flashes. Alex had picked up the message from Ludmila taken the previous day, when Mrs Ferguson was asking Alex to get back in touch with her. Luckily, earlier that morning, as part of her general work catch-up, Alex had at least tried to call Sammy Ferguson back. The phone was engaged so Alex left a simple message that she had called as requested.

'Morning Mrs Ferguson,' said Alex, getting her retaliation in first. 'I did call you this morning. Honest. Check out your messages.'

Sammy ignored her.

'That foreigner woman with the funny name that you lot normally have sitting here, did she tell you what it was all about? Wessex Constabulary. Always had it in for I and my family. What are you lot going to do about it. And where is Mr Wright to? Not here? Again? If I was buying a house or was one of those coffin dodgers come in to make a Will, then he would be all over me like a rash. He doesn't care about us lot.'

Alex knew that most solicitors would have given up on Mrs Ferguson a long time ago and that she would not be welcome through the door. Alex also knew that Sammy Ferguson had figured that over the years WHW Legal had done far more than could have ever have been expected in looking after both her and her family's liberties. However, on each and every meeting it had become necessary for Sammy Ferguson to go through her introductory rant. Rant over, Sammy Ferguson was now able to move forward.

'How can I help?' asked Alex.

'It is our Henry. Being harassed every day. What the Wessex Constabulary is up to is outrageous. He has fucking done nothing wrong as well. Suspect that your foreign colleague didn't understand properly.'

Biting her lip, Alex explained that Mrs Ferguson would have been understood by everyone in the office. However, Alex used the opportunity to advise her client on what to do if her son Henry was stopped in the future and that if he was ever arrested then she should call for Alex without delay.

'At least I get something done with you Alex,' retorted Sammy. 'More than I ever get from that 'too good for the likes of you' Mr Wright. Happy Easter and see you soon.'

With a click of the door and a brief wave and smile, that was it and Sammy Ferguson was gone.

Alex had little doubt however that she would indeed be seeing Mrs Ferguson soon.

After lunch, one of the firm's conveyancing clients came in with a query as to why the agents had not yet released the keys to their new property. Alex got a message to Douglas Wainwright who said that he would come down and sort. Two minutes later, the concerned looking clients were ushered in to the waiting area by Mr Wainwright and after a phone call had been made, everyone was happy and the clients were leaving through the door with smiles on their faces.

'You really look in your element and like you are having a great time,' commented Alex.

'Absolutely,' said Douglas Wainwright. 'Never actually realised how much I miss work. You should also know, that I have just taken a direct call from the bank's Mr Curtis. Nice chap. He said that he had yet to hear from Eaun but as I have a very personal interest in what is happening, including personal guarantees, he thought that we should know that the bank's international desk in London has just received over 5 million Euros in their Holding Account. He confirmed that the amount was from an account at the Banca Calvia in Mallorca. He also confirmed that the amount received is nearly everything that was originally taken, less some commission charges. It hasn't sunk in yet. We are still not yet out of the woods, there is still a long way to go, but this is absolutely marvellous news. No idea what Eaun and Ludmila have been up to in the Balearics, but it has made me a very happy man.'

Alex could see that Douglas Wainwright was threatening to become emotional. It was hardly surprising. He also had everything to lose.

'That is brilliant news!' said Alex. It was indeed brilliant news for everyone.

'Have two more completions to do and also to pass on the great news to Madge and Felicity,' responded the consultant and former owner as he sprang up the stairs to what was now surely Julian's former office.

Before returning to her work, Alex heard her mobile buzzing in her handbag. She retrieved her phone and looked at the screen. It was a text message from Ludmila.

~ ~ ~

On the journey from Julian's villa back to Calanova, all of those inside Jan's pick up truck were buzzing. Eaun picked up the few bits of English, but most seemed to be in excited Russian, Spanish or Polish. Eaun was happy to be left alone for a while.

He felt physically and emotionally completely drained. He could hardly believe what he had witnessed. His feelings towards Julian were still stuck on utter puzzlement. After over 20 years, why had he betrayed Eaun and all his other colleagues? He had to assume that Julian thought that he had got away with it. Another day and the millions would have been safely hidden in a Swiss bank account. But why trash his reputation? That could never be recovered.

He was equally as puzzled about Rita Thornham. He still had the image of her staining and spreading Julian's sofa with the sun oil as she sought to sit as far apart from her lover as possible. Maybe he would learn more over the passage of time.

In the meantime, Jan's vehicle had arrived back at his lock up and the shutters had already started to roll up as they approached. Five minutes later and everything, including the tin bath was safely stored away in the workshop.

Before anyone had time to disperse, Jan made an announcement.

'Right, everyone down to the Bellver Restaurant,' he said. 'You all know where it is, just down past the yacht harbour on the front. Ludmila says that another one of her bosses, a Señor Wainreed is paying. Hurrah for Luda's bosses! Luda, go down with the boys and I will get Reme and the kids and join you in five minutes.'

Ludmila nodded but first pulled Eaun aside. 'Right, don't worry about the money, Douglas gave me Euros so that we could at least look after people at this end. Jan, Maxim and Georgi have already become irate at any suggestion that they be paid. Anyway, they all say that they had the best time ever!'

'Before you decide to join in the party,' added Ludmila, 'you need to make those phone calls to Mr Curtis at the bank, the fraud squad man and also that Mr Facker or Mr Fucker at the Solicitors people. You might also want to call the insurance people as well. You know who I mean. I will contact the office and let them know what is happening. Now off you go, find a quiet place to make your calls and see you at the restaurant in a few minutes.'

There was a kid's playground down the hill just before the road running parallel to the yacht harbour. However, there were no kids. He looked at his phone. Just after 4pm Spanish time. They must still be having their siestas or were at home anyway playing on their computer games like kids everywhere else. In England it was still mid-afternoon.

After what they had tried to do to him, Eaun was struggling as to why he cared at all about Rita and Julian in particular. He just did not want them to come to physical harm or even worse.

After finding some shade to protect his ever reddening scalp, he called Steve first, Denise's colleague at the fraud office at the Wessex Constabulary HQ whom he had spoken to on Wednesday evening. 'I am now big buddies with my new Interpol mate Rafa in Palma. As well as discussing the relevant merits of Luis Saurez since his latest move, we have also been exchanging notes on who has to cope with the biggest crims,' said Steve. 'Think that he may be ahead on points,' explained Steve.

'Well, how has your holiday been?' Steve went on to ask Eaun.

Eaun explained that all had gone well and it looked like most of the money had been hopefully retrieved. At least those were the words he used to Steve.

'Rafa says that the local Guardia Civil are all set to go. Just waiting for the call,' said Steve. 'It is going to take days to get all the paperwork over to Spain. That will include a full and detailed statement from yourself. Until we have all this they cannot make a formal arrest, but Rafa reckons that the boys from the Guardia Civil will make it all look fairly scary, going round there mob handed in their riot kit and all properly tooled up as well. Just to shake them up a bit first before they are properly lifted and brought in at a later date.'

'Great,' replied Eaun. 'Your mate Rafa might want to warn his colleagues that both the suspects may be somewhat immobile. It would be even better if they could get to the villa as soon as they are able.'

'Immobile? What do you mean 'immobile'?' chortled Steve. 'You haven't got carried and done anything silly have you? Like take a chain saw to their legs?'

Eaun did not say anything.

'No worries,' replied Steve. 'Assuming that the address that Denise gave me is the correct one, Rafa says that the boys will be there in a few minutes. Their nearest base is actually in this place called Anthrax. They should be there in no time.'

Before putting the phone down, Eaun had Steve promise that he would call him back after Julian's villa had been visited by the Guardia Civil.

It turns out that the next phone call he need not have made. It was to Mr Curtis of the bank. Eaun had never thought of bank officials having emotions, but Mr Curtis sounded overjoyed and almost tearful with delight. Yes, he was very pleased to confirm that the sum of Euros 5,267,874 had safely arrived at the bank's main international office in London earlier that afternoon, Mr Curtis also went on to say that he had already called Mr Wainwright at the WHW Legal office and that he was now fully appraised as to what was happening. Eaun thanked him profusely and ended the call.

The next telephone call that he had to make was to Mr Farquhar. Once again, Eaun got straight through.

'I am calling you as promised,' Eaun told Mr Farquhar. 'Pleased to say that all or nearly all of the diverted funds have now been returned to their proper place. Mr Curtis will be able to confirm all of this to you. You should also know that the local authorities here in Mallorca are also now taking a direct interest in Mr Darby-Henderson. The Wessex Constabulary and myself shall of course keep you fully posted, but that may now be after the weekend.'

'Thank you indeed, Mr Wright,' responded Mr Farquhar. 'I am extremely pleased to hear that. We shall indeed no doubt have to be speaking again in the near future, but in the meantime, Happy Easter.'

Eaun thought that Mr Farquhar almost sounded as friendly

as the bank manager.

That just left the firm's professional indemnity insurers. His contact there was not taking calls. Had probably left for the weekend. This could probably all wait till Tuesday in any event but for the sake of compliance and due diligence, Eaun left a brief message in any event saying that the monies had been retrieved. The bit about the Guardia Civil could wait.

All of the necessary calls made, Eaun sauntered down to the main road by the yacht harbour. The Restaurante Bellver was easy to spot, from the noise created by the large party of adults and children under the awning. Eaun could spot Lumila holding one of Jan and Reme's children on her lap whist the other toddler played with their toys on the table. Bottles of wine, beer and water were waiting to be poured in to the waiting glasses.

'Hurry up, we are just about to order,' said Ludmila.

As the food arrived and the beer and wine started to flow, Eaun could hear several languages being spoken, except English. However, Eaun used the opportunity to reflect on what had happened. By now the Guardia Civil would have swooped on the villa, but Eaun had heard nothing from Steve. Perhaps something dreadful had happened? At least the money had been returned and he might not be totally ruined after all.

By the time orders were being taken for the desserts, Eaun had moved his thoughts on as to how he would cope with life without Victoria. He was wondering to himself why he did not feel distraught and completely devastated when he received a big hug from Jan.

'I am just so sorry, Eaun,' said Jan.

Sorry, sorry about what, thought Eaun. After all, he had got the money back and as long as Julian and Rita were at least still alive, then the day would have been near perfect.

'Ludmila has just explained to me. Everything was moving so quickly that we did not have enough time to explain everything to you,' continued Jan. 'I am mortified. Let me put your mind at rest in case you think that we are all ruthless mafiosa.'

By now, the other conversations had stopped and all eyes were on Jan and Eaun.

'The acid bath. There was no acid. We used the old tin bath just to scare the two of them. The liquid inside the bath was just filthy drainage water, cleaning fluids and of course the piece de resistance from Ludmila, her bath bombs.'

'Bath bombs?' queried Eaun as he stared at Ludmila.

'Yes,' replied Jan. 'She brought them from England and in the disgusting water they were perfect, gurgling, fizzing and bubbling like real acid. Even frightened me.'

'But, what about the rat?' queried Eaun.

'We have Maxim to thank for that,' explained Jan as Maxim nodded in acknowledgement. 'When he is not working for me, Maxim runs his own what do you call in English, stripping of pine firm. It is all the fashion these days. Pine stripping business. That is what you call it. No one is supposed to have tanks of acid these days, so his work shed is just outside Santa Ponsa with no business neighbours nearby. The rat was real. Maxim found it in his shed last night, it was already dead. Probably poisoned. Anyway, to add a little realism Maxim let the dead rat have a few minutes in the real acid bath. As you were able to tell, it all worked!'

There were worried looks all around the table as everyone realised that Eaun must have thought that Julian and Rita were being confronted with the threats of a real acid bath, and having their skin and flesh burned off to the bone like the unfortunate rat.

Eaun was taking it all in. Looking back, as he was so tired and exhausted, he realised later that it could have gone either way. It started with a quick giggle before developing into a fit of uncontrolled laughter. Having started, the two children then followed Eaun and then the rest of the adults at the table, slapping each other's backs and holding their sides in mirth as the two robbers, Julian and Rita had been foiled by a plan that was smarter than theirs.

'Thank you. Thank you…' muttered Eaun for much of the

rest of the evening. All that he now wanted to make the day perfect was for Julian and Rita not to be dead.

More drinks all round were ordered.

~ ~ ~

As the end of the working day approached, the steady string of calls and visitors did not decrease but Alex did squeeze in enough time to read the text from Ludmila.

'Yeah!!! Tell everyone. Mission accomplished. Luda xxxxx'

Alex smiled and was still smiling when once more the front door opened. It was not a client. It was Frank, Rita's husband.

Frank did not look good. He always used to look smart but this afternoon looked as if he had slept in his clothes. He also looked like he was starting to grow some stubble, but more by default than design.

'Look, please do not try to fob me off and insult my intelligence,' said Frank directly to Alex. 'Where is your boss Mr Wright? Not here I suppose. Never is here. No wonder the place is falling apart.'

Alex could not stop Frank.

'You know what I heard this lunchtime, that your other boss Darby-Henderson had kidnapped my Rita and taken her off somewhere secret. I have been to the police. Three days missing but unless they are presented it on a plate the lazy sods don't want to know. So, where is my Rita being held prisoner?'

'And what is going on about my boy Nicky? Rita disappears and suddenly the police are smashing down the front door and rifling through all Nick's things as if he is a common criminal. I tell them about the kidnap though and they just look at me. I have really had enough.'

Alex sensed that Frank really had had enough. Alex wondered whether Frank had just wandered down from the Black Dog. But no, there was no smell of alcohol. He looked genuinely at the end of his tether. She decided to ignore the reference to Nick Thornham, of which she knew quite a bit.

Even if it was not for confidentiality, Alex thought that it was best that Frank did not know what his son was up to.

'Look Frank, I can't tell you where Rita is as I honestly don't know,' said Alex. I imagine that she just wanted a few days away. Happens to all of us. I can also assure you that she most certainly has not been kidnapped by Mr Darby-Henderson or indeed anyone else as far as I am aware. Look, let me have your mobile number. You are quite correct, Mr Wright is not in the office today either, he is away on urgent business but he will be around tomorrow I believe. I will telephone him now and even though the office is closed on Good Friday, get him to call you tomorrow.'

Frank looked as if he was going to say something else but had run out of material.

'Okay, he had better,' replied Frank, said more in hope than as a threat.

Alex sighed and smiled as Frank retreated to the front door and out in to the street.

It was nearly closing time for the office. Unusually and happily, Alex had not been called away from the reception desk. The phone rang once more.

'I don't suppose that Mr Wright is there?' asked a smooth and slightly cultured voice. 'Still in Spain I suppose.'

Alex started to panic. How did everyone suddenly know where Eaun was.

'Look, let me get straight to the point,' continued the caller. 'My name is Gustave Paterson, my wife is Anabel Paterson. We own Sedgeton Grange.'

Alex knew all about Sedgeton Grange. The Sedgeton Grange. Posh boutique hotel and eatery during the weekends and a place where all sorts of shenanigans allegedly went on during the midweek. No one had ever invited Alex to enjoy either of the establishment's two very distinct facilities.

'I understand that Mr Darby-Henderson will be indisposed for a period. We normally deal with him. Delighted to see Mr Wright though. In fact, it is Mr Wright that we really need to see. Enormous amount of legal stuff that we need to get through. Big changes afoot. When can we see him?'

Alex was desperate to ask how this Mr Paterson knew about the two partners. However, after bringing the fee earner diary up on the screen, she offered an hour on Tuesday the following week with Mr Wright which was accepted with alacrity.

'See you next week,' said Mr Gus Paterson.

Madge appeared from the stairs door.

'Have to leave on time tonight. Have two on a sleep over so unless I am back home within ten minutes I will be calling you out when I have Social Services on my back.'

Both the women wished each other a Happy Easter and commented that neither of them had ever experienced a day like it. Alex told Madge about the text from Ludmila.

'Looks like I might be seeing you next week for work after all!' said Alex.

With a smile and a grin, Madge was out of the front door. Alex was about to put the latch on for the evening, when there was one last person who brusquely pushed the door open.

Broad, squat and with a balding head, the man stood opposite Alex.

'Kendrick Maclean. Dougal Kendrick Maclean. Bradstock Farm. Sorry, Manor,' stuttered the visitor.

'We are just about to shut the office for the Easter weekend,' explained Alex. Bradstock Farm, she thought. This was familiar. Of course, it was where her client Charlie Battingsdale lived. Or at least he had told Alex and the police that that was where he lived.

'Look, I just need to fix an appointment with two of your people here. I understand that Mr Darby-Henderson who we normally deal with will be away for a while.'

Kendrick Maclean pulled a piece of paper out of his gilet pocket which Ronnie had given him. He read the script.

'Yup, I need to speak to a Mr Eaun Wright. I know that he normally does wife trouble and stuff like that but we need to speak with him about our business and we need someone who knows what the hell, sorry, apologies, knows their way around. We are told he is the best.'

Still looking at the slip of paper, Kendrick Maclean continued.

'We also need to have a word with someone called Alexandra Hilton,'

''That is not a problem,' responded Alex. She still had Eaun Wright's diary on the screen in front of her. Tuesday afternoon, say 4pm?'

'Perfect,' said Kendrick Maclean.

'How about this Alex woman?'

'Ha, that is me!'

'But the Alex that we need to speak to is a proper solicitor, not a receptionist.'

Alex explained that she was just covering for the day and that she really was a fully qualified solicitor.

'Apologies again, then,' replied Kendrick Maclean. 'I think that I may well have caused you a bit of grief yesterday morning when you were representing my youngest, Charlie, at the Keynsham nick. Think I sent some dick head fancy-pants brief called Axelby thinking that he was better than you. Full apologies. It was out of order.'

Alex remembered the humiliated and humbled Mr Axelby receiving short shrift the day before. She smiled at Kendrick Maclean.

'That is not a problem,' said Alex. 'It might be best if I saw you at the same time as you are seeing Mr Wright? It's OK, we won't charge you double rates. I suppose that you will be bringing Charlie with you? A nice lad. Hope that he has not got in to trouble again.'

'No, nothing to do with Charlie. It's our other boy, Tarquin. Think that he is in deep shit, sorry, trouble. Basically, we need help.'

'That's fine,' smiled Alex. 'See you all Tuesday 4pm. In the meantime, Happy Easter!'

'And to you,' responded Kendrick Maclean as he headed for

the door, followed by Alex, getting ready to finally put the latch on the door and turn off the reception lights.

At least we have not yet been taken over by the SRA and are able to lock the office front door ourselves, pondered Alex.

HOMEWARD BOUND

I T WAS 15 minutes past midnight and the Departures board had just announced that the Bristol flight would be 30 minutes late. Ludmila seemed to have spent half her adult life in airport lounges. 30 minutes was nothing.

Next to Ludmila, her boss Eaun was trying to get comfortable on the plastic Palma Airport chair, where discomfort was a design feature. Poor Mr Wright. After the Bellver restaurant Eaun had followed them all back to Jan and Reme's flat where everyone then continued the party, except for Mr Wright. He kept staring at his phone and eventually took up Reme's offer to crash out on one of the kids' beds, even if it was a bit too short for Eaun's legs.

Eventually, it was time to head back to the airport. Jan had long ceased being in any state to drive, so a taxi was ordered, with Ludmila's brother insisting that he accompany them.

When the taxi pulled up at the flat in Calanova, Ludmila spilled many tears at saying goodbye to Reme and the two children. Promises of seeing each other imminently were made. Jan was sitting in the back of the white taxi with Mr Wright next to him, still with his phone in his hand. Jan was apologising once again for not telling Eaun beforehand that the tin bath, the rat and the bath bombs were all part of the subtle plan and of course no one was actually going to dip Julian's feet in to a real acid bath, although Jan did add that if what his sister had told him about Julian and this Rita woman, then he deserved everything that was coming to him.

The taxi had just left the Via Cintura and was now on the main road to the airport, when Mr Wright's phone sprang in to life. Ludmila turned around. 'Yes, Eaun Wright speaking. Steve? Wonderful! I have been waiting for you to call. Yes, just on the way to the airport. Hang on, let me put you on speaker.'

It took Eaun a few moments to find and press the Speaker button.

'Right, you are on speaker now,' said Eaun as he pointed the phone in the direction of Ludmila, with Jan listening in.

'Yeah, just had my even bigger mate Rafa ring me back with an update. Sorry about the delay in getting back to you, but things turned out to be more complicated than everyone thought. Denise described you to me as and I quote 'a quiet really nice country solicitor' but it sounds to me as if you have been on the rampage and been a very busy boy indeed. The Guardia Civil team from Andratx were fully prepared to be dealing with terrorists when they left their garrison. When they raided Mr Henderson's villa, they were armed to the teeth with assault rifles, grenades and machine guns. It seems however that they were greeted with chaos and carnage. Your partner was tied up, curled on the sofa gently sobbing to himself. His missus apparently ignored the scary SWAT team and continued to abuse, hiss and spit at Mr Henderson, even more so when they finally got the ropes off her. Someone had it seems tied them both up. There was also mention of a skinned rat but I think something must have got lost in translation. Funniest thing was though that someone had put a Jag convertible in to the swimming pool. I don't suppose that you know anything about this would you? I thought probably not. Rafa said that the Guardia Civil Comandante who was leading the raid was in near tears. Turns out that he is a petrol head and he welled up at seeing what he described as a priceless 1966 Roadster model resting at the bottom of the pool.'

Eaun asked DI Steve Dibley that he pass on his profuse thanks to his mate Rafa for the information.

'What is odd is that when the Guardia Civil got there, your friend Mr Henderson started mouthing off and not just about a rat. The Comandante's English is not perfect but he could have sworn that Mr Henderson was shouting that he had been tortured and threatened with drills and a bath. Yes, a bath, I know. The woman then started to scream at Henderson who mentioned no more about any torture,' continued Steve. 'From then on, neither of them could recall how they got tied up. The lovely Rita, when she had stopped attacking her lover suggested that they were just 'playing games'. The Jag at the bottom of the pool was just an accident. Anyway, think that the boys from the Guardia did a great job, they duly terrified Romeo and Juliet and took away piles of paperwork. They even threatened them both with a gentle slap if they didn't behave. As I think that you already know, Interpol and the Spanish authorities are not yet in a position to take either of them in. This will take a few days, but everything will be handed over to the local financial and fraud teams in Palma next week. Think that their passports may have got muddled up with the papers that were seized so that no one is going anywhere. Only disappointment was that when a computer was eventually found, it was sharing the bottom of the swimming pool with the Jag.'

However, it seemed to Ludmila that Eaun was only interested in one thing.

'Neither party has come to any harm, though,' enquired Eaun.

'Happy to confirm that physically both Rita and Julian seem to be alive and well with no visible signs of any acts of torture, if that is what you mean,' confirmed Steve.

'That is great, thank you so very much,' responded Eaun.

'All the pleasure of the Wessex Constabulary, Interpol and our friends in Spain,' came the response. 'I have just looked at the rota, I see that Denise Halloran is in tomorrow so I will brief her on events. Also have to say on a personal note that you are incredibly fortunate on getting the money back. Nice one. If you had left it another day, the money will have been in Switzerland en route to the black hole of a Cayman Islands account. Probably best that I don't know what happened out there, but one day I will get Denise to let me know your secret.'

After more profound thanks from Eaun, the call ended.

Immediately, Ludmila noticed that the mood of Eaun had changed completely. It was as if a huge weight had been lifted off his shoulders. For the rest of the journey to the airport he was now smiling and joining in on her brother's still semi-drunken jokes.

Sitting next to Eaun on the airport chairs, Ludmila looked across at her boss. His neck was at an acute angle and his head was nodding up and down like one of those dogs that the English sometimes placed in the back of their cars. He was also starting to slowly dribble.

As the effects of the alcohol consumed at the restaurant and Jan and Reme's began to wear off, Ludmila started to reflect on her own involvement. In the airport there were several patrolling Policia. Would anyone be looking for her wanting to speak to her about torture and criminal damage to a James Bond car? She had heard Steve the policeman say that neither Julian nor Rita wanted to file a complaint, but the seriousness of what she had become involved in was starting to sink in.

What she could not understand at all was how and why Eaun was most of all concerned about the well-being of his partner and employee who had tried to rob him of nearly £5 million. If it was left to her, she would have poured a real acid bath.

Before the dribbles from Eaun reached his shirt, the flight to Bristol was at last called.

No Policia had put their hand on Ludmila's shoulder and even more important, Ludmila would be back home in Somerset in time for the promised family Easter Egg hunt on Saturday.

~~~

The easiest part of getting home had been the flight itself, although on the return journey it was Eaun's upper left arm that was utilised as take off comfort by Ludmila. On arrival at Bristol

Airport, it took well over an hour to travel the hundred yards from the passport check to the arrivals lounge. Matters were not helped when 4 flights arrived within a few minutes of each other, stretching the resources of Bristol's International Airport to breaking point. The post Plague and Brexit complications simply added to the wait.

In the arrivals lounge Eaun went to pay for the parking. Initially, he thought there must have been an error. He only wanted to pay for the time that he stayed at the Short Term car park. He did not actually want to buy that part of the car park. Eaun made a mental note that next time he should read the signs more carefully and head for the Long Term car park.

As Eaun carefully snaked his trusted Volvo through the dark narrow roads of the Mendips he eventually passed one of the signs for Sedgeton. He then thought to ask of Ludmila what he had seen in the town a couple of days ago.

'Bit random,' said Eaun. 'I have been meaning to ask yourself or one of the girls, but on Wednesday I saw the demonstration outside St Christopher's. I understand what they are protesting about but one of the signs that a demonstrator was holding said 'Hippies Go Home'. Another sign was a lot more forthright. I didn't understand it.'

Ludmila sniggered.

'You have been living in this town a long time Mr Eaun, you should understand this!'

'It is really quite simple,' said Ludmila. Especially since Covid, there have been many new people coming to Sedgeton, particularly from London. Nothing wrong with immigrants. I am one! But the new immigrants from London bring with them their different cultures. For me, I love Sedgeton. Particularly the schools and the education. But all of the, what is the word, newbies, want to send their children to the Free School where they do what they want. It also means that fewer children attend the 'normal' schools like St Christopher's which is now threatened with closure. That is why people get fed up.'

Eaun nodded, but Ludmila had started.

'Grzegorz, the girls and me live in a nice house. We love our home. But it is rented. Even with our two salaries we could not afford to buy our terraced house with three bedrooms and a postage stamp garden. Yet, this week we have a man and his family, the same hippy whose brats trash my plants, saying that he has loads of money to buy what he wants. Isleworth. I have never heard of bloody Isleworth. Hippies now are not like the old lot, all peace, love and flowers. They now come with £750,000 in their bank account. And attitude.'

Ludmila had got herself worked up but Eaun thought that it probably was not worth explaining the geography of Middlesex and the Thames. At least he now understood why there were demands for hippies to return home, whether to Isleworth or elsewhere.

Eaun did not fathom why, but he then went on to tell Ludmila about Vicky leaving him. He left out the other bits concerning the reason for her departure.

He would after all have to tell everyone eventually in any event.

Ludmila just went quiet and after a short time she just said that she was so very sorry. Without thinking, Eaun replied that he was not particularly sorry and it was probably all for the best.

They were soon outside the Nowak family residence.

Eaun retrieved Ludmila's rucksack from the back and went round the Volvo to open her passenger door. As Ludmila turned to face the front door, from nowhere she flung her arms around Eaun's neck and squeezed him with a tight hug.

'A huge 'thank you' and you look after yourself,' whispered Ludmila. With a couple of pats on Eaun's back, she was gone behind her front door.

Eaun got back in to the car. He had not had time to say a proper 'thank you' to Ludmila. He owed her so much. He also reflected that whether by choice or inclination, the hug from Ludmila was the first hug that he had had since before The Plague.

Luckily, Ludmila had not patted Eaun on his upper arms. At least the bruises should now be matching, thought Eaun.

A few minutes later, Eaun was driving up to his own house. Instinctively, he looked for Vicky's Fiat, but of course it was not there. Why would it be.

He retrieved his own bag from the back of the Volvo. He also picked up three large boxes of ensaimadas, helped kept secure with string tied around them. He had broken a habit of a lifetime to actually buy something in an airport departure lounge. He felt good about it, as he reflected on surviving the day not having been struck off, made bankrupt or even arrested in a foreign country. All things considered, compared with the events on Wednesday, the last day had been a triumph. Now, he just wanted to go to bed.

Door unlocked and alarm code keyed in, Eaun opened the door and noticed his work brief case on its habitual spot. Eaun then spotted the previous day's edition of the *Daily Mail* neatly stacked by his brief case. DI Colin Thompson had obviously declined Eaun's offer to help himself to the newspaper. Eaun cursed that of course once Victoria had gone, the wretched paper people actually deliver the correct title. However, it was probably unfair to completely blame the demise of his marriage on the negligent delivery of the local newsagent.

The police inspector turned pet minder had also scooped up from the doormat some delivered mail which he had neatly placed on the hall table. He would tackle that in the morning. He was exhausted.

Before going up to bed Eaun walked towards the kitchen and flicked the light on.

There, lined up in front of the kitchen table were not two, but three cats. Behind them, were three cat food bowls, all of them empty. Vlad and Ivan were of course in attendance, but joining them was his old adversary, the mangy tom that Eaun was certain had been responsible for the most recent hit.

There was however no stench of any cat spray, although Eaun thought that he could still detect a slight whiff of floor polish.

He wondered why there were three cat bowls. He then

realised, he had never told DI Thompson how many cats there actually were. When he came round to feed them, he must have seen the 3 animals and obviously thought to feed all three.

Eaun was too tired to care. He simply piled more cat food into all three bowls and for good measure also poured out a large saucer of milk for consumption, a treat never offered by Vicky on the grounds that milk was not good for cats.

Eaun then trudged up the stairs.

Things were starting to change.

~ ~ ~

Just 650 to go now, but DC Denise Halloran had thoroughly enjoyed the last couple of days. It was the first time that she had ever had to don fancy dress as a detective constable. She had also greatly appreciated relating to her work colleagues all the goings-on at Caligula's Roman Orgy, deliberately exaggerating what she had really witnessed, just to ensure that they were all sick as pigs with envy. Her husband had also wanted to know all the details and even asked for the dates of the next planned orgy. In his dreams. There was no way that Rod Halloran would ever be let out of Wells on his own.

It was just gone ten in the morning. It did not really bother Denise that she was working on a Bank Holiday morning. She had the Easter Monday off plus the following two days as well. After years of working shifts, weekends and Bank Holidays had long ceased to be special and merged with every other day.

Extracting the information from the Patersons about the whereabouts of their mate Julian Darby-Henderson had been cracking good fun. It was not every day that a police officer had no option but to keep her warrant card in her knickers. Denise thought that it was unlikely that she would ever have to do again. A shame.

Just a few minutes earlier, Denise had put the phone down on Steve from the fraud office at HQ. He had given Denise a full de-brief on what had happened out in Mallorca the day before.

She had already received a brief text from Alexandra Hilton during the evening saying 'Thank You!!! Xxx' so imagined that whatever had been planned had been successful.

She was however deeply relieved to hear from Steve. In truth, she had no idea what was going to happen out in Spain and if anything had kicked off and anyone had got hurt, then the fingers would have been pointing at Denise, something that she did not want happening with only 650 days to go.

She believed Steve when he said that Eaun Wright had been incredibly lucky to have been able to retrieve his firm's money before it disappeared within the criminal labyrinth of offshore accounts. For once, it seemed that the good guys had actually won.

However, Denise could still not get her head around how a priceless E Type convertible belonging to Eaun's business partner ended up in the deep end of a pool. Even if he had been outrageously deceived, as he had, Denise could just not see the Eaun Wright that she knew ever doing anything as uncharacteristic as drive a Jag into a swimming pool. Curious. Very curious.

Before putting the phone down, Steve said that he did not have a great deal to do and he was the only one in his section actually at work that day. If Denise was OK about it, then he was therefore going to do a little digging around on Julian Darby-Henderson and the delectable Mrs Thornham. Leaving everything behind in the UK and putting everything at risk for £5 million somehow did not all properly add up. If he found anything then he would get back to Denise by the end of the day.

Denise now started to concentrate on her task for the day. The Sedgeton Grange Hotel.

Denise had checked out all the local police logs about any complaints being raised following Wednesday's extravaganza. There was nothing, from either those belonging to the club or members of the public. She was not surprised.

Denise had found the whole of the Roman orgy hilarious.

Cavorting around in the nude or semi-nude was not really her scene, or, as she both trusted and hoped, something that her husband would ever want to indulge in. If folks looked forward to a good night's spanking or whatever was their thing, then good for them, thought Denise. They are plainly doing no harm to anyone and if no laws were being broken then it should not be the concern of the police. It also seemed to Denise that the weird sex pest with the white pony tail and no bottom was a genuine loose cannon, not something that was ever planned or intended to happen during the evening's entertainment.

Denise had already briefly visited Gustave and Anabel Paterson the day before, the Thursday afternoon, just to make sure the frighteners were kept on and that the two proprietors were kept on their toes. Denise had also demanded and duly received all of the hotel's personnel files which she took away with her. The Sedgeton Grange was by then getting ready for their weekend guests. There was a quiet bustle from the staff as they applied the finishing touches to the change around. Denise assured Gustave that he would get his HR files back the following day.

So, first thing on Friday morning, Denise had rang the hotel and said that she wanted a meet with the two owners. It was Gustave to whom she spoke. He sounded fraught but quickly agreed a meeting for the late morning. Denise confirmed that she would be returning a large pile of buff personnel files.

'Fully recovered from Wednesday evening's fun and games?' asked Denise with a smile on arrival at the hotel. The two owners just looked at each other miserably, thought Denise.

'Look, you can relax. Unless we get any complaints of law-breaking from anyone, I am not concerned what goes on in the Dungeon or the Sex Heaven or whatever they are called. However, what I am deeply concerned about is the use of The Sedgeton Grange and your club as a drugs supermarket.'

Denise saw both Gus and Anabel look at each other. It was clear that neither knew what she was talking about. Denise imagined that Gustave probably had his proboscis stuck so far into his profit and loss account sheets that he was oblivious to what was happening in his own establishment. As far as Anabel was concerned, her preoccupation with style, content and the whole client experience meant that like her husband, she was blind to what was going on right under her own nose.

'I can assure you officer that there are no drugs issues here,' piped up Anabel. 'This is a respectable membership.'

'What are you able to tell me about Tarquin Battingsdale, one of your respectable members?' retorted Denise.

'I know the name and probably the face but I really do not know a great deal about him,' answered Anabel.

'Like everything else around here, what was available was all top of the range stuff, from Moroccan Gold, to Special K and Snow. And no, Mrs Paterson, the Special K on sale Wednesday evening was not what you would put on the hotel buffet breakfast bar,' quipped Denise.

'Look, I know that we may not have got off to the best of starts earlier on,' interjected Gus. 'However, I assure you that we do not allow any illicit drugs to be bought or consumed here at Sedgeton Grange.'

'Orders for drugs are taken right here, and quite openly as well, Mr Paterson,' replied Denise. 'Individual orders are taken, just like you can order a tequila sunrise and then arrangements made later for personal delivery to the customer, your private club members.'

Both Gus and Anabel Paterson were silent. There was nothing that they could really say.

'I tell you what,' continued Denise. 'You just make sure that your friend Mr Battingsdale comes nowhere near your establishment again or you will be down in custody for a formal interview for being concerned in the supply of Class A drugs.'

'I do remember Tarquin now,' Anabel then piped up. 'All the staff were inundated last night. Tarquin has always been a helpful and kind lad. I thought that he was just assisting the staff take orders for drinks.'

Sadly, Denise believed Anabel. Gustave was just shaking his

head.

Denise started to gather her papers together and get ready to leave.

'Aren't you going to ask us about the HR files you have in front of you?' asked Gus.

'Maybe next time,' said Denise. She had more than enough on her plate as it was. 'Until then, it might be worth both of you taking a very long think on what is actually going on here. There are going to be other people besides me looking on to see what is really happening here.'

Now, back in the peace and quiet of her own office on this quiet Bank Holiday, Denise knew that there was only one route for her to take. The day before she had left Sedgeton Grange knowing that both Gus and Anabel had been really shaken by what had happened in the previous 48 hours. However, she also knew that the drugs issue was potentially huge and would mean serious investigation. Instinctively Denise hated passing on work to other officers, but she also appreciated that with threatened turf wars becoming ever more likely in the West Country, now was the time to pass the papers on Mr Tarquin Battingsdale over to her specialist colleagues in the drugs squad.

Denise checked out a number on the directory and picked up the office phone.

'Drugs squad? Billy Matheson? Brilliant. You owe me one. I have some quality work for you boys to get stuck in to.'

~ ~ ~

It was now just after lunchtime on Good Friday and The Sedgeton Grange Hotel, formerly the Cloisters Preparatory School for Boys, was heaving with their holiday weekend guests as well as locals who had booked a place in the dining room. All of the downstairs reception rooms had guests in them. Gus did not fancy being in the goldfish bowl that was his office, so after grabbing the right key and whilst en route rescuing Chef from a lecture from Anabel, Gus then headed for the door marked

'Staff Only', turned the key and together with Anabel entered the forbidden midweek only territory of The Dungeon.

'We need somewhere quiet and this is the only place,' explained Gus.

With the flickering neon lights above and most of the accessories stored away until the next Members' Club evening, the Dungeon was hardly recognisable from Wednesday evening's action.

Gus approached one of the large oak tables down in the part of the Dungeon that was affectionately referred to by the participating membership as Purgatory Parlour. There were still some feathered handcuffs on the top of the table which Gus then swept to the side before drawing up a couple of stools for them to sit on. There was still a slight iciness from Anabel, as Gus figured that he had still not been forgiven since their meeting the day before.

'Right,' commenced Gus. 'We need to move forward. I promised that I would produce a plan and this is it.'

Gustave then unfolded large pages of print outs. These, he announced, are the business plans for the next six months. Anabel remained seated, stony faced.

For the next 20 minutes Gus explained what they would be doing. The only serious accusation that he believed the Hotel faced was the alleged selling of drugs on their premises. Not only could this produce major legal issues, but at the very least it would also create severe reputational damage as well. To therefore deflect any future complaints from the local constabulary, Gus proposed that an immediate letter of expulsion be sent to Tarquin Battingsdale, citing behaviour likely to bring the good name of the Club and Hotel into disrepute. To reinforce and enhance the Club's standing with the authorities, Gus said that he had already drafted an email to be sent to all club Members letting them know that the Club maintained a strict 'No Tolerance' policy in respect of either possession or use of any prohibited drugs.

With regards to the quite appalling behaviour of the

stand-in speaker for the evening, a letter had been written to Piers Hudderston advising him in no uncertain terms that his presence would in the future not be welcome at Sedgeton Grange. It went without saying that the promised donation to the Wessex Monuments & Historical Buildings Society would of course no longer be honoured. Without being specific on names, Gus mentioned to Anabel that he had already spoken to several guests who had contacted him regarding the antics of the Hon Sec and how their evenings had been ruined. He still had a couple of other calls to make in order to apologise profusely and to state that no such thing would ever again be tolerated.

Gus then moved on to the issue of the alleged under age employees serving alcohol. Gus assured Anabel that all that they had to do was to ensure that each employee had a notice from their employer stating that at no time, if indeed they were under the age of 18, should they be involved in either the serving of alcoholic beverages or be involved in any Members' Club evenings.

'I know that you especially adored the boys and girls showing off their pert little bottoms at Wednesday evening's Caligula evening,' proclaimed Gus. 'However, as far as I can see there is absolutely no reason why we can't allow exposure of the posterior at future events, provided that all the staff sign a consent form that they are over 18 and that that they are doing so voluntarily. Anabel, my dear, the bottoms will still be on display, but just legally in future. In fact, you should know that I have already booked an appointment with Eaun Wright and his team for the beginning of next week, to ensure for starters that we are fully up to date and compliant with all our Members' rules. We both need to go along. In the light of what we have been told about poor old Jools, looks like we should now ride with the winning horse Mr Wright and we do not want news of what has been going on recently at the Club to be divulged to other unknown lawyers.'

Anabel managed a weak smile, which was the first afforded to Gustave in nearly two days.

'Think that on the employee front, I am fairly sure that following today's meeting with her and despite having access to all our HR files, DC Halloran is not particularly interested in pursuing this particular matter. Bigger fish to fry no doubt.'

However, Gustave had not finished.

'I think that in future we just need to be a little more savvy on how we plan things. Maybe just give the orgies a miss for a little while.'

Anabel's already weak smile disappeared completely.

'However, you are brilliant at what you do, Anabel. Everyone knows that. Of course we can have more orgies in the future but in the meantime it may be more prudent for a short period to market an event like a Pyjama Party rather than a full-blooded orgy. Ages ago you also mentioned the idea of a Country Club.'

In fact, as far as Gus was concerned he had just thought of the idea, but already he could see a real smile return to Anabel's face with her mind already planning ahead on what could be devised.

'Go on, Gustave!' asked Anabel as her voice echoed around The Dungeon.

'It is simple,' responded Gus. 'There is no mention of the events of Wednesday, there does not have to be. Instead, we just quietly implement one of your brilliant re-brands, as seamlessly The Sedgeton Grange Members Club becomes the Sedgeton Health Spa and Country Club.'

'We both go to Sedgeton every day and we see the explosion of all these cottage industry health and well-being businesses opening up everywhere. What is this Mindfulness business all about, by the way? It may well be that it is all pretentious rubbish but it is pretentious rubbish that pays. We want the punters coming here, not to some flea-infested one-man-band hot and sweaty pit in the middle of the Artisans' Quarter. We already have most of the spa facilities here.'

'Downstairs, this place the Dungeon can double as a snooker room. Following lockdown, snooker is now the boom sport once more and the dungeon is perfect, although we may have to do something with the hanging shackles. We don't want anyone missing the crucial black because their mind begins to wander.'

'Seventh Heaven? Obvious. Yoga is now the new sex. It is not just all the yummy mummies who are at it, but men as well. I have been reading up. There are now hard men, even athletes such as rugby players, who employ their own personal yoga trainer. There is hardly any money that needs to be spent on the attic, just some mats and we pinch all the best teachers from the Artisans' Quarter. This will be our new cash cow.'

However, just in case there had been any wobbles in his pitch, Gus had listed his clincher for the end.

'It will be the 10th Anniversary in a few months' time when we bought what is now The Sedgeton Grange at auction,' enthused Gus. 'Think that this will need a proper celebration and an event for everyone to remember. Perhaps you can jet off to Amsterdam again or even somewhere a bit different to buy something memorable for our new Health Spa & Country Club to maybe even replace the iron shackles. If there is no hen party going on you can even take a guest or even guests with you!'

'What an absolutely splendid idea,' responded a beaming Anabel. 'I will take you away for a genuine dirty weekend just like we had ten years ago. You are so brilliantly clever! I love you!'

Anabel then quickly approached her husband, accidentally knocking the pink feathered handcuffs on to the floor before grabbing him in a huge hug, arms around him and with her face buried in the side of Gus's neck.

'Thank you,' said Anabel directly into the ear of Gustave.

Gus was already thinking ahead into the future.

~ ~ ~

Easter Sunday 21st April

Eaun had now been back in Sedgeton for several days. He had been busy.

On the first full day back, the Friday, he had slept through most of the morning. When he did eventually wake up, he found himself curled up in a foetal ball on his side of the bed. There was of course no sign of Vicky. It took him several minutes after waking up to register that his wife had dumped him for a younger woman. Try as he might to become enraged by this act of betrayal, Eaun still couldn't. After he got up and headed downstairs, he leaned over the bannister. There was no whiff of anything unpleasant. Eaun had remembered on this occasion to slip on his dressing gown. However, the Friday edition of the *Daily Mail* had been delivered through the letter box many hours beforehand. Of course, with Vicky now departed, the right newspaper was being delivered like clockwork on a daily basis. The *Mail* would however still have to go. Eaun made a mental note to pop on down to the newsagents later, pay the final bill and cancel the subscription. After recent events the newsagent would no doubt be delighted to rid himself of the Wright account.

There was also the pile of post that he had ignored when he had arrived back home in the early hours. He carried the items together with the newspaper in to the kitchen with him. The latest roll call of the three cats was lined up ready for their breakfast, with the mangy ginger joining his new mates, Vlad and Ivan. Eaun filled up the three bowls and poured some more milk into the saucer. Crucially, there was still no sign or scent of any violation that had been committed whilst he had been away. Eaun also thought that ginger now started to look less mangy and had even started to put on weight.

All that was in the bread bin for Eaun's own breakfast was what remained of the granary wholemeal bread that Vicky collected twice weekly from the Olde Somerset Wholemeal Bakery in the town's Artisan Quarter. What was left was however going a bluey green as the mould was starting to spread everywhere. Eaun dumped the remains of the loaf in the food recycling bin. No more visits to the Artisan's Quarter for bread and Eaun would now be able to enjoy white sliced bread again. Things were not all doom and gloom.

As Eaun turned the kettle on to make himself a coffee, he dumped the *Daily Mail* in the paper recycling bin and picked up the bundle of post, flicking through the various items. All of the post joined the unread and unopened *Daily Mail* in the recycling bins, except for a handwritten envelope without a stamp which had been clearly hand-delivered. It was in Vicky's handwriting.

The back of the envelope had a strip of sellotape across the back as if it was some sort of royal seal. Eaun picked up one of Vicky's prize Sabatier knives and slit the paper at the top of the envelope. The letter was short, but even when they first started going out together, Eaun had never known Vicky write any letter more than a few paragraphs.

The letter was undated.

Dearest Eaun,

I came round to see you earlier today but there was no one here. As usual your office did not know where you were but I heard there was talk going round that you might have gone to Spain on a holiday with some woman. I hope that it all works out for you both. It is good that you are able to move on and I hope that you are happy together.

I have taken what I need. Everything else you can have. Perhaps in a week or so we can sit down and talk through the mechanics of what happens here (you are however not an easy person to pin down!). In the meantime, can you please look after the two boys. You will be pleased to know that I will not be applying for custody of them. Chris is allergic to cats.

I have also spoken to Alison and Cassie. As predicted they have both been very grown up about everything and wished us both luck for the future. I am really sorry that things did not work out between us. It was just one of those things really. I am very happy in my new life and I am sure that you will be as well.

See you soon. Hope that you had a great holiday.

As always,

Love

Vicky x

PS I know that you will be worrying about this but when I do have to go and see a solicitor to sort out my share of everything for Chris and myself, I promise not to use those ghastly people down the road from your office that you do not like. Mr Robinson? Maddison?

The water having boiled, Eaun made himself the best of the instant coffee that was on offer. With Vicky having departed, perhaps he could now even treat himself to an upgrade in the domestic coffee making facilities. The positives of life without Vicky were slowly beginning to multiply.

Eaun was pleased to hear the bit about his wife not going to see the reptilians at Maddison and Robinson. He was however a little disconcerted about the reference to 'my share of everything for Chris and myself'. What share? Still, she had at least contacted the girls as promised although Eaun could not understand the reference to him going off on holiday with some woman. What holiday? What woman? The rest of the day Eaun spent in the house, ceremoniously dismantling the matrimonial bed and smashing the mattress slats. He just made it to the town skip in time for him to dump the remains of the bed and the mattress from both the inside and from the roof of his Volvo. When he got home, Eaun inspected the near empty former matrimonial bedroom with satisfaction. Tonight, he would sleep in the guest room.

On the Saturday, Eaun had decided to designate his time and energy on his two daughters, Alison and Cassie. He duly phoned his daughters at their flat in Baldwin Street in Bristol. The place actually possessed a land line. For students this was almost unheard of. Alison was out with 'her bloke' (Eaun did not even know there was a 'bloke'). Cassie proclaimed that both of them had been fine and Alison was coping marvellously on hearing the news about their mother and Chrissie. Eaun knew that this really meant that she was not coping at all. Eaun mentioned that he was going up to Easton in Bristol the next day, the Sunday, to get some stuff from IKEA. Could he pop in to see the girls at their flat? It seemed that Sunday was not a good time and Monday might also be difficult. Eaun suspected that for a multitude of reasons they just did not want their father visiting their hovel of a death trap flat. Eaun was then inspired enough to suggest a barbecue at the family home in Sedgeton on the afternoon of Easter Monday. Cassie thought the idea was splendid and upon Eaun promising that he would pay for the train fare and pick them both up at the station, that was enough to seal the deal for the Monday barbecue. Eaun spent the rest of Saturday cleaning the family home from top to bottom, something that he had never done before. In fact, he had never done a great deal of cleaning but his chosen task of cleansing every room in the house became strangely empowering and therapeutic. With no one around to complain, Eaun performed his cleaning tasks whilst his favourite Pink Floyd tracks thundered from the downstairs sound system. The three cats had chosen to disappear for that part of the day.

Exhausted but exhilarated by the day's labours, in the evening Eaun treated himself to a long bath instead of his customary shower (mercifully Vicky had not appropriated all of the soaps, bubbles and lathers), followed by a delivery from the Sedgeton Alhambra Curry House, consumed whilst watching a top of the table clash on Sky Sports. Retiring to the guest room for the night, Eaun enjoyed his best night's sleep for a very long time.

Straight after his instant coffee breakfast earlier on the Sunday morning, Eaun had once more collapsed the rear seats of the Volvo Estate and headed off to IKEA with his order list for himself in his new post-Vicky life. Inevitably, he had ended up buying items in the store that he either already had or did not want. Matters were also not made easier when he had forgotten to take with him the Scandi name of the bed that he was supposed to be buying. After a few test bounces on the double bed that he thought was the one that he wanted, he decided that it would do and wrote down the aisle where both bed and matching mattress were to be picked up at the exit, ready to be taken home for assembly.

On the way back from Bristol, Eaun had thought of doing a surprise visit on the two girls in Baldwin Street in the middle of the city. However, they were probably still in bed (Alison possibly with her 'new bloke') and Cassie had made it clear that their father should stay away. In any event, Eaun remembered that the new mattress was tied down to the roof of the Volvo. Given the area in central Bristol where he would have to park up, Eaun did not fancy the chances of survival for the mattress if it was left on its own for more than five minutes. Eaun therefore headed towards the A4 and then on towards Bath and then Sedgeton.

Back home, the heavy brown IKEA boxes were hauled up the stairs with Eaun sweating at the effort. The mattress then barely made it round the top of the stairs. Regretfully, the afternoon had been nowhere near as successful as the dynamic morning expedition had been. Eaun had unpacked everything and lined up all the parts to the new bed on the ridiculously clean carpet of what was now the former matrimonial bedroom. Eaun was pleased to note that there were the correct number of legs and the right Allen key tool had been supplied. Gradually, over a period of a couple of hours, the parts to the bed lay scattered over the carpet, some joined together but most discarded and hurled in despair. Eaun could at this point feel the rage swell inside him. It was time for a deep breath and a coffee in the kitchen.

Eaun took a sip of the coffee. It was far too hot to drink. Eaun knew that he had been putting everything off since he had got back from Mallorca. Waiting for the coffee to cool, this was an opportunity for him just to stop for a moment and take stock. Even Eaun realised that the manic actions since his return were simply masking over the reality of what had really happened to him. On the Friday afternoon he had the landline disconnected from the plug on the wall. He did not want to speak to anyone. He had also turned off his mobile, only turning it on to speak to Cassie and to place his take away order. Eaun now took a deep breath and turned his mobile telephone back on.

The notification pings took well over half a minute to tell Eaun that he had dozens of emails and many missed calls, most from numbers that he did not recognise. There was also scores of unread texts.

Nearly all of the communications were concerned with Eaun's well-being. There was nothing else to clean in the house and it was time to come to terms with what had happened.

On the end of his marriage, Eaun felt almost guilty at not feeling utterly grief-stricken. However, Eaun found himself returning to just two big concerns. First there was his daughter Alison. Eaun had tried to imagine his best friend at university announcing that he had fallen in love with Eaun's Mum and was going off to live with her. Eaun's stomach started to heave at the thought. He recognised that all of the pain on this would be with Alison and he was delighted that he had at least managed to arrange for Alison and her sister to come down for a barbecue the following afternoon. His second big concern was the dread of every professional; another solicitor, a rival, poking over the detritus and embers of a failed relationship, where letters, invoices and inner secrets would all be disclosed to scrutiny. Eaun hoped that his wife was going to be as good as her word and not instruct those leeches at Maddison and Robinson. However, as he now knew with Victoria, he could no longer feel secure with anything.

No, the big worry for Eaun was his reputation. He had no idea what was going to happen. Yes, the bulk of the stolen money may have been miraculously returned but the theft itself had happened under his watch. As a partner he must therefore be held accountable. It was all about trust and that trust been breached by the firm having nearly £5 million stolen from its coffers. Eaun thought of the Daily Newsletter of the *Law Society's Gazette* that landed in the Inbox of every solicitor in the land, with a headline featuring his name alongside the words 'Struck Off', an article that would be read by all his many friends who were lawyers, his colleagues and of course his rivals. Eaun was aware that everyone makes mistakes whilst in practice. Most do not see the light of day. But what was undisputable was that if a solicitor or a doctor had been struck off, then what was certain was that something really bad must have happened. Eaun was now having to face this truth. The *Courier* may now be deceased, but Eaun had no illusions and imagined that his ruin and public humiliation at being struck off would be even worse as the news spread on social media. Eaun wondered what on earth was 'social' about spreading news about the misery of others.

As he ploughed through the many messages for him, there was one that caught his attention. It was from Douglas Wainwright. He had left a voicemail saying that there had been 'significant developments' and that they should speak. Could Eaun please call him as soon as he got this message.

Eaun felt something within him start to spur in to action. He still had a responsibility to others.

As Eaun headed towards making another coffee for himself, he started writing down a list of all those that he had to phone back. The first call was to the landline at the flat in Baldwin Street. He had completely forgotten about his daughters' expertise at putting together flatpack furniture. They were the original flatpack queens. He left a message. Could the girls get an earlier train tomorrow and he would pick them up? He was having a small issue with some IKEA furniture and if they could sort it before the barbecue that would be great.

Eaun then placed the call to Douglas. Unknown to Eaun, things were starting to happen faster than he could ever have imagined.

~ ~ ~

Kendrick Maclean knew that his wife Ronnie loved it when she had the whole family round the table. She had for years tried to make Easter Day a spring version of Christmas Day, but neither of the boys had really caught on to what Ronnie was trying to create.

For this Easter Sunday, it would just be her husband and

herself sharing the leg of lamb. The cut of lamb was far too big for the two of them, but had been purchased at the butchers in Sedgeton by Ronnie in the expectation that she would also be feeding her two sons.

Kendrick Maclean had spent much of the last three days asking questions, digging around and generally making enquiries on issues regarding his family. At the beginning of the week, he was a highly successful entrepreneur creating a new and exciting project in his adopted county of Somerset. A few days later, everything seemed to be on the precipice. And none of it was down to him.

Ronnie knew bits of what was happening, but Kendrick Maclean had promised his wife a full update of what had really been going on with the two boys. Over lunch on Easter Day at Bradstock Manor, all would have to be explained.

'First, Charlie,' started Kendrick Maclean. 'As you know well Ronnie, I love both the boys to bits, particularly Charlie, even though they are not my own flesh and blood. However likeable he may be, Charlie has always been a bit of a plonker. He mixes with all the wrong crowd, and comes under the influence of toe-rags far too easily. Certainly does not get that from you.'

'I have spoken to Charlie and I know that you have as well, Ronnie. He has told me everything that went on in the police station plus the advice that he got from his brief. I have also made a couple of phone calls to former colleagues of mine back in town, and their view is the same as mine. Whether with the Met or here with the Wessex Constabulary, the police have got fuck all actual evidence against Charlie. He is on bail, but the police have to do that. He will walk.'

'No bad language at the table,' chided Ronnie, whilst offering Kendrick Maclean the opportunity of finishing off the roast potatoes.

Her husband apologised for his lapse and then duly accepted the last few roasts.

'Where do we go from here, then?' asked Kendrick Maclean. 'Your idea was brilliant. A masterpiece. And you actually got

Charlie to accept. Fantastic. I know that it will probably cost me in real money, but having Charlie officially and properly work for me as part of the project team is spot on. He knows that he will be working like a dog and I have already told him that at the end of the day he will be begging to crawl in to bed as he will be physically shattered. I will also be paying him proper money as well. At least there is now every chance that he will keep his nose clean till he is off to Warwick University in September. I have also told him what I will do if I see his mate Nicky Thornham or his ilk ever step foot on Bradstock Manor. Sorted.'

'How about Tarquin, Dougal? What is going on?' enquired Ronnie.

Kendrick Maclean was aware that Ronnie did not know everything about what her eldest son had been up to. On a personal level, Kendrick Maclean reckoned that both Charlie and Tarquin, Tarquin in particular, had picked up some bad habits in the old genes department from their father and Ronnie's first husband, Gerald Battingsdale. Kendrick Maclean had once described Mr Battingsdale senior to Ronnie as a 'nutter' and was the main reason why both boys 'behaved a bit funny'. Since that incident, Kendrick Maclean had been banned from ever referring to Gerald Battingsdale again. There was no way therefore that he was going to mention now, that in his humble opinion the current troubles were mainly down to the boys' biological father.

This was going to be a difficult conversation. He would try and shield Ronnie as much as he could, but unfortunately there would be some things that she would have to be told. However, it was Ronnie who wanted to know more.

'Let's start with what happened on Wednesday evening, with you running off to some fancy dress do. What was that all about?' asked Ronnie.

'Ah, yes. You already know that Tarquin was going to a fancy dress party that evening. He had told us. I went to check what was happening. Turns out that the so-called fancy dress party was an excuse for a Roman orgy. Don't get me wrong,

Ronnie, I am as broad-minded as the next man but there were things going on there that shocked even me. Right here, in the middle of Somerset. It was disgusting. Anyway, managed to track down Tarquin. When I got there I just knew that he was up to no good. I will admit that I arrived feeling a little bit angry. All these middle aged fuckers wandering around with their bits hanging out. I have no idea what Tarquin gets up to in his social life, but I am pretty sure that it does not involve seeing over-weight old people getting it off with each other. Inside and outside I might add. There were also special rooms where even worse things were happening, but I was too embarrassed to go in.'

'Then how did you know that 'worse things' were happening in special rooms?' enquired Ronnie. Kendrick Maclean ignored the question and carried on.

'I made sure that Tarquin did not see me when I arrived. First of all I was taken in and I thought that Tarquin was just helping the bar staff with taking orders. I then asked around and asked some of the punters who were speaking to Tarquin what was going on. They explained that he was the 'go-to' man in Sedgeton to order your drug of choice and anything else that you needed. It also seemed that Tarquin was now part of the local thriving gig economy, within a matter of days arranging delivery of the order direct to the door. In short, our son is a drug dealer.'

'Before we get on to the next bit, not sure whether I want to see my missus with her clothes hanging off her at one of these orgy things. I know that we have only just been accepted as members at Sedgeton Grange Private Members' Club, but we might now have to review that membership.'

'Just get on with it,' ordered Ronnie.

Kendrick Maclean knew that his wife must have guessed what Tarquin was up to, but he was nevertheless nervous of going on to the explain the next part of his discoveries. However, he also knew that not telling everything was futile as well as dangerous.

'It all goes back to the crucified badger. There was me thinking that this was a warning sign for me personally to go away. Having invested two mill already in Bradstock I am not going to allow myself to be harassed off my own property. After going through a rogues' gallery of dodgy local tradesmen, I rapidly came to the conclusion that the warning to 'Fuck Off' was not actually meant for me. Despite being naïve and just plain stupid, it was also not meant for Charlie who bottom line is involved with no one and in no iffy dealings. And I am assuming that you did not upset your Book Club members enough to incite this level of intimidation. That leaves Tarquin.'

'I know that most of the family don't like Griff, but during the last week he has been invaluable. He can access places and people that I have no chance of ever reaching. With a hefty bonus payment in this week's wages envelope, what Griff has managed to find out is this. This is a bit depressing and it sounds more like Hackney or Peckham rather than here in rural Somerset, but turf wars are happening in our own backyard, literally in our case. On Wednesday night back at his flat, I shouted and screamed at Tarquin to tell me what was happening. Of course, he didn't. As always, you were right. A quiet word in his ear from yourself and on Saturday morning once again at his flat I had probably the longest conversation that I have ever had with him. Basically, he is scared shitless. I actually felt really sorry for him, he had no idea what to do or where to turn. He believes that he is going to get very seriously hurt. Ronnie, this is all a different world with different rules from anything that we had to cope with.'

'Tarquin explained that when we were still living in London he 'dabbled', whatever that means. He set up his own legitimate property business. We know all this because we helped him with some set-up cash. However, like most kids these days he wanted everything now, today. I think that he really wanted to emulate me, except that I have been grafting for thirty hard years to achieve what I have.'

'So, basically, in order to make everything happen a bit

quicker, he had dipped his toe in the drugs world and had got gradually sucked in. By the time we moved down here, Tarquin had cash but he also owed his suppliers back in London even larger amounts of money. You and I may have thought that Tarquin had been a huge success down here. It turns out that everything is mortgaged to the hilt, with even his credit cards maxed out. The flash motor is leased not owned. Tarquin told me that what with his new style delivery service together with selling the more expensive gear, there was every chance that he could have paid off all of his debts by the end of the year. However, that was before he discovered that he had managed to tread on some very big toes along the way. So far so good?' enquired Kendrick Maclean.

His wife nodded.

'Tarquin admitted to me that it was a mixture of both plain ignorance and stupidity that made him start selling his wares in Somerset. The county is no different from anywhere else in the country. Through Griff, I managed to get the registration number of the vehicle that took delivery of the dead badger. The badger had actually been found and supplied by the local travellers' community and for a small fee handed over. Working in the insurance and re-insurance sector is not always as boring as people imagine. A couple of phone calls back to my old office and within the hour I had the registered owner and his address in Redland, just off the Whiteladies Road in Bristol. The Mercedes Estate it turns out belongs to some established drugs baron who has been successfully running supplies in to Bath, Somerset and even down as far as Dorset for years. Some people refer to it as County Lines – call it what you like, with the baron resting up in the big city and his teenage minions doing all the selling, collecting and taking the risks further down the line. Of course, our man in Bristol does not want his quiet and well-oiled business messed around by some arrogant young whipper snapper down from London. Thus, the crucified badger was posted as a stark warning. There are two schools of thought why the badger ended up here at Bradstock. Some say that as his brother, also called Battingsdale, lives here, there was a presumption that Tarquin also lived here. I personally do not buy that. Everyone in town knows who Tarquin is and how to get hold of him. He has to be high profile and it is easy to find his apartment in Sedgeton. Only trouble is that the entrance to Tarquin's residence is by a shared glass front door. To the sort of people that Tarquin had got mixed up with, how a message is delivered is really key. Nailing a badger to an oak door hundreds of years old sends a very clear, personal and unambiguous message. You can't nail anything to a plate glass door, particularly if that front door serves five other properties. Even I understand that. The badger's message was aimed at Tarquin. And almost certainly nailed by the boys from Bristol.'

'There has been a great deal happening, as you can see. I have also made some executive decisions of which I hope that you approve. However, I had to move fast,'

'Go on,' said Ronnie.

'There was no way that I was going to visit any alleged drugs tzar at his lair in Redland. I realise which league that I am in and you will be pleased to hear that at least some of the fees for sending me on that Anger Management course have been paid off. You do not need to know how, but through Griff and his contacts, I managed to get a message to our friends in Bristol that once again they have a monopoly on their market in this part of the county and that Tarquin would not be bothering anyone again. Via the same channels that I was using, they curtly acknowledged receipt of the message earlier this morning. I know, there is never any guarantees dealing with the dregs but this was business and hopefully there will be no further threat from that particular source.'

'We still have the serious issue of Tarquin's debts. Once you had the head to head with him, telling him to let me have all the information that I needed, he spilled everything. The amount of debt that he is in for is enormous, namely £175,750. The illicit drugs sector seems to be very specific when talking about things like debts, even down to the last pound and penny. At a later date you can sort with Tarquin as to how he pays us back everything. What Tarquin is terrified of is the fact that as he is no longer trading in the sector, he is unable to service that debt. His next payment is due on Friday next week. What I have therefore done is told Tarquin that we will pay off his debt, provided that he does exactly as you, his mother, tell him. I want to make sure that there is no blowback on any of this. The boys in Vauxhall know people who know other people who will arrange payment of the debt in cash, in full, on the strict understanding that that is in full and final settlement. The next few days are likely to be a little uncertain, so I have also arranged for Tarquin to disappear up in town for a few days till all the loose ends are tied up. Even I do not know where he is.'

'Finally, as far as Tarquin is concerned this just leaves the issue of the Old Bill. Seems that yesterday afternoon someone from CID was knocking on the door of the apartment in Sedgeton, enquiring as to Tarquin's whereabouts. That is not a problem. Before the holiday break I managed to get an appointment for this Tuesday to go through with the lawyers exactly where Tarquin stands and what is the best way out of this mess. Whatever does happen, he will be in the very best of hands.'

'Think that is about everything,' concluded Kendrick Maclean.

The chair that Ronnie was sitting on scraped on the old flagstones on the kitchen floor as she stood up and walked round to where her husband was sat, before presenting him with a lingering and surprisingly gentle and tender kiss on the lips.

'Thank you,' said Ronnie.

THE DAFFODIL FAIR,
BARBECUES & OUR HENRY

E AUN HAD been invited to Douglas Wainwright's for an early morning breakfast. Douglas lived in a small village called Mells, between Radstock and Sedgeton. The village still miraculously boasted a school, church, shop and even a public house. Mells was also the venue for the annual Daffodil Fair, when the village was closed to traffic and attracted thousands to its Morris dancing, competitions, beer tents, dog shows, civil war battle re-enactments as well as exhibitions. It was also the venue for every local trader in the village and beyond to show off their wares in the main street.

True to his word from their conversation the night before, Douglas had warned the security people at the village entrance that Eaun was arriving early and he should be let into the precincts of the village where he could park up in Douglas's drive.

As was often the case at the Fair, by the time the event had come round on the calendar, the actual daffodils had either died or were on the point of expiry. Astonishingly however, it was not raining and the sun was even shining.

Once he had parked up at Douglas' drive, Eaun walked to his front door where he was greeted by a generous man hug from his host.

A short while later, Eaun had consumed his first home cooked food for days. Since the death of his wife Peggy, Douglas had told Eaun that he had been on several cookery courses and that putting together scrambled eggs and smoked salmon with herbs was incredibly easy. Eaun made a mental note to ask Douglas later for the details of the courses. He had also spoken at length with Douglas as to what was happening in the future. Douglas suggested something that was already exciting Eaun. But what about the bank and the SRA? They were still a very long way out of the woods.

'I agree, said Douglas. 'It would have been easier if you had kept your phone on over the weekend, although I do not blame you having an enforced 3 day radio silence. Mr Curtis and Mr Farquhar have been desperately trying to get hold of you. After liaising with Alex, they both agreed to speak to me on the agreement that I would immediately pass on to yourself what they were saying. The bank is as you know a few thousand down on the original amount that was stolen, mainly caused by commission and interest rate fluctuations. I have already covered that balance. Western Provincial are therefore up to their full compliment. Yes, I know, I will need to be repaid by the firm. I have full faith in you, which is just as well! We can sort the re-payment details shortly. More important in many ways was my conversation with Mr Farquhar. He did not comment on what his inspection team found on Thursday, but I very much suspect that they had nothing material to report. Besides the gross dishonesty of Julian, there have been no other breaches of trust. Mr Farquhar was never going to tell me what was going to happen to you and the firm. He did however intimate strongly that there would be no Intervention. That would have been the end. There are of course no guarantees, but this language is certainly in the tone that we want to hear. Mr Farquhar was never going to say what his recommendation would be for yourself. In any event, any final decision needs to come from the Solicitors' Disciplinary Tribunal. However, one advantage of being my age is knowing people in the profession. I have been doing some phoning around. There was a huge risk in chasing our friend out to Mallorca. However, it clearly worked and the general consensus seems to be amongst my colleagues who specialise in professional disciplinary proceedings is that at worst you are probably heading for a fine or similar.'

'Struck off?' asked Eaun.

'Again, there are no guarantees on anything in life but no one even mentioned this as a likely income. So, let's plan for the future,' said Douglas.

And that is precisely what the two men did, before Eaun had to leave in order to be able to drive out of the village before the Daffodil Fair crowds arrived and clogged the roads.

Before leaving, Eaun had asked Douglas to come along to the barbecue at his home that he was going back to prepare for the afternoon.

'Wouldn't miss it for anything, old boy,' came the response. 'Shame that you will miss the vintage car exhibition at the Fair. Saw them park up a Jaguar E-Type roadster in readiness earlier this morning. Think that you would have enjoyed seeing that.'

With a wave and a smile, Eaun started his short journey home to Sedgeton in his faithful old Volvo.

~ ~ ~

Alex Hilton arrived at Eaun's house on the outskirts of town, having been given a lift in by Madge. She was grateful for the lift, particularly as the sun was now actually threatening to become warm. It would be an easy 20 minute walk back home to the old Brewery building when the barbecue came to end. Alex had spent much of yesterday and most of this morning on the telephone and she knew that all of the office would be there this Bank Holiday afternoon.

Madge and herself were the first to arrive. A badminton set, croquet and outdoor furniture had been strategically placed around the extensive garden. Smoke was rising from smouldering charcoal pieces on the old-style barbecue itself. Alex knew about Mrs Wright's departure from the scene. She had also heard something about Victoria now living with someone else much younger than herself. However, that was none of her concern.

Alex spotted Eaun talking to two young women inside the house. She presumed that these were his two daughters. Alex had seen both of them only briefly before, when they had come into the office, usually seeking what they euphemistically called 'change' from their father. She liked them both.

'Let me give a proper introduction,' said Eaun. 'This is my eldest daughter, Alison. She is currently at Bristol on her final year. This is Cassandra, or Cassie, still in her first year at UWE. They currently both share a luxury penthouse suite overlooking the docks in the middle of the city.'

'I wish!' said the eldest, Alison. 'The only view is from a skylight at the top of the stairs and it is impossible to go to sleep until the dance clubs below shut their doors at 4am. You can understand why it is easier for us just to go clubbing instead of sleeping.'

Everyone was laughing.

'The girls have been fantastic. If you are being served chilled beers and great food then that is all down to their preparation. This is all after they managed to put together a brand new IKEA piece of furniture in less than 10 minutes.'

Eaun had his arms around both girls and was clearly proud to show them off.

Alex noted that all of the office seemed by now to have arrived for the barbecue. Ludmila had come along with her husband Gregor and her two girls, Julia and Natalia. The two girls headed for the croquet set and with venom started smashing the wooden balls with the mallets. Everyone waved to everyone else as Alison and Cassie supplied the filled glasses and the bowls of appetisers that they had earlier told their father to collect from Waitrose. There was a good and happy atmosphere, which given the week that had just past, was indeed remarkable.

Eaun then clinked the top of his wine glass with a spoon, calling everyone to attention.

'I will not be long and I know that we all want to get stuck in to the barbecue,' started Eaun. 'However, I need to say just a few words first. All of you who work in the office will know what has happened. What many of you may not know the full details of is that Mrs Wright and myself are no longer together. If she was, then she would be inside, tossing the salad and directing when I should put the chicken thighs on the charcoal.'

There was a nervous laughter on those assembled on the grass and listening to Eaun.

'What I will say now, just so that all of you have heard it from myself, is that Mrs Wright has found someone far younger and more attractive than myself.'

Again, there was a nervous but by now subdued wave of laughter.

'Who can blame her?' laughed Eaun. 'We are now well in to the 21st century and the fact that she has decided to live with another lady is neither here nor there.'

Alex noticed that both Alison and Cassie were definitely not laughing and were tightly holding each other's hands.

'These things happen,' continued Eaun. 'We part with each other's genuine best wishes. One door slams in your face and another door opens. During this week there have been a multitude of doors opening for which I will be forever grateful.'

Alex had never been particularly fond of Victoria but she could only imagine what Eaun and his two girls were going through.

'As those doors have opened for me, I owe everything to all you fantastic people standing in front of me now,' said Eaun, who Alex thought was about to crack up. 'You know what you have done for me and in the next few days and months I will want to say a proper and very personal 'thank you' to all of you individually. Whilst the doors have been rapidly shutting and opening, a great deal has been happening at WHW Legal over the weekend. Douglas, over to you,'

Brilliantly handled, thought Alex.

Douglas moved to the front of the crowd, looking dapper in cream linen suit and blue open neck shirt. Douglas had revealed to Alex earlier that this outfit was his 'Number Two's' kit.

'I expect that most of you already know this, but the

wonderful news is that our former partner Julian Darby-Henderson has voluntarily made the decision to return the money that he took back to its rightful owners,' he said.

'You will also all know that we have had several people in from the SRA. They are there to protect our clients and ultimately to help protect us from rogue players,' continued Douglas. 'There is no knowing what final decisions they will take, but my instincts tell me that in a week's or even a month's time we will all be here alive, well and still very much in business.'

Not for the first time that week, Douglas received a round of applause from the assembled.

'To ensure that we enjoy a smooth passage into the immediate future and until such time as we are able to recruit the candidates that we deserve, I will work on a full time basis. Have to say, I am thoroughly enjoying myself although I think that Eaun is already working on at least one candidate to come down and join the team!'

Alex suspected that Felicity Lawton was already on her second glass as she started to whoop and clap. At this point Douglas invited Eaun to come forward again.

'Thank you Douglas. Indeed. An old friend of mine who is a property and private client specialist, Robbie Carmichael, has always wanted to come down to live and work in Sedgeton. Assuming that we get over this SRA malarkey, I have once again invited him down to work with us. I am quietly hopeful but we shall have to see.'

'With Rita now opting for a different career path, it has been necessary to appoint a new Practice Manager. I am therefore absolutely delighted to appoint Ludmila Nowak to this new role, starting tomorrow Tuesday morning. Ludmila has people skills, inside out knowledge of the firm and how we work. What she also has and I did not know until she told me as we were queueing at one of those interminable lines at the airport, was that following her degree she took a post grad professional course in management accountancy. I have also seen at first hand how quickly and accurately Ludmila can feed financial information into a laptop under the most severe pressure. I can tell you all more about this at a later date. And thank you Gregor, Julia and Natalia for allowing Ludmila away for that short time. Without her, Jan and the Russians, none of this would ever have happened.'

Alex was still not very sure who the Russians were.

Gregor and the 2 children clapped and cheered Ludmila who was clinging to her husband's arm with tears running down her cheeks.

Eaun continued.

'With Ludmila promoted upstairs, we need a new receptionist. So, for the next two weeks Alison and Cassie will be helping out during their Easter break from university until we can find a permanent replacement. They both need some distraction from making sure that their old man manages to look after himself properly at home. Whilst they are around, I will also be buying as much furniture from IKEA as I dare.'

There was general laughter and the two daughters were now joining in.

'Last but not least, again subject to getting the green light from the authorities, we have a new partner in the firm. Congratulations Alexandra Hilton!'

Alex felt genuinely moved and intensely proud as those around her cheered and patted her on the back.

'We can go into the details later, but with court closures and the difficulty of making any money at all with a criminal defence practice in the middle of the countryside or indeed anywhere else, Alex and I may have to re-shape the area of expertise that we are able to offer.'

Alex found herself nodding to her future partner who then nodded back with a smile, whilst inviting Alex to the front to say a few words.

It was Alex's turn to be waved forward. She was used to speaking in front of a crowded open court, but this was more nerve-wracking.

'Eaun and I spoke at length yesterday and of course I knew

about the offer of the partnership and what he was going to say this afternoon. I am very touched that there is all this trust put in me and I will do everything that I possibly can not to let anyone down.'

'Before we get stuck in to the excellent spread that the Wright family have put together, and Eaun is let loose on the barbecue, it would be good to let you all have a brief update on what has been happening since both Eaun and Ludmila went international.'

'I took a telephone call this morning from DC Denise Halloran. She would love to have been here this afternoon but instead has asked me to pass on her very best wishes to Eaun for the future. I am not sure what this means Eaun, but she mentioned that you are the only man to have found out what she really keeps in her knickers.'

There were some guffaws and fingers pointed at Eaun who raised his hands and was smiling, indicating that he knew nothing.

'Happily, I have no idea what she is talking about,' continued Alex. 'However, she also mentioned that she had just had an update from her mate Steve Dibley in the fraud office who in turn had just received the latest report from the Spanish police and Interpol on what has been happening in Mallorca.'

'It seems that when the Guardia Civil raided Julian's property on Thursday, initially there were vociferous complaints made about aggravated assault and even torture. The Comandante duly returned to Julian's villa yesterday afternoon. It seems that the assailants who allegedly assaulted and roughed up Julian and Rita were Batman, Pluto and some other Russians. Donald Trump was also apparently involved. The two were also insisting that they were not terrorists. Someone it seems had accused them of being involved in terrorism which sparked the big heavy para military response. When the Comandante explained that they could follow up their complaints when they were to be formally interviewed by the financial police authorities and others at the head police office in Palma this Friday, it seems that the complaints were then immediately and formally withdrawn. There is still a Jaguar in the swimming pool although no one is quite sure how it got there. Steve said that the Jaguar will be raised as soon as they ae able to get a wrecker that is big enough to haul out the sunken treasure. In any event the vehicle will then be immediately seized by the authorities.'

Alex could see Felicity Lawton from the corner of her eye, quietly jumping up and down and clenching her fists in triumph.

'It also seems that the love story of Julian and Rita will continue to run. Steve Dibley went on to say that initial investigations have revealed that Julian had mortgaged his Oakhill property for nearly two million and that he also has other properties and assets in the UK and abroad which he has already sold or mortgaged. All of his assets are being frozen. Julian and Rita will be formally arrested and interviewed when they report later this week. It seems that there is also a growing interest in our love birds from several other forces in the UK, including the Met. The latest from Steve is that an Investigating Magistrate in Paris is now looking at allegations of money laundering. With their passports already seized, I guess that neither Julian nor Rita will be going anywhere fast for some time.'

'Just one final point,' said Alex. 'Eaun and Douglas have been assured that all of the firm's bank accounts are now ring fenced and Julian will not be able to inflict any further material damage. However, there will inevitably be at least some initial damage to the good name of the firm. What was really interesting during my time as temporary receptionist last week was that we had two clients contact us to make appointments for next week, a Kendrick Maclean and the people from Sedgeton Grange. Both parties it seemed would have had good reason to go elsewhere for their legal business, but they chose not to and instructed WHW Legal. If I was like Monty Python's Brian and believed in the signs, I would say that this is definitely a good omen for our firm's future. Time for Eaun to get those steaks on the barbecue!'

With that, everyone in attendance then concentrated on the reason that they were there and started to enjoy the flowing drinks and the excellent food. In tandem with his two daughters, Eaun was able to put on a wonderful barbecue in the Spring sunshine. To round off the afternoon, Eaun then produced several boxes of something called ensaimadas which he had been introduced to in Mallorca. The contents of all three boxes disappeared within minutes, with enquiries being made on where and how the next delivery could be dispatched.

Once all of the guests had left, Alison and Cassie started to clear the garden of the discarded toys, sports equipment as well as disposable plates and cups. The two girls eventually retired inside the house, leaving their father and Alex chewing the cud seated outside on the folding family picnic chairs.

'I forgot to mention Frank,' said Eaun. I called him last night. After I had persuaded him that I was not involved in kidnapping his wife, I let him know where he would be able to locate Rita. After telling me that he was therefore flying out to Palma immediately to 'do in that little fuck Darby-Henderson', on reflection perhaps I should not have told him. The poor chap has not had the best of weeks. It seems that his son Nicholas has been involved in some drugs territorial dispute with the result that Frank also had his front door smashed in by the police and his house turned upside down.'

'I had heard,' commented Alex. 'What I still do not understand is how and why Julian and Rita got together. Two of a kind? Animal magnetism? How come we all managed to miss what they were both up to?'

'I genuinely do not understand any of it,' responded Eaun. 'Why destroy a lifetime's reputation and risk everything for a slap and tickle with Rita whilst wearing a pair of budgie smugglers. Perhaps in the days and weeks to come we will get an inkling on what on earth was happening. Some things you just cannot legislate for.'

Alex and Eaun sat quietly for a while, taking in the sound of the clinking serving bowls and glasses being washed in the kitchen inside. Out of the corner of her eye, Alex noticed a sleek ginger cat dash away from the barbeque with what looked like a large piece of red meat in its mouth, being chased by two other cats. Eventually, Alex made her excuses and said that she was walking home. It was only a short downhill journey into the middle of town. After a warm embrace and hug with Eaun followed by a wave and shout of 'cheerio' to Alison and Cassie in the kitchen, Alex was on her way striding across the garden lawn.

As Alex reached the gates at the end of the drive, there was a tall gentleman who looked as if he had just been playing golf coming in to the property.

'Hi, my name is Colin,' he said. 'Eaun asked me round for a quick drink as a 'thank you' whilst he was away.'

Alex smiled and pointed towards where Eaun was before heading down the hill and back home.

~ ~ ~

Tuesday 23rd April: Morning

Ludmila had woken up at 3am, 4am and 6am. She then gave up, got out of bed and told her-half awake husband Grzegorz that he would be in charge of getting Natalia and Julia up and ready that morning. Today was her first day as the new Practice Manager at WHW Legal and she was going to be first into the office.

On arrival at the office, the first thing that Ludmila did was inspect her stricken rubber plant. Alex had indeed done a remarkable job. It really did look as if it might survive the previous week's assault by River and Marley.

Ludmila felt nervous as she then waited for all the others to arrive for work. She wanted to be there to personally greet them as they stepped through the door.

The last to arrive at the office had been Alison, Mr Wright's daughter. Ludmila had been spending the last ten minutes tutoring her on how the telephone system worked. A couple of minutes before 9am, Ludmila switched the system from taking messages to going 'live'.

'You going to be OK?' queried Ludmila as she started to head for the stairs and then to Rita's old office, where she was going to complete the removal of the embossed 'Rita Thornham- Practice Manager' signage on her new office door.

'Ludmila, us young ones understand tech. No worries,' came the response from a smiling Alison.

As the wait began for the first call of the day to arrive, Ludmila hovered at the bottom of the stairs just to see how Alison was going to cope. However, before the telephone console had an opportunity to show signs of life, the front door to the office opened and in entered a large shape.

It was Sammy Ferguson. Her footwear this morning was another but differing pair of bedroom slippers. What looked like a red nylon dressing gown had been thrown over a grey track suit. Sammy was out of breath and gasping for air.

'Good morning Madam. How can we help you today?' asked Alison.

'Give me a minute, have ran all the way here,' exhaled Sammy as she advanced towards Alison, gulping in as much air as she could, oblivious to Ludmila who was semi-concealed at the bottom of the stairs. Sammy waited till she had enough breath.

'Where is she to then? That foreign woman been fired, has she?' exhaled Sammy eventually. 'Useless she was. Tell Mr Wright and the Alex woman that there has just been another dawn raid. They came mob-handed this time when it was still dark and smashed down my door, or what was left of it after the last time. The filth have taken away our Henry. He is innocent. This whole thing is just taking the cunting liberty.'

Ludmila listened as Alison calmed Sammy down, persuading Sammy to take a seat in the waiting area whilst she arranged for either Mr Wright or Ms Hilton to come down immediately and help sort the latest outrage perpetrated by the

Wessex Constabulary.

Everything was just going to be fine.

Lightning Source UK Ltd.
Milton Keynes UK
UKHW022250311021
393171UK00010B/270

9 781914 407154